MW01591737

BOOKS BY NORMAN HARTLEY

Shadowplay   1982

Quicksilver   1979

The Viking Process   1976

SHADOWPLAY

SHADOWPLAY

Norman Hartley

Atheneum   New York   1982

Library of Congress Cataloging in Publication Data

Hartley, Norman.
  Shadowplay : a novel.

  I. Title.
PR6058.A69497S47   823'.914   81–69137
ISBN 0–689–11249–1   AACR2

Copyright © 1982 by Motorium Limited
All rights reserved
Composition by American–Stratford Graphic Services, Inc.,
Brattleboro, Vermont
Manufactured by Fairfield Graphics, Fairfield, Pennsylvania
Designed by Harry Ford
First Edition

FOR CHRISTINA

SHADOWPLAY

1

Paul Sellinger was a master of the arts of corporate warfare. An hour before the opening of the World News centenary celebrations in New York, I was standing at my office window watching the first guests being sheepdogged from their limousines into the shade of the awning in front of the main entrance, when Paul sent me a message on the violet channel of the agency's Electronic Information Network.

Violet messages had overriding, drop-everything priority. They were intended to be extremely rare and unignorable but Paul abused the system constantly; he used it to bypass my secretary, break into meetings, or just to keep a timed printout of sensitive material for his own records.

I pressed the receive key on the E Net desk terminal and watched the message print out on the small VDU screen:

To: John Railton, President, World News Agency
From: Paul Sellinger, Senior American Director

John. There have been more disturbing developments in the Allenby scandal. There is no longer any doubt that it is going to break soon or that you will be deeply implicated. I strongly recommend that you cancel your Colorado trip and return to London immediately to brief your lawyers. I will continue to do what I can to protect you, for Nancy's sake, as well as for the agency, but in fairness I must point out that my own position is becoming increasingly difficult in view of the Family's current commitments. Paul S.

The style was classic Sellinger: a savage attack disguised as good advice. At least most of the board members wouldn't mistake it for a gesture of friendship when it turned up as part of the dossier Paul would prepare for each of them when he finally disclosed the precious information that I was involved in the Allenby affair. Paul and I had been locked in around-the-clock warfare for months and decoding our battlefield communications had become a favorite WN pastime.

En clair, this one was saying that Paul was almost ready to use the scandal to finally oust me as president and chief executive of World News. Nancy was mentioned as a little psywar touch—to remind me that he had already taken my wife from me, as he now intended to take the agency. The other references were straightforward too, for insiders. The Family—always capitalized in Paul's communications—was the Sellinger dynasty, headed by the patriarch Jacob, the Swiss-born arms dealer who had founded the Sellinger Corporation, now one of America's big four defense contractors with Paul's elder brother Robert as president. No one needed to be told either why the Sellingers wanted control of World News. In dollar terms, their media interests were a sideshow, but a vital one, given what Paul's message coyly referred to as the Family's current preoccupation: the development of the Starburst missile system as the successor to Cruise for the 1990s. The U.S. army had just formally accepted Starburst, an event to be celebrated by the missile's first "public" test-firing in Colorado the next day, but politically, there were harder roads ahead. For Starburst to become the heart of Western defense, as was intended, it had to be accepted also by America's NATO allies and the Sellingers needed World News to help create the climate of acceptance. Paul's job was to deliver it. The Family's chain of newspapers and TV stations didn't have the international prestige and influence for the task of backing Starburst, but they had given Paul the presidency of the Global News Agency with which we had merged. Now the Sellingers were one stage away from what they wanted, and I was the last obstacle.

They had maneuvered well, but there was one flaw in their scenario: I hated Paul too much ever to let it happen. He had left his footprints on my neck once—over Nancy—and I was

4

never going to let him do it again, least of all by destroying the agency I'd spent twenty years helping to create by turning it into a public relations division of the Sellinger Corporation.

I buzzed my private secretary, Mandy, and told her Paul was coming. She knew I'd been avoiding him and she sounded relieved when I said I would see him immediately. She would have tried to stall him if I had asked, but like most of the former Global staff, she was afraid of him and she had too many friends who knew from direct experience how vindictive he could be with staff who crossed him.

Within minutes, I heard him entering noisily into the outer office and Mandy had barely had time to announce him when the large teak door slammed open. He pressed forward into the room, without greeting, and moved straight to his favorite position, facing me across the desk, feet astride, ignoring all the chairs around him.

Physical dominance played a big part in Paul's business style. He was a huge man, well over six feet tall, with a big jowly face and beetle brows; 250 pounds, a third of it gut. As far as I knew, he had never hit another man in anger, but he always tried to imply that by disagreeing with him, you were putting yourself in physical danger. In fact, he wasn't fit enough or fast enough to handle half the opponents he appeared to threaten, but he assumed—and he was right—that to most people, the idea of striking a member of the Sellinger family was unthinkable *lèse majesté*.

With me, it was different. Paul squared off against me regularly, but warily. Just when he seemed at his most aggressive he would give himself away by glancing at my broken nose which reminded him that, despite my English gentleman's shell, I was much closer to being the roughneck he would secretly have liked to be. Once, at the height of the divorce wrangling, when he had been goading me about how quickly he intended to marry Nancy, I had threatened to throw him down the stairs of the World News building in London, breaking both his arms first so he would roll better. Though he hadn't taken me literally, I was sure the image had haunted his dreams, as I'd intended.

"You got my message," he said. "The Allenby situation is getting out of control. You'd best get on a plane tonight."

5

I was used to the Sellinger theatrics and I ignored the dramatic tone and biting stare.

"You've got it wrong, Paul," I said. "You must have very bad sources. I'm in close touch with London and the signs are all good. The editors are getting cold feet; two have backed off already."

I'd no idea whether it was true or not. Sellinger had deliberately left me no time to check whether there really had been any developments, but I'd learned that it was always better to bluff him with the big lie rather than engage him on his chosen ground.

"Bullshit," he said. "You really think Allenby's lawyers are going to scare the British tabloids? What is it you Brits say in Fleet Street—there are some stories that are too good to check?"

"They'll check this one."

"Yeah, and then they'll run it. You want me to start writing headlines for you? How about 'Heiress dies after sex and drugs orgy. Media chief named.'"

"Don't be ridiculous," I snapped. "You know damned well I had nothing to do with Louise Allenby's death."

"You were there. You're involved. You'll all go down together."

Sellinger was right, of course. If the scandal did break I couldn't survive. He'd been needling me for days and I hadn't given him the satisfaction of seeing even a hint of how worried I was, but he wasn't fooled. He knew how vulnerable I'd suddenly become. He planned to use it to break me, but before that, he was making it his all-purpose tool and currently he was using it to try to stop me from attending the Starburst test in Colorado.

"Paul. Let's get to the point," I said. "All this crap about new developments in London isn't fooling anyone. You don't want me to go to Colorado. Well, I'm going. My decision's final." I smiled. "You can hardly blame me for wanting a ringside seat at what your own PR people are calling the military event of the decade."

"Don't get cute," Sellinger said angrily. "That's not the point and you damned well know it. The issue here is that you're trying to humiliate me and humiliate the Family. Do you know what Ray Welland of the *Post* said to me this morning? 'I hear John's going to Colorado to keep you all honest.' Christ, the bastard as good as said that if you didn't go, our people would start interfering with the coverage."

"Ray jumps to conclusions too easily," I said evenly. "It's a good thing he doesn't see documents like this."

I reached into the top drawer of my desk and handed him a copy of a memorandum he had sent to Jim Eisenhardt, the WN chief defense correspondent, who was in charge of the Starburst coverage.

The Colorado test was intended to put an end to criticism that the U.S. army had been pressured into accepting Starburst before it was fully proven, but it was probably only going to intensify the controversy. Eisenhardt had prepared a thoughtful and well-balanced curtain-raising feature which set out the political issues around Starburst and stored it in the E Net for release on the eve of the firing. Paul had retrieved it and had sent him a memorandum, alleging that the piece had serious errors in it and the criticism was set out in such a way that it would have seriously harmed his career.

"How did you get this?" Sellinger said.

"Eisenhardt showed it to me."

"When?"

"While I was in Washington. We live in an electronic age, Paul; you can't pull the old 'Slip one past him while he's out of town' number. Jim put it on the E Net."

"What! That was a personal note for his private guidance."

"On board notepaper?" I said. "With a copy to the World Service Editor, putting a hold on the story, and a copy to Eisenhardt's personal file?"

"Jim made some very stupid mistakes in the article. You're too soft. You have to record a man's failures as well as his successes. It's damned lucky for World News that I happen to have the inside knowledge to be able to put him right."

"Inside knowledge and I'm afraid inside bias, Paul," I said calmly. "I read Eisenhardt's article very carefully. I thought it was an excellent, well-argued piece. I said so in a note to the WSE when I canceled your hold."

"You mean the piece has gone out?"

7

"This afternoon."

"Dammit, that article contained some very damaging and ill-informed comment. Parts of it were downright hostile."

"That wasn't my judgment. The hold is canceled and I've made it clear to the WSE that Eisenhardt and the team have had the benefit of your inside knowledge and it will be reflected in their coverage"—I paused—"without any further memoranda being necessary."

"You're a fool. You'll make yourself a laughingstock," Sellinger snapped. "It's unthinkable for a chief executive to get involved in the day-to-day output of the agency."

"Yes," I said, "I agree. In all the years I've been with WN I've never known a chief executive to do it before. But then I've never known one to have to. Jim Eisenhardt came to me because he received what amounted to a severe reprimand from board level which he disagreed with and wanted to ignore. I was the only person with the authority to arbitrate and to overrule you. I've done so. If you try to reverse it, you'll make a fool of yourself."

"So you're admitting it," Sellinger roared. "You think you *are* going to Colorado to keep us honest."

In the early days of my fights with Paul, I might have fallen into a trap like that. But not now. The rule with Paul was no admissions, ever—not even something that was blatantly obvious. Admissions were something Paul could play back to the board with the context distorted.

We both knew what was going on, but I didn't think that even Paul realized this time just how far I had gone to undermine him. I had, in fact, shown the Eisenhardt memo to Ray Welland personally, and to a number of other editors whom I trusted. I'd done it to let them know that I was aware how bad the situation was; that I understood that our coverage of the Starburst firing and its aftermath was the biggest test of our objectivity since the merger and I was putting my own personal reputation on the line as a gauge against Sellinger interference.

"There's no question of my going to Colorado in that capacity," I said calmly. "I'm going to Colorado strictly as an observer. I have complete confidence in Eisenhardt and the team."

8

I stood up.

"Paul, I have to break this. And so do you. The ceremonies begin in half an hour. You'd be better employed in the auditorium making love to a few clients. My decision stands. I've no reason to change my schedule. I'll continue to monitor developments in London and I'm grateful for your promise of continued support."

Paul hesitated, which wasn't like him. He knew me well enough to recognize a dismissal line and he rarely wasted time over lost positions; his style was to retreat quickly, then swing back in later from another angle. But he seemed reluctant to leave and I had the distinct feeling that it was because he wanted to tie me up for a little longer.

I got the confirmation quickly enough. Mandy buzzed me and before I could pick up the receiver, Paul tried to reopen the argument and stop me from taking the call.

I ignored him and picked up the handset.

"I'm sorry to interrupt," Mandy said. "Security has called from the gatehouse. There's a big fight going on. Cox is there. Security says he's making a terrible scene and wants you to come down."

"What's that bastard doing now?" Paul snapped.

"I don't know," I said, "but I expect he's on to something."

Cox was my executive assistant but he had spent most of his career as a foreign correspondent. His journalistic instincts seemed to have been fully formed before he left kindergarten and as a correspondent he had the one gift which counted above all others, including writing ability: he could read a situation quickly, sort through the bullshit and the smokescreens, including the ones being laid down by those in authority, and decide what was really going on. It wasn't a characteristic to endear him to a Sellinger.

"Where is he?" Paul said.

There was something odd about the way Paul put the question.

"He's at the main gate," I said, watching Paul's eyes. They always darkened when he was bothered by something and I could see that Cox had gotten himself involved in something Paul knew about already.

"I'm going out there to see what's happening," I said.

9

"Don't be a fool," Sellinger said. "For Christ's sake learn to delegate. You're as bad as Milner."

It was an easy cheap shot. My predecessor Ted Milner had been unable to delegate even the choice of the agency's toilet paper and he had dissipated most of his creative energy on trivia. But when Paul used that attack, it was a certain giveaway: it meant there was definitely something going on out there that I shouldn't know about.

I didn't argue. I told Paul I'd meet him in the auditorium in time for the welcoming speeches, and when he had reluctantly left, I called for my car to come to the side entrance.

The World News complex is set in a large, almost treeless, green wasteland in a remote section of the New Jersey peninsula. One of the dubious advantages of the computer age was that a news agency no longer needed to be located in high-rent Manhattan, and Global had secured several hundred acres in a suitably zoned industrial park ready for future expansion. I missed being in the city, close to decent restaurants and good-looking women, but it had made good economic sense to move our own New York operation and in the early June heat wave that had been building up for several days, it was some consolation to be away from the baking downtown streets.

The main drive was almost a mile long and it was already carrying a steady flow of visitors' limousines. I didn't want to create a scene by racing up it in the opposite direction, so I took a roundabout route, and approached the main gate from the side. As I skirted the perimeter fence, I glanced back and I wasn't surprised to see Paul's Lincoln, fifty yards or so behind.

I knew it was pointless to try to stop him. If I challenged him with the absurdity of telling me not to bother with trivia one minute, then doing the same thing himself the next, he would simply stonewall and tell me he thought I might need his support.

God, I thought, what a circus all this was turning the agency into, but I could see no escape. In the weeks after the merger, I'd done my best not to be drawn into this time-consuming and damaging personal struggle, but I'd learned very quickly that the price of not playing Paul's game was to have him erode the structures of the agency around me.

As we approached the gate, I spotted the place where the

10

scene was taking place. About fifty yards from the main gates, along the perimeter road, a mobile TV van was parked close to the fence. It had a rooftop camera platform and a full rig of relay aerials, but, unusually, there was no logo on the side to indicate which channel or network it belonged to. Around it was a small crowd of people, and in the middle I could just glimpse Cox. He seemed to be faced off in a toe-to-toe argument with a tall, lanky man in an oatmeal-colored safari jacket and a chartreuse neck scarf. The man appeared to be the leader of the TV crew and I could see he was angry enough to hit Cox but he seemed to be holding back—probably, I thought wryly, because he was afraid of being charged with assault on a juvenile.

Cox's appearance is, to put it mildly, misleading. He is thirty-two years old but looks about fifteen, and a fragile, boney fifteen at that. There is nothing about him to suggest someone whose collected reporting on Vietnam has become a standard text for understanding the war or who had just come back from four months of playing tag with Soviet troops in the mountains of Afghanistan.

When I'd assessed the situation, I wasn't worried about Cox and I decided to deal with Paul first. His car had drawn up behind mine and I hurried back and put myself in front of the chauffeur before he could open the door.

"Paul, I think it's better if you don't get out," I said.

"What!"

"I don't think we'd better be seen disagreeing in public," I said pointedly. My eyes carried the message to him. Paul knew there were times when I would not be pushed and if he didn't want to be put in his place in front of strangers, he'd be wise to stay on the sidelines.

I walked back toward the crowd and a WN security guard pushed his way out to meet me.

"What's happening here?" I said. "What the hell's going on?"

The security guard gestured helplessly toward Cox. "I think he'd better explain it, sir." The guard made a passage through the TV crew and introduced me to the man in the safari suit.

"Marvin. Ray Marvin," he replied. "ATL-TV Enterprises."

I turned to Cox. "What's happening?" I said.

"What's happening, Mr. Railton," Marvin interrupted angrily, "is that this kid here is preventing us from setting up and he's damaged some of our equipment."

Cox gave me a quick grin. "Nothing's damaged, Marvin. I just pulled out a few cable leads to give us time to discuss the issues here."

"The issue here is that we've got written authorization to film inside the grounds, and if you don't get the hell out of my hair I'll use the leads to string you up on that goddamn fence."

"Chief, I'm sorry to get you involved in this," Cox said, "but you'd better look at the authorization."

He handed me a letter which had become tattered and crumpled in the struggling, but I knew before reading it what I would find. It was on board stationery, from Sellinger's office and over his signature.

"What are you here to film?" I said to Marvin.

"We're making a TV documentary about the centenary celebrations."

"Chief, it's a setup," Cox interrupted. "They're Sellinger Corporation flacks."

Marvin whirled on Cox. "What the hell do you mean by that?" he said angrily. "ATL is an independent television newsfilm company."

"They're Sellinger Corporation flacks," Cox repeated, unperturbed. "They're waiting for Big Brother."

Big Brother was the house nickname for Paul's elder brother Robert, the president of the Sellinger Corporation.

"When Robert arrives, they're going to interview him at the gates. Robert's got a speech prepared. Here are the camera notes."

Marvin made a try to grab them from Cox's hand, but Cox was too quick for him.

He handed me a TV cue sheet which laid out the main points of Sellinger's speech. Robert was currently being talked about as a potential Secretary of Defense and he had already begun to take soundings about a political career that the Family fully intended might one day end in the White House. The speech laid out his current line: Starburst was the weapon to make America strong again; the Sellingers were giving America that strength.

"Check the eighth line," Cox said.

I read it and saw that Robert was planning to announce a speeded-up delivery date for the first Starburst to be deployed operationally. It was a front-page news point and would inevitably become the lead to any stories about the WN ceremonies if Paul announced it here. Robert was, in effect, planning to hijack the media coverage of the celebrations, on top of which, World News would be directly linked on coast-to-coast TV with the Sellinger Corporation.

Carefully, I tore the authorization into four pieces, looking straight at Marvin.

"If any of your crew have guild cards, there'll be a press conference at 7:30 which they're welcome to attend. Otherwise, you have five minutes to get this rig off World News premises."

Before Marvin could reply, I turned my back on him and walked back to Paul's car.

"I won't bother to brief you," I said when Paul had lowered the dark-tinted window. "I'm sure you're aware of the situation. But I'd like you to deliver a personal message to your brother from me. Tell him that if he opens his mouth this afternoon to say anything other than hello and goodbye, I'll shut him up publicly and personally, whatever embarrassment it causes to him or to World News."

2

I waited until Paul left so that he couldn't countermand my instructions to Security, then I drove back with Cox, using the perimeter road. I was glad, anyway, of a chance to talk to him; a few minutes in his company was always a welcome break from wrestling with the Sellingers.

In normal circumstances, Cox would have placed 140th or lower on any short list for the post of exec. He was a brilliant correspondent but strictly a loner without enough corporate discipline even to be put in charge of a major bureau. Ideally, he should have been left as a solitary warhorse and paid bonuses never to set foot in the head office, where his irreverence and free and easy ways often shocked the kind of men and women who made up the agency's "ground crew." But I liked his humor and I had wanted to use his promotion to encourage the younger correspondents, and most of all I needed a man like Cox—who was about as concerned for his career pattern as a Tibetan monk—as a buffer against Paul, who exerted relentless pressure on my personal staff. There had been a lot of kicking and screaming about the appointment—much of it from Cox—but since his return, he had complained only humorously. In conversation, he loved outrageous exaggeration and gossip but in his work, he had a puritanical regard for integrity which made him a driven man in pursuit of truth; with Cox around, there was no danger of my becoming the kind of leader

14

who lost touch by hearing only his own views played back to him.

"By the way," I said as we sped along the edge of the complex, "how did you get onto Robert's TV number?"

"I have a new friend among the meeters and greeters."

"Not Sally Anne?" I said with a grin. "She's only been back from Beirut for two days. Give the poor girl a chance to catch her breath. Anyway, you were head over heels in lust with that research librarian up to this morning."

"I have a lot of catching up to do," Cox said. "Those puritans in Afghanistan have very nasty folk remedies involving sharp knives and sensitive parts of the body, if you mess around with their womenfolk."

Cox looked at his watch. "Five to six," he said. "Better get a move on. We don't want to have to start treating the guests for frostbite."

It was a standing joke in World News that the building was always too cold, because, it was said, the computer which controlled the air conditioning was in love with the main computer in the news processing division and couldn't be reached by mere humans. Beneath the joking, there was very real hostility to the building, which was a technoparadise designed by a man whose concern for people was limited to leaving just enough space for them between the computers and the rest of the communication-age toys. The outside, too, was dispiriting. The plain gray facing and tiny arrow-slit windows, which were meant to facilitate temperature control and cut costs, gave the building a secretive and threatening look, even in the brilliant late afternoon sunshine—superb symbolism for an organization dedicated to the free flow of information.

It was exactly six o'clock when we entered the main doors. Bill Marshall, who had been in charge of the welcoming party, was on the steps and he looked relieved. He didn't say anything but he was slightly out of breath and I guessed that he'd been chasing around the building looking for me.

"We're all set," Marshall said. "The auditorium's packed. We're holding the elevator for you."

Cox grinned. "He means 'Where the fuck have you been, chief, you're holding up the show.'"

Marshall looked at me nervously but I laughed too. "It's okay, Bill," I said. "Something important came up. I'm sorry if I've messed you up."

When we reached the auditorium, most of the people had taken their seats but there were still little knots of guests standing in the aisles chatting and getting each other drinks. In the audience, besides about two hundred WN staff, were the heads of many of the world's leading media institutions—publishers, editors, owners of TV and radio stations, the chiefs of our rival agencies, together with our big financial clients, the bankers and stockbrokers who really paid our bills by subscribing to WN's computer-based economic and financial services. Most of them knew each other and many of them were my personal friends, some of them going back ten or twenty years.

In the little corridor at the entrance to the auditorium, I spotted Jean-Jacques Thoraval, the head of the French publishing house, Chebard.

He raised his glass.

"*Salut*, John. Welcome to the tiger's cage."

He didn't need to explain. His house had just been taken over by a French conglomerate which was big in defense manufacturing and already he was having to fight off interference with his celebrated children's encyclopedia; his new bosses said it didn't adequately reflect French innovations in defense technology—meaning the conglomerate's products.

I greeted several more guests as I walked down the side aisle to the front row, but almost as a reflex, I scanned the audience to see where Nancy was. I spotted the familiar, slim, blond figure near the back, dressed in an exquisite white dress that had probably cost more than her entire clothes budget for any one year of our marriage.

Never look back, I thought. The folk singers know it so well. Travel on. No regrets. But I did have regrets, as Paul knew well enough, even though our marriage had been unofficially declared over before he had come on the scene. Nancy gave me a brief, rather arch smile of recognition. I expected no more; she was seated next to Robert Sellinger and I knew that members of the Family were always furious at even the faintest signs of lingering intimacy between us.

A British news magazine had once described Robert Sellinger

as the acceptable face of corporate capitalism—in unstated contrast to Paul. Robert looked like a slightly deflated copy of his younger brother; similar in shape, but smaller, healthier-looking, and more amiable.

Nancy, I knew, got on well with Robert. He had done a lot—or so I'd heard—to make her welcome in the Family, especially among the rather bitchy womenfolk of the Sellinger tribe.

As well as being president of the Sellinger Corporation, he was also the family diplomat and he gave me a warm, full-toothed smile, even though Paul must already have delivered my message and he would be seething with frustration at having a major PR project undermined.

I glanced around, looking for Paul, but I knew he would appear only at the last moment. He hated having to take a supporting role at the centenary celebrations, in front of people who all knew how much he wanted to be president.

Worse still, most of the guests knew the full story; how my appointment had been intended as a deliberate personal insult to Paul by the British side during the merger negotiations: the last face scratch of a reluctant bride.

The original World News had grown weak under my ineffective predecessor, Milner, and though we still had an unmatched reputation for news integrity, we lacked capital. Global, under Paul, had a lackluster reputation but a strong financial base, and they had seen the chance to buy World News. Paul had assumed that he would automatically head the enlarged agency, but this had been the last sticking point in the negotiations. As their final condition for recommending the merger to their shareholders, the British directors had insisted on naming the first chief executive and I had been given three years, as one unofficial directive put it, "to make us rich but honest instead of poor but honest." Out of pride, Paul had refused the vice-presidency and taken only the title of senior American director. It didn't make him any less influential but it did give me a slight maneuvering edge.

Because of the film, the people who were speaking at the ceremony were in the front row facing the screen instead of on stage facing the audience, and Paul's absence was not particularly noticeable, especially as I had insisted on having no line of guests of honor in order not to create a pecking order among clients and friends. Generally, though, I wasn't very happy with the centenary arrangements. I had been in Japan when the program had been made final and there were too many signs of the "corporate communications expert" Paul had brought in to advise. The centenary film itself was boring and conventional, full of idiotic sequences showing telex machines being installed to the inspirational sound of violins. I wondered if I should make a joke about it in my welcoming speech but I decided against it; it was intended to be an official WN publicity film and the director was in the audience.

As it turned out, I never got the chance anyway.

I saw Paul slip in by a side entrance and I looked at Don Westerman, the head of American Financial Services, expecting he would take it as a signal that it was time to introduce me.

But when the houselights dimmed and spotlights came on, it was Cox who got up to face the audience, even though he had not been scheduled to speak.

"Ladies and gentlemen," he said, "I hope you won't object, there's been a slight change of program. We were to have shown you the new WN film *A Hundred Years in the Life of a Great News Agency*, but we figured you'd all be seeing that soon anyway, if our PR people are doing their jobs properly, so we thought we'd give you a little surprise.

"Many of you know already that this week is the fortieth birthday of our president, John Railton, and the staff has put together a filmed tribute to him. It's called simply *The Correspondent* and a lot of you folks out there figure in the film too, which I hope will get me off the hook, if anyone objects."

Cox smiled in Sellinger's direction and I saw that he was glowering furiously toward Shelagh Coombes, one of his aides, who should have been in charge of the screening.

Then the spotlight went out and I felt a shock, as though someone had thrown cold water onto the small of my back.

There on the screen was an image that I recognized instantly, even though I had never seen the film before. It showed a figure poised on top of a high wall, looking out over a dusty African square filled with tanks and armored cars. The figure was me, aged twenty-two, during one of the Nigerian coups that had preceded the Biafran war. It was eerie looking at the scene from below, but I recalled instantly how it had looked from the top

18

of the wall. Everything came back: the sounds of the gunfire in the distance along the coast road; the shouting and screaming as police boxed a crowd of demonstrators into a side street; the bizarre vignette of the panicked police horse kicking in the side of an official car full of politicians scrambling to escape before the news of the change of government was announced.

I had been inside the Prime Minister's Residence by chance when the coup was launched. I was the only journalist who had seen his assassination. I knew exactly how he had died and who had done it, but if I didn't get off the top of the wall in the next few seconds, I knew I was going to feel a bullet in my back.

That moment had stayed with me for nearly twenty years. I could still feel the fear, the adrenaline pumping, and the sucking breath from the wall climb, and remember the moment when I had looked down at the armored cars in the square and seen the one sight I hadn't dared hope for—the little white Volkswagen beetle with Nancy at the wheel.

In the film, I could assess calmly just what a risk she had taken. She had been parked literally under the guns, within feet of the soldiers on the front turrets. When she had seen me, she had fired the engine and swung the car right along the line of tanks and started her dash for the wall. As I had seen her move, I'd tried to find a place to drop safely, but there had been nowhere and I remembered the moment of blind fear as I had launched my self off the wall. On the film, the camera went into freeze frame when I was halfway to the ground, and the audience broke into spontaneous cheering. That was a picture most of them had seen before, on the cover of *Life*, with the caption "Portrait of a World News Correspondent on His Way to the Telex."

Then the film showed me for the first time just how close Nancy had come to being killed. As she had reached the Residence wall, a machine gunner had opened up and the bullets had swiped alongside the beetle, inches from her side of the car. I hadn't been able to get the door open and I couldn't fit through the open window and I'd ridden out, half-jammed against the windshield, scrabbling desperately to keep my feet clear of the speeding ground.

As the sequence ended, I turned back to look at Nancy and

I saw with pleasure that she was also looking in my direction. I smiled at her in the darkness and she smiled back. There was no attempt to be discreet; it was a grin from the old days and it made me feel a little sick at the back of my throat. I turned back to the screen, remembering the night of the escape, in Dahomey, after we'd managed to cross the border to file the story and secure a worldwide scoop, and how we'd lain in the bedroom of the little French hotel, listening to the sea, locked in frenzied release. I could feel her skin again, slippery in the unair-conditioned heat, and taste the wine and garlic in her mouth.

The film continued, following loosely the thread of my life, but it was a stylized, artificial life: an exercise in hero making, highlighting the great moments and cutting out all the depression, failure, and fear.

And I soon saw that it was much more than a "Hail to the Chief" tribute. Artistically it wasn't polished, but whoever had cobbled the film together from old TV and newsreel clips had obviously had a much deeper purpose. In its crude, loosely edited way, the film was a tribute to the ethos of the foreign correspondent and, as Cox had said in his introductory speech, it was touching many people in the audience besides myself.

Many of the faces on the screen were also faces in the amphitheater. Before long, there were little cries of recognition as old men recognized the younger men they had once been. Soon the audience was alive with laughter and chatter and one scene almost brought the audience to its feet. Half the editors and publishers in the auditorium had been there when World News–TV had filmed a riot at the Berlin Wall and the East German guards had tried to confiscate the film. The cameraman had thrown his Bolex over the heads of the guards and I had caught it and started to run. More guards had closed in, unwilling to shoot but determined to have the camera. I had lobbed it to a colleague, feinted, then taken it back again and sprinted for the edge of the crowd. There were closeups too of half the VIPs in the audience who had risked a rifle butt or a jackboot to carry the camera for a few yards even though they knew it would be a World News scoop.

By the time the film was over, there was not a single member

20

of the audience who hadn't understood what it was saying. My birthday was only the pretext. The film was to remind everyone that all these people had taken risks for the sake of information. It featured none of the Yellow Press cowboys who processed news as entertainment; the film was about the ones who agonized to get it right, as far as that could be achieved in the rush of events.

Now, as older men, they were almost all struggling against rising costs and commercial and advertising pressures, and the film was intended to stiffen their backs a little against the Sellingers of the media world.

For the Sellingers, information represented money and power; it was a commodity to be tailored to the needs of profit. When Paul had first become involved with Global it had been because they wanted cheap foreign news to fill the pages of their third-rate papers, which were little more than profitable adjuncts to the local chambers of commerce in small towns across the United States. Then the Sellingers decided that it had more value to them as a world news agency they could use for public relations and propaganda. In the phrase Paul had flung at me once across the boardroom, "We needed a fine reputation. So we bought one. Yours. That's the way of the world. You buy what you need."

The audience had understood, but just in case anyone missed the point, the film also included a clip of a speech I had made at the World Press Council calling for a determined fight against the faceless moneymen of the media.

I turned to Cox, who had crept up in the darkness and taken the seat beside me.

"Cox," I said, "was this your doing?"

"No. Don Westerman did a lot of it. I just got elected as the sycophantic asshole who's brown-nosing his way into the chief's favor."

He paused. "Seriously though, a lot of staff—Global and World News—were behind the film. They wanted to tell you they understand what's going on and they're behind you."

I had noticed and I knew it was true. Seventy-three percent of the revenue of World News now came from financial and commercial information services, but the general news correspondent, especially the war correspondent, was still the folk hero. The age of the accountant as hero might be coming, but it wasn't there yet.

When the film was over and it was time to make a speech of thanks, I knew there was no need to draw any morals so instead I played it lightly.

"Ladies and gentlemen," I said, "that was quite a birthday present. Like many of you in the audience, I must admit I never really thought I'd make it to forty. I always promised myself that if I did get there—despite all the stray bullets and wild rides on unspeakable airlines—I would draw a line and call everything afterwards my second life. This week marks the beginning of that second life and also a new life for World News, combining the traditions of two fine news agencies. But I can't let the film pass without a word of thanks to a woman who is here in the audience, my former wife, Nancy."

There was a lot of rustling and murmuring in the audience as everyone wondered how I would handle the situation.

"Some of you may be too young to know that the woman driving that white beetle was that lady sitting here in the audience and if she hadn't been so astonishingly brave, for better or for worse, World News would probably have a different chief executive."

I smiled into the audience, looking directly at her.

"Nancy, I saw that film for the first time today and I never really knew just how close those bullets came to you."

I paused.

"As most of you know, Nancy and I have decided to go our separate ways, but at least my colleague Paul Sellinger has had the good sense to keep her in the World News family. I think we should all be grateful to him for that and if she isn't going to be a part of my second life, then at least she will continue to be a part of this great news agency."

The applause lasted several minutes and I had the added pleasure of seeing Paul Sellinger look angrier than I had seen him in weeks.

But I wasn't sure how Nancy would take the speech and I felt a little twinge of nervousness as I saw her coming toward me down the aisle.

She smiled. "Thanks for the tribute. It made you a lot of friends."

"You didn't mind being used tactically?" She was far too bright to lie to.

"No. I understand. You haven't lost your touch."

"I lost you."

"I meant with your job. They love your style. That's what they want, you know. All these young and not-so-young romantics. A leader with style. Don't disappoint them."

"You mean the way I disappointed you."

"Don't spoil it," she said. "It was a simple compliment."

"I know. The film shook me a bit, that's all. Seeing the old beetle made me wonder just how big a price I did pay to sit in this chair."

Nancy's look was completely neutral.

" 'What might have been' is the most destructive game there is. You can't afford to play it. You said it yourself. This is your second life. Enjoy it."

"I don't play it often," I said. Then I added, because of the film and because I always tried to be honest with her, "But it would be easier if I didn't have to look at you quite so often."

3

From the moment we arrived at the Fort Benedict Missile Proving Ground in Colorado, there was no mistaking the kind of welcome the Sellingers had arranged for me. In the great catchall military phrase, we had been classified as hostiles.

Superficially, we were given VIP treatment: a field-rank Buick with its red plaque covered to take us from the airport to the base; crisp salutes and snappy door opening; stiff, deferential body movements from the Missile Corps driver. But you could read it in people's eyes and in the tone of the greetings: I was on someone's blacklist.

It was a fiercely hot desert morning with a dry wind which seemed to close the pores and prevent even the relief of sweating. The limousine was air-conditioned but the drive was short and we were soon at the guardroom, where the delays began. There was no doubt they were deliberate. The provost sergeant's eyes looked straight through me as he apologized for having to make a special check with Base Security. His behavior was as impeccable as his turnout. If I complained, there was nothing with which he could be reproached, but his eyes said I was just so much unappetizing dead meat.

As we waited for Security to call back, I sat in the car at first, but the cool quickly dissipated and I got out and strolled with Cox along the perimeter fence. The delay didn't seem to bother Cox and I noticed how at ease he seemed in the military environment. With his childlike, owlish face and fragile frame and single protective earring, he looked like an alien creature—of a different race from the muscular, sweating men who were repairing a huge sign which read: "Fort Benedict: The Home of Starburst." But as we stopped and chatted, they seemed to recognize something in his manner which told them he had been in a few of the spaces they knew about. I envied him that because I felt no such ease. Just the sight of the guardroom and the provost sergeant made my scrotum tighten. Everything I had hated about the army was all there in one little vignette— the stance of the MP, the impeccable white gaiters and belt, the heavy nightstick and sidearm, the helmet set deliberately a shade too low over the eyes; the whole regalia of fear, carefully assembled to intimidate soldiers who weren't easy to scare.

As we turned back toward the guardroom, Cox noticed my tension. He grinned. "Bad memories?"

"Yes."

"Did you tangle with the MPs when you were in the service?"

I hesitated. There was no point in lying.

"No," I said. "I was one when I was in the service."

"A cop?"

"Yes. I was a redcap for two miserable, unforgettable years." I tried to say it lightly, but Cox could see that even after so long it wasn't an easy memory to bring up.

"I gather you weren't a volunteer?"

"No. I was hijacked."

"Hijacked?"

"Yes," I said, "it was quite deliberate. The MPs wanted me. I'd just come down from Oxford with my national service still to do. I'd boxed for the university and the MPs had one of the best military squads. They knew I'd never volunteer, so they rigged the paperwork. You know the army. No appeal. No redress. They might just as well have thrown a sack over my head and dragged me into a car."

"So what happened?"

"I got mad and rebelled. Refused to box for them, so they decided to break me. But I survived basic training, so they blocked my application for a commission and had me assigned permanently to the depot in Aldershot where the CO could supervise my career personally."

"Sounds like someone had been reading *From Here to Eternity*."

"Maybe," I said. "But it was a neat twist. They never needed to get me in the stockade. In the MPs they can make your life hell while you're still supposed to be one of the good guys."

As I went on with the tale, it became as it always did, harder to tell. I mentioned it rarely but, with practice, I'd compressed it down to a tight little anecdote. I even raised a laugh with it occasionally, but it was still a bitter memory. I'd held the record for punishment duty during my specialist training and when I still wouldn't fight, I'd been assigned to permanent provost duty, which meant seventeen months of brawling in bars, night after night. The parachute regiment had been in Aldershot at the time and so had the Camerons and the Irish fusiliers. I was strong and fit, but at first I didn't have the cunning or the ruthlessness to deal with the nightly manhood rituals. On my second night on patrol, while I was still giving a formal warning to a "poisoned dwarf" from the Glasgow slums, he had nearly taken my eye out with a broken beer glass. That set the style, and on top, the CO used to give little chats to my so-called partners. "Don't forget, Railton has to learn how to take care of himself. He's a big boy now. Too big for his boots in fact. Too high and mighty to box for a shitty corps like the RMP."

"Is that how you got the nose?"

"Yes. That was a bar stool. We were in the middle of cooling out a grudge fight—paras versus a visiting navy display team— when my partner turned his back at a crucial moment."

"And did you ever box again?" Cox asked.

"No. Not in the army and not afterwards either. It's probably just as well. University boxing is pretty gentlemanly stuff. When the MPs had finished with me, about all I was fit for was fighting all comers in a fairground tent."

We passed the guardroom again and there was still no word on the clearance so we walked in the opposite direction to look at the installations.

Inside the gates, it was hard to tell where U.S. army property ended and the Sellinger Corporation's began. Though it looked more like an air base, Fort Benedict was an army research facility and for five years it had been "The Home of Starburst" under a joint development scheme. A photographer for a radical magazine could have shot a complete library of illustrations for attacks on the interweaving of the military-industrial complex.

Five minutes passed, then the sergeant called us back. There had been a mix-up over the clearance. "No problem now. Sorry about that, Mr. Railton." The apology wasn't too curt, but I had gotten the message: I was an unwelcome alien in Sellinger country.

From the gate, we were driven to the Missile Control Center, a huge tinted-glass tower with panoramic views over the vast complex of hangars on one side and hazy, red-hued stretches of desert on the other. Our ID was checked again and Cox was told to stay with the driver and be taken to the press center, where he was due to join Jim Eisenhardt and the World News team covering the firing which was due in about three hours' time.

I was taken to an observation lounge near the top of the tower and was surprised to find that I was almost alone. I was greeted by a Missile Corps major, given a tepid gin and tonic with no lime or lemon and a tiny shard of ice, and left staring out over the base. I asked the major a few questions, got no worthwhile answers, ordered another drink, which this time was warm, then stood by the window quietly fuming.

At first there was no movement on the airstrip immediately below, but there were two sleek executive jets with Sellinger Corporation markings parked on the tarmac, and after a while some crewmen appeared and started to prepare one of them for takeoff.

Then a huge bus drove up between two hangars and slid slowly toward the aircraft. It was an enormous vehicle and inside it appeared to be laid out as a mobile restaurant-cum-bar. The seats were not in rows but grouped around small tables, and even at that distance I could see champagne and racks of liquor bottles and buckets of ice.

The bus drew up next to the jets and Robert Sellinger got out, followed by Paul, at the head of a long file of dignitaries, some of whom looked almost too drunk to stand. I recognized most of the faces immediately. There were three of the most powerful men in the Senate, including Karl Tallman, the head of the Armed Services Committee. Behind them were the governor of Colorado, the president of the United Bank of America, and a three-star general I was sure was the commandant of West Point.

I walked quickly over to the major.

"Major, what's happening over here?"

"Sir?"

"I should be with that party out there on the tarmac."

"No, sir. I don't believe so, sir."

"Why not?"

"I believe that's the A group, sir. They're about to fly over the proving ground. I believe you're with the B group, sir."

"I'd like to go down," I snapped.

"I'm sorry, sir. I'm afraid that's impossible. You have to have an escort to go through the building."

"Then you escort me."

"I'm sorry, sir, I have no clearance for escort duty." There was no point in arguing. The major's was a world of unquestioned orders; his job was to keep me up there, sipping tepid gin while the VIP party swilled iced champagne and flew over the proving ground.

I strode angrily back to the window and there they were—the brothers Sellinger—center stage on the tarmac, Robert in command, chatting with each guest as he handed them out of the bus and then passed them on to Paul who escorted them to the plane. The sight was too much. I always seemed to be hemmed in by bloody Sellingers. They occupied my every day. It had gotten to the stage that I couldn't plan a trip or even go out to dinner without wondering what they would be up to behind my back. All the plans I'd developed over the years, ready for the moment when I might become chief executive, were in danger of slipping to the sidelines. It really was too much. I had no business being stuck in the Colorado desert worrying about overseeing news coverage; I should have been in Los Angeles, chairing the final sessions of the teletext review committee whose decisions could save or lose three quarters of a million dollars for the agency.

I looked down at the Sellingers and said softly: "All right, you bastards. You may be able to play games with me on your missile base, but World News is my home ground and you're not going to win so easily there."

But even as I said it, my resolve faltered. I thought of the Allenby business and of Paul's sneering words: "You'll all go down. Everyone who was there will be implicated."

Why, why had I given Paul such an edge against me? Why was human sexuality such a bizarre set of impulses? I thought suddenly of Jim Mossman, who had destroyed himself just as he was about to be named Treasury secretary. A brilliant man who would certainly have been the best secretary for a decade. He had worked for the post throughout his career, yet even when it was within his sights, it hadn't prevented him from risking one night in a gay bar in Hamburg where he'd been seen, allowing himself to be led around naked on a dog lead and slapped by youths in Nazi uniform. My own folly was tame by comparison, but in Sellinger's hands . . .

I couldn't bear to think about it. The coach was almost empty now and the last of the VIPs were boarding the plane. It was almost too late. The Missile Corps officer was standing by the bar watching me as I fretted at the window. He looked relieved. His job was to stall me, and he knew he had almost won.

But not quite. I strode over to him and put my hand on his forearm, in a deliberately bruising grip.

"Major," I said, "we're going to catch that plane. You have a straight choice. You can either escort me, or you can decide now that you're going to physically hold me back . . ."

4

"John, what on earth are you getting so upset about?" Sellinger said, shielding his eyes from the glare of the tarmac. The heat bouncing off the runway was already beginning to crinkle my suit again and Sellinger's bulk left no room for me in the shadow of the aircraft tail.

"I'm sorry about the delays at the gate," Sellinger said, "and I'm sorry there wasn't enough ice at the bar. Major Kilburn told me how upset you were. I'll see it's put right, but everyone's pretty tied up right now."

"Paul, to hell with the ice," I snapped. "That's not the issue here, as you damn well know. Why wasn't I on the flight to the proving ground?"

Sellinger looked surprised.

"That's where we're going now, if you'll calm down," he said. "We're just waiting for the other passengers." Adding, after a deliberate pause, "Everyone has to have a special check on their clearances."

He gestured vaguely across the field to where the first executive jet was completing its takeoff circuit.

"I assumed you didn't want to go with all those drunken politicos, so I put you in the B group. You'll be getting top-grade technical briefings instead of the mush we have to pump out to the As. I thought you'd rather have the serious information. But I will try to see the drinks are cold too."

I had to admit it was round one to Sellinger. He pointed toward the foot of the Missile Control Center.

"Here's the rest of the party. Come on, I'd like you to meet General Morton Haxler, Jr., our Director of Public Information. He'll be with us on the flight."

Sellinger took my arm and started to lead me across the tarmac. "Take a tip from me, John," he said confidentially. "Go easy on the gin. Morton's our chief lobbyist. Doing a fine job in Washington. Likes to come on as a homespun old redneck, but he's a real sharp animal. You'll need to be sober to match wits with him."

Before I could hit back, Haxler was striding toward us. He was a chunky man of fifty with a high-domed bald head and a lot of muscle packed into his lightweight gray civilian suit. He greeted Sellinger and thrust his hand out toward me.

"Mr. Railton? Pleased to make your acquaintance, sir. Paul's told me a lot about you."

He took my hand in an overhand grip and applied the kind of pressure that could have dislocated a finger if I hadn't been wary. But I've been playing those games since I walked into my first gymnasium and I let off some of my anger with a counter-grip that made him catch his breath. I released it just as he was getting flushed and he pulled his hand back quickly.

"That's quite a grip, Mr. Railton, quite a grip. Are you a military man, by any chance?"

"No," I said. "Just a simple civilian."

Sellinger saw Haxler's discomfiture.

"John's being too modest," he said. "He spent two years in the British army."

"That doesn't count," I said. "It was strictly peacetime soldiering. Never saw a shot fired in anger."

"Still does a man good," Haxler said, trying unobtrusively to shake his fingers to get the circulation going again.

"What rank did you reach?"

"Corporal."

Instantly, Haxler looked gratefully at Sellinger for raising the subject.

"What went wrong?" he said. "Bad day at the officer selection board?"

"No. I didn't apply for a commission."

"Why was that?"

"General," I said, "I don't think my military service of twenty years ago has anything to do with anything. Shall we go on board?"

Haxler nodded. "Of course." But his smile told me he would return to the topic when he needed to regain an edge.

Paul wanted me to go on board immediately, even though there was no sign of any other passengers, but I was partway up the steps of the aircraft when Robert Sellinger appeared from under the belly of the plane, looking very angry. Paul gestured to me to carry on, but I paused to watch the scene below. Robert took Paul aside and it wasn't easy to work out what was going on. It was a tenet of the Family—laid down by Jacob with absolutist authority—that Sellingers were always united in public, and the argument on the tarmac was conducted like a street brawl between professionals in which there is no swinging and cursing, only tight, close-in grappling. But reading body language is one of a correspondent's basic skills and I had had plenty of practice at reconstructing situations at a distance, from the wrong side of a police cordon. I gathered that the argument was about Haxler, who had paused at the foot of the aircraft steps. Robert didn't want Haxler to come with us and Paul was blocking Robert's attempts to take him away. As I watched, it occurred to me that I hadn't heard any aircraft taking off in the past few minutes and the VIP plane must still be on the tarmac, waiting, I guessed, for Robert to take Haxler over to it. The argument lasted several minutes then Robert gave in, clearly with bad grace, and disappeared behind the tail plane. I went on up the steps and Haxler followed.

The plane was a thirty-seat Piper Worldrover, arranged inside like a small conference room. At the nose end were three high-backed chairs facing the cabin; the rest of the seats were in a normal configuration except that small note-taking tables had been added to the armrests.

There were several men already seated in the cabin. They all looked military despite their civilian clothes, but there was no one I recognized. A Sellinger Corporation attendant showed me to a front-row seat, directly facing the cluster of three chairs.

Haxler stayed by the cabin door, then Paul came on board, accompanied by a youngish, bland-faced man in a creaseless white suit whom I recognized immediately. His name was Ralph Inman and he was the Sellinger Corporation's house zealot, a lobbyist and publicist who presumably worked under Haxler but who was well-known in his own right as one of the carriers of the flame of neo-McCarthyism on Capitol Hill. Currently he was acting as advisor to a bipartisan coalition that was trying to push a resolution through Congress which would commit the United States to achieving and maintaining nuclear superiority over the Soviet Union, but his role was much wider. The Sellinger Corporation, in concert with a number of other defense-oriented corporations, kept a voting index of members of both houses who supported pro-defense and anti-Communist bills and amendments. Inman kept the score and channeled the rewards—as well as the punishments.

The team in charge of the briefing was already looking pretty high-powered; then, after several more men I didn't recognize had filed into the cabin, Robert Sellinger appeared at the door. Paul and Robert said nothing to each other and there was no discussion of the seating arrangements. Haxler, Paul, and Inman took the three seats directly facing me and Robert sat down at the end of the front row after giving me a curt and, I thought, rather embarrassed greeting.

By the time we took off, I was beginning to feel very uneasy. The composition of this passenger list was all wrong. Twenty minutes before, I'd been irritated that I wasn't getting enough attention; now I seemed to be getting far too much. Apart from Inman and the Sellingers, there was no one who had ever come to my attention in the media, which was absurd given the invitation list for the test firing. As far as I could tell, there were no congressmen, no obvious military brass, no one in fact who seemed surprised that I should have been given the place of honor.

In the other plane were some of the best-known names in American politics. Admittedly Paul was probably right when he said they were more interested in champagne than in missile data, but they still should have had Haxler with them. Instead we had him, as well as his notorious deputy, not to mention

Robert himself, who had apparently decided that it was more important to keep an eye on what was happening in our plane than to look after his principal guests himself.

When we were airborne, a steward served drinks and General Haxler proposed a toast.

"Gentlemen, I give you Starburst—the greatest weapon ever placed in the hands of our armed services. The missile for the twenty-first century that is ready now."

The steward refilled the glasses, then Inman announced that General Haxler would continue the briefing with the history of the development of Starburst.

After a few polite preliminaries, Haxler began with the Cruise missile, explaining that it was a form of flying bomb. Launched from the ground or from the air or from a ship or submarine, and armed with a nuclear warhead, Cruise flew toward its target by normal inertial navigation. Then, for the last five hundred miles or so, it navigated by an ingenious terrain-following radar known as Tercom. A computer memory in the nose of the missile carried a "map" of the territory it was flying over. It flew low—sometimes as low as a hundred feet— to avoid enemy radar, and it used its own radar altimeter to scan the ground below and "match" it to the map in its nose, so that the missile "knew" where it was, to an accuracy of a few feet.

"Cruise was the beginning," Haxler said, "but Starburst took over where Cruise left off. Whereas Cruise flew at about five hundred miles an hour—just below the speed of sound—Starburst is a variable-speed missile. It can fly up to twice the speed of sound, or it can hover almost stationary if the guidance system needs to verify a location; but when it decides it knows where it's going, boy, no radar in the world can spot that baby."

"You mean it's invisible to the enemy, General?" someone asked from behind me.

The general grinned. "No, sir, we do not make unwise claims of that nature. We do not say that Starburst is invisible. We just say you can't goddamn well see it."

The exchange irritated me. It was as obvious as the stooge shareholder primed to ask at the annual general meeting how the chairman saw the future of the company. Worse still, the whole briefing seemed to be a charade, gone through for the

34

form, teaching no one, including me, anything they didn't know already. While Haxler had been talking, I had glanced around several times and noticed that most eyes were on me, not on him.

I decided it was time to take the initiative. Coming all the way to Colorado to be baited by the Sellingers was bad enough, and I certainly didn't intend to go away without at least trying to get at some of the crucial issues surrounding Starburst.

"General Haxler," I interrupted, "can we talk about trees?"

"Trees?" Haxler said. He gave me an ironic little smile as though he was being patient with the irrelevant questions of a nonexpert, but he knew very well what I was getting at.

"Yes," I said. "I want to talk about the Starburst guidance system. As I understand it, General, the information in the computer memory of Starburst's guidance system—TIM, Terrain Identification and Matching, isn't it?—comes from satellites which take high-resolution photographs from twenty-two thousand miles up. The images picked up by the radar altimeter when Starburst is skimming over the ground a couple of hundred feet up aren't in the same form. You're not comparing like with like. I gather the problem's much more difficult when the missile has to navigate across great flat snow-covered expanses, or thousands of miles of forests in Eastern Europe with the trees looking completely different on satellite pictures with their leaves on and off."

"The problem's been cracked," Haxler said. "We've done tests in Northern Canada. A first-rate simulation of Soviet forests."

"Yes, but you're feeding the missile data prepared by the U.S. mapping agency. Highly accurate stuff. Far better than any satellite picture you have of the Soviet Union."

Haxler looked at me angrily.

"You seem to know a lot about our system, Mr. Railton."

"I've learned what I can," I said. "I came here to try to learn more."

"What you're asking for is classified information."

"I don't want details," I said irritably, "I just want to get some sense of the progress you've made with the problems that have bedeviled Starburst—and Cruise before it, for that matter."

35

General Haxler's eyes darkened.

"Mr. Railton, why the hell don't you just leave that stuff to the experts and get on the goddamn team? There's great work to be done. A message to carry. Why won't you help us convince all those damn pinko governments in Western Europe, our so-called allies, that they'll be irradiated ducks without Starburst?"

"Starburst's public relations are your field, General," I said. "Mine is to look for facts and make objective judgments."

"Bullshit," Haxler roared. "There are two teams. Us and them. You've gotta choose sides, Railton."

"I've chosen my side," I said sharply. "But being a patriot doesn't mean giving carte blanche to the defense industry."

I glanced at Paul and I could see he was enjoying the baiting session he had set up, especially with Haxler coming nicely to the boil. But Robert wasn't enjoying it; he was leaning forward in his seat, frowning, watching intently.

"Morton, I think we should deal with the issues in a more general way," Robert said finally, looking hard at Haxler.

Haxler grunted. He was obviously irritated at being reined in, but as a military man he understood hierarchies. Paul might be the natural leader of the Sellinger pack—if Robert and Paul had been jungle rivals instead of brothers, Paul would probably have snapped Robert's neck with a single heedless bite—but as president of the Sellinger Corporation, Robert was still the boss.

Making an obvious effort to sound more reasonable, Haxler turned back to me.

"The big problem," he said, "is that it's very hard to farm out subcontracts for Starburst components in Europe. She's really a homegrown baby. If we could just find a way of dividing up the cake a bit—help the European economies create a few jobs—we'd be home free, don't you agree?"

Even in the interests of preventing another flare-up, I couldn't let that pass.

"General Haxler," I said drily, "there are a few other objections to Starburst in Europe."

"Like what?"

"Like the fact that Starburst can only function if it's programmed by information from U.S. surveillance satellites. If it's deployed in Europe, America still calls the shots. The Euro-

36

pean nations want some control of the system that's defending them. Your people say that Starburst will make Western defenses more flexible than ICBMs, creating a middle ground between surrender and Armageddon. A lot of Europeans are saying that's fine except that Europe will *be* the middle ground and it doesn't make them very keen on theater nuclear weapons, especially wholly American-controlled systems like Starburst."

Ralph Inman leaned forward in his seat.

"Tell me, Mr. Railton," he said in a calm, almost unnatural voice. "How do you feel about that personally?"

"What do you mean?"

"I mean how do you feel about that as a European?"

"Mr. Inman, my views are not the issue here." I said it with the kind of bluntness that either stops a conversation dead or flares into an argument, but Inman's stare didn't flicker. I knew the look well; there was no arguing with such people. He had the kind of distant gaze that parents are terrified of seeing in their children as they come home to announce that they've seen the light and must serve God through whatever idiotic prophet is currently holding sway in the true-believer department.

"Mr. Railton, it's not your decision whether your views are an issue," Inman said. "Other people have to make that determination. We have to identify our critics. There are too many people gnawing at the fabric of our great country."

"Inman, do grow up," I said angrily. "You're not talking to some thickheaded anti-gun-control lunatic."

"So just who am I talking to?" Inman said, preparing to bear down. "Some kind of pacifist who wants the Russians to walk into Europe? Is that it? You'll let them take over, then work on their better natures while they're the occupying force?"

I whirled on Paul.

"What the hell is this? A briefing or a loyalty hearing? Call off your dogs."

Before Paul could answer, Robert Sellinger stood up.

"Ralph, you're getting carried away here," Robert said. "John's a good friend of the Sellinger Corporation. If he has doubts, it's our job to satisfy them. I think it's time we took a break."

He glanced out of the cabin window.

"We're well over the testing ground. I have to communicate

with the control center. Paul, I'll need you standing by during the call. And you, Morton. Ralph, perhaps you'd like to explain the slalom system to John."

It was all very blatant; there was no room for subtle maneuvering in the aircraft cabin. He wanted to read the riot act to Paul and Haxler, but I still hadn't worked out the dynamics of what was going on. Paul had brought in Haxler and Inman to do their Grand Inquisitor number to bait me, perhaps, to throw me off some scent, or even drive me away from Fort Benedict. But Paul couldn't really believe that I would quit that easily, and why was Robert on my side? He seemed to disapprove of what was happening—and who were the rest of the nondescript group on the plane? They seemed to be some kind of jury at the inquisition, but no one was paying them any particular attention and they didn't seem particularly subservient to the Sellingers.

When Paul and Robert and Haxler had gone into the pilot's cabin, ostensibly to talk to the Control Center, Inman began to explain the landscape we were flying over. He wasn't happy about the situation. He reminded me of a Doberman who has been prevented from tearing an intruder apart and told, "Friend! Sit!" Inman was sitting, because that was what he had been ordered to do, but he didn't believe I was a friend and he assumed his masters would soon come to their senses and issue fresh instructions.

We were flying over a flat stretch of open desert, a plain with boulderlike formations on the horizon in each direction. Inman pointed down at a metal structure that looked like a pair of radio-transmitting aerials.

"One pair of pylons," Inman said. "One hundred and fifty feet apart. Like gates in a slalom. Starburst will fly through the gates like that, on a twisting, four-hundred-mile course over every kind of terrain. You're going to see Starburst navigate those gates and find a target no bigger than a normal building."

I was tempted to say that Starburst must have flown the course so often it could probably find the mess hall with the guidance system switched off, but I decided against it. I would get nothing out of Inman and there was no point in bickering for the sake of it.

Apparently the slalom gate was the first on the course, and as we had flown in a direct line from the center, we were almost at the launch area. It looked like a tiny desert township situated at a crossroads, except that the low buildings were all painted in drab military greens and grays. On the edge was a huge fenced-off parking lot, with three missile-carrying vehicles parked in a row, about fifty yards apart. I recognized Starburst immediately. The whole unit was no bigger than one of the big interstate rigs which thundered along the desert highways. The missile itself was barely thirty feet long and was fully enclosed in a rectangular, boxlike structure.

I looked the launch area over carefully, but there was little I hadn't already seen in publicity pictures issued by the Sellinger Corporation. For the moment, I was more interested in what was going on in the pilot's cabin and I could see Inman was too.

When the Sellingers reappeared, Robert was smiling his political smile, Paul looked cross, and Haxler had the neutral look of a man caught in the middle of something he couldn't control.

The plane banked gently to begin the return flight and we all took our seats again and more drinks were served.

"Well what do you think?" Haxler said, when we were all settled again.

"Very impressive," I said. "It should make a spectacular test."

Haxler's eyes narrowed. "By that you mean great to watch but nothing like battle conditions?" he said. "Just what the hell do you want? You want us to fire simulated Soviet missiles at it? Lay Colorado waste for your entertainment?"

I saw Robert wince and I thought, Christ, that truce didn't last very long.

"I'm telling you this baby is ready for battle," Haxler said. "Anywhere. Any time."

"And the guidance system is secure?" I said. I was needling him deliberately now, pinpointing the core of the Starburst controversy. Most of the guidance problems had been known about since the earliest days of the Cruise program and most experts figured that Starburst had solved them—but at a cost. In order to deal with the complexities of matching the images on featureless or confusing terrain, the TIM in the missile nose cone had become so complex that it was—the critics said—too fragile and easy to interfere with. In the early days of the

Starburst program, it had been attacked as the missile that could fly faster than it could think. In response, the design team had given Starburst the capacity to slow down in flight, almost to a standstill.

In theory, if the missile got "lost," with its radar no longer recognizing the terrain over which it was flying, the engines cut out, then a booster rocket fired to restart them once the on-board computer had made adjustments to the readings and found out where it was again. It was a brilliant system—that much was generally acknowledged—but the critics were still insisting that it had become too complicated and therefore vulnerable to Soviet countersystems which might be able to jam or disorient Starburst. The Europeans, who didn't want the missile deployed anyway, had seized on this as their main reason for seeking delay. Meanwhile, the Black Eagle missile was being developed by a consortium of European countries. It was similar to Starburst in basic concept, but it had a number of extra features: it was made of lightweight plastic to increase speed and range and reduce fuel load, and it was supposed to have a guidance system that was invulnerable to all fooling devices. But in the consortium's most optimistic forecasts, Black Eagle was five years away. If Starburst really was ready, as the Sellinger Corporation claimed, it was the obvious choice of weapon; if it wasn't, then Black Eagle probably had a significant edge. I was inclined to favor Starburst, but I didn't want World News used as a pawn in the Sellingers' hard-sell campaign if there was no evidence to back up their claims.

I'd expected my remark to provoke an outburst, but the response by my Grand Inquisitors almost caught me off my guard.

"Mr. Railton," Inman said quietly, "how far do you feel the Soviets have gotten in developing countermeasures to Starburst?"

"How could I possibly know that?" I said irritably.

"I'm asking you as an informed observer. The head of a great news agency. Do you believe the rumors that the Soviets are developing a jamming system that can upset the Starburst guidance system?"

"I've no idea."

"But you think they could develop ways?"

"Obviously they could."

"Well, how soon do you think?" Haxler interrupted. "How much time before the Russkies can throw out a few signals and confuse Starburst? You must be aware of the speculation on this, being right at the heart of the news business."

"That's an intelligence matter. Not journalism."

"Aren't the two linked?"

"No, dammit, they're not."

"You sound angry," Haxler said.

"Dammit, I am angry," I said. "I don't like being interrogated."

Haxler smiled and put his hand on my arm. "There's no need to be sensitive, Mr. Railton. You're not being interrogated."

But I was. This time there was no doubt. These questions were being asked for the record. Every eye in the cabin was on me and I could almost hear the tape recorders turning.

I decided to take the Chinese approach. If a meeting is going badly, break it off. Give the other side nothing whatever to work with; don't let the gears mesh at all.

"Gentlemen," I said, "I have to go to the can."

The method was crude but effective. If I said nothing further at all, there would be nothing to twist or misinterpret, nothing the Sellingers—or anyone else—could use. It might look cowardly, but the baiting was taking a sinister turn and I needed time to discover what was going on.

I settled down in the toilet at the rear of the cabin, determined not to emerge until the plane was landing.

As I took a Sellinger Corporation publicity magazine from the rack, a phrase came to mind that I had seen once on a police file: "Subject using toilet. Interrogation interrupted."

5

The Starburst test was beautiful. No other word fits. It was an aesthetic experience more than a military one and it proved very little—except that the Sellinger Corporation's public relations people really knew their job. We were being invited to witness and applaud an exercise in technical perfection, and it wasn't presented as reality but as a dream sequence in glorious Technicolor. The end product wasn't a nuclear holocaust; it was a firework display of surreal, complex, beautifully directed theater.

And we were seated as for the theater, in the dome at the top of the Missile Control Center with breathtaking views across open desert. The foreground had been cleaned of airplanes and any other distractions to the eye. There was only one focus, three thousand yards away: a dark, menacing structure in brown concrete, a mock-up of a Soviet missile silo. It was ugly and massive with huge buttresses and a roof open to the sky, like the dome of an observatory through which, we were told in Disneyland commentary, SS-36 missiles were being directed at urban complexes in Western Europe. Its only decoration—unlikely but effective—was a gigantic red hammer and sickle covering almost the whole side of the bunkerlike structure.

As soon as you entered the Missile Center's dome, you were taken over by the atmosphere: the glass wall, tinted green to reduce the glare, which gave the desert an unnatural brilliance, and behind and to the sides of the rows of seats, a series of enormous television screens which would record the progress of Starburst from the launch area, around the slalom course, and onto the target.

We were seated and given drinks and welcomed by the ringmaster of the giant electronic circus, the test director, who introduced himself as Dr. Myron Weizman and gestured toward his team of young, shirt-sleeved technicians as though inviting them to stand up at their monitoring consoles and take a bow. Our chairs were on swivels and after the introduction we were invited to turn our backs to the panoramic window and focus our attention on the first television screen. The screens were all blank but as we turned, the first one was filled with the colorful image of the little township we had flown over an hour before. It looked unchanged, except that it looked more exotic as a TV image.

In front of me, the A group were ranged in the first three rows of seats. I presumed that some of them were, by now, very drunk, but the great glass amphitheater gave them an air of dignity and the TV coverage of the launching would show no unseemly scenes to the voters back home. Behind them were two rows of mainly military figures, including a sprinkling of women officers. I had a seat in the third section, with a group of men who I gathered were engineers and technicians serving at Fort Benedict.

The voice of the test director came crisply over the faultless sound system. "Ladies and gentlemen, the red alert has been sounded. A Soviet attack is judged to be imminent. The U.S. missile commander has been ordered to make a preemptive strike against predetermined Soviet military targets. Starburst is under target orders."

On the screen, the little township seemed to be going about its business unaffected by the red alert. There was some traffic in the town center but no sign of any emergency and still no military activity. Then, without warning, the camera zoomed in on the parking lot and focused on a large silver truck, a refrigeration rig with the words "Colorado Meat Processing Plant" stenciled along the side. There was a whirring sound, deliberately amplified by the sound system, and the roof of the truck began to rise quickly to an angle of forty-five degrees. As it tracked upward, the nose of a Starburst missile appeared,

43

remaining parallel to the rising roof which had now taken on the appearance of a metal shield.

"The missile commander is in a firing situation," the test director intoned. "Five seconds to firing. Five, four, three, two, one . . ." The word "zero" was lost in a dramatic hissing sound. The silver sides of the rig which had looked so solid only seconds before quivered like aluminum foil then the whole vehicle disappeared in a cloud of white smoke.

By the time the smoke had cleared, the missile was airborne and streaking upward: a gray torpedo-shaped tube, caught by the camera in perfect silhouette against the blue sky.

"Booster burnout complete," the test director reported.

The tracking camera kept the missile in close-up, giving an astonishingly detailed picture of the short, stunted wings that were emerging amidships and the four tiny fins splaying out on the tail.

"Stabilization ailerons in position," the test director said, adding in a more conversational tone, "Well, I guess we're off and running. Ladies and gentlemen, the first part of the flight has been kept short in order to reduce the size of the test area. In battle conditions, Starburst can fly up to two thousand miles, powered by its turbo-fan engine—a thoroughly tested form of propulsion which does not need to be demonstrated in more than token form. For this demonstration, Starburst is assumed to be within three hundred miles of its target."

The second screen came alive and the test director resumed his magical incantations.

"Approach guidance system activated. Acquisition confirmed. Ladies and gentlemen, that means Starburst has recognized its path to the target. Our baby knows where she is and she's on her way home to roost."

Suddenly all the remaining screens came alive at once, showing different stages along the slalom course. As the missile passed from screen to screen it seemed to be growing larger, and it took me a moment to realize that this was an illusion created by the TV director's art. At each stage, the camera had been placed closer to the point where the missile was passing, so that Starburst seemed to be growing ominously before our eyes, as we swiveled our chairs, degree by degree, mesmerized by the missile's progress around the course. No detail had been overlooked. The backgrounds at each stage of the flight illustrated a different type of terrain and they had been designed as carefully as if each were a Starburst commercial, imprinting a lingering, fascinating image on the eye. There were no featureless tracts of scrub. The missile began its progress with an elegant swan dive, plunging down from its simulated long-distance trajectory, then flattening out at less than two hundred feet to begin its low-level radar-evading run to the target. With the cameras tracking it, the missile twisted and turned eerily, following first a riverbed, then a canyon edge, then turning suddenly to avoid a boulder outcrop. As the terrain grew more complicated, the missile slowed and it really did look as though it were "pausing for thought," in the test director's phrase. Then a rebooster fired and the missile sped on—its demonstration of "hovering" complete—looming larger and larger until it was one screen away from the moment when it would appear in direct vision through the panoramic window.

It was tribute to the image-makers' art that when Starburst did finally come into direct view, the illusion was so gripping that the panoramic window seemed to have been transformed into a gigantic television screen. There was an amplified whine which set nerves twanging in my spine, then a flash and a roar, and a split second later the familiar red cloud began to billow skyward in chilling mushroom shape.

The effect was awesome: a vast fiery column which seemed about to burst open and engulf the whole of the desert beneath. Like the rest of the audience, I was hypnotized by it, then the applause began, at first a ripple from the technicians close to me, then quickly taken up by the rest of the amphitheater. People rose in their seats and someone cheered, then—with no sign that it had been rehearsed—the technicians started to sing "God Bless America." I watched, fascinated, as the dignitaries joined in group by group, until half the audience was standing stiffly, as if saluting the ever-growing mushroom cloud in the desert.

I felt a tap at my elbow and I turned, irritated at being distracted from this extraordinary moment.

It was a young hard-faced man in civilian clothes, wearing on his lapel a large identification tag bearing a color photograph.

"Yes?"

"Haig, sir, Base Security. I'd like you to accompany me please."

"No," I said, "not now. I want to watch the end of the firing."

The man edged closer and said in a quiet but determined voice, "I'm sorry, Mr. Railton, I have to insist. I've instructions that unless you agree to accompany me, I am to place you under arrest."

6

I was taken to a small rear elevator and the journey down the tower was like a personal descent into hell. It began in the brilliant bowl of light of the observation dome and ended five minutes later in a dingy corridor at least three levels below the ground. I tried to argue with my escort, but his eyes simply glazed over with an "only obeying orders" look. I didn't have a single friend or ally in the dome and I knew they wouldn't let me call Cox. Two other obvious security men were hovering close by and there was no doubt I was going to end up in the elevator. If I went kicking and screaming, it could hardly help my standing as chief executive of World News. Sellinger would be counting on that. I had no doubt at all that he was behind whatever was going on. This might be a U.S. military base, but it was Sellinger country and it wasn't reassuring that the Family could manipulate military security to do their bidding. No doubt the "misunderstanding" would be cleared up later when the Sellingers had gotten enough mileage out of my "arrest." For the moment, I could only bide my time and, as consolation, I spent the ride down in the elevator rehearsing some of the more brutal military police tricks I could use against the fragile parts of Paul's body.

When we reached the sub-sub-subbasement level, I made another try at protesting, bringing in every threat I could think of that might possibly redound on the young soldier's career.

He let me finish, then he said, "Mr. Railton, I was told that if you continued to protest, I was to tell you to 'think of it as going to the OK Corral.' I presume that means something to you."

"Yes," I said, "it does."

The words changed everything. If the man who had sent me that message was involved, then there was a lot more to this than psychological warfare by Paul Sellinger. The soldier saw my change of mood, but realized that I wasn't going to tell him what the message meant and led me down the corridor to a brown metal door. Inside, it looked like a maintenance men's restroom. There were a long metal table, some canvas chairs, a line of pegs with overalls hanging on them, and a large coffee-vending machine with a sticker pasted across it on which someone had scrawled, "This machine is in its nonfunctional mode again."

The officer stood uneasily by the door, watching as I walked around inspecting the room, then, as the door opened again, he almost knocked over a chair as he came to attention, snapping his neck so far back that he was looking right over the head of the man who came into the room.

Bob Ryder nodded at him. "At ease, soldier. That's okay. You can leave us." I smiled. I couldn't help it. Bob Ryder was such an unlikely figure of awe. He was small, slightly built, and walked with a pronounced limp. Now that he was the CIA's deputy director of operations, young agents usually assumed that he had acquired the limp during one of his many covert operations and that his spare frame concealed vast reserves of strength. But I had known him since we were both no older than the kid who had just left; I knew the limp came from childhood polio and that Ryder was exactly the kind of nonphysical intellectual he looked.

"Some fucking corral," I said, gesturing around the room.

"It'll grow on you," Ryder said. "Want some coffee?"

"It isn't working."

Ryder walked over to the machine, pulled a ballpoint pen out of his pocket, and inserted it into a slot by the selector panel.

"Black or white?"

"White."

Ryder manipulated the ballpoint and a plastic cup dropped

and started to fill with coffee. He had always had healer's hands with anything mechanical.

"Bob, I know there are budget problems in the CIA, but this is a helluvan office for a Deputy Director."

"There are reasons."

I didn't press him. I knew Bob would not play games with me, but his tone reminded me that although he was a close friend, he was also a man I would always prefer to have on my side, not as an enemy.

In the latest shake-up, he had become number three in the Company. His position wasn't very secure, but throughout his career it had always been like that: he was a survivor, but always out of step. In the days when covert operations had ruled the CIA, Ryder had been considered an intellectual who held on to his position in the field only by ingenuity and personal courage. Now, in the age of the electronic spy, when the unthinkable had happened and a former head of the rival National Security Agency had been named as director of the CIA, Ryder was identified with the no longer fashionable "black ops boys" when he was in fact more cerebral than most of the youngsters who were rising in the new regime.

The bond between us was almost conventional, in his world if not in mine: I had once saved his life.

It had happened in West Africa, during Ryder's first field assignment—a posting he had wangled despite having failed Ranger training and all the other physical tests that were normal for operational agents. There had been an attempted coup and, in the aftermath, while observing troop movements, he had almost been shot by a drunken soldier with whom he had been unable to deal physically. I had come on them by accident and managed to get Ryder to safety. The incident would have ended his career—probably in ridicule—especially as his would have been almost the only blood shed in a virtually bloodless coup. It could also have damaged mine, as I would have lost all credibility as a neutral observer.

His private joke about the OK Corral was a reference to the vow he had made after the West African incident never to need such help again. He was still not a physical man but his small-arms skills were near perfect, and he had become a devotee of what he called The Doc Holliday School of Interpersonal Relations, which, in his own phrase, relied heavily on the concealed derringer and the "shoot 'em in the back while they're still at the bar" approach to physical confrontations.

And he had changed in other ways too. Though we were contemporaries, his hair showed more signs of gray and his face had acquired a permanently wary look, that of someone who had been too long in the jungle.

"So what the hell is going on?" I said when he handed me the coffee. "How did you get involved? And why did you have to pretend I might be arrested?"

"There's no pretense," Ryder said. "I had to get permission direct from Langley to bring you into this basement. We're here because this meeting isn't official. What's said within these walls is on my personal responsibility. It's still not certain that you'll be able to leave Fort Benedict without being arrested."

"Bob, this is getting completely surreal," I said. "What in God's name could I possibly be arrested for? Is this something to do with what happened on the plane? With Haxler and that mad red-baiter Inman?"

"That's part of it. But it goes back much further. I've been involved from the beginning."

"What beginning?"

"The Allenby business."

That stopped me for a moment. Then I said, "What has Allenby got to do with the CIA? For God's sake will you tell me what is going on here?"

"Yes," Ryder said quietly. "I'll tell you what's going on. I'll tell you what happened on the plane and why you're in danger of being arrested, but it won't make any sense unless we start with Allenby. First, I want *you* to tell me what *you* know about the Allenby affair. You're talking only to me. There are no bugs. I give you my word. I've swept the place personally."

"What do you want to know?"

"I want to know what *you* think this is about," Ryder said. "Pretend that the scandal is just about to break and I'm your lawyer. Brief me."

"Well, first off, I hardly know Louise Allenby," I began. "Until this started, I didn't know much more about her than most people who read the gossip columns: that she was the

daughter of Kent Allenby, the Louisiana shipping magnate—
Louisiana, that is, as in Panama and Liberia. I knew Louise
was supposed to have been very much her own woman, thirty-
ish, career of her own as a fashion designer until she was killed
in a car crash in London, very stylish, a looker, her own best
clotheshorse. Then, about a month ago, a journalist called
Fred Wint—an Australian freelance, drunken, vicious bastard,
as unreliable as hell—started peddling a story around Fleet
Street about how Louise Allenby died. Officially, she was supposed to have been knocked down by a car one morning while
she was shopping in Chelsea. Hit and run. Driver never found.
Inquest gave an open verdict."

"And how did Wint say she died?" Ryder said.

"He claims that it didn't happen at around nine-thirty in the
morning, as it was supposed to. He says the police found her
body at five A.M. and though there were tire marks on her, she
was dead before the car touched her. Wint says there was a
cover-up and he's acting as intermediary for someone who can
prove it. He's been to just four editors—all the biggest-spending
populars—and he's talking big money: bids over fifty thousand
pounds to open. He's offering lots of titillating detail but not
the whole story, and no proof. He wants money up front first."

"What kind of titillating details?" Ryder said. "What are the
police supposed to have covered up?"

"A lot of stuff to make a tabloid editor salivate. Wint says
Louise Allenby was wearing a five-thousand-pound fashion fur
from one of her own boutiques, but a cheap chain-store dress
underneath that was three sizes too big for her. And nothing
else. No underwear, no jewelry, no shoes, no stockings or tights.
And Louise Allenby was known, apparently, for her chic and
the fact that she never ever wore anything she hadn't designed
herself."

Ryder nodded. "Anything else?"

"Oh yes. The police are supposed to have overlooked the fact
that she was doped up to the eyeballs."

"Is the idea that she OD'd?" Ryder prompted.

I gave him a tight grin. "If only," I said. "No, this is the
point where the tabloid boys go into orbit—or would if Wint
weren't so unreliable or if their own people could turn up anything. The story is that Louise Allenby had been at a party—a

very wild, crazy party with plenty of dope, booze, and sexy fun and games and a lot of very well-known people."

I paused. "Including Mr. John Railton."

"Did you know she was at the party?"

"Vaguely. I glimpsed her once, but I didn't know that I was directly involved in the way she was supposed to have died."

"Which was?"

"Wint's version is that she died in a sleeping bag—while raising money for charity." I managed a grin. "At this point the tabloids have to order special type to get the headlines big enough. Louise Allenby and a number of other women volunteered to let themselves be raffled off. One hundred pounds a ticket. Each one hid inside a sleeping bag; they crouched right down inside to conceal their identity. Wint says Allenby was high and suffocated herself."

"While you, presumably, were a couple of sleeping bags away?"

"More or less. But I didn't know who the women were, except for the one I drew."

I broke off and took a sip of almost cold coffee. Even knowing Ryder as well as I did, it was impossible to convey the real atmosphere of the party. In the newspapers, the story would run on stylized lines, all the triggers to excite the reader as predictably as food to a lab rat: police corruption, cover-up, orgy, group sex, drugs, mate swapping, heiress dead . . . you could take your pick for the heads and subheads. But I wasn't managing to convey to Ryder the friendly, good-humored atmosphere of the warm, firelit rooms, the feeling of coziness with the long drapes closing out the winter bleakness. In other circumstances, I would have admitted to Bob that it was one of the most enjoyable nights of my life, a memory I had relived, scene by scene, countless times. My own mood had been crucial and I couldn't explain that adequately either. The divorce was dragging on and I was tired of the worry and the depression and the constraints the court and the lawyers were trying to put on me; I wanted Nancy back and I had just found out about Sellinger. The merger talks were beginning and I thought the divorce had killed any chances of my getting the presidency and I'd gone to the party feeling rebellious, angry, and raunchy and just ready for the excitement of the sleeping-bag game.

I'd known the hostess, Kate, for years and slept with her joyfully once after a party at Oxford. We had never repeated it, but we had remained friends and I trusted her and liked her crazy ways which had taken her a couple of times around the world and through several marriages. She had told me about the game, and led me by the hand, laughing, demanding my check. Then she had squeezed the hand and whispered: "Trust me. It's strictly for fun. The women are all in the mood, and they're all free agents." Then she had added, with a final squeeze, "And they're all worth winning."

"Did you see Louise Allenby at all during the game?" Ryder asked.

"No."

"Did anyone tell you the names of anyone who was playing?"

"No."

"So you saw only the woman you won?"

I smiled. "It sounds funny to think of winning her. Later, there was so much more to it. Her name was Jennifer Ross. We had an affair. It didn't go on for long but . . ." I stopped, looking for words.

"Bob," I said, "a friend once said to me that with sex, the vocabulary is hopeless, so when something is superlative, it's best to bypass all the clichés and just say 'It was nice.' The affair with . . . Miss Ross was nice." I didn't tell him my nickname for her: Seagull.

Bob grunted.

"And you were so wrapped up in the beginning of this superlative affair that you didn't notice anything that was going on in the other sleeping bags?"

"We weren't even there," I said. "I took her away to another part of the house."

As I said it, I had a sudden image of myself carrying Seagull, still in the sleeping bag, to an attic bedroom at the very top of the house. I thought how the papers might put it—or a witty lawyer: that I'd behaved like a dog who had been given a very special marrow bone and carried his treasure as far away as possible so no one could see it or take it away.

"And you didn't come down again?"

"Once. To the kitchen to get some drinks."

"And you didn't see anything?"

"Let's say I saw a lot of very interesting human configurations here and there, but I didn't see Louise Allenby."

"That's it?"

"Just about."

Ryder shrugged and changed position on the edge of the desk.

"That's about what I figured," he said. "You're still at version A."

"How do you mean?"

"I'll call it version A for convenience. That's the story Wint first took around Fleet Street. Now he's come up with another version. He took it to one editor only, Herbert Rice-Williams of the *Express*. He claimed he's just received new documents; that he still didn't know whom he was acting for, that he was doing it for the money. Rice-Williams read the documents, saw there was a lot more to it than some well-known people screwing around in sleeping bags, and contacted SIS."

"And what was this version B?"

"The punch line is that Louise Allenby didn't suffocate accidentally. She was murdered."

"Did Wint say who did it?"

"No. But he did claim to know why: he said it was because she was working for us."

"For the CIA? Christ. Was she?"

"It's a tricky one," Ryder said carefully. "She had worked for us several times, as a freelance. At the time of her death, she was supposed to have been working on something she thought we'd want: in your business, you'd call it developing an outline before trying to sell the story."

"And what was the story?"

"You're not going to like this," Ryder said quietly. "She was supposed to have been investigating you. Specifically, she was trying to prove that you are the man the Soviets are counting on to feed them information about Starburst."

"For God's sake!" I exploded. "This is some kind of put-on. You can't be serious." I stopped short. "Bob, I'm beginning to get the nasty feeling that I know what's happening here. I have a feeling you may just have been suckered into the latest round of the war between Paul Sellinger and me. I think I may just know who's feeding this crap to Wint."

"No. That's not it," Ryder said. "Forget Sellinger."

"Bob," I said irritably, "there's no way I can ever forget Paul Sellinger. I'm at war with him twenty-four hours a day and I'm telling you. I *know* just how far that bastard would go to discredit me."

"John, we go back a long way," Ryder said slowly. "Long enough for you to know I'm not a complete clown."

"Yes. I know that."

"Then give me credit for knowing what's going on in World News. If there was no more to this than Paul Sellinger putting Wint up to floating crappy stories around Fleet Street to discredit you, you don't seriously imagine I'd be here, do you? So sit still and listen to the rest of it, because your career—and a helluva lot more—depends on it."

This time the tone really made me uneasy. He was serious as well as irritated and there was no trace of friendship.

"We'll start with the background," Ryder said. "For almost two years we've been getting feedback from behind the Curtain that the Russians weren't too worried about Starburst. And the reason they weren't worried was because they were counting on an intelligence breakthrough: leaked information that would enable them to neutralize the whole system. It was good feedback, from sources I personally trust. Then worse came. It was fleshed out by a defector who came over to the West Germans. He claimed that the KGB had a mole in London who was being prepared as the conduit for the Starburst information."

Ryder smiled wryly. "A mole in London isn't exactly a novel idea; they've already uncovered enough to form a cricket team. But the defector said this one was special, off the usual nets— not in the intelligence services or the government where the vetting had been really screwed up tight after the previous shambles, but someone highly placed in the media."

Ryder paused and took another sip of coffee.

"According to the defector, the mole had already won his spurs with Moscow, especially on dissidents. He claimed that really delicate stuff—names of dissident scientists, details of how their networks functioned, stuff like that—was known to a very few trusted Western correspondents and had gotten back to the KGB via the mole in London. He said the mole had

55

passed other information too—about U.S. activities in the Gulf and South Africa and the Horn—but that he'd been allowed to go inactive to cut down the risk of him being spotted before Starburst, which was his big task."

Ryder reached down and picked up a large black briefcase he had left resting beside his foot.

"Now, one of the reasons we're here in this sleazy basement and not in the base security office is that I wanted to scare you: and the best way of doing that is to show you a few documents you aren't supposed to see. So don't explode, or protest or rave at me. Just sit quietly and read."

7

Ryder opened his document case and took out three manila folders. Without speaking, he handed me the first one. I opened it and before I was halfway through it, Ryder had achieved his purpose: I was well and truly scared.

The file contained several Soviet official documents, with U.S. government translations attached. The translator had called them Investigation and Arrest Summaries, but they were quite simply the official file of a purge.

One document described how a group of scientists met every Sunday in a Moscow flat to brief Jewish and other dissidents who had been banned from working, and kept them up to date with developments in various scientific fields. Many dissident scientists were afraid to attend and the information was passed on to them through what was known as the "network." I knew about the briefings already: a former World News Moscow bureau chief, Jay Wellesley, had been one of those trusted by the network and they had fed him information about the condition of the leading scientists in the labor camps and in prison.

The document listed seventeen arrests and the names were all familiar. Wellesley had called me when I was chief of correspondents and asked to be pulled out of Moscow because he feared he might be interrogated by the Soviets. I had agreed and I could still remember Wellesley's relief and gratitude when we had met in Vienna and he had told me the situation and how he was sure he had gotten out hours before being arrested himself—and he had given me the names.

The translation of the document said that the arrests had resulted from information received from "our regular contact in London," who had passed it to the KGB Vienna station.

The other documents were similar. It was eerie seeing the most sensitive information I'd received while chief of correspondents being replayed in stilted Soviet officialese. It all fitted perfectly. I was being framed, and it was being done with devastating thoroughness.

The file even contained a letter from a Moscow University student detained in a labor camp. It was addressed to his former professor, the dissident physicist Yuri Arlov, and warned him "not to say anything to Wellesley; he is the source."

I looked at Ryder. "You know Wellesley's dead, of course. He was killed in a car accident five months ago."

"Yes. But it probably wouldn't have helped. He couldn't prove you didn't pass them the information back."

"Bob, I passed nothing." As I spoke, I realized how subdued my voice had become; the documents had shaken me badly and Ryder could see it.

"Those are some of the documents that Wint showed to Rice-Williams; he told SIS he didn't know who gave them to him. They haven't been able to break him down. He said he's been told to expect more."

Ryder picked up the second folder. "This file will show you that opinions are divided on what to do about you."

As I read the contents of the second folder, I felt my face flushing and my skin starting to crawl.

Ever since Wint had walked into Rice-Williams' office, I had been under total surveillance—in London, Washington, and New York. There were accounts of my movements, my contacts and associates, the meetings I'd had and the restaurants I'd eaten in. It was a thick file and I started to get angry again when I saw that my phone calls had been tapped and some of them subjected to Voice Stress Analysis—which effectively gave me a lie detector test without connecting me to any machine, using simply tapes of my voice. As I turned to the section marked Evaluation Reports, Ryder interrupted. "You needn't bother to plow through that," he said, "I'll give you the highlights. U.S. Military Intelligence favored having you arrested in London and charged with passing information to the enemy. The Brits don't want another mole scandal—but they don't want another mole cover-up scandal either."

"And the CIA," I asked drily. "How do they feel?"

"Divided also. A three-way split. One school says have you arrested and charged to put you out of action, another says leave you in place and let you hang yourself, and there's a third—led by me—which happens to believe that you aren't a Soviet agent."

"And what do you believe it's all about?" I asked, as calmly as I could manage.

"Let me put the question back to you. If I handed you that file, plus everything I've told you—the defector information included—and I blanked out your name, what would you think of Mr. X?"

"I'd be very suspicious of him indeed, though it's mostly circumstantial."

"And if, for the sake of argument, you *know* the man is not the mole, what would you think of the file?"

"Obviously I'd say that he—that I—was being set up, probably to take suspicion off the real mole."

Ryder grinned. "Which happens to be what I believe—though it may end up costing me my job if we can't prove it."

"The 'we' includes how many people?" I said. "Do we have any allies?"

"Would you believe Paul Sellinger?"

"Now that really reassures me. With Paul as an ally, I'll probably end up taking Rudolph Hess's place in Spandau."

Ryder shrugged. "Oh, he'd like to see you hung out to dry. But not for this. A mole preparing to leak Starburst secrets is something the Sellingers don't need, believe me. When Wint started pushing the first version of the scandal, Sellinger thought he had you. He was all set to nail you to the mast Then when Wint went to Rice-Williams with the mole story, the whole thing blew up in his face. The Sellingers have billions riding on Starburst—and maybe eventually the top office in the United States, if Robert's political career takes off. There's no way they want an intelligence scandal remotely connected with Starburst. It could scuttle the whole program. So far, Paul's backing me all the way. He doesn't really believe it's you; he just wants the real mole found and quick. The reason Paul didn't want you to come to Colorado was that you were more likely to get arrested here, on military property."

"I don't believe it."

"Believe it," Ryder said emphatically. "Military Intelligence is itching to get its claws on you. This is an ideal place; all kinds of special security regulations can be invoked. Paul helped me fight them off. That's what the plane trip was about. The military wanted to pick you up as soon as you set foot on the base. Paul persuaded them to continue the investigation without actually arresting you. He arranged the grilling by Haxler and Inman. It was all on tape and VSA, of course. No definite conclusions, as usual. You didn't cooperate."

"Bob, I just don't believe Paul is on my side," I said. "And what about Robert?"

"Robert's not happy. He's undecided about having you arrested. He wants it suppressed just as much as Paul does, but he thinks Paul's way is going to get the Family too directly involved. He wants the military to handle it. That's pretty typical of Robert."

"Bob, I'm hearing you," I said, "but I just don't bloody well believe all this."

"It's gone beyond the point where it matters what you believe. We have to get some proof of your innocence."

"So what do you want me to do?"

"I want you to retrace some of your steps," Ryder said.

"What steps? What do you mean?"

"I want you to go back and see your KGB contact."

I looked hard at Ryder, looking for a smile—some sign that he was joking.

There was none and I said sharply, "I thought we'd agreed I had no KGB contact."

"No. I said I didn't believe you were a Soviet agent. I didn't say you hadn't been in contact with them. You have been associating with someone we believe has very strong links to the KGB."

"Who, for God's sake?"

Ryder opened the last folder and handed me a photograph. "You recognize the lady of the sleeping bag? Ms. Jennifer Ross, nicknamed by you Seagull?"

I stared incredulously at the pretty oval face and the broad, curving smile.

"Tell me what you know about her. Just briefly, a couple of lines."

"Age about thirty-five," I said, shaken. "British. A painter. She specializes in nature drawings. Illustrates textbooks and catalogues. Flowers, birds. Had been married before I met her. Went to art school."

"Doesn't sound very threatening," Ryder said. "So perhaps this photograph might surprise you. Wint showed it to Rice-Williams."

It was Seagull again, but taken when she was about ten years younger. She was dressed in more formal clothing than the artist's gear I was used to seeing her in and she was standing on the parapet of a castlelike building looking out over a city I didn't immediately recognize.

"The city's Ankara," Ryder said. "The man is Colonel Igor Korapkin of the KGB. Odd sort of contact for a nature illustrator."

Before I could say anything, Ryder handed me another photograph. Seagull again, this time with a woman about her own age.

"That was taken in Stockholm," Ryder said, "and the woman with your beloved Seagull is Anna Kirov, the senior KGB station officer in Scandinavia. She's a very mysterious lady, your Seagull. Her curriculum vitae, as they say, doesn't quite add up. We've confirmed some details of her life—birthplace, early schooling, and so on, but there are problems. There's no record of any marriage; and there's something funny about her art school career. The dates don't quite add up. It smells wrong."

"I can't help you," I said. "I admit I know hardly anything about her. It was just a casual affair. You know how we met."

"Yes, but I want you to get to know a lot more about her. I want you to see her again."

"I've no idea where she is."

"She's in the south of France, in St. Tropez. We traced her two days ago."

"Well, pick her up," I said.

"We have nothing to hold her on." Ryder smiled drily. "We

61

have a lot more on you. I want you to go and see her. Tell her about scandal . . . tell her what you like. Just get alongside her again and see where it leads."

"Bob, I can't," I said. "I can't just leave World News and chase off to France. I'm supposed to be in Brussels this week and Amsterdam. I've got a news agency to run. I'll be missed."

"You'll need Paul Sellinger's help. He's willing to give it. He'll cover for you."

"No, Bob," I said. "Dammit, no. I will not be helped by that treacherous bastard."

Ryder looked at me steadily and picked up the phone beside him on the small table.

"There isn't a choice, old buddy. I know how you feel about Paul, but I don't think you'll like the alternatives any better."

Ryder spoke quickly into the phone and I realized he was sending for Sellinger. He gave me no chance to interrupt and I sensed suddenly that Ryder was more nervous than he was admitting. He didn't feel in control of the situation, and it wasn't reassuring.

Ryder put down the phone and smiled wryly. "Your ally is on the way. He's been talking to the Military Intelligence people. They're still not happy about turning you loose. I asked him to help cool them out."

"Bob, you've no right to ask Sellinger for favors on my behalf."

"John, there's more at stake here than your pride—more than your career too. You're so wrapped up in your feud with Paul, you don't seem to realize that Starburst is a damned fine weapon system which this country—and NATO—can't afford to lose. If there's a mole we have to find out who the hell it is, and frankly if you have to eat humble pie with Paul Sellinger to help do that, then that's your tough luck. Now do you get the picture?"

I knew Ryder was right; if anyone else but Sellinger had been involved, I'd have been grateful for the help. The files and the photographs had shaken me badly. It didn't take much imagination to project myself forward into the dock of the High Court, but why, dammit, did I have to count on Paul?

Ryder did his best to stop me losing my temper. He offered

me another cup of coffee and went through the routine with the ballpoint pen again, and I did manage to calm down—until Sellinger arrived. He walked in the door, and said to Ryder, without looking at me, "It's okay, Bob, I've won him a week. We can go ahead."

It was all there in one phrase. The condescension; his infuriating habit of pretending that he was the center of every situation; always the controller. He somehow managed to convey in a few words that he was in alliance with the CIA and the U.S. government and I had become his pawn. The hypocrisy, as always, was stunning. There was no suggestion that he needed to find the mole as much as I did. Well, I might need his cooperation, but I wasn't taking that kind of shit.

"Paul, cut the crap," I said. "You'd better start praying that I can find out who your blasted mole is before your entire family fortunes go down the tubes."

Paul ignored me and continued talking to Ryder.

"But seven days is tops," he said. "The Director of Military Intelligence won't risk any more."

Finally, with carefully judged timing, he turned to me.

"John, you're lucky to have good friends," he said. He paused just long enough for me to rise to the idea that he was including himself, then he added quickly, "Like Bob here. It's a pity you don't have as much luck with your womenfolk."

Sellinger grinned at Ryder. "First he marries a beautiful woman he can't satisfy, then he finds a consolation prize in a sleeping bag and it all goes sour on him."

Ryder glanced down at my hand, which was clenching tightly. The taunt about not being able to satisfy Nancy was the oldest psychological wound in the world and the easiest to inflict. It wasn't true, but you couldn't fight back without making the most ridiculous and humiliating protestations of virility.

But Ryder interposed himself quickly—almost physically blocking me off from Sellinger.

"Paul," he said sharply, "the feud between you and John is in abeyance. And that's official. I'm running this until my director decides otherwise. Your only role is to help John get to France before anyone tips off the woman."

"It's all in hand," Sellinger said airily. "John was due to fly to Brussels for a lunch meeting with the president of the EEC. I'll go in his place."

"You damn well won't," I snapped. "I'm not having you taking over the talks on the European expansion program."

"You've no choice, John. What do you want to do, just not turn up? We've spent six months getting him ready to support us in the European stock-exchange services deal."

"You mean, I have."

"It really doesn't matter at this point," Ryder interrupted. "John, you have to go to St. Tropez."

I knew there was no point in arguing.

"I'll need Cox," I said.

"No," Sellinger said. "Better if you go alone."

"It may be better to go alone, but I'm still taking Cox," I said. I'd no intention of leaving myself isolated and more vulnerable than necessary, and Cox didn't need to be in London or New York to stay in touch. "Bob, you can give him a security warning or whatever's necessary."

"Yes. I'll do that."

Sellinger stood up. I could see he'd read my mood. There was no more mileage to be had from this line of taunting and he never wasted even a minute of his time.

"Aren't you going to wish me luck?" I said sarcastically, as Sellinger turned to leave. "Don't I carry the Family's good wishes with me?"

"Just worry about yourself," Paul said brusquely. "If you can find out from this woman what's going on, you might just have a chance to survive. The Family will survive whatever happens; you can count on that."

When he'd gone, Ryder said quietly, "Does this go on all the time?"

"Twenty-four hours a day."

"Jesus Christ."

Ryder hesitated. "Before you go . . ."

"What?"

"There's one thing I have to say. Before we leave the corral and this becomes official again."

"What's that?"

"Kidding aside, I know how rough the Sellingers can play.

And because I know, I'll level with you. Just watch your back, old buddy. Paul's on your side because he has to be. But if the Sellingers ever decide the situation's getting too messy, they won't necessarily leave it to us to clean up."

"Thanks," I said. "My mother used to say you should always send someone off on a journey with a word of reassurance."

Ryder grinned and put on his mock Southern drawl.

"Well, that's right. So y'all just have yourself a wonderful trip to St. Tropez, y'hear?"

8

On the journey between Denver and Paris, I managed to master my panic. It didn't hit immediately; the departure from Fort Benedict was too unreal for that. After the conversation with Ryder, I simply slipped away and, as far as World News was concerned, I vanished on a special negotiating assignment. There were several WN problems I wanted to deal with first, but Ryder wouldn't allow it and his anxiety to have me leave quickly, before the trip could be queried, made me realize how shaky my position was.

I traveled alone and anonymously, via Chicago and Montreal, then, on the Air France flight to Paris, I almost lost my nerve. I was overtired and irritable and as I slept fretfully, the nightmares began to merge with black daydreams as I imagined how the situation could turn out. Once the panic started, I knew I had to let it run, so I lay back, sweatily gripping the armrests of the airline seat, letting my imagination devise scenarios of the worst that could possibly happen. I went all the way, through humiliation and ridicule in the media to dismissal, arrest, and imprisonment. I scripted the total erasure of John Railton, personal and professional, and the eclipse of World News by having its head branded as a spy. And it didn't just concern World News. After my disgrace, no international journalist would ever be quite free of the taint of spying—spies and foreign correspondents had always fished the same waters. Three times in my own career I'd been wrongly arrested by suspicious Third World governments that hadn't recognized the line between the two. Now I was singlehandedly going to rub out the line.

After that, my imagination turned on my friends and colleagues and by the time I was halfway over the Atlantic they had all coalesced into a single gigantic conspiracy to frame me. Ryder had warned me in Colorado, "In a climate of suspicion, everyone is suspect," and as I sat, unshaven, scared, and stiff-eyed with exhaustion, I decided that he was right. How could I possibly trust anyone? There was simply no way of finding out in time which of my friends or professional colleagues might be doing this to me. I even began to suspect Cox. He had traveled separately and would be waiting for me in Nice, and I imagined him laughing at my naiveté; briefing his principals, whoever they might be, about my movements, grinning as I stumbled deeper and deeper into the maze that was being constructed around me.

It was when I reached that point that I realized how paranoid I had become, and I knew the worst was over. I washed and shaved carefully, ate a sandwich and some nuts, drank a double Courvoisier, then slept soundly for the last two hours of the flight and by the time I reached Charles de Gaulle airport, I was back in control.

I struck lucky and got a first-class cancellation on an immediate connecting flight to Nice, without having to use WN influence, and when Cox met me at Nice, he said, "You're looking very fit. Anyone would think you'd arrived for a few days of chasing sun babies."

I grinned. "There's no point in panicking. All we can do is to take this on one step at a time."

But I could see Cox wasn't relaxed and when I asked him what was the matter he said simply, "Brussels," and I knew from his tone that it was serious.

"Sounds like time for a second breakfast," I said. "Let's find a café."

Cox had already rented a Peugeot 505 and he drove us to the industrial edge of Nice well away from the airport. The café had a pleasant little terrace opposite a street market where the housewives were beginning their early morning shopping, and we could have been in a different city altogether from the

67

luxury tourist hotels of the Promenade des Anglais which were only a couple of miles away.

We ordered coffee and croissants and Cox waited for a signal from me that I was ready for the bad news. When I gave it, he said, "Sellinger didn't turn up in Brussels last night and no one's canceled the lunch with the EEC president. It looks as though he plans just to have you not show up."

"You're sure."

"I called the number two in the Brussels bureau, Rob Neilsen. He's a close friend. He told me he'd heard a rumor that you were ill but wouldn't admit it."

"Our beloved ally didn't waste much time, did he."

Cox grinned. "You know what they say. Sellinger gets up early so he can be a bastard for a little longer each day."

As usual, Sellinger had made a stylish thrust. If he wanted to score some quick points off the situation, this was by far the best way to do it. The purpose of the Brussels talks was to renegotiate a series of unprofitable contracts with five European stock exchanges. Milner, my predecessor, had gotten us into them because he'd been overanxious to break into a new market, and as well as our losing money on them, they were also weakening our bargaining position elsewhere in Europe. The Belgians had been stalling renegotiations on the grounds that they were bound by EEC regulations, but I'd found some loopholes and after a lot of careful negotiation I'd managed to get Ludwig Gerstein, the German president of the EEC, to support my claim that circumstances had changed enough for there to be no bar to renegotiation.

If I brought off a new deal, it would put our European stock-broking services back on a viable footing and within World News; it would prove that although I was a "general news" president, I knew how to defend the Economic Division's interests. If Sellinger had gone in my place, he could well have taken the credit which would have been infuriating, but this was far worse. If Gerstein took offense, or simply lost interest, the Chairman of the Belgian stock exchange, Jean le Mesurier, would simply backtrack and insist that the old contracts must run out their life. On top of which, the meeting with Gerstein, though technically a private working lunch, would be well publicized, and if I simply failed to turn up, with no reason or excuse, there would be a lot of damaging talk.

I drank another cup of coffee, went over the situation carefully once more, then nodded to Cox.

"Ready?"

Cox took out a small note pad.

"Call your secretary in New York. Don't tell her where you are. If she wants to know, say you're in Geneva. Get her to send a telex to Gerstein, personal from me, saying I have complete confidence in Sellinger and hope talks go well. Then ring your friend in Brussels. Tell him to call Gerstein's secretary and ask if the message arrived. Tell him to say that I sent it because Gerstein knows how much I hate Sellinger and didn't want him to feel I wouldn't stand by any decisions made.

"Then call my secretary in London. Tell her to send a telex to our Brussels bureau chief, Anne Mitchell, for onpassing to Sellinger." I reached into my briefcase and pulled out one of the documents I'd prepared for the Brussels trip. It contained a list of queries and the numbers of the files where I'd found the answers.

"Tell her to list these file numbers in the telex and mention the queries and make it look as though I'm passing the information on to Sellinger ready for the talks. That should put the ball back in Sellinger's court. Even if it's too late to stop the embarrassment, at least everyone will be asking where Sellinger is instead of me."

I grinned at Cox. Now for a bit of bastardy.

"Call the chairman of the Belgian stock exchange, Jean le Mesurier, direct. I'll give you his private, unlisted number. Say you're calling on my behalf. Say I'm worried because I've had to let Sellinger take over the talks but I'm still taking a personal interest and I'll stick to our deal. If he drops his opposition to renegotiation, I'll do my best to see that the British reconsider their opposition to him in the International Stockbroking Commission elections in October."

I grinned.

"He'll be a bit surprised because we haven't made any such deal, but he'll recognize blackmail when he hears it; he uses it often enough himself. But be blunt. He's a thick-skinned old bastard and you have to really hit him over the head if you want to make a point."

I noticed that Cox had taken only very sketchy notes but I knew he'd get all the details right. He had an excellent short-term memory and, like many reporters, he only used notes as a reminder over the next half hour or so.

When he came back he was grinning broadly. "I enjoyed the call to le Mesurier. He seemed to feel I was blackmailing him. Can't think where he got that idea."

I grinned. "No. Neither can I. That takes care of Brussels. There's nothing else that can be done before the lunch is supposed to take place. We'll worry about fence-mending afterwards. Anything else needing attention?"

"Not that I know of. Do you want me to check your signals? I've got my E Net terminal with me."

All WN correspondents carried these terminals. They could be hooked to telephone lines in most countries for filing copy or receiving service messages stored in the system. By using my private code letters, Cox could retrieve, on the café telephone, any signals that my private secretaries in either London or New York had left in the system for my personal attention.

"If you use the E Net the Paris bureau will know where you are."

"I've arranged a bypass."

"How?"

"Someone in London will retrieve your messages. Then I'll go on-line to her and, as they say, computer shall talk unto computer."

"Her? Who is she?"

"Mary Rainham."

Rainham was another correspondent, and a friend of Cox.

"That was risky," I said sharply. "How much does she know?"

"Nothing, except that it's a confidential assignment."

Cox paused and looked at me evenly. "You trusted me. You made a snap judgment. I made a similar judgment. I know everyone's suspect, but there has to be some trust, otherwise the whole thing will just stall. You can't cut yourself off from the network."

"Yes," I said. "You're right. I'm sorry. But don't call her yet. Save it until there's more in the store. It's time to go and tackle Seagull."

Cox nodded. "Hadn't you better tell me a bit more about her?"

"There isn't a lot to tell, I'm afraid. The affair didn't last all that long and we had a pact not to talk about the past. There were reasons that seemed good at the time—I was coming up to a divorce I didn't really want and didn't want to talk about. She told me she'd been married, that it had turned sour, and it suited her not to go into her past. So we lived in the present. Sex, friendship, each other's company. It seemed natural while we were living it." I hesitated. "After Ryder's photographs, it makes me look like a gold-plated, diamond-studded asshole. But that's something I'm learning to live with.

"However." I managed a grin. "The facts, such as they are. The lady Seagull. Real name—verified by Ryder—Jennifer Elisabeth Ross. Age, also verified by Ryder, thirty-six. He traced her birth certificate. Born in St. John's Wood, London. There's a record of her attending Maida Vale Primary School up to the age of eleven. Then a girls' boarding school in Norfolk—Exton House. After that comes the London College of Art and her career as a freelance nature illustrator, but Ryder's people say the details don't quite hang together. I couldn't help Ryder at all really. Jennifer and I never lived together, though I often stayed at her flat and she stayed at my place in Little Venice several times, often for a week or more at a time. She dressed well, very casually, jeans, shirts, very good taste but nothing expensive. Same with the flat: comfortable, very colorful. Really nice, in fact, but nothing indicating big money.

"She insisted on going dutch a lot—we never spent that much anyway, ate in out-of-the-way pubs, little restaurants outside London. She liked to drive in the BMW. Didn't own a car herself."

"How about some basic description?" Cox said.

"What can I say? You know how meaningless police-type descriptions are. I have no photos. About five feet eight inches, slender, short dark hair which she could have grown down to her waist by now. It's more than a year since I saw her last.

71

Good muscles, strong, lithe, very athletic. Moves beautifully. Though I hate to say this, I could just see her on some KGB assault course or in a gymnasium learning self-defense."

Cox grinned. "Reassuring."

"Very."

"What about the painting?"

"I loved her work. I haven't a very educated eye but I could have looked at it for hours. Exquisite, delicate drawings. Birds. Flowers. Every detail perfect, but when you stood back, there was always more than just a paintbrush playing at being a camera. Cover or not, she was an artist."

"Anything else?"

"Nothing important."

"Give me a capsule description," Cox said. "Never mind the police forms. Come on now. Quick, what do you remember about her? Three lines."

"Capable of arousing me at a thousand yards on a foggy night. Didn't see anything odd in giving up hash for Lent, and puts her feet on railway carriage seats."

Cox grinned. "Thanks. That helps."

"No," I said, "it doesn't. The psychiatrist games don't help because we may be dealing with an illusion. There are a hundred things I could tell you about her. Little intimate details. What she likes, her attitude to this or that. But everything I say has to be qualified—'apparently this,' 'she seemed to believe that.' If she's a professional, I may know nothing about her at all." I stood up. "Let's head for St. Tropez."

"Tell me one thing," Cox said as we walked down to the parking zone. "Why Seagull? Did you give her the nickname?"

I hesitated. "Yes. I gave it to her. But there was no special reason. It was just a nickname."

Cox knew I was lying, but he didn't pursue it. There was no point in telling him it was because of the soft, mewing sound she made during lovemaking when things were happening to her that she especially liked. Or how she'd insisted with good-humored naturalist's pedantry that it wasn't accurate and seagulls had much harsher, higher-pitched cries.

There was a lot more I'd held back in the café: how much I'd cared for her, how much I'd enjoyed making love with her, how proud I'd been—in the worst kind of cliché way—of how

I'd conducted the affair. It had been my proving flight after the crash with Nancy. I'd shown myself that I could attract a beautiful woman, love her as she wanted to be loved, then end the affair without bitterness to spare her involvement in the divorce. A perfect episode, a memory I couldn't bear to have spoiled; yet now I had to face the surreal possibility that it might have all come out of a KGB training manual, that even the mewing might have been done on cue, as part of a programmed fantasy seduction module IIA—the affair as confidence builder, suitable for use on middle-aged men suffering from predivorce depression.

Intellectually, I knew such things happened. I'd known personally at least three men who had fallen into similar traps in Moscow, Prague, and New York, but I still couldn't believe it. The ego fights against such humiliation beyond all logic, yet the pictures were there and I could think of no innocent explanation. She might have been a KGB target instead of a collaborator, but why would senior officers of the KGB bother with a young woman who illustrated books of roses and garden birds? And what had she been doing in Ankara and Stockholm and at the World Peace Congress?

I closed off the train of thought. It could only lead to depression and anger when what was needed were simple, logical steps: find her, talk to her, try to find out what the connection was. No prejudgments.

As we got in the car, I turned to Cox.

"There's one role you have in this that we haven't talked about."

"What's that?"

"Keeper of the royal objectivity. Right now, I'm calm and I'm thinking clearly. But it could get messy. Personal. I may be finding out things about her, and myself, that I don't want to know. You may have to help keep me straight." I grinned. "I don't want a confessor. That's not my style. Just a kick in the butt from time to time, if I seem to be going off track."

Cox looked at me seriously. No smile. No wisecracks.

"I understand," he said. "You can count on it." Then his face cut into a grin. "What can a correspondent lose kicking his boss in the butt? I've always wanted to work out of the Reykjavik bureau anyway."

9

Cox took Autoroute 8, the Marseilles tollway, as far as Le Muy, and for the first part of the journey we discussed tactics for making the approach to Seagull.

The doctor she was living with, Yves Guerard, was an intern at a fashionable clinic on the outskirts of St. Tropez specializing in plastic surgery and other medical concerns of the ultra-rich. He had apparently twice done summer internships there and Ryder's people had the impression that he was more dedicated to acquiring an annual tan than to developing his professional skills. She shared a little flat with him but the CIA reports said they never seemed to be there and Seagull apparently spent a lot of time in the hills of the St. Tropez peninsula doing drawings of Mediterranean flowers. Guerard didn't sound like a very flattering successor, but for all I knew he could have been another KGB assignment, and if he wasn't, it sounded like a typical Seagull living arrangement—casual and impermanent, with painting and sex in about equal proportions.

"What do you think?" Cox said when we had compared notes from our separate briefings with Ryder.

"I think an approach away from the flat," I said. "If we go there and they're out—which seems likely—it'll tip her off that someone is looking for her. If she's there, and she really does have reasons to avoid me, she can stall better from inside her own place; refuse to let me in, make a scene, set a jealous boyfriend on me, call the police. There are all kinds of options, assuming she was desperate enough."

"And away from the flat?"

"Still risky. She can still make a scene, but if we plan the approach carefully, we should be able to cut down the chances of her getting away." I grinned. "Especially if you look after Guerard."

"Ryder described him as a young, fit sun worshipper who spent more time looking after his own body than other people's. Leaving aside the fact that he may have a black belt in something or other, he probably has a gang of friends—French kids always run in packs on holiday."

"Don't worry. You'll think of something," I said. "That's why you're a highly paid exec—resourceful, quick-thinking." I grinned. "And replaceable in case of damage."

Cox laughed. "Let's start at the clinic. I'll make the inquiries. Friend of a friend, looking for advice on behalf of an ugly sister. How much would it cost to put her nose back in the middle of her face? Some rubbish like that."

We came off the motorway at Le Muy and started down the winding road through the woods and limestone outcrops to join the coast road. Immediately the traffic started to build up, and by Ste. Maxime, we had been swallowed up in a bumper-to-bumper line of holiday traffic crawling through the town.

"I thought the French were all supposed to start leaving the roads about now to have lunch," Cox said. "What happened to a great tradition?"

"I don't know," I said, "but at this rate, we're going to miss Guerard at the clinic. My bet is he'll spend the afternoon at the beach like everyone else in these latitudes."

Once through Ste. Maxime, the traffic began to speed up and we got directions to the Clinique Barbotin. After the first try, Cox learned not to pull off the road when he was asking a passerby, as forcing our way back into the line again practically needed a motorcycle escort. After the third attempt, we had our information—and I also began to get the feeling that we were being followed. At first I didn't say anything. Silently, I rehearsed the words, "Cox, I think someone is tailing us." Immediately my "stop before you make a fool of yourself" mechanism sounded the alarm, but I decided to trust my in-

75

stincts. When I've looked back on most of the serious blunders of my life, the post mortem has usually shown the cause wasn't recklessness but a failure to trust my "feel" for a situation.

"Cox," I said cautiously, "do you remember what they used to say back in the sixties?"

"What?"

"Just because you're paranoid, it doesn't mean no one's following you."

Cox nodded. "You mean the silver Citroen CX?"

"You noticed?"

"Yes. But it's hard to tell. I make it two men, thirties, darkish-skinned. Cruising very slowly in places, but could just be girl-watching."

"When we stopped the first time, they stopped too."

"Yes. The passenger got out to chat with that topless teeny who'd just wandered off the beach to buy some cigarettes."

"You don't miss much," I said.

"No. But it could have been genuine. Two guys on holiday, looking to fill the passenger seats." He grinned. "If we weren't on a mission to save the West from Ming the Merciless, I'd have stopped too. The young lady had a nice hungry look."

"And the second time we pulled up?"

"I didn't see them."

"No," I said, "neither did I, but we were stopped a couple of minutes and they should have gone by us. And they're still behind."

"There was some congestion behind us when we stopped. They might have just caught up to us. What do you want to do?"

"If the old lady was right," I said, "the clinic is well back from the coast. If they're following, they'll have to leave the main traffic stream. If they do, we'd better watch out. Whatever else they're doing in St. Tropez, they aren't looking for plastic surgery."

But when we found the clinic, I could see no sign of the Citroen. It didn't turn with us and though Cox paused, then did a complete circuit of the clinic building, it didn't reappear.

"I'll meet you at the port," Cox said. "I'll take a taxi." As he spoke, a teenage French girl on a bicycle, wearing white shorts and a breast-hugging sailor shirt, rang her bell and waved across at him.

Cox waved back, then looked at me seriously. "Don't worry, Chief. I'll keep my mind on the job. I happen to agree with Ryder. Starburst is a good missile. I think we need it. I wouldn't like to see the Soviets or anyone else shove it down the tubes."

"Interesting," I said. "This is something I'll have to get used to."

"What?"

"This sober, patriotic, thoughtful Cox, who turns down passes from sun babies and believes in Western defense."

"I've always believed in it. But don't worry, I won't break the code again. Serious without being solemn. The correspondents' watchword. Anyway, at least this Seagull person has had the good taste not to hide out in Paraguay. Any assignment that brings me to St. Tropez on expenses can't be all bad, even if there isn't time to enjoy it."

I left Cox at the clinic and drove into the port of St. Tropez and parked the Peugeot by the yacht basin. I hadn't been there for four or five years but nothing seemed to have changed. The port, even at lunchtime, was given over to the same stylized, ritual craziness. It was such a phony town, but I'd always liked it because everyone knew it was phony and never really pretended otherwise. There were more middle-aged tourists than when I'd last been there, but it was still a good people-watching place. The clothes were fun, the women were pretty, and the deep suntans helped along those who weren't. I couldn't defend my liking it rationally. Really, I suppose I just liked the sun and the women. I've always liked climates you don't have to defend yourself against and when I want to laze around in the sun, I'd rather be surrounded by beautiful, half-naked women—even if they are posturing and showing off—than by desolate rocks and lonely seascapes.

By the time I'd walked the length of the yacht basin and chatted with a few of the people who were eating lunch in the wells of the smaller, less fashionable yachts I was feeling almost cheerful, but it didn't help when I glanced at a magazine rack to pick up something to read while I waited for Cox, and the first face I saw was Nancy's. She was on the cover of an

American women's magazine over a caption promising, inside, the story of "Nancy Sellinger, the country house lady who likes to keep her feet off the ground."

I bought a copy, took it to the terrace of the Café de la Marine, and opened it at the article. It consisted mainly of photographs of what the headline called Nancy Sellinger's twin loves—the English countryside and flying her own plane. The first pictures were the most painful. It showed Nancy standing in the rose garden of Samman's Farm, the house in Kent halfway between London and the English Channel where she spent much of the year.

The caption mentioned that the house, which had not been a farm since the seventeenth century, was being lovingly restored under Nancy's direction—but tactfully didn't say that the house had once belonged to me. I had inherited it, struggled to keep it up without adequate means, and finally lost it to Nancy in the divorce settlement. Paul, who had been spending as much time as possible in Europe since the merger, attempting to win friends among the World News associates, always used it—not because he liked country life but because he knew how much I hated his being there. Paul understood the importance of personal symbolism. He used the house because for me, Samman's meant defeat. It reminded me of my last efforts to hold on to Nancy and keep my career and private life in some kind of balance. Having it go to Nancy after the divorce had sealed Sellinger's victory.

The other pictures were mostly of Nancy with her Piper Comanche, including one aerial shot of her skimming over the White Cliffs of Dover. Over a subhead which read "The Sellinger Lady in a Hurry," the article said that Nancy had already broken two flying club records, for the shortest time to go solo and the shortest to reach twin-engined rating. Flying had always fascinated her but when we were married she had not been able to afford it. Now it seemed she was making up for lost time.

I always hated seeing her referred to as Nancy Sellinger, and seeing her in the glossy magazines, as I often did now, only underlined how far she had moved away from me.

Her wealth seemed to seal the gap between us. She had been

born well-off—her father was a New York insurance broker with a house in Manhattan and a summer place in New England—but when we had married, she had slipped easily into my own modest life-style. She had never made any formal renunciation of her money; she simply hadn't used it, or talked about it, but when the marriage had begun to falter, I had measured her alienation by her gradual return to it. There had been trips first—back to her parents, who had retired to Maine—with no bill for the ticket, then longer trips, and clothes I could not have afforded. Now she had gone all the way, leapfrogging over her upper-middle-class upbringing into the Sellinger world of conspicuous ease.

The article said Nancy flew almost every day, often across the Channel to France. Nancy had always hated the French after some bad experiences during her student days, but of course, I was reading about another woman now: Nancy Sellinger, not Nancy Railton. If she were to come to St. Tropez now, she would have no contact with the French. It would be to one of the ungainly rich men's toy boats moored in the main harbor—the ones with carpets and mock-Regency furnishings which could never actually put to sea because the salt spray would kill all the plants twining around the salon.

I stood up suddenly and walked to the edge of the café terrace and threw the magazine into a trash can on the edge of the road. I knew too well where that line of thought would lead and it was too destructive and depressing.

It was time to concentrate on Seagull and to pray that "the consolation prize I'd won in a sleeping bag" hadn't really turned sour, as Sellinger had taunted.

I ordered another gin and sat mindlessly watching the passing parade until Cox came back, looking pleased.

"Didn't think it would be that easy," he said. "Seems Guerard is a creature of habit. Doesn't sound very overworked. I gather his father's a professor at the Paris Medical Faculty. Yves is the clinic golden boy. Condescends to put in a few hours each morning, then lunch, then beach. Always the same place—Le Windsurf Club near a village called Gigaro."

Cox paused. "And always apparently with his girl friend, the lady Seagull." He smiled. "Incidentally, if we ever need to swear in any deputies to get Seagull away from Dr. Guerard, there are a couple of nurses in there who'd really put their backs into it."

"So it's the beach then," I said. "Could be a good place, if we're careful. Do you have the right clothes?"

"No."

"We'll buy something now," I said. "These tropical suits are too conspicuous. In St. Tropez, you might as well be wearing a morning coat."

When we got back on the coast road, we watched for several kilometers for any sign of the Citroen but neither of us could spot it. To play doubly safe, we went twice around all the major traffic islands and did a further check at the La Croix hypermarket complex, where we stopped to buy bathing suits and T-shirts and beach trousers to put over them. By the time we had changed and checked yet again for the Citroen, we had wasted another half hour, and it was past three o'clock when we reached Gigaro.

It was the prettiest of several beaches we'd passed on the way and it was also the most popular; the after-lunch crowd had already slotted themselves between the all-day sun worshippers and the sand had more or less disappeared under a uniform layer of bronzed bodies. Unlike the earlier beaches, almost ninety percent of the women were topless and though there were still plenty of families—including a good number of English and German tourists—it seemed to be mainly a young people's gathering ground.

The Windsurf Club was at one end, separated from the public beach by a high windbreak made of laths and green reeds. We scouted it first without getting out of the car, but we ended up blocking traffic on the narrow beach esplanade, so we parked and walked back and sat in a café terrace within sight of the club.

Judging from the cars in its private parking lot, the Windsurf Club was an expensive place to work on a tan, but it wasn't immediately obvious what the members got for their money. The scrappy laurel hedge didn't provide much privacy, and there wasn't much in the way of club buildings either—just a beach bar with a thatched awning, a restaurant which was now deserted, and a row of hutlike structures which were presumably showers and changing rooms. The sand was slightly less crowded than on the public beach but the club didn't have its own stretch of water and the wind-surfers merged in among the hundreds of sails crisscrossing the bay as soon as they left the shoreline.

"Well?" I said, when we had both finished examining the terrain.

"Doesn't seem to be any control on the gate," Cox said. "There's no shade for the watchman's booth. He's probably in the water, if he's got any sense."

"Yes, I'm sure we'll get in all right. Problem is getting Seagull away from Guerard."

"We could wait until he's at the clinic tomorrow."

"We can't afford the time," I said. "I must try and get this over with in time to get to Rome. If I miss many more engagements, Sellinger will start making noises about WN needing an interim president."

Cox got up from the table. "I'll go in first," he said, "but before I go, do me a favor."

"What?"

"Smile."

"About what, for God's sake?"

"About anything. I know you're angry and I know you're uptight about seeing Jennifer—Seagull—again. But if you approach her looking like that, you'll scare her shitless."

"Even if she's a trained Soviet agent?"

"Don't prejudge," he said. "Be gentle. You're an old lover who's come back to talk to her because you're worried about the scandal and you want to coordinate stories in case the *News of the World* cowboys start getting in touch with her."

I grinned. "You mean I'm not supposed to stride up to her and seize her by the throat and say, 'Madam, are you now or have you ever been an agent of the Soviet intelligence services?' "

Cox grinned back. "That's better." He pointed across the road to the public beach. "Just relax. Enjoy the scenery. I'll be back as soon as I've found out if she's there."

The scenery he was pointing at consisted of two whitish-looking teenagers in matching G strings, who were smearing barrier cream around each other's nipples to protect the newly exposed areas.

When they'd moved on, I watched a group of English people: a family commanded by a fearsome-looking matron who, though topless, looked oddly overdressed in the ample bottom half of a two-piece made for more inhibited beaches.

The thought made me wonder about my own clothing. I'd bought a pair of white drill trousers and a blue T-shirt which, with the rope-soled canvas shoes, were fine on the esplanade, but, not surprisingly in the baking heat, I couldn't see a single man on the beach wearing anything but swimming trunks. There were several with shirts on—obviously as a protection against blistered shoulders, but if I wanted to remain even moderately inconspicuous, I would have to get rid of the trousers.

I was just wondering where best to leave them when I saw Cox sprinting out of the club. He'd obviously had the same idea as he had stripped to his bathing suit and was having trouble in bare feet on the hot concrete of the esplanade.

He signaled me urgently to come and I paid and ran across the road.

"What's the matter? What's wrong?"

"Nothing," Cox said. "A bit of luck. They're both out windsurfing but she's coming in without him. If you move it, you may be able to catch her while he's right out in the bay."

Cox ran ahead, guiding me through a narrow passageway beside the restaurant away from the immediate area of the clubhouse, and as soon as we were on the sand, I saw Seagull. She was right by the water's edge, with one foot on her surfboard, guiding it through the small tidal undertow. She was completely absorbed in controlling the sail so that it didn't become waterlogged as it lay flat on the surface of the sea.

Once I had spotted her, Cox stopped and I hurried on, slowing down just enough not to kick sand over the rows of sunbathers.

There wasn't time to rehearse a greeting. I simply walked up to her and said, "Hello," then added spontaneously, "You look incredible. A seagull dipped in chocolate."

She was wearing two tiny triangles of lilac fabric linked by a

82

plaited thong and she was uniformly tanned a deep resident's bronze.

"John. What in heaven's name are you doing here?"

There was no point in pretending it was an accidental meeting. My skin color would tell her I'd been on the coast only a few hours.

"I came to find you," I said.

"Just like that?"

"Not quite. I need to talk to you."

"You didn't pick a very good time." She glanced out to sea. "I'm not alone."

"I presumed not," I said. I gave her a little smile. "A seagull would need a barbed-wire barricade to stay alone in St. Tropez."

"I'd rather not pick up any old threads," she said. "It's never a good idea."

I'd expected some awkwardness, but there wasn't quite enough surprise in her voice to be convincing. I was sure she had been at least half-expecting me and the thought wasn't reassuring.

"John, I don't want to talk," she said, turning slightly away on the pretext of maneuvering the sail.

"It's important."

"To you perhaps. For me the past is past. I don't want to reopen it."

"It's not that easy," I said. "It isn't a matter of just deciding you don't want to."

"Yes, it is easy," she said. "It's very easy. I just get on my surfboard and while I'm out in the bay, you catch a plane to London, or New York, or Hongkong, or wherever you're going next."

Considering that she gave me a cue line, I should have moved more quickly, but I hesitated just a fraction too long as she hauled up the sail. Though the mast was flat on the water, there was no water on the canvas to weigh it down and she was at just the right angle, too, for the wind to help it rise. She caught the guiding ring smoothly and the board was several yards offshore before the sail had reached forty-five degrees. I lunged after her but I missed the back of the board by a foot and ended up soaking and floundering ridiculously in the low broken surf along the waterline. By the time I'd gotten my footing, she was twenty yards out; the sail was high and she was preparing to run tight with the wind. She was completely at ease on the board and the maneuver she'd used to get away from me told me there was no chance she would fall. Once she got out of the shelter of the promontory she would catch a stiff breeze which was making whitecaps on the dark-blue water in the middle of the bay. Nor was she even limited to the bay of Gigaro. She could go around the headland and come ashore in any three or four smaller beaches up the coast. After that, she could simply disappear and I'd have no hope of tracing her in time.

I looked around desperately. There were wind-surfers for hire, but I wouldn't have lasted ten yards and there were no other boats inside the club. But just beyond the windbreak there was a jetty and I could see two inboard speedboats, rigged for towing water-skiers. There wasn't time to go around by the road. I stripped off my trousers, grabbed my wallet and keys in one hand, and plunged into the water. I needed to go only up to my knees, but even that depth of water made running ungainly and it took me three or four minutes to make it to the jetty.

The boatman had watched me coming, and there was no point in trying to hide the fact that I wanted a boat at all costs. But as he started to bargain, I snapped in French: "Don't be stupid, you haven't had more than one water-skier all day." I was only guessing but I knew wind-surfing had almost killed water-skiing as a vacation sport and the price I offered in the next breath was big enough to settle the argument.

I pointed toward the club beach but the boatman shook his head, indicating a line of buoys marking the inshore limit for boats. "Go around," I said. "Stay parallel with the shore. I want to catch that board—the one by the point. With the blue sail."

The boatman headed straight out to sea at ninety degrees to the shore, then swung in a dramatic, heeling arc and put the boat into high gear. The marker buoys lasted less than a quarter of a mile, then we were in open water and closing on Seagull fast.

84

I wondered if Guerard had been watching, but for the moment it didn't matter. If we could just get alongside, I knew I could get her into the boat.

I had no intention of hurting her, but I was quite prepared to play rough; there was too much at stake for niceties and her lack of surprise at seeing me had shocked me out of any tender desire to relive old times.

But I hadn't counted on her determination either. I gave instructions to the boatman to approach her astern, on the windward side, so I'd have room to reach out and grab her if she refused to drop the sail. When she heard the roar of the engine, she turned and glanced over her shoulder, then she started to look around. I could guess what was in her mind. If she went out farther into open water I might not get her immediately, but I had only to circle and wait until she gave up. If she headed around the promontory, I could reach the shore as quickly as she could and there were no inlets small enough to keep the speedboat from following. Her only chance was to head back the way she had come and try to play tag among the other wind-surfers where the speedboat would lose its edge, even supposing I could persuade the boatman to risk losing his license by getting dangerously close to shore.

With a better boatman, she might even have gotten away with it, but, like me, she assumed his competence and that was where we both made a mistake.

Her try at escaping began beautifully and it would have been a very stylish maneuver. She needed to turn into the wind, but sharply so that she could free-run toward the beach and build up a lead, while we were making our turning circle. I saw her moving slowly toward the bow of the board, ready to do the elegant little two-step around the mast necessary to go about into the wind.

I signaled to the boatman that she was going to turn—believing that he would have worked it out for himself anyway—and gestured to him to cut the engine and swing his nose around when she had passed. I made the gestures clear enough, and anyway it didn't take a master mariner to figure out how to come alongside her immediately after the turn. Or so I thought.

She began to go about and the next thing I knew, we had

sliced the nose right off her board and sent her spinning into our bow wave, her head inches from our hull.

For a second I thought we'd killed her. I couldn't believe any professional seaman could have done anything so stupid. I stared desperately into the wake, then I saw her head appear in the flurry of foam and saw that she was still conscious. I jumped over the side and grabbed her before she went under, and signaled to the boatman to cut his engines so I could haul her aboard over the flat transom without getting tangled in the screws.

This time he got it right, but it took us both all our strength to manhandle her and by the time I'd followed her in, she'd gotten enough of the water out of her nose and lungs to start yelling and throwing punches.

There was no time to be subtle. I grabbed her in a bear hug which looked very approximately like a tender concern, for the boatman's benefit, but which in fact pulled her arms into her body so tightly she started coughing and choking again.

"Quick," I said, "get her back to the beach. Leave the board. I'll pay you to come back for it later." The boatman didn't argue. He'd obviously been expecting me to blame him for the accident, and he turned his back on us before I could begin and I concentrated on holding Seagull immobilized, using a military police hold. I forced her into a rough fetal crouch, with her head buried in my chest so she couldn't shout, which was fine in the boat, but I'd no idea what was going to happen once we landed. She had only to shout rape, or even start to struggle, and I'd have the police or the lifeguards on me in seconds.

If they'd seen the accident the lifeguards would come anyway, so I decided to have one more try at persuasion.

"Seagull," I said, "I'm sorry. I didn't mean to hurt you. I need to talk to you. Really need. Wouldn't have done all this if it didn't matter."

When she didn't answer, I looked down and realized she was unconscious. I knew instantly what I'd done. I'd pressed too hard on her neck veins while trying to keep her head covered. I'd practiced often enough applying the hold without too much pressure and twice I'd accidentally put a partner out in the RMP gymnasium. I eased myself around to shield her fully from the boatman's view and checked her eyes and her breathing. She would be all right, but she could be out for several minutes and I was going to have a lot of explaining to do when we got to the beach. But I'd underestimated Cox. When the boat touched the landing stage he was there, ahead of the lifeguards, waving a set of car keys.

"*Docteur, Docteur,*" he shouted in French. "This way. The car's waiting. You can take her straight to the surgery."

I picked her up gently, stepped out of the boat, and said quietly to Cox in English, "Stick my wallet in my trunks. Pay the boatman to get the wind-surfer, then wait for me in St. Tropez. The Bar du Port."

Cox nodded, signaled to the boatman to wait, then started to clear a path for me across the beach. The lifeguards stood back at the magic word "doctor"—no one in France ever harasses the professions—and I was halfway across the beach with Seagull in my arms when I heard Cox hiss behind me, "Chief. It's Guerard. Just coming ashore. The red sail with the white stripe."

I looked back and saw the sail. On the board was a tall, fit-looking man in his thirties with long, dark wavy hair and a deep tan.

If we'd been alone, there would have been no problem; he looked too vain to be much of a fighter. Even as he skimmed toward the beach, believing he had to deal with some emergency affecting his lover, he still made a point of making a stylish and unnecessary maneuver as he passed by the raft full of teenage girls moored just offshore. But if he once reached us, I couldn't see any way of getting off the beach. The lifeguards and others at the club would know he was a doctor and I couldn't brazen it through with the idea of taking Seagull to my imaginary surgery.

It was Cox, as usual, who came up with a solution. Before Guerard had even beached his surfboard, Cox ran back to the water's edge, grabbed hold of his arm.

"Yves, Yves," he shouted in loud, piercing French, "don't leave me for that man. He's old and ugly," he shouted, pointing at me. "And look, he prefers women. Can't you see he's not for you?"

The scene stopped even me dead in my tracks and Guerard

just stared at Cox in disbelief. It wasn't just surprise; he had no idea at all how to deal with this outburst of homosexual jealousy by a frail-looking, bony man he had never seen before.

First he stood still, uncertain whether to try to throw Cox aside or reason with him. I stood still also, not wanting to provoke him into action, waiting for Cox's next move.

Cox went on yelling, then started to pull Guerard back into the water as a crowd of fascinated sunbathers started to close in around them. When Guerard saw his way was being blocked by the onlookers, he made another attempt to get free of Cox's nagging grip.

Cox let out a high-pitched wail and started flailing at Guerard with both fists. I watched fascinated. Anyone who didn't know Cox would see only a pathetic flurry of blows from an apparently hysterical gay youth, but I could see that Cox knew exactly what he was doing. He was obviously a skillful boxer with the speed and intricate footwork of a featherweight and he was placing blow after blow under Guerard's half-hearted guard, straight into the gut.

I knew Guerard's wind wouldn't last long. And I knew Cox well enough to be sure no one would get them apart without killing him. It was time to move and, when in doubt, it's usually best to do the simplest thing—so I picked Seagull up again and ran straight off the beach.

10

When Jennifer eventually came around, the first words she said were, "God, I need a cigarette."

"Seagull," I said gently, "you've only just got the water out of your lungs."

She turned sideways in the front passenger seat and watched me drive.

"John Railton. In the last half hour you have almost split my head open with a speedboat, almost drowned me, almost choked me to death, and as a bonus you've also scorched my back by dumping me wet on a red-hot leather car seat. I'll worry about my health. Just give me a cigarette."

"I'm sorry. I don't have any."

"Well, bloody well stop and buy some." She looked around angrily, trying to get her bearings. "Turn left at the next fork, there's a *tabac* about half a mile on."

We were already well out of Gigaro. To avoid being caught in traffic, I'd taken a minor road, straight up the hillside into the woods above the bay. Across the valley I could see the Saracen village of Gassin, but I wasn't sure exactly where I was in the confusing network of roads crossing the St. Tropez peninsula.

Seagull closed her eyes again and didn't answer when I asked how she felt. I drove on, found the *tabac*, and stopped the car. I hesitated before getting out and, without opening her eyes,

Seagull said, "I won't run away. I'm too wrecked. Just get me a packet of Gauloises Filtres and a box of matches."

As I bought them, I watched her through the window of the little grocery store, but she didn't stir. When I gave them to her, she lit one and said, "Follow the road marked Amarin. Take the first left, then a right. The signpost says Vallieres."

"Where are we going?"

"I have a place up there."

I was going to say something about the flat but I decided against it. It was going to be awkward enough explaining how I'd found her and it wasn't the moment to let her realize she'd been under detailed surveillance.

I followed her directions and we began to climb more steeply, making several hairpin turns around trees which formed a shady canopy over the road. Already I could make out four separate hills on the peninsula and see the sea on both sides. On the horizon, I could see an aircraft carrier outside the bay. I knew it was the U.S.S. *Dwight D. Eisenhower* on its way back from an Indian Ocean flag-showing cruise to take part in the NATO exercises. For the first time in more than a decade French troops were taking part, and the papers I'd seen at Nice airport had carried reports of protests in Paris and Lyons.

I wished suddenly that the whole Starburst nightmare would just evaporate and I could be left sitting beside this beautiful, bronzed, almost naked woman, with no other problem than to find her a shirt so I could take her to dinner in one of the hill-top villages and watch the sunset.

I had no idea how I was going to begin to question her. Even "wrecked," as she put it, she was still far too bright to be led sideways into an issue, and there was a real chance that she would simply say "No, I don't want to talk about it." I could then assume her guilt, but where would that leave me? Should I have her arrested? And anyway, could I? And if I did, was my career irretrievably lost? Or what if I did nothing? I'd been turned loose on a very tight rein to try to unravel some threads that Ryder's men hadn't managed to do. If I couldn't undo even the first skein, would I simply be formally interrogated and forced to resign?

I was thinking about the options when suddenly a completely naked woman stepped out into the middle of the road. I could hear laughter coming from under the trees at the side of the road, and the sound of clinking glasses. There was obviously a party going on in the grounds of the red-tiled farmhouse, and the woman had gone to get something at the main house. I braked and she waved and continued her crossing unruffled, and disappeared behind the wall. It was an extraordinary sight and yet quite natural. She seemed to be simply part of the wildlife of the peninsula—like the deer in Windsor Great Park.

Jennifer didn't react. She stared ahead through the windshield as though she hadn't noticed and I knew it was her way of telling me she was still angry. She had told me once that she liked to amuse herself by trying to see things through a man's eyes, and normally she would have made a joke or a teasing sexual allusion.

I stopped the thought short, knowing I was being ridiculous. I was recalling a woman who probably had never existed. The reality was this sullen, angry creature slumped beside me whom I had somehow to provoke into responding to me.

"Look, Seagull," I said, finally, "I'm sorry about what happened at Gigaro. I know it doesn't make up for it. But what else can I say?"

When that didn't get any reaction, I added, "And I'll pay for the surfboard."

She drew on her cigarette.

"Cash or by installments?"

"What do you mean?"

"Last time we met, you were worried that your divorce was going to ruin you. I gather it didn't, finally."

I managed a smile. "It left me enough to buy a wind-surfer."

"How bad was it?"

"The settlement?"

"Yes."

"About what you'd expect."

"Did it help my not being there?"

"Yes. Though they knew about us, in the end. I wanted to give Nancy most of what I gave her. I felt I owed it to her. But if I hadn't, Sellinger would have seen she took it."

"But it helped? My going away?"

91

"Yes."

"Then why didn't you keep your side of the bargain? We had a deal. We promised each other a nice smooth ending. You didn't want me to get involved in the divorce. So we parted. Two free beings. Now you're back."

"Seagull," I said gently, "let's stop playing games with each other."

"What games?"

"Plowing through dialogue about divorce and partings and free beings. You know very well I didn't come here to try and pick up where we left off, or interfere with your life here."

"Then don't interfere. Just go away."

"Seagull, we've been through this once."

"So what are you going to do? Drive another speedboat over me?"

She leaned forward and pointed through the windshield.

"Break. Bell. End of round one," she said. "We're there. That's my place."

I looked up and saw a small campsite and beyond it, half hidden in some trees, a Provençal cottage with a red-tiled roof.

"The house? How do I get to it?"

"No. Not the house. The tent. Just drive straight across the field."

I did as she said and parked beside a big orange "bungalow" tent big enough to sleep five or six people. The flaps were closed but there was an awning projecting forward on two poles, making a terrace, with three canvas chairs grouped around a plastic table.

"Help me open it up," she said. "It'll be as stuffy as hell until we get a breeze through it."

Though we had to be several hundred feet up, the air was dry and the breeze felt hot on the skin. The grass was so brittle that it crackled as we walked over it, and I noticed a sign on the tree beside the wall warning of the dangers of fires. As a further reminder, there was a grove of charred trees lower down the slope.

She saw me looking and said, "They caught that one in time. Over at Cap Marie they weren't so lucky. Forty thousand hectares went up in smoke. That thing doesn't leak fuel or anything, does it?" she added, pointing to the car.

"Not as far as I know."

I checked quickly under the tank, then went back to help Seagull open up the flaps of the tent.

"Welcome to my studio," she said. The interior of the tent was divided into four segments: a kitchen, a sleeping area, and what would normally have been another "bedroom" and an eating area, but which here were a clutter of artist's materials, discarded sheets of paper and board and piles of paint-stained rags.

"You haven't changed," I said, remembering how I used to have to step over the same kind of clutter in her Hampstead flat.

"I clean it up every night. I have to take most of the stuff away each time I come or it would get pinched. I leave the easel and the biggest board."

"You don't sleep here then," I said. I stepped into the sleeping area, waiting to see whether she would mention Yves. She'd been unconscious through the confrontation on the beach but she must have guessed I knew. However I had traced her, I would presumably have found out about the flat in St. Tropez.

"I sleep here sometimes. If I'm on a good streak." I looked around the bedroom for some kind of indication of how much she used the tent; I didn't know what it would prove, but I wanted to stall to leave her to make a move.

She noticed my eyes scanning the small rack of washing beside the camp bed.

"You haven't changed either," she said. "Still looking for your frivolous woman?"

It was an old joke. She'd teased me once in Hampstead about being interested in her washing line. I'd told her how we used to look at everyone's washing on the way to school and tell one another with boyish bravado that it never did any harm to know which houses had a girl with a frivolous taste in undies. It had amused her then as casual pillow talk, and I remembered kissing her and telling her I knew better now. I had never known a more sensual woman than Seagull, yet she always wore little-girl underwear—cotton bikinis that felt wooly to the touch from too many washings.

Now the joke seemed silly and strained, a reminder that

93

there is nothing as awkward as sex gone sour. Which brought us back to the same nightmare question: Had there ever been anything to turn sour? Nothing she had said since I had spoken to her at the water's edge had sounded right. She had been scared when she saw me and she still was, but she was also angry and not, I was sure, just because of the accident with the boat.

I decided it had to be faced. At least we were alone here— to talk, or to fight if we must—but we could easily be interrupted, by Yves or by someone from the house.

"Seagull," I said, "it's time for round two."

"Yes." The tone was cold, deliberate, not helping.

"Seagull, I know about Yves. And your life here. I'm not trying to disturb any of that."

"How did you know where I was?"

I smiled. "Seagull, come on. I have two thousand-odd employees. Many of them get paid to find out simple things like what the President of the United States really said to the Pope during his state visit to Italy."

I didn't know whether she believed it, but it was plausible: I could have found out.

"But the real question is how you knew I was coming."

"What do you mean?"

"You weren't surprised to see me, and as for being worried at what a new lover will think because an old one drops by, Seagull, it was nonsense. You can handle that sort of situation in your sleep. You knew I was coming and you knew it wasn't just to relive old times."

Seagull paused. "All right," she said, "we'll talk. I'll get dressed. Get us some drinks; there's a cooler in the kitchen."

Dressing consisted of putting on a muslin shirt, and she was already arranging the chairs on the terrace when I had finished finding out what was cool enough to drink. There was no ice, but I had found some tonic floating in the melted water of the cooler, and some gin, and anything was welcome in the baking heat. The sun would be starting to go down in less than an hour, but the tent was still stifling from being closed up during the day and the little terrace wasn't shady enough to deal with the glare from outside and the accumulated heat within.

94

We sat facing each other uncomfortably and before she took a drink she stroked her neck.

"Does it hurt?"

"Yes. But it'll be okay." She paused. "Yes, I've been expecting you."

"Why?"

"Your men who are so good at finding out about Presidents and Popes don't cover their tracks very well. I knew they'd been making inquiries in London."

It was lie number one. She could well have known that someone was inquiring, but no World News people had been anywhere near her. But I couldn't challenge it without revealing my own lie and admitting that the CIA was involved.

"I'm sorry if my people embarrassed you."

"At least they didn't try to choke me to death."

"There'll be others," I said. "Reporters. Not just World News. Police too, if they haven't already been. That's why I came to see you: I wanted to warn you. Tell you what's happening."

When she didn't react, I decided to plunge on. I was getting nowhere. I had to get into it. I gave her what Ryder had called version A: how the party was going to turn into a scandal, because of stories being peddled in Fleet Street; how Louise Allenby was supposed to have suffocated in a sleeping bag while she was high on dope.

She listened, still with no sign of surprise, then she said quietly: "So what do you want from me? Do you want me to lie? Say you weren't there? That I met you somewhere else?"

"No. That's not possible."

"Then what?"

I knew I was in a corner. She was too quick, too abrasive. I still didn't know why she had been expecting me and already version A was useless. I wasn't ready to jump straight to version B, so I decided to improvise a middle ground.

"I do need an alibi," I said. "The police aren't satisfied that Allenby died accidentally. They believe she may have been murdered."

"And you think you're a suspect?"

"Yes. It's possible. I knew her slightly."

95

"So there's no motive?"

"I'm open to suggestions. So apparently are the police."

"You've been questioned by the police?"

"Not officially. Not directly about the murder. Only hints."

"Then why do you think they're after you?"

"The hints were very strong. And I've had other information."

"And you want an alibi."

"Possibly, yes."

She smiled. It was what I had learned to call her Seagull smile, a warm laughing smile which set the edges of her mouth into an unusually steep curve. It was the first hint since I'd arrived in St. Tropez of the woman I had thought I'd known.

"No problem at all," she said, "I'll be glad to help." She paused, then said in a mock Cockney accent she had used before to tease me: "Yes, your honor. You see, we was in this sleeping bag and we never got out because he'd won me, see, and, I mean he wouldn't want to pass up free nooky, I mean, would 'e? So he couldn't have done it. We were in there fucking our brains out the whole time. Er yes, your honor, he did get out twice . . . once to go to the loo and once to get some more grass. No, your honor, he wasn't away long. Not long enough to kill anyone, I'm sure. The grass? Yes, your honor. Marijuana. No, it was mine. When I said he went to get some more, I meant from my handbag. Yes, your honor. He likes to smoke but he never buys his own, on account of 'im being respectable."

She broke off, still laughing. "Did that sound all right, or should I rehearse some more?"

But her smile didn't last.

"And you talk about me playing games," she said angrily. "You wanted to talk straight. So talk straight."

"All right," I said, stung at being taken in by the smile. "Let's start from the beginning. How did you know I was coming here?"

"There were questions in London, I told you."

"That's not good enough."

"No, it bloody well wasn't good enough. Whoever it was, they weren't just looking for my new address. They've been to Scotland asking questions about my mother. They've been to my schools; places I grew up; they've been sniffing round friends. Yes, they could have been reporters, but they weren't, were they? They weren't just asking about me. They were asking about us. And they weren't just plain old-fashioned coppers either, were they?"

"What do you mean?"

"What do I mean?" she sneered. "I mean that if it were an ordinary murder inquiry, I wouldn't have Americans, posing as reporters, asking questions about me right here in St. Tropez. For God's sake, John, don't be naive. St. Tropez, my St. Tropez, is a village. You might as well try to make discreet inquiries in Chipping Magna. And if I hadn't worked it out for myself, I'd have known anyway that intelligence were involved."

"How? How would you have known?"

"A phone call," Seagull said. "A phone call from Kate. A Kate in total panic who'd just skipped out of Cairo because the CIA were about to get the Egyptians to arrest her. She wanted to know what the hell you'd done." She smiled. "That can't surprise you. You know Kate. She's never short of men who care about her welfare. One of them was in Egyptian security."

I listened with growing alarm. People as far on the fringe as a security official in Cairo knew I was being investigated; it might be only days before hints started appearing in the press. The French scandal sheets would float anything. They'd probably announce I was also the Queen's secret lover as well as a spy, just for good measure. And still I was no further with Seagull. Everything she said was plausible. The CIA and MI6 could have been that clumsy; they were in a hurry and Ryder had admitted they were desperate. Kate could have called Seagull; they were supposed to have been friends since school. Or it could all be a professional's defense, one so carefully constructed that I would have to believe it.

I knew it was confrontation time. I got up from the chair. "Seagull, could I have another drink? I want to get something from the car."

She read my look. "So we're getting to the nitty-gritty at last? I'm getting through to you?"

"Yes," I said, "you're getting through to me."

Copies of Ryder's photographs were in a document case in the trunk and as I walked over to get them I wondered how I should show them to her. Would she be expecting this? Had she a defense for this too? Though the sun was already low on the horizon and the first cicadas were beginning to crackle in the woods, it was still hot enough to feel my pale skin tingle through the back of my shirt. In the bay there were more whitecaps than before, but the woods around the house were sheltering the tent from the stiffening breeze. There were more cars too in the lane we had driven up, presumably the beach crowd dispersing to villas in the hills. I watched for a moment, enjoying a break in the tension of fencing with Seagull, then I saw the Citroen parked under some trees about a mile down the hill. Or at least I saw a Citroen roof, a fragment of metal caught by the sun. There was no way of being sure. The model was one of the most popular larger cars in France and metallic silver one of the standard color options. If we hadn't noticed the Citroen outside Ste. Maxime, I might well not have noticed this one. There were other cars parked on the hillside—lovers perhaps, or people enjoying the view from one of the deeper patches of shade.

I heard Seagull's voice behind me. "Well, what do you have to show me?"

I wondered suddenly if she was speaking for the record. Could the Citroen be watching out for her, with a gun mike trained on the tent, waiting to step in if her defenses didn't convince me?

I took the document case from the trunk and went back to the little terrace of the tent. Seagull had poured another drink but it was tepid and the tonic had gone flat.

I left it on the table and reached down for the document case, glancing down the valley to see if the Citroen was still there. At first I thought I saw the roof, then I realized it was a trick of the sunlight; the Citroen had gone.

"What's the matter?" Seagull said.

"Nothing."

"So what do you have to show me?"

"Some photographs," I said, laying them out on the table. "I came to ask you to explain these." It was impossible to tell if she went white; her tan was too deep to betray any change in skin tone. But her eyes and her mouth were enough to tell me how scared she was.

"I've nothing to say," she said. "Those photographs belong to the past. They have no connection with the party or Louise Allenby or you."

"Seagull, I want to believe that," I said. "But saying it isn't enough. You have to explain."

"They're the past," she said. "The past is closed."

"It's being reopened. By me, now. By others if you won't tell me."

"I won't reopen the past. Not for you, or anyone. Take the photographs. I don't want to see them."

I turned, looking for words that would get through to her, trying at the same time to control my own anger.

Then the dart hit the back of my thigh.

Darts are supposed to sting, but this one felt as though an iron bar had been laid across the muscle. I yelled "Shit" and stumbled forward, the leg buckling under me. The pain seemed to go both up and down, affecting my toes and stinging right into my groin. I remember thinking, I'll get Seagull for this, then I saw the second dart hit her. It struck her in the softest part of the hip and the impact tore a hole in the muslin and actually took fragments of fabric into the hole it made in the skin. When the blood came, the hole seemed to explode like a lanced boil and she screamed and put her hand over it and pitched forward onto the floor.

I was already losing consciousness when I saw the flames in the tiny kitchen of the tent. I'd no idea how they'd started; my head was swimming and I couldn't focus or hear properly, but I could see the fire catching the end of the canvas partition. Seagull was on the tarpaulin floor of the terrace; I had fallen inward and my head and shoulders were inside the tent. I was closest to the fire, five or six feet away at most, but the difference was academic; with the breeze and dry canvas and grass, the tent would be our funeral pyre. But whoever had shot the darts and started the fire had reckoned without my father. Later, as I lay delirious in the hospital, I said a prayer to him, telling him it was finally all right. We were finally quits.

As a child of five or six, he had once summoned me sharply

as I sat playing by the hearth instead of coming for a meal; scared by his voice I had gotten up too quickly, tripped over the curb, and plunged arms first into the fire. I'd been almost a year in the hospital and it had grieved my father right up to his death that he should have left the fire unguarded and caused me so much suffering as well as giving me a fear of fire that had never left me. Over the years I had tried to master it, but in battle zones it was always the flamethrower or the burning building that made my guts dissolve, more than any shelling or machine-gun fire.

In the tent, it was the fear that saved me. As the flames approached, blind panic fought with the effects of the drug and gave me the strength to drag Seagull and myself out of the tent, when I should have been lying helplessly in the path of the fire.

I remember nothing clearly about the escape, but one image was strong and sharp: that kitchen was the blazing hearth and I could not, would not fall into it again.

The rest was fragments in a delirium. With hindsight, I can put them into a kind of sequence; at the time, there was only confusion and strange shapes and noise.

The monstrous black shape soaring over the trees I know now was a twin-engined Canadair rigged for fire fighting. Later I saw press pictures of two of them doing their spectacular water-collecting belly flops in the bay of St. Tropez before skimming back to the hills and opening their gigantic bomb doors to let thousands of gallons of seawater spray onto the blazing trees. When I first became aware of the plane, I must have known subliminally what it was because I remember trying to turn face upwards. I wanted water, refreshment, and though my arms were almost paralyzed from the drug I tried to roll over and turn Seagull so that she could enjoy it too. Then there was the roar of the engine and I saw the doors opening over the tree tops like a vision in a science fiction movie and I thought, "No. That's not right. This is going to hurt. It's too heavy." As I tried to turn back, I remembered stupidly the Bob Dylan song, "A Hard Rain's Gonna Fall." And I thought I was shielding my face when the water did fall, but I must have hardly moved my limbs except in my imagination because the rain fell on my back, stinging and cutting.

After that I lay still, enjoying the slippery feel of the soaking grass until I looked up and saw more fire, still in the trees, and I somehow got the idea that my chest was soaked with blood, not water, and I tried to move so I could wipe it away.

The next fragment was an argument. I could see, just, but it was like the view through a car windshield in a storm when the wipers are not working. I was in an ambulance and someone was trying to get in the back doors but a male nurse with a Red Cross armband was barring the way. Outside, I could hear French voices shouting angrily and someone else, a woman, crying and there were sirens and the sound of horns honking. It was a tableau I could make no sense of at all and I had to be told much later that the ambulance bringing us from the fire had been involved in a traffic accident; an injured man was being put with us, but the driver was refusing to let the relatives in. The nurse told me afterwards that I'd raised an arm and said petulantly, "This is my room. I paid for it. Go and sleep somewhere else."

After that, there was the hospital. The first time I opened my eyes, I saw Seagull lying in a bed next to mine and I thought stupidly, "If this was an English hospital, we'd be in separate rooms," then Cox appeared, blurred but reassuring, and said, just as I fell unconscious again, "It's okay, Chief, you're not burned. Neither is she. You made it."

The second time I came to, I thought I was still in the middle of a bizarre dream, because Armand Celestin, the WN Paris bureau chief, was standing there, looking as he always did as though waiting for the long-overdue summons to the Quai d'Orsai for his appointment as the next French foreign minister. Cox again, I thought. The ever-resourceful Cox. If you needed someone to browbeat the local gendarmerie, who better than Celestin, the diplomat manqué, friend and confidante of three French presidents.

When I slept again, the journalist in me took over my dreams and I found myself writing press reports of the fire. "Police in St. Tropez said tonight they were waiting to question two English campers in connection with the forest fire which destroyed several thousand hectares of forest in the Var Department yesterday . . ." and so on. I started an argument with myself at one point about whether names should be used in the story: local reporter versus Paris bureau chief; one wanting a good byline story, the other concerned about libel if police had gotten the foreign names wrong, as they often did. Then the dream faded and I imagined the Canadair dropping fire bombs to dry out a wet forest, and the next thing I remember I was on a stretcher being put into the back of a camper van.

The stretcher was halted with me halfway into the van. I could see the French license plate and the "F" plaque, then Celestin came into view, then Cox, then another stretcher with Seagull sleeping soundly, her face flat on a narrow white pillow.

I remember Celestin looking distastefully at the camper van. He had never, I'm sure, vacationed in anything less comfortable than a five-star hotel, and he seemed uncertain that a human being could be allowed to travel in anything quite so inadequate.

Then Cox came over to the stretcher, holding a piece of paper.

"Can you hear me?" he whispered.

"Yes."

"Last-minute formalities. You have to sign this. The police are letting us take you away, but you have to sign a medical release."

I managed a nod, but found I couldn't move my arm.

Cox glanced around, then shifted his position so that his back was between the stretcher and the policeman and scrawled a signature on the form. "I've done Seagull's," he said. "Okay, we're all set."

"Where are we going?" I said, hearing my voice sounding faint and hoarse.

"Italy. Over the frontier via Menton. Quickest way of getting you out of French jurisdiction. It was a helluva fire. Everyone's very jumpy."

"Cox," I whispered, "have you ever considered getting a job as someone's exec?"

Cox grinned. "Not fucking likely. I'm for the quiet life. Give me El Salvador any time."

11

By the time I was fully conscious and able to grasp events again, the camper van had transformed itself into the cabin of a Lear executive jet. We were on the ground—I had no idea where—and I could hear the engines warming up for takeoff. I was in a berth and, for the first time since the fire, I felt comfortable. I had a slight headache, but the pain had gone from my leg and I could see clearly and I felt quite cheerful—until I saw Cox.

When he stepped through the partitioned door into the cabin, he looked more worried than I had ever seen him. There was no sign of the relaxed, wisecracking Cox. He looked tired, which was understandable enough, but there was obviously much more wrong than that.

He sat down on a folding seat beside the berth and leaned over as though to talk confidentially. When I tried to thank him for what he had done in France, he brushed it aside and said, "Chief, there's no time right now. All hell's breaking loose." I was going to make some comment about where had the "serious but not solemn Cox gone," but I could see that whatever had happened had really gotten to him.

"What's happened?"

"What hasn't."

"Where are we?"

"Genoa. We're taking off for Stelstead. It was the nearest quiet field to London."

"Where's Seagull?"

"In the other cabin. She hasn't come around yet. Dr. Richardson is with her."

"Richardson?"

Mervyn Richardson was the company physician, an eminent private specialist who was World News consultant in London.

"He flew out with the Lear. He says you'll be fine, by the way."

"What about Jennifer?"

"All right too, probably."

"Thank God for that."

Cox hesitated.

"Chief. We have to talk about Jennifer. I've been in touch with Ryder. He's in London. He wants to know immediately what you found out about her in St. Tropez."

"Nothing conclusive," I said. "She was scared when she saw the photographs. She said they were part of her past life and she wouldn't reopen it."

"Do you think she was lying?"

"I'm still of two minds," I said. "On the one hand it's pretty damning. But I'm still nagged by the idea that if she's a professional, and I was an assignment, why didn't she go back to Moscow or at least farther out of reach than St. Tropez? And if it was the Russians who tried to kill me with the fire, why kill her too? They could have tranquilized me and let her escape while the fire was starting."

Cox shrugged. "Assuming it was the Soviets, maybe she was being punished," he said. "Maybe she was supposed to go back to Moscow and ran off to St. Tropez with Yves instead. Maybe they just decided it was safer to have her dead too."

"Cox," I said, "your tone tells me you know more about Jennifer than I do. Has Ryder found something?"

"No. But he thinks he's close. Chief, you'd better prepare yourself. Ryder's people are convinced her background story isn't right. Ryder's as good as told us to stand by for bad news." Cox managed a little smile. "As though we didn't have enough already."

"Like what?"

"Like they're going to test Starburst in Europe during the NATO exercises. In about three weeks."

"What! They're insane."

"So a lot of people are saying. But the President has put the screws on NATO. A big political blackmail number. Agree to the missile test or we start pulling U.S. troops out of Europe. I've done you a full briefing document. But I don't have to tell you the bottom line. The situation—your situation—is coming to a head. Whatever's supposed to happen is going to happen soon. There are other signs too."

I smiled. "Have pity on a poor invalid," I said. "Break it gently."

"It's not good however it's broken," Cox said seriously. "In some ways it's worse than the announcement of the test firing. It's about the scandal."

"You mean it's broken?" I said. "Why the hell didn't you say that in the first place?"

"No. It hasn't broken. But someone's warming up the house, as the comedians say. Take a look at this."

Cox reached down to the floor of the cabin and handed me an Italian newspaper. It was the previous night's *Messagere* and when I saw the headline, I almost dropped the paper. Two thirds of the front page was taken up with the announcement of the Starburst test, but it was the right-hand headline that Cox was pointing to.

"IL SCANDALO INGLESE," it read. "L'AMORE E LA KGB."

As I read it, I realized that the story had nothing to do with me, or the party or Starburst. It concerned a former British ambassador to Moscow who had had an affair with a woman interpreter. The story was more than ten years old. The man had confessed at the time and resigned immediately; now it had all been dragged up again quite gratuitously.

Cox watched me scan it.

"It has to be deliberate," I said. "There's no other reason for bringing the story out now. Poor bastard's been quietly running a boat-repair firm in Poole for the past ten years, eking out his pension and trying to persuade his loyal wife that it was just a mad moment of passion."

"Oh sure. It's deliberate, all right," Cox said. "And the papers had a field day. I've had the press digest on the E Net. Story is fronted in a dozen countries. It's unbelievable. Cartoons. Sanctimonious shit about 'How can the Russians be so vile?' and

105

acres of 'How could he be so stupid?' editorials. Catty quotes from the wife of the next ambassador saying what a tart the interpreter looked. And friend Wint's already done the rounds of his editors. No prizes for guessing his line: 'If you can sell extra papers with ten-year-old rubbish like this, think what you can do with an exclusive with top people leaping in and out of sleeping bags for charity and Russian agents killing heiresses during drug and sex orgies to protect their mole.' "

This time, I did manage a smile. "Cox," I said, "I do wish you could put a slightly better construction on the evening than that."

Cox grinned back, obviously relieved that I hadn't been uprooted by his news.

"So we have to get a move on," I said. "How long is Seagull going to be unconscious."

"I don't know," Cox said. "I'll get Richardson."

As Cox opened the partition, I caught a brief glimpse of Seagull. She was lying with her head sunk deeply into the small pillow. She looked very peaceful, even though her eyes were dark under the tan and there were exhaustion lines crinkling her face. No, she didn't look like a tart, I thought. But it would make no difference. "Beautiful Soviet agent seduces news agency executive while she acts as conduit for his treason." That was story enough.

Then Dr. Richardson stepped into the cabin and closed the partition door. We had already completed our takeoff. There was no turbulence and Richardson stood with the same air of relaxed calm as he did in his consulting rooms in quiet chambers just off Fleet Street.

I had always liked him. When I'd first been treated by him as a young correspondent, I'd been impressed by my first taste of rich man's doctoring and realized that it was different in much more than the sumptuous appointments of his surgery. It was a matter of attitude. Richardson dealt with high achievers and he accepted that achievement, like aging, had a price in physical deterioration. He never moralized, or told his patients to stop overworking; he simply assessed the deterioration, prescribed a treatment, then laid out the requirements for a complete cure and the specific consequences of ignoring his advice. The value judgments were left to you. He lived, as far as I could judge, a very quiet life and his main interest was rare books and he enjoyed his occasional sudden—and lucrative—excursions into the strange situations that came with the World News consultancy. It was typical of him that he expressed no particular surprise that the chief executive of World News should have been hit by a tranquilizer dart.

"It was a substance called Androloxine," he said as he sat down beside the berth. "Developed for tranquilizing giraffes, I understand. You're lucky, really. There's a stronger version for use on elephants."

When I asked him about Jennifer, he ignored my insistence that I had to talk to her immediately. "She'll be fine. I've done all the necessary tests. But she'll be out longer than you were. A matter of body weight and female chemistry. It's now nine o'clock. We shall be in London by noon or soon after. By then, she should be awake and beginning to be coherent. But I wouldn't expect you to be able to have any serious conversation with her before tonight."

I have never argued with Richardson. He knew that I would ignore his advice if I had to, but I knew that his judgments were rarely faulty.

When Richardson had gone back into the other cabin, I took out the briefing document Cox had prepared on Starburst. As usual it was succinct and thorough and though he always used a casual, racy style, I also knew it would be accurate both in detail and in tone.

"First announcement of the European test of Starburst made in Washington (State and Defense simultaneously)," it read.

Starburst will be fired during NATO summer exercise "Mighty Shield" to demonstrate its readiness for a battle-field role in Europe. (WN trailed Reuters, AP by six minutes.) Firing confirmed by NATO military planning council in Brussels. (AP one-minute lead over WN.) Missile will be fired from Britain, but Defense ducked questions on details. Big fight broke out immediately over exact kind of test firing. To stop fight blowing up further, Defense called second press conference. Spokesman said it would be fired in a "simulated invasion situation." In other words, it'll be presumed that Soviet tanks have rolled over the Iron Curtain borderline and are on West German soil. Starburst will be targeted to land on exercise battle-field in West Germany, as part of counterattack.

Background

New York Times, Washpost say U.S. blackmailed Euro allies into agreeing to test because Sellinger Corporation backed by several other elements in defense lobby, acting through Haxler and Inman, put screws on President. They threatened to set Senate/Congress motion rolling accusing President of going soft and reneging on campaign promise to "make America strong again"; also of going back on pledges not to let Europe go on sheltering under U.S. nuclear umbrella for free; sliding out of their share of worldwide defense commitments etc.; resolution would also have accused President of letting U.S. arms programs drag.

NYT says President sent special envoys to Bonn, Paris, London, etc. saying that unless Starburst could be tested, U.S. would start pulling out any U.S. troops in Europe that host countries refused to pay for, causing widespread panic in various European treasuries. *Times* says Britain agreed to be the base for firing the missile because President threatened blow whistle (with chapter and verse) on British backsliding on defense commitments—pulling rug out from under PM's supposed strong defense posture.

DPA, Frankfurter Allgemeiner say Bonn agreed after horse-trading in which U.S. agreed to reduce extent of land maneuvers during Mighty Shield if West Germans accepted the test firing. (German farmers been saying NATO maneuvers will ruin harvests; highway department saying tanks on roads during summer will wreck Autobahn system, screw up tourist season, etc.)

Antinuclear protests

News of Euro test sparked biggest antinuclear protests seen in Europe for a decade. Two hundred thousand people out in Trafalgar Square last night; same kind of numbers in Rome, Bonn, Paris. Firing seems to have provided catalyst to really cement the new Movement for Nuclear Disarmament (MND) as successor to CND. Demonstrations very impressive, especially in London. Headlines all stress "dignified, peaceful protest," but fringe crazies also starting to get active. Animals—Antinuclear Militants—have announced formation of a London chapter.

I glanced up from the document. The Animals had so far been active only in West Germany and France. They specialized in colorful and aggressive street theater. In Frankfurt they had arranged a simulated nuclear explosion using colored smoke and had sent crowds panicking through the city center in the rush hour. They didn't like the quiet, dignified approach of MND and they tried whenever possible to provoke the police into clashing with demonstrators to give the impression of an authoritarian attempt to put down the antinuclear movement.

"Next big fight is going to be over the firing site," Cox's note continued.

Already there have been small demonstrations outside various U.S. air bases in Suffolk and Cambridgeshire but no one will say where the Starburst will be fired from. Also some panic about missile getting hijacked by terrorists or going amok over the Channel.

I talked to Ryder about this. He says there's no danger. According to Ryder, one Starburst will be flown over from the States the day before the test to a base where there are no nuclear weapons (so no protesters). It'll be fired from inside the base, over well-programmed course, with air space totally cleared, at low altitude and low speed. Missile will be tracked all the way and will come down on top of a cardboard tank or some such in the middle of a plain in West Germany. If it should go astray, it'll be destroyed immediately from the ground, and it'll be tracked by aircraft the whole way as well. Ryder says if it does come down, without a warhead it will do a lot less damage than a small plane crash.

Sellingers don't want that kind of detail published because it will give impression that test will be pretty Mickey Mouse, not really simulating battle conditions, so we may well get some press hysteria building up . . . also MND antinuclear protesters roaming around looking for somewhere to protest.

As I was on the last page, Cox came back into the cabin. I'd just reached the section on the details of the test and I said: "Cox, we have to make sure World News gets the balance right on this test. We mustn't go along with any Sellinger Corporation hype suggesting that the test will be like the real thing."

Cox didn't answer immediately and I saw that his worried look had returned.

"We have other problems, Chief," he said.

"What's wrong now?"

"I'm afraid it's Seagull," Cox said quietly. "I've just had a message from Ryder. There's no doubt she's a phony. She was never at the London College of Art. The diploma she used to get her first freelance assignments, the dates and details of her art school career, and the details she gave as a reference for the flat in Hampstead are fakes. They relate to someone else—a woman who's now in India. Ryder says there's no doubt she's taken on someone else's identity."

12

When we landed at Stelstead, my only concern was to hide Seagull. I was determined to have the truth about Ryder's photographs before I went to the World News building, or made any other moves, but I ran into a snag I hadn't anticipated: Dr. Richardson didn't want to let me take her out of his care.

We touched down late, just before one o'clock, and as usual his prediction was accurate. She started to come around as we were circling the field, and though she was still very shaky, she managed to walk to the lounge of the Executive Air Charter building on Richardson's arm. We exchanged only a few strained words and I could see Richardson was deliberately putting himself between us to ward off any confrontation.

She could have been acting. I no longer felt I knew anything about her. For all I knew she might be fully alert and feigning drowsiness as she planned her next move. I had the feeling I was walking beside a blow-up doll with the shape and features of someone I had once cared about.

In the lounge, I led Richardson aside and told him I planned to take her to Cox's flat. He glanced over to where she was sitting, fumbling with a cup of coffee.

"Professionally, I'm not sure I can allow that. She's still very unsteady."

"I have to talk to her," I said. "I'm going to sit with her for the rest of the day and the rest of the night if necessary."

"I'm sure you have good reasons, John," Richardson said quietly, "but I'm not a clockwork toy doctor World News has bought. You can't just bring me in to patch someone up and then turn me around and send me tick-tocking off over the horizon. She's had a very heavy dose of animal tranquilizer. It hit her very hard; she's a long way behind you in recovery."

"Mervyn, are you certain?"

Richardson looked at me coolly. "You mean is she faking?"

"Yes."

"It's possible. However, there's nothing in our consultancy agreement which precludes a second opinion. Shall I recommend someone, or would you rather choose for yourself?"

"I'm sorry. I had to ask. I wasn't really questioning your professional judgment."

"It sounded remarkably like it."

Richardson took my arm and led me farther away from Seagull.

"John, I've been your physician for very many years, and your air of masterly calm, which I know impresses the World News staff, does not necessarily impress me. At this moment, you are a very agitated and very angry man. And your self-control is not without limit. We both know that."

"For God's sake, I'm not going to hang her on a meathook."

"Perhaps not," Richardson said. "But there are other forms of violence. Browbeating someone in her present condition, for example, could have very serious and lasting effects."

"Mervyn, I give you my word—my personal undertaking—that I will not harm her. I won't question her until she can take it."

"And if she doesn't give you the answers you want?"

"Then I'll hand her over to the authorities. You have my word."

Richardson nodded. "Where will you be?"

"I'd prefer not to say."

"And I'd prefer to know."

I gave him the address of Cox's flat in Bayswater. "Give it a couple of hours," he said. "Just leave her. Let her doze; she'll keep coming around and nodding off again. You did the same in Genoa. I'll go and get her settled in the car."

After that I was determined to waste no more time, but when Cox came into the lounge, he wanted another delay. The bodyguards he had ordered from Mills Security, the firm we used in London, had not turned up. He had phoned and they were on their way, but I was adamant. Stelstead had been a good choice of airport—close to London but with no airport stringer bureau of the kind that would have noted my arrival routinely at Heathrow. It did handle a steady flow of executive charter traffic, though, and I could easily meet someone I knew; also I was afraid Seagull might have a relapse and Richardson would try to change his mind.

Cox had arranged for my own driver, Herbert Walker, a man I trusted, to meet us in a rented car and he'd chosen an inconspicuous brown Volvo from the fleet of a firm we used for overflow transport. Its anonymity was spoiled a bit by being parked next to Richardson's ancient black Daimler which needed only a white ribbon to be ready for a 1950s society wedding; but we got away quickly without, as far as I could tell, being spotted by anyone.

No one said much. Seagull dozed off almost immediately but I was reluctant to talk to Cox, who had taken the front passenger's seat, in case she could overhear.

Instead, I glanced at my afternoon paper I had picked up at the airport. The Moscow ambassador scandal had moved into the inside pages but the front was full of military news. The Warsaw Pact had brought its own autumn maneuvers forward to coincide with the NATO summer exercises, and the two sides were preparing to play children's games of dare on a massive and terrifying scale across the demarcation line between East and West.

I glanced across at Seagull and wondered about her background and training. How early had someone spotted the strong, resilient body I'd loved so much to hold? Or had it been the quick, intuitive mind that had first caught her masters' attention? And now, it seemed, she was dispensable. She had been a target too, there was no mistake about that—she hadn't been caught up accidentally in an attempt to kill me.

The thought brought Sellinger's face floating into my mind. I remembered Ryder's chilling words at Fort Benedict: "If the Sellingers ever decide things are getting too messy, they may not leave it to us." Was it possible that the Sellingers had decided in St. Tropez that it was simpler just to get us both out of the way? But that made no sense; there had to be a real mole somewhere and I didn't believe I'd outlived my usefulness yet in trying to find out who it was.

I looked again at Seagull, and thought, Damn the sleeping-bag game. I'd lost Nancy because of my ambition, now I was going to lose my career through self-indulgence and desire—not exactly an original pattern. And it was all likely to be over very soon. If Seagull was a Soviet agent, pleading my innocence would be a waste of time. There's no greater sin for a journalist than being naive. And if she simply stonewalled, as she had in St. Tropez, and I had to hand her over to Ryder, I wouldn't hold out much longer anyway against Sellinger's pressure. I'd be obliged to resign, "pending further inquiries," pleading ill health probably, which Paul would make sure sounded plausible enough after my absence from Brussels. At least when I thought about the EEC talks, I realized what a minor problem they had become; I no longer cared whether Gerstein was angry, or whether the stock exchange contracts were renegotiated. I just wanted the Seagull business settled.

I was really working myself into a foul mood and because of it, I had no warning of the crash. Cox saw the Jaguar coming out of the side turning, but before he could do anything, he was trapped by a buckled door. My own reaction after the car hit was completely reflexive.

We were on Western Avenue, the main arterial road into London. The traffic was heavy but the flow was steady and the driver was keeping to the nearside lane, anticipating some maneuvering in the outer lanes, in preparation for a major right turn ahead.

The Jaguar was a gray XJS, almost new; an expensive car for the two young, tough-looking kids in the front seats. It appeared from the side turning without any warning and, making no attempt to brake, it smashed into our near side, at the level of Cox's door. The Jaguar's bumper caught in our wheel arch and the two cars skidded together, careering into the guardrail down the center of the road. There was a screech of brakes behind us and the car immediately following grazed the curb as it swerved close to the pedestrian walkway. The crash knocked Walker to the floor and I saw from the corner of my eye that he was bleeding from a graze on the side of the temple.

Cox seemed to be all right, but he was jammed in tightly and Seagull seemed to have rolled with the impact because of the tranquilizer. The two men in the Jag seemed to have suffered no damage and they were already halfway out of the car. I saw the look of determined anger in the face of the driver and in the split second before I reacted, I read into it much more than the fury of someone whose car had been hit.

He was coming for me, I was sure of it, but I'd had one rehearsal for my death on the hillside in St. Tropez and this time I was not going down easily.

If there's one lesson I learned from my two brutalizing years in the military police, it was "Get in first": get the advantage. If you lose the initiative, you'll probably lose the fight.

I presumed they had guns but I didn't care. Inside the car, I was a static, framed target; at least in the street I could create some confusion with movement.

The nearest of the two was the biggest, a heavy, broad-shouldered man in his mid-twenties with hooded eyes and the slightly hunched stance of a boxer. Once I was out of the Volvo, there were only feet between us and I hit him with a shoulder charge that sent him staggering back against the Jaguar. Before he could regain his balance, I got in a kick at his kneecap. It wasn't a direct hit but it made him scream an obscenity and he started to slip back against the car door. I had the advantage of height now and I stamped downward at his extended leg and caught him square on the ankle. He screamed again and tried to reach downward to protect his legs and as he leaned forward, I hurled him upward again and heard his head crack solidly back against the window.

I knew that was it, and only just in time for me to deal with the second man scrambling over the hood of the Jaguar. It was a mistake. He should have come around. It was quicker to come over the top but he could get no purchase on the polished metal surface and he was in too much of a hurry to check his momentum as he prepared to leap on my back. I turned and managed to get under him, grabbing him savagely by one lapel and his tie. It wasn't really a throw that I executed; I more or less hauled him down onto the roadway, half choking him into submission, half relying on the force of his impact on the concrete surface.

I was vaguely aware of a crowd forming and shouts and a woman screaming. I did hear someone call "Dial 999" but by that time I was straddling the second man and beating his head against the curb.

When I was sure he was unconscious I turned back toward the Volvo. Cox was struggling to move Walker, who was wedged under the steering wheel, so he could get out of the driver's side. Seagull was still in the back seat and I yelled at Cox to keep her there, that I was all right and it was all over here.

There was a crowd several lines deep now and the traffic seemed to be backed up as far as Heathrow, but no one tried to stop me as I knelt on the roadway and checked the second man's breathing.

Then I saw the police car approaching, against the line of the blocked traffic, two wheels on the pedestrian way, with horn blaring and headlights flashing despite the bright sun. Two uniformed policemen got out. Someone pointed at me and shouted, "That's him. That's the one"; but the older of the two officers had already worked that out from my rumpled suit and sweating face and before long I was sitting in the back of the stationary police car.

The constable was young and soft-faced and as I waited for him to get his notebook out, I sat stupidly—with the adrenalin ebbing—thinking of a cartoon I'd seen recently of a cherubic-looking policeman saying to his partner: "I sometimes have the feeling the public's looking younger every day."

I gave him a cursory statement, trying to fudge over my position in World News by giving my home address and describing myself as managing director of an "information company," but the constable wasn't put off. After comparing notes with his partner, who had called an ambulance for the two men and talked to several witnesses, he said, "Sir, I'm afraid your story about a fight breaking out after the car accident is not supported by other eyewitnesses. They are saying that it was an unprovoked attack by you on the two men. What do you have to say to that?"

I tried to stall further, saying I believed that I was being attacked and had acted in self-defense, but he clearly wasn't satisfied, and when all the statements had been taken he an-

116

nounced, as I'd expected, that I would have to accompany him to Chiswick police station. I was taken in the police car and though the constable said it was so he could continue taking my statement, very little was said on the journey and I presumed it was to prevent me from concerting statements with Cox, Seagull, and Walker. I'd no idea how bad the situation was legally; my first concern was to stop word from getting out. I was already having doubts about whether the crash had been another attempt to kill us, but if the press got hold of the story immediately, it would be academic anyway: I would be linked with Seagull.

The Jaguar was being towed to the police station but the Volvo was drivable and Walker, who had only been grazed, was following us, with Cox and Seagull. I wasn't certain of the law, but I was fairly sure that the police could not detain anyone but me. I was counting on Cox to stay with Seagull whatever happened, but he probably wouldn't be able to handle Walker as well and the driver's first reaction would, I knew, be to call the head office.

At the station, the isolation was the most irksome part of the procedure. Once we had got past the desk sergeant, I had no idea where the others had been taken and I was "processed" on an upper floor. When I was searched, I asked if I was being arrested, but I was told that it was standard procedure for "persons detained at the station" and I didn't argue. I was taken to a small bare interrogation room furnished only with a table and three wooden chairs, and I sat with the second policeman who told me that "CID would be handling the matter from now on."

I'd expected the matter to be dealt with initially by a young detective constable—everyone I'd seen in the building seemed to be under twenty-five—but the man who came in was in his mid-thirties and he introduced himself as Detective Inspector McMurdy. I soon saw why. My fudging about the "information company" hadn't lasted five minutes; from the other statements, they'd learned who I was and the inspector, a shrewd, aware man with bright red hair and a distractingly high forehead, knew exactly what that meant in terms of prestige and status, and had even seen me on television, at the ceremonies in Lon-

117

don to mark the World News merger. After some quick preliminaries, he gave me a formal caution and came straight to the point.

"I'm told by the officers who attended the scene of the accident," he said, "that several witnesses have stated that immediately after the collision, you leaped from the back seat of your car and attacked the two men, kicking, punching, and wrestling them to the ground. I should warn you that the extent of the injuries inflicted has not yet been determined, but in any case this constitutes a serious unprovoked assault and I should like to know why you acted in this way."

In the time since the accident, I'd already planned my strategy; in the long term, the court case, if there was one, would be nasty, but I would have a far worse and more immediate crisis on my hands if any hint leaked out that I was afraid for my life because of an attempted murder in France. With the scandal already bubbling, and my name possibly already being mentioned in connection with it, even a hint of a story like that would bring the whole Fleet Street pack to my doorstep. So, though I knew it sounded feeble, I went on stalling. I said I had a good explanation for my behavior; that I was convinced that if I hadn't struck first, the two youths intended to attack me. I had good reasons for that belief but I wasn't in a position to disclose them.

The young PC took notes and when I'd finished, the Inspector said, "I'm sorry, Mr. Railton, but I'm afraid I must point out to you that it is very much in your interests to give me those reasons."

We sparred for a while and the inspector asked me if it was a security matter. I said it wasn't, not knowing whether he believed me. We argued again, then he said, "Mr. Railton, if you maintain this position, you leave me no alternative but to charge you with a criminal assault."

I knew he would have to charge me, but at least the situation seemed to be still within reasonable bounds; then, just as the inspector was making what I guessed was one final appeal for more information, I heard Paul Sellinger's voice in the corridor outside. He wasn't near the interrogation room but there was no doubt he was intending his voice to be heard all over the building. I gathered he'd forced his way past the desk sergeant and was being physically restrained from looking for the CID office. He was shouting and cursing and I knew him well enough to know that his tone was calculated.

Despite his naturally aggressive manner, Sellinger had a keen sense of occasion; when it suited his purposes, he could be subtle and quietly authoritative—the approach he well knew was the right one to help me in the present situation. Instead, he was being deliberately offensive. He was, by the sound of it, being half-dragged back down toward the staircase, and he was thundering abuse at the officers for their incompetence. I winced as I heard the damaging phrases booming out, one after the other: they had no right to detain a man like John Railton. Didn't they know whom they were dealing with? He would see the Home Secretary; he would have questions asked in the House. Eventually, they must have got Sellinger downstairs and the inspector made a point of not acknowledging what was going on; then, just as we were about to resume the questioning there was a knock on the interrogation room door. The inspector, who was by this time noticeably irritated, opened it and I heard him say, "Tell the sergeant I'll come out when I've finished interviewing him and not before." There was a pause, then I heard the policeman at the door say, "Sir. He's asked for a complaint form. He says it's outrageous that you won't see him and he's asking for your name and rank."

The inspector cursed quietly and went downstairs. I was left with the young policeman, who stared at the wall rather than be drawn into conversation, and when the inspector came back he was badly rattled. I didn't need to be told what had happened. It had taken me months to learn how to cope with Paul Sellinger in full cry; he was capable of an imperious arrogance which seemed to place the Sellinger family's concerns above all possible challenge; and he could bear down on you, hectoring and harassing in such an unjustifiably violent way that it left you speechless.

When the inspector sat down, I knew Sellinger had done what he had set out to do: I had lost all possible chance of the benefit of any doubt.

He spoke very formally and I could see he was having trouble controlling his temper. "Mr. Railton, if you persist with your present attitude, I have to advise you that I shall have no alternative but to charge you under section eighteen of the Offenses Against Persons Act with causing grievous bodily harm with intent. This is a very serious charge which would be dealt with at the Central Criminal Court and could carry a sentence of up to life imprisonment. Have you anything to say to me?"

I saw that Sellinger had boxed me in securely; without spelling out the details, the inspector had inferred in the earlier conversations that I was making it difficult—but not yet impossible—for him to deal with me under another section, on the much lesser charge of causing bodily harm but without intent. Thanks to Sellinger, I had now gone straight to the head of the table and it was going to take more than formal stalling to get me down again.

"I'm sorry about the interruptions," I said. "They weren't of my doing. If I were able to give some indication of the reasons, would it change the situation?"

"It could affect the situation, yes."

"I would need to talk to someone first," I said. "Will you allow me to make a phone call?"

The request was a lie, but I didn't see how it could make matters any worse. I knew I still dare not give my reasons and a lawyer probably wouldn't help, but there was one man who might still be able to undo the damage Sellinger had done.

I called his number, praying that he would be in, and I could feel the relief unknotting my nerves when I heard the familiar deep, gravelly voice.

"I'll be right down," he said before I was halfway through my cautious explanation. "What's the DI's name?"

"McMurdy."

"Is he there?"

"Yes."

"All right, John. Put him on."

I handed the phone to the inspector.

When the call was finished, McMurdy looked at me quizzically. "So you know Jim Pike?"

"Yes," I said. "We were in the army together."

It sounded feeble, like saying we were old school chums, but there was no way of conveying to the inspector how much I owed to Pike.

I'd told Cox in Fort Benedict that I'd survived the military police, but I hadn't said that it was mainly due to Jim Pike. He had been my sergeant and he had decided, after making, as he always did, his own personal assessment of the situation heedless of all the pressure from his superiors, that I was getting a raw deal.

There was nothing he could do to change permanent assignment to provost duty, so he had helped me in the only other way he could: he had taught me how to look after myself. Painstakingly, he had shown me all the things that seemed to come naturally to him: how to be streetwise, how to read a situation in a bar and know who presented the real threat and who were the blowhards who could be cooled out with a sharp word, and above all he had taught me all the self-defense shortcuts which appeared in none of the manuals. Jim had left the army soon after me and I'd always felt that my treatment by the CO had played a part in his own disgruntlement with service life. Instead, he had joined the Metropolitan Police and had just retired after one of the most spectacular careers the force had seen in postwar years, rising to become detective chief superintendent in charge of the Flying Squad, which dealt with armed robbery and major violent crime.

Though my own profession had helped debase the word, he had been in a real sense a legend in the force, a folk hero to young policemen and one of the last of the old-style Scotland Yard governors, before—in Jim's own private phrase—the CID had been monkeyed about with by the ponces from Uniform branch.

When he walked through the door of the interrogation room with McMurdy, I noticed that the young constable beside me half-rose out of his chair. It was a natural response to a man whom I had seen disciplining a military police platoon with only a stare across a barrack square.

He stood almost six foot four inches tall and his bulk was emphasized by a thick leather car coat which he wore open over a somber, dark-blue suit. But his eyes were his source of his authority as much as his size. They had told many a violent robber: Don't bother reaching for that shotgun, mister, because I'm going to get you, and you may as well accept it. I noticed too that he was wearing the discreet blue tie with the bird motif, just in case anyone in the Chiswick station was too young to remember that they were looking at the man his colleagues had called Mr. Flying Squad.

I couldn't help smiling at the contrast with Sellinger. Pike was almost diffident with McMurdy. I gathered that the inspector had once served under him, but there was no more than a hint of that in Pike's manner. I'd seen him use the approach before. "I think it's time to pour a little oil," he would say with a wink and proceed to charm the victim with devastating man-to-man frankness and a dash of Cockney humor.

But I knew it wasn't going to be straightforward. Jim was a policeman above any other loyalty and he would never put McMurdy into an awkward situation by asking him to break a law as a favor.

The inspector had obviously agreed already to let us talk alone and when the inspector and the constable had gone, Pike said gruffly, "Well, you've got yourself into a right one here. What the hell have you been doing?"

I made a sign, asking if he thought the room was bugged, but he shook his head. "Just give it to me straight and we'll see what we can do."

I told him almost everything, describing the attack in France and the problem with Seagull, but without going into all the details of Starburst. "I saw her downstairs," he said. "She's with your man. Cox, isn't it? She still looks a bit dopey but they were talking."

"Then we've got to get a move on," I said. "I've got to talk to her."

"Now just hold on. You're not going to be walking out of here that easy, especially after what that American ponce has been up to." Pike grinned. "I'll tell you something, if he comes back again to plead for you, we're all going to end up in the fucking Old Bailey."

When he'd asked a few more questions, he said, "You say you can't give any reasons at all. But how much could you tell the Director of Public Prosecutions, if I could persuade the DI to let it go that route?"

"Nothing," I said. "At least not yet."

"Then we have got a problem," Pike said thoughtfully. "If you won't even talk to the D of PP, McMurdy's in a spot. He's got a signed statement from an independent witness saying you launched an unprovoked attack; we might be able to get him down to section twenty, but if we're going to get you off the hook altogether, we need a new angle. I'll go and see if I can get McMurdy to hang fire a bit, while I go and talk to the two lads in the car." He looked at me hard. "Now you've had time to think, do you think they were after you?"

"Jim, to be honest, I've no idea. I believed it at the time, but they didn't handle themselves like pros. I could have gone off half-cocked."

"All right. Just sit tight. I'll go and see what I can do."

I stayed in the interrogation room and I was brought a cup of tea. McMurdy's attitude seemed to have softened slightly, but the waiting didn't improve my nerves. Jim was gone over an hour and a half and when he came back, he talked in private to McMurdy for another half an hour.

Finally, he came back into the charge room.

"John," he said, "you are a very lucky feller. You have just been very close to disaster, mister, I'm telling you."

He sat down and lit a cigarette and gestured toward the door. "The DI's just doing the paperwork. He's letting you go. You'll be out in about ten minutes."

"Christ, Jim," I said. "How ever did you manage it?"

"You were lucky, that's all. I went over to the hospital and saw the two kids." He grinned. "I told the nurse I was 'Ex-Detective Chief Superintendent Pike,' but I managed to slur the 'ex.' Anyway, they weren't after you. You scared them shitless, as a matter of fact. But they weren't hurt as bad as the DI thought. One fractured ankle and a few nice bruises between them. The Jag belongs to the driver's dad. He's a bookie over in West London. They'd had a few drinks and anyway, the kid wasn't insured to drive it. I explained that there could be a few nasty moments for him in court if this thing went ahead. I couldn't make any deals of course, but I said I was sure you'd be more inclined to pay for the Volvo and not make any countercharge of dangerous driving, if he forgot the whole business. The DI could still have insisted on charging you, but he's a good lad. I had him on my team at Harlesden."

I started to thank him, though I couldn't think of any words to say it properly, then I heard a sound of a scuffling in the corridor. The door opened and Cox came in, looking very agitated. McMurdy was close behind him.

"What's wrong?" I said.

"Chief, I'm sorry, Seagull's gone and I think she's with Sellinger."

"How with Sellinger?"

"Apparently he came back. Very quietly. There was no fuss. No scene. I was being questioned again. She was in the waiting room when I went in. When I came out they were both gone."

"And he took her?"

"I can't be sure. The desk sergeant says Seagull left first."

"So there's a chance she isn't with him."

"Yes," Cox said, "there's a chance, but Sellinger left a note with the desk sergeant." He handed me a slip of paper handwritten on a sheet torn from the entry pad. "John, don't worry," it read. "I'll take charge of Ms. Ross."

13

It seemed obvious, once we had talked the situation through, that if Sellinger did have Seagull, he would take her to Kent, to Samman's Farm—the one place I would have least wished them to be.

It was the obvious place. It was remote—not overlooked by any of the handful of cottages in the same valley—and it was large enough for him to interrogate Seagull in complete privacy, even if Nancy were there, and she probably wouldn't be in this perfect flying weather.

There were no dissenting voices when we discussed it at a council of war in a drinking club called the Hunter's Den close to the police station: a shabby basement room with mock tiger and zebra skins on the walls and pairs of crossed spears stained with excess polish and with fragments of polishing cloth still adhering to the dented edges.

But Pike didn't agree that I should go down there as quickly as possible to confront Sellinger. When I insisted, he raised his beer mug to eye level and peered at me quizzically over the rim.

"You've still got that little soft streak, haven't you?" There was no point in pretending I didn't know what he meant.

"I'm not going soft," I said. "But if Seagull has to be thrown around by the hair to find out what's going on, I intend to be the one to do it."

Jim shrugged, unconvinced. "I won't argue," he said. "You're not going to change."

But I knew I couldn't bet only on Samman's and I knew too that I was going to need help. I asked Jim, tentatively, if he'd be willing to come on the World News payroll, initially to help look for Seagull if she wasn't with Sellinger.

"I did promise the missus I'd build her a patio," Pike said, then his face broke into a grin. "But my arm could be twisted. But finding her isn't going to be easy if she's not at this farm place. We'd need some help. I've got some mates, men who were with me on the squad. I figure I could round up a posse—if you can afford it."

It was a better offer than I'd dared to hope for, but when I tried to thank him properly, he said gruffly, "You always could use a decent minder about the place. You're still a bit too nice. I never did manage to make you into an out-and-out bastard."

I left Cox with the delicate job of stalling Ryder, to buy me a little more time before the authorities stepped in.

"But don't contact him immediately," I said. "I'll phone you here at the Hunter's Den when I'm almost at Samman's. Then you can call Bob and break the good news that we've lost Jennifer."

For the journey to Samman's I borrowed Pike's three-liter Rover and I really put my foot down on the motorway leading down toward Kent. It felt good to be free of the police station and to be doing something—anything—rather than sitting around a table speculating, and I was relieved, too, to have someone as competent as Jim on the team. But once I was off the motorway and into the last fringes of outer suburbia, I felt the world closing in on me again and the old fears of Sellinger coming to the surface. The bastard was winning; there was no doubt about that. And if you'd back me against a wall and made me admit what I really feared most, that was it. I tried to tell myself that it was Western defense that was important, and my career and the standing of World News, but the bottom line was always the same: most of all, I didn't want Paul Sellinger presiding over my downfall.

I tried to take my mind off it by driving the Rover to the very limit of its ability to hold the road, but when I overshot a hidden police observation point, I came back to my senses. All I needed was to be arrested for dangerous driving. When the police let me pass without giving chase, I braked down to sober speed and cruised fast but legally into the Kent countryside.

I paid the call to Cox from a phone box right on top of the Pilgrim's Way looking down toward Samman's. The clay sub-soil of the ridge had obviously shrunk and subsided in the intense early summer heat and the box was heeling over absurdly. The angle was so steep that I had to lie back, resting full-length on the glass, like the pilot of a space capsule, and when I'd given Cox the instruction to call Ryder, I stumbled out with the feeling that I'd probably made the last call before the box finally toppled into the ditch beside the road.

Only in England, I thought as I sat down on the grass to collect my thoughts for the confrontation with Sellinger. Yet it was a reminder, too, that though I was less than thirty miles from London, this was a genuinely rural area, of farmland and hop gardens, with only a few insignificant pockets of high-class commuter homes clustered around the outlying railway stations. It was almost seven o'clock and the heat of the day was just beginning to ease, and the Kentish landscape looked magnificent. The prolonged heat wave had given the valley an almost Mediterranean tinge of yellowish-red instead of the familiar mixture of a hundred shades of green, but there was still enough grass and woodland in every direction to soften any signs of drought.

As I looked down toward Samman's, I remembered how much I'd once loved the house, in childhood first, then when I had inherited it from my uncle. If I'd been richer, I might have gone on loving it, but once I became the owner, the dream house had turned into a financial nightmare. My uncle had bequeathed it freehold and clear of mortgages and with a legacy intended to pay for its upkeep. But by my standards it was a huge property, and in inflationary times the money barely had covered the first two years' maintenance. Then a major roofing problem had taken most of my savings from World News, and after that maintaining the house had become an obsession.

I should have sold it, but I held on because Nancy loved it so. Partly I stayed out of stubbornness and partly because I wanted her to live where she wanted to live, as a compensation for my increasing absences as I rose in World News. In the end, it had gone to her in the divorce settlement, and in a gesture timed deliberately to annoy me, Sellinger had paid off the mortgages I had been forced to raise, as heedlessly as if he had been buying an extra dress for the honeymoon. In addition, he had done in six months all the repairs and restoration that I had wrestled with for almost seven years. That part, though, I'd only heard about secondhand; since the divorce I'd kept a private vow never to set foot in Samman's again.

Until today. The thought stirred my anger again, and I drove the last five miles through the lanes at crazy speed, knowing there were never any radar traps and that the brakes of Pike's Rover, which he kept in Flying Squad condition, could deal with any tractors or groups of hikers that might appear round the half-blind corners overgrown with Queen Anne's lace and elephant grass.

When I reached the last house at the top of the hill above Samman's, I felt my stomach tightening and I roared down the last, long curving lane touching almost eighty. Instinctively, I braked extra hard at the bottom, ready for the turn into the unpaved private road that led to the house. There was a sharp little edge where the macadam met the old cart track and the potholes of Samman's Lane had to be negotiated prudently at the risk of a broken exhaust.

But when I turned, there were no telltale drop and no potholes. The lane was still paved but it was white and smooth with a thick surface of roadstone of a grade I had always thought of as a private standard of unattainable luxury. Old reflexes made me cost out the repair: five tons at least of number-one washed roadstone; eight men for God knew how many days to remake all the ditches and grade the surface. Two thousand pounds at least, perhaps three. Then I saw a discreet little board on the shoulder announcing that the work had been done by Masons' of Edenbridge, the best and most expensive contractors in the district. So double the first guess; no rough and ready handshake deals on the black economy for Mr. Bloody Sellinger. God, how I hated that man and his money. And if he had Seagull too . . .

As I slowed to take the last bend before the house, I suddenly saw Nancy. She was standing at the gate of the walled rose garden. When she saw the car she signaled me to stop and I realized that she must have been waiting for me. I parked the car out of sight of the house and Nancy motioned me to come through the gate. She was wearing a short sundress in a clinging, shimmering material which turned almost blue when the light caught the folds as she moved.

"Nancy," I said gently. "How nice. I thought you'd be off flying somewhere."

"John," she said urgently. "Never mind the niceties. I've only got a few minutes. I came to tell you that Jennifer's not here."

"Nan, I don't understand," I said.

"Of course you do. Paul knows she's missing. He left you that note at the police station to try and get you down here. It's a trap. He's set a little scene. He'll be all calm and offhand; you arrive in a fury, thinking he's kidnapped Jennifer; he provokes you a bit, then gets you to admit you've lost her. He's been planning it with Robert. I overheard the call."

"And what then?"

"If you admit you've lost Jennifer, they're going to have you arrested. But the board won't be told about the intelligence angle. They'll use the scandal, tell the board you've been chasing around the South of France after a woman who would have compromised you; got so agitated you beat up those kids on the way back from Heathrow; came down here looking for her. You thought she was coming to Robert for protection or some such. You'll either have to go along with it, or admit publicly that you're being questioned as a potential spy."

I reached out and gave Nancy's hand a little squeeze.

"Thanks," I said. "It's another one I owe you. One of so many."

Nancy quickly withdrew her hand. The gesture wasn't abrupt but it was firm. "John, I'm not trying to go down memory lane," she said.

"Then what?"

"I just wanted you to know that I didn't think you deserve all this. I don't care about Jennifer, or the sleeping-bag business. I know how you must have been feeling and that's all in the past anyway. I won't insult you by saying I know you're not a traitor. That's too absurd. I'm just sorry at how it's all turned out."

She broke off. "You'd better hurry. Paul's waiting for you."

"I wish there was one way I could thank you," I said.

"There is." She gave me a grin that took me back a lot of years. "Just don't let the bastard win."

As I got back into the car, I thought how absurd it was to feel so cheerful. I'd just been told that I was a step away from being arrested. I'd lost Seagull and I'd no idea whether I would find her again, and I'd almost made a total fool of myself by falling into a very simple Sellinger trap.

But Nancy's smile wiped out so much and it had given me one last extra little incentive to win the war against the Sellingers.

I drove the final stretch of Samman's Lane at close to sixty, scattering the new roadstone savagely into the ditches, and I made the last turn with a deliberate skid that cut deep black wheel marks into the elegant white surface.

As I braked and turned into the driveway, I saw Paul standing in the kitchen garden at the side of the house. He was dressed in what he probably thought of as garden clothes: lily-white flannels, whose line was spoiled only by the bulk of his gut; and a matching silk shirt, topped by a stupid tennis umpire's hat which flopped over his ears. He was holding a stainless steel trowel which didn't have a scratch or a soil mark on it, and a designer version of an old-fashioned barrow with a couple of weeds laid pathetically on the rim.

Even without Nancy's warning I would have recognized it as a piece of scene setting, but after what she had said I could just hear Paul describing my arrival in a confidential chat with a board member. "Christ, John was agitated. First he beat up those two kids on his way into London. A really savage beating. Put them both in the hospital. Then he lost the damned woman and thought he'd blown his last chance to keep his name out of the papers. Came roaring down to Samman's looking for her. Caught me when I was in the garden . . ."

But thanks to Nancy, I was ready for him.

Paul strode over to the car.

"John. Are you all right?"

"Yes. Of course."

"What happened? Are you out on bail?"

"No. I've been released. There won't be any charges."

Paul hid his disappointment well, but I could see the cloudy look coming into his eyes.

"Thank God for that," he said. "I'm glad I was able to bring those cops to their senses."

Short of hitting him, there was nothing I could say to that, so I waited for his next thrust.

"So what's happened with this Jennifer woman?" he said. "What's the situation?"

"I thought you were in charge of the situation," I said sarcastically.

"You mean my note. I was afraid they wouldn't let you out. But my people couldn't find her."

"That's because they're not as quick off the mark as mine are," I said airily. "She tried to walk out of the police station. We picked her up within two minutes."

Sellinger's eyes darkened. "Who did? How?"

"I've hired Jim Pike. He's put together a special team. You'll have heard of Pike, of course. Ex-detective chief superintendent. Best governor the Flying Squad ever had. Jennifer didn't have a chance."

"Has she confessed?"

I looked at Sellinger carefully; it was time to use the big-lie technique he had so often tried on me.

"No," I said. "And I don't think she's going to have anything to confess. My guess is we'll clear her."

"But you haven't done so already."

"Not finally, no. But that's hardly surprising since someone shot her full of bloody giraffe tranquilizer. She's only just coming around. Pike's handling the interrogation. It won't be long."

Now that Nancy had tipped me off that Paul was not concealing any ace in the hole, I could bluff as well as he could.

"So why did you come down here?" he said. Attack, attack, attack, I thought. With Paul, always attack.

"I'm not happy with the way your people are handling their side of the investigation," I said. "My part is almost done. I've found Jennifer and we'll have that side settled soon. Either way, I've no doubt that what she'll say will confirm that I'm not a Soviet mole. So if there is a mole, it has to be someone in the Starburst program. From what I hear, you haven't been doing a damn thing to find out who it is. You're always bleating about wanting to help me. Well, I came down to tell you that it's time to get your ass in gear and do some real helping. Get your internal investigations moving."

Paul grunted. "We'd better go and have a drink," he said. "Come on, we'll use the west terrace."

He led me around the side of the house and I wondered if he had chosen the route deliberately so that I would have the best view over the estate. The gardens probably hadn't been in such superb condition since the man who built the house, Sir Thomas Wetherby, had created them in the sixteenth century. The magic wand of wealth had passed over the unkempt jungle with which I had once struggled. Trees and fully grown shrubs had appeared, by landscape contractor's conjuring trick, and the lawns had been rolled and chemically prepared and cut by a massive professional mower, to judge from the width of the immaculate stripes.

But I was more interested in watching Paul. Thanks to Nancy, I had the initiative, but I was still surprised that Paul was fighting back so feebly. He had planned for my arrival carefully and it wasn't like him to be so easily thrown when he was acting through a piece of theater. For the Sellinger family, public life was always treated as theater, and Paul had had plenty of practice. Jacob, the patriarch, always demanded of his sons a disciplined, polished performance, even when someone departed from the script, as I had. Paul wasn't giving a true Sellinger performance and I was curious to know why.

As we turned the corner by the west terrace, Nancy appeared on the path beside the fountain, and immediately I had the feeling that she had had something to do with it. Paul almost jumped when he saw her, and as she approached I could see his neck muscles tensing as they did when he was violently agitated. For a moment, I thought he had guessed that she had already spoken to me, but I dismissed the idea; if Paul had known about the talk in the rose garden, he would have handled my arrival quite differently.

As Nancy approached, she looked at me calmly and said, "John. What a surprise. I didn't expect to see you at Samman's." Before I could answer, Paul interrupted brusquely.

"Something urgent has come up. Nan, do you mind leaving us to have a little chat."

"Well at least let me give John a drink," Nancy said. "If he's come down from London in heat like this he must at least feel like a gin and tonic."

"I'd love one," I said, but Paul's face clouded with anger.

"I'll take care of the drinks, Nan," he said sharply. "I said it was urgent. Leave us to talk. Would you mind?"

"What's the matter?" Nancy said. "Are you afraid we'll start fighting again?"

Paul's look left no doubt that I'd been right. It was something that had happened with Nancy which had put him off his usual stride.

"I'm sorry if I interrupted a quiet family afternoon," I said. "But it is urgent."

Nancy looked hard at Paul. "It wasn't exactly quiet," she said. "In fact, Paul and I were tearing each other's throats out."

"Our domestic quarrels are no concern of John's," Paul snapped.

"But it wasn't a domestic matter," Nan said equally sharply. "It was a World News matter. In fact, it's more John's business than mine. John, did you know Paul had fired Sally Menzies?"

"No," I said, "I didn't."

I was surprised, both that Sally had been fired and that she'd been the subject of a fight between Nancy and Paul. Sally was Paul's London private secretary and she had worked for my predecessor before the merger.

"Nan, for the last bloody time, I did not fire her," Sellinger roared. "She quit for personal reasons."

"That's not how I heard it," Nancy said, squaring off to Paul head on.

"That's quite a turnabout," I said, looking toward Paul. "I'd always thought of her as one of our best secretaries. What happened?"

I thought I might as well try stirring up the quarrel, but I didn't really have much hope. This was the point where Paul would normally have sent Nancy scuttling, even though she was in a defiant mood. I was fully prepared for him to recover his composure and swing back into the attack against me.

Instead, Paul flared at Nancy, "Nan, I ordered you to leave it alone."

"I don't take orders," Nancy snapped back. "I hate capricious men, especially when they're powerful. From what I heard, you fired Sally on a whim."

I listened and I simply couldn't believe it. For all my bravado, I was still on shaky ground over Jennifer. If Paul could just compose himself, he could still ask me some very awkward questions, but instead he seemed completely consumed by a fight over his secretary.

"This is becoming absurd," Paul said. "Nan, you're making a fool of yourself." He turned to me. "John, do you mind leaving? There's no point in you getting involved in this."

"Paul, we have to talk," I said, putting on a reasonable show of irritation. "I need some answers from you about your investigations."

"I'll be in touch," he said. "Nan and I have some matters to settle."

For a moment I was almost tempted to insist, but I decided not to push my luck. I'd had a lucky escape, first thanks to Nancy's tip-off and now thanks to a quarrel I didn't understand.

"If you say so," I said. I smiled at Nan. "It was nice to see Samman's again. I'll take that drink another time."

14

The firing of Sally Menzies nagged at me all the way back to London. In all the years I'd known Paul Sellinger, I had never seen him lose his grip on a situation like that. The firing of a secretary just couldn't be that important to him. More likely, the quarrel with Nancy was a symptom of a much deeper break between them. All the signs were there. And I had been there to gain by it. But how would Nancy feel when her anger wore off? Would she be sorry she'd gone so far? . . . Really, I knew it was best not to think about it. I mustn't fall into the same trap that Sellinger had and let myself be distracted from what really mattered. The Family was clearly becoming reconciled to my arrest. Until I found Seagull, nothing was going to come out right.

When I got back into central London I called Cox at his flat, where I'd told him to make our base, and the news was all bad. Ryder had been furious and given me virtually twenty-four hours to find Seagull, after which his director would take the matter out of his hands. Pike had managed to round up five ex-Flying Squad men and they were working in three teams. They'd already covered almost all the contact points on my list and turned up nothing. Seagull was remembered in several places, but no one had seen her for five months, when she'd been about to leave for France. I waited in a pub in Fulham, sipping a cloudy pint of bitter, until Pike called in his whereabouts to Cox and I drove out to join him. We met in a pub

135

in Hampstead, had a quick drink, then cruised around the area near Seagull's former flat, in the hope that I'd remember some person who knew her, but we both knew that it was only a way of keeping my spirits up.

By half-past twelve, reaction to the day was beginning to set in and I felt exhausted. Pike said he and his men would carry on the circuit but I decided to break off and go to bed. We had a final disconsolate coffee in a late-night student café in Swiss Cottage and I told Pike everything that had happened at Samman's, including the way Nancy had gotten me out of trouble. Pike wasn't impressed. "All very touching, mister," he said, "but you shouldn't have gone in the first place. And the Sellingers are on the warpath. If we don't find Jennifer, you're a stone dead duck."

Pike was contacting Cox every half hour, and at one o'clock I said I would make the call. I picked up the phone, to report that we'd still found nothing, but when Cox came on the line he said excitedly, "Chief. She called. She came through the WN switchboard. She wants to see you. She gave me an address."

When I went back to tell Pike, he said, "So that's the game, is it? Sounds like a very nasty little trap."

"I have to go," I said. "I'm not walking away from it." Pike's gravel voice showed no emotion.

"Nobody said you were, mister, but we'll have a little think first."

The address was in Belsize Park and we held a council of war in Pike's car, in a side street near Swiss Cottage. The three teams parked separately in adjacent streets and the squad men came over one by one and slid into the Rover.

Despite my agitation, Pike refused to be hurried.

"Anyone know the place?" he said. "Bill, that used to be your ground, didn't it?"

A slender, flashily dressed man who looked more like a bookie than an ex-CID officer nodded. "Yeah. That's where we picked up Dizzy Richards that time. Had to chase him all over the fucking gardens. Service flats. About six in one of those converted Victorian jobs."

"Any porter?"

"Yeah. May even still be the same old boy. Been there donkey's years."

Patiently, Jim continued the questioning until we had a picture of the house. I could visualize the kind of old converted mansion it was, but this one was apparently different in that it had a big rear garden which was shared by the tenants and was full of sheds and small outbuildings.

"Don't like the sound of that much," Pike said.

"Is he going in wired for sound?"

The small, rough-looking Irishman asked the question straight across me; it was obviously not my decision. This was a familiar assignment to them and I was part of the problem, not part of the solution.

"He's not going in at all until we've been through the building," Pike said. "We'll wire him up, if he does go in, but you're going to comb that place like you're searching a baby for nits. If we're dealing with the same people, they didn't mind burning down half of St. Tropez to get him last time."

"Don't forget they got Seagull too that time. Are you saying she's back with them again now?"

"I haven't the faintest fucking idea," Pike said gruffly. "Let's just take it one step at a time."

We drove to the house and I was left in the Rover with one of the team, a former Flying Squad driver called Terry Mitchell. He was obviously used to doing the backup chores, and while the rest of the team surrounded the house, he fitted a microphone and tiny transmitter under the waistband of my trousers.

The street was quiet but there were still, at 1:30 in the morning, a few homegoing residents parking cars or walking back from the restaurants and cafés of Hampstead a mile or so away beyond the park. The house was exactly as Bill had described it: a detached red-brick house with a high-peaked slate roof framed by wooden eaves. There was a low wall in front, and a straggly hedge, and at the back the wall doubled in height to enclose a large, badly kept garden.

"Don't worry, sir," Mitchell said. "There's no one knows his job like Jim Pike. They won't let you go in there if there's going to be aggro, and Jim can sniff trouble ten miles away."

He described the routine they would be going through; Bill

would be talking to the porter while the rest of the team would be going quietly over the grounds, shed by shed; checking for every catch-hole or hiding place. If they were satisfied, Pike would take the decision about the rest of the flats.

"She's on the top," Mitchell said. "I doubt if Jim'll let you go without checking her floor and the one below it. Paddy'll do the roof. He's like a cat up there. You needn't worry about anyone hearing him."

Half an hour passed and I began to get impatient, but Mitchell didn't seem concerned. "Check like this could take an hour, easy. More, if they do all the next-door gardens."

Then, suddenly, Pike reappeared. I'd expected him to come sliding out of the bushes, but instead he walked out of the front door of the building, crossed the road, and leaned into the car window. "Interesting situation," he said. "We've done her flat. It's clean. You can go on up now. She's waiting."

"You've been in her flat and talked to her?" I said incredulously. "What excuse did you give?"

"Didn't need one," Pike said. "She invited us in. We talked to the porter, got him to take us up to the floor below hers. We talked to the people right under her. Old couple. No problems there. Then she came out on the landing and said, 'You'd better come up. It's quite safe.' " Jim paused. "We've been through her flat. Every inch. Nice place. Full of flowers. No sign of trouble. She just watched us, smiling, then she said, 'Will you let him come up now? I really want to talk to him.' " He shrugged. "Decision's up to you now. They could be planning to blow you both sky-high, but if they are, I don't think she knows about it. I wouldn't say she's in a suicidal mood. Bit tense. But I don't know what to make of it." He grinned. "She's a good looker, though, isn't she? I can see why you fancied her."

"I'm going up," I said.

"I presumed you would," Pike said. "We'll be recording. Paddy's on the roof and Mike's with the old dears in the flat below. Any sign of trouble, we can be in there in about ninety seconds."

The porter let me into the building and led me nervously up to the top-floor flat; he obviously hadn't enjoyed renewing acquaintance with the Flying Squad again and he scurried back down as soon as we reached the upper landing.

138

I knocked and Seagull opened the door. For a second, while the door was ajar, I thought it was someone else, then it opened further and I thought, Good God. It's Seagull in Nancy's clothing. She was wearing a long silk Liberty's kimono tied loosely at the waist; it wasn't the same color or pattern, but it was exactly the kind of garment Nancy used to wear and I had never seen Seagull in anything like it before.

She saw my odd look and smiled. "No, it's not really me, is it? I borrowed the flat from a friend who's away in Scotland and I had to borrow a few clothes to go with it."

"You look beautiful," I said. "Truly beautiful."

"A Liberty's robe and a tan does wonders."

The interior of the flat was expensively furnished with leather and stainless steel chairs and modernistic wall hangings and, as Jim had noticed, it was full of flowers. There were flowers in little baskets and buckets and vases; tall sprays and delicate arrangements in miniature glass ornaments.

"The flowers are my contribution," she said, and added in an oddly quiet tone, "I use them to keep me steady. They're a great consolation when things feel as though they're getting out of hand."

She didn't suggest where I should sit, but I noticed that we both, independently, ignored the stylish armchairs in the center of the long room and chose two upright chairs at a side table close to the window. Neither of us needed to say that it was how we used to sit in her tiny flat in Hampstead.

"Would you like some tea?" Seagull said. "Your doctor said we should stay off alcohol."

"I've already had a drink. It did wonders."

"Wine then? There's some here you'll like."

"Yes. Please."

As she crossed to the kitchen, I was still distracted by the image of Nancy. But there was no mistaking the walk; she moved with a subtle sway that made her flow along the floor, and I felt the stirrings of arousal that had been missing in St. Tropez.

She brought a bottle of claret and poured me a glass, then a second one for herself and put it by her elbow.

She crossed her legs and I watched the kimono slide open. She wasn't teasing; that was her usual way of sitting, but I noticed that she was wearing sleek, satiny pants that matched the kimono. She caught my look and smiled. "Your style," she said. "You always did like your women to look like a cross between a snake and a seal. I wasn't indulging you. It's the only kind Anna has."

I could see the banter wasn't really playful. She was very tense and I guessed she was slipping into our usual ways as a cover for her unease. She noticed again as I glanced down at her thighs and at the wine.

"If you're thinking that I'm tense, I am," she said. "But I think we have a problem."

"Oh?"

She smiled. "I read a book once called *Blue Movie*. It was very funny. And very instructive too. I learned from it that you get a really spectacular sound effect if you put a microphone close to the activity you have in mind."

She touched my hand. "Don't lie. I don't mind your being wired up, or whatever it's called. I brought it on myself. I've been very stupid. I'm sorry."

She took my other hand. "So no gentling, please. But I wouldn't mind if you held my hands. Tonight I'm not the tough old Seagull you always said you admired. But I'm ready to talk. I know it's serious. I won't run away from it again."

She broke off. "Would you like to smoke?"

I made a small gesture toward the microphone. "I'd love a cigarette, yes." She grinned, immediately picking up the emphasis.

I watched her prepare the joint without speaking, enjoying the delicate movements of her hands. When she had finished taking the stalk and the seeds out of the little pile of marijuana, I almost forgot the microphone and said, 'Don't put too much tobacco in it,' but I remembered in time and let her finish without comment.

She lit it and we both drew in deeply, then she sipped the wine and for the first time, I managed to think of the photographs Ryder had given me without feeling anxious.

"There are so many apologies to make," she said. "Do you mind if we skip them?"

"Of course not."

"I'll just make one. I'm sorry I tried to run at St. Tropez.

I could have saved us all this. I thought I was much stronger than I am."

I didn't hurry her for an explanation. I knew it was coming and I could see the grass was dissipating her tension. It wouldn't be long before I had the answers; there was no need to press.

"Seeing you did make me angry, though. The parting was bad enough."

"I thought the parting was what we both wanted. We both agreed."

"I knew it would make the divorce easier, but agreeing is not the same as wanting."

She paused.

"But it wasn't just that. When they started asking questions about me in London and then in St. Tropez, I didn't know what it was about but I knew it would involve raking up the past. I didn't want that."

She took a long pull on the joint. "John. It would help if you can tell me what you want to know. I mean exactly. I know it's about the photographs and intelligence, but it would help if you could tell me why you came to St. Tropez."

I took only a second to decide. If it would help her tell me more of the truth, I gained; if her answers weren't right, Pike would have her arrested anyway. I had accepted that, and it was also part of the deal I had made with the Squad team to cover their own position.

I told her almost the whole story—the allegations about Louise Allenby's murder, her supposed connections with the CIA, ending with the claim that mattered: that Seagull had been helping to prepare me as a sacrificial mole.

She smiled at the phrase, then she added quietly, "You must have hated me a lot, if you believed that. I would never have done that to you. But I know how it must have looked."

She took a sip of wine.

"I'm not very good under stress," she said. "I cracked once— in a previous life. I ran away because I thought I might crack again. But I'll start at the beginning. When you checked on me, I must have seemed a very mysterious woman."

"Yes. You did."

"I'm sorry. I'm quite ordinary really. I went to school at Exton Hall. You must know that. I was expelled actually, but that wouldn't show in the records. I ran away a couple of times because it was so boring, and they allowed my parents to take me away. I went abroad for a year. Hitchhiked. Played around. Then I got bored again and I decided I was wasting my life. I was in France, and I signed on at the Sorbonne to study Russian. After I left school, I called myself Elisabeth. I didn't like the name Jennifer. I'll come later to why I started using it again. Anyway, I stayed three years at the Sorbonne. Got a good degree and came back to Britain. By that time, I'd got the bug and my language was in first-class shape. I did a postgraduate degree at Birmingham, then I came to London and joined the Royal Institute of Military Studies. I was a research associate, translating and editing Russian material and working for my doctorate."

She paused, and I could see we were coming to a point where the story was causing her distress.

"That was when it all started to go wrong," she said. "When I met Malcolm Tyler. You may have heard of him vaguely. Minor defense expert. One book, *The Politics of the Strategic Balance*. I fell in love with him and we started to play house together. I told you we were married but that was never true. Anyway, we started to have problems."

She smiled slightly. "We're coming to the embarrassing bit. I don't like saying it, but the story makes no sense unless I do— the problems really started because I was very much brighter than he was. I became his assistant as well as his lover and it was fine at first, then people began to notice that he had a very mediocre mind"—she hesitated—"and, unfortunately, I didn't. The situation got out of hand very quickly. His book was a disaster—well, not really. It just sank without a trace. I started getting offers he should have gotten and there we were: all set for one of the classic modern domestic dramas. Brilliant woman threatening lover's ego, and all played out in a tiny flat.

"And in a tiny world too. Defense studies is a cozy club. We could have separated, but neither of us could make a career elsewhere, so we hung in and fought. We could have resolved it, of course, but by that time I had a child, a son, Hugh. We went on fighting and the child got ill, a nervous complaint, brought on, they said, by the tensions at home. I was getting pretty ragged too—we fought round the clock practically; at home, at the Institute, then back home for another round. Finally I cracked. I was exhausted from working hard and looking after Hughie as well, and I had a nervous breakdown. I spent a year in a clinic in Wales, a whole damnable miserable year. When I came out, Mal had managed to get a fellowship and my great-aunt had taken over Hughie, and it was made pretty clear that if I wanted either my job or my child back, I was going to have to learn how to crawl.

"I didn't crawl, but I went into a real decline. Depression, frustration, guilt, fury—the classic mixture. I got mixed up with a feminist group. Second Chance, they were called. They helped me make the break. I'd always been able to draw well, though it had only been a hobby. They showed me how to make money at it and set me on a different path. They're responsible for the phony records, too. They believe that your second chance works better if you can rub out the traces of the original crash." She grinned. "They're really very slick at it. Pinching records, getting a sister to doctor a file here and there. The slogan's true, you know. The sisterhood is very powerful." She smiled ruefully. "Actually, there's no great trick to it. Ninety-eight point seven percent of all the secretaries in the world are women.

"With me, it was especially easy. There was a woman called Sarah Ross who'd been helped by Second Chance. She'd remarried and gone off to India. She didn't care about her art school diploma, so they changed the initials on her records at the college registrar's office. I took my own file out of the Defense Institute, but I must have been vetted. You'll find all the details. If you start looking under Elisabeth Ross, you'll find everything you need eventually."

"Now tell me about the KGB," I said. "Every detail. Every contact."

She looked up, as if surprised.

"John, there isn't that much to tell. If you knew about defense studies, you'd have known that. It was absolutely routine. I was target material, even though I was always in Malcolm's shadow." She paused. "They probably had me tagged as someone who would become important in my own right eventually. It was so standard it was almost a joke. I went abroad often; a dozen conferences at least, either with Mal or as an interpreter. The KGB always made contact. Korapkin's funny. Very solemn and Russian but a bottom-pincher at heart. Really, it was blanket coverage. They kept in touch with everyone in the field and all the more so with me because I was doing my thesis on missile deployment and disarmament. And they always, always take photographs.

"My love, that's it," she added. "If the Soviets wanted to frame you, they'd have a choice of people. I'll bet they have photographs on a dozen people you've met as a correspondent or a news executive. I don't know about your past girl friends, but I'll guarantee I could find at least one man or woman in World News who's gone into journalism via something like defense studies and has had the KGB contact treatment."

"Seagull, I believe you," I said, "but can you help me prove it? You said if we look under Elisabeth Ross, we'll get the details eventually. But eventually isn't good enough."

"I managed to get my own records out of the Defense Institute," she said, "but I was vetted enough. MI5 must have a file."

"They should have traced you already," I said.

"Maybe. But even with computers they're not infallible." She smiled. "Or should I say especially with computers."

"Anyway," I said, "I need corroboration urgently."

"You mean because you could still be framed?"

"Yes," I said. "And you along with me." I hesitated but she finished the sentence for me.

"You mean especially if we're dead."

"They won't have it easy now," I said. "With what the boys downstairs have on tape, no one's going to go racing into court. But if they're desperate, they might still try to do it by the scandal and through the media. If the Russians are going to get information about Starburst, that means they do have a mole. They could still try to sacrifice us—even if it only held up long enough to muddy the waters. What we need is a solid dossier, documenting everything you've told us."

"I already have a lot of stuff: documents Second Chance stole. They're at my mother's in Edinburgh. I thought one day I'd be strong enough to start again. But when I panicked in St. Tropez, I learned I'm not there yet. And you can talk to Malcolm. He's in Canada, at the University of Toronto."

144

Jennifer refilled the glasses and I noticed the tiredness in her eyes.

"Is my interrogation over now?"

"Yes, my Seagull. And I'm sorry I was the one who had to open the wounds."

"It was probably as well. I'd been kidding myself I was growing tough again, but I was just getting brown."

"Will you ever go back to Yves?"

"No. He was just a way station. There'll have been a couple of successors in my bed by now."

"So what next?"

"So I'll think about it, but can we please turn off that microphone? I feel drained and empty and I want to sleep—in your arms—if you still want to. I will get strong again. But not tonight."

She got up. "I'll be back in a minute. I prepared some food. I'm hungry and food helps. Like the flowers."

She went into the kitchen and I reached under my belt to fiddle with the microphone.

When she came back, I was laughing. Seagull smiled too, as though grateful to pick up my mood. "What's the matter?"

"I've just blown a hallowed moment in spy films. The hero is supposed to turn off the microphone, so Control won't hear him making love to the heroine. Only I can't turn the bloody thing off. It doesn't seem to have any switches."

I was still smiling when Pike knocked at the door, and when he opened it, he was smiling too.

"Right bloody copper you'd make, mister," he said. "Here, just give me the whole thing." He grinned. "I'll go and brief Ryder. We'll officially allow you over the side until oh eight hundred."

I thought he was going to add a rough policeman's joke about having fun in Seagull's arms, but instead he said with surprising gentleness, "Be careful with her. She sounds like a nice lass. We'll get the file and do some checking, but I believe her."

"Yes," I said, "so do I. And don't worry. Now I know I'm still dealing with a Seagull, the one thing I do know how to do is to apply tender loving care."

15

At seven o'clock the next morning I was enjoying a luxurious postsexual drowse—my first moment of true ease in days—when someone started pounding on the door of the flat. Seagull was in the kitchen cooking breakfast, dressed only in a Victorian camisole top which was supposed to protect her upper half from splashing fat. I was still a bit jelly-limbed, but I managed to snap myself awake, and I was already helping to barricade Seagull into the bathroom when I heard Terry Mitchell's voice.

I opened the door and said, "I thought I was supposed to be OTS until eight o'clock."

"Sorry, sir, Jim sent word. You're to come right away."

"Where?"

"To Mr. Ryder. Seems there's been some good news. Best you get over as fast as you can. We'll take good care of the girl."

I shaved as Seagull was finishing off the breakfast and I was careful to keep my nose free of soap so I could enjoy the smells coming through the bathroom door. She was the only woman I'd ever known who flavored breakfast eggs with thyme and when they were ready I said with a grin, "I hope I never have to be psychoanalyzed."

"Why's that?"

"If I do a word association test and they say 'Thyme,' I'll

say 'Fantastic, glorious, unbelievable sex' and they'll lock me up for ever."

She laughed. "Great sex or not, you're still leaving."

"Yes, but I'll be in touch the minute I can. Terry and the boys will make sure you're safe and by lunchtime, every security agency in Britain and the States will know you're not KGB."

"And after that?"

"After that," I said, "we'll play it by ear. As we always did." When I got down to the car, Mitchell opened the door and I was surprised to find Pike inside, with Paddy.

"I thought you were with Ryder," I said.

"I was. But he's out at Whitestones now."

"The SAC base in Buckinghamshire?"

"Yes."

"What's he doing there?"

"It's a long story," Pike said. "Bob will tell it to you. Paddy will have to get a shift on. I'll keep an eye on Miss Seagull."

He got out of the car, and Paddy revved the engine enthusiastically. "Just like old times," he said. "I've been given a special assignment number by the Yard. If any coppers stop us for speeding, it's as good as having my old warrant card back."

I sat in the back and pretended I wanted to doze. If we were going down the Flying Squad's version of memory lane, we were obviously going to break every speed limit between Hampstead and Whitestones and I didn't want to distract him. Also, despite the general air of cheerfulness, I was feeling a bit uneasy. Everyone seemed to know what was going on except me, and Jim and Bob seemed to have become very close, even though they'd known each other for barely six or seven hours. There weren't two men I trusted more in the world, but I still didn't like the feeling they were organizing everything for me. I didn't know what a Yard special assignment number was, but Jim and his team had obviously acquired some kind of official status. A lot had been happening while I was lying in Seagull's arms and I wasn't going to feel comfortable until I knew what it was.

But despite myself, I did enjoy the drive. I'd already gathered that Paddy had been the best driver in the Squad but I realized as we sped out to Buckinghamshire that I'd never actually seen

147

driving of this caliber. There was no rally stuff; no broadside drifts, or wheel-screeching skids of the kind you can do only when the roads have been closed to all other traffic. There probably wasn't any single moment when I was less safe than when I drove myself, but neither was there a single moment when we weren't going at the absolute top limit that road conditions would allow. We did thirty miles in forty minutes, all of it through back roads and suburbs, twisting and turning to avoid the bottlenecks of London's early-morning rush hour. It was as exhilarating as a roller coaster ride, yet I could almost have read a book.

When we got to Whitestones, Paddy winked at me. "Sleep all right, sir?" I winked back. "Yes," I said, feeling my heart still racing. "I'm quite refreshed now, thanks."

At the guardroom, there was none of the runaround I'd had at Fort Benedict. A pass was waiting, together with an escort, and within minutes I was with Ryder in the base security office. He was alone, but I gathered that Cox was also on the base. "He's rounding up a change of clothes for you," Bob said. "We're going on a little trip."

I could see that Bob was so happy he was almost high, but despite it, I almost screamed at him that I didn't want to go on any trips. I was beginning to feel like the Flying Dutchman, doomed to race around the world, never touching any home port. I'd woken up that morning with one desire above all others—to get back to the World News Building in Fleet Street where I was completely at ease in my skin—but when I told Ryder that, he said only, "You'll think it's worth it, when I brief you."

The base security office was a small room on the end of one of the wings of the complex which ran alongside part of the runway. Through the window, I could see several small military aircraft, and in the distance, the shadowy outline of a huge G-36 long-range nuclear bomber.

We couldn't talk immediately, as people kept rushing in and out, apparently making preparations for the trip, but eventually Bob glanced at his watch and locked the door behind a departing airman.

"We haven't much time," he said. "The first bit of good news is that Jennifer is okay. Her story checks out."

"Jesus," I said, "you didn't waste much time."

"Had her mother out of bed in Scotland an hour after Jim came to the Embassy. Special Branch really pulled out the stops. She had all the documents Jennifer told you about. We've done some checking in London too. She's clean, John. You can stop worrying about her." Ryder smiled. "MI5 is pretty red-faced about the whole business. They didn't like being confused by a feminist organization."

"And the second bit of good news?"

"That's more complicated." Ryder sat down in the wooden armchair behind the cluttered desk and I stood by the window looking down at his grinning face.

"For you, the Jennifer thing is a real break," he said. "It doesn't solve anything, but it sure as hell helps. It looked damning and it was phony, so it's going to be a lot easier to convince everyone that the dissident stuff is phony too.

"It's good news for Jennifer too. It makes her safer; there's not much point in killing her now. Even dead, she'd be hard to frame as an agent. And for me," he went on, "it was also terrific news because it got the director off my back. I wasn't kidding when I said that backing you dented my credibility a bit. Now I've scored some brownie points and I've got my freedom of action back."

"To do what?" I said.

"To follow up the one lead I've got that might take us to the real mole."

"You mean you have a suspect?"

"No. That's too strong. But I have suspicions, and I also have a place where I think I can check them out. That's what the trip's all about."

Ryder grinned.

"Tell me," he said, "if you had to name your own enemy, the guy who's doing this to you, who would you want it to be?"

I didn't even hesitate.

"Paul Sellinger."

"Why?"

"To simplify life. As an ally, he's so treacherous he's already an enemy. If he was behind this, I'd only have one adversary to worry about."

Ryder grinned.

"Pretty good rationalization for this time in the morning. Now tell me why you really want it to be Paul."

I smiled. "Because I hate the bastard more than I've ever hated any other human being, and if I could prove that he was a Soviet agent and a traitor I'd go to my grave happy."

"Better," Ryder said. "Much better. That's much more like it."

He paused. "So you wouldn't be too upset if I told you that in the past eighteen months, Paul Sellinger has made four ultrasecret trips to Prague and on three of them, he's gone straight on to Moscow. As far as I can find out, the trips had nothing to do with World News and they were not known to anyone in the Sellinger Corporation."

It was an exquisite moment. I felt the shiver run all the way up from the small of my back.

"Ooh," I said. "I like it, Bob. I like it. You're quite sure."

"Yes. I got it from a man in Prague that I trained personally and put in place ten years ago. While you were in St. Tropez. He believes Sellinger is collaborating with the Soviets."

"I want to believe it," I said. "But why? What possible motive can he have?"

"The word I have from inside the Sellinger Corporation is that the rift between Paul and Robert is much more serious than I'd realized. I have it from a source I trust that Robert is trying to freeze Paul out altogether. Jacob seems to be going along with that. If that's true, I'm sure Paul is capable of using the Soviets to scuttle the Starburst program to destroy Robert."

"You think?"

"John, I've watched the Sellingers for years," Ryder said. "Longer than you have. Long before the merger brought you nose to nose with Paul. They behave like gods. They really think they stride the earth like giants. Their passions, their emotions get out of balance too."

"One thing fits," I said.

"What's that?"

"If it were Paul, he'd never do it without setting up a sacrificial mole. There's no way Paul's ever going to finish up in a grace-and-favor flat in Moscow with some dreary *dacha* for weekends."

"No," Ryder said, "that's for damned sure."

"And you think you can get proof?" I said.

"Yes, there's a good chance. Do you know who the ID people are?"

"Yes, more or less."

ID stood for Intelligence Dissidents. The group operated out of Athens and seemed to consist mostly of ex-CIA employees who had quit the Company because they believed it had itself become subversive and unconstitutional. The name was also a play on words, since the ID people's main activity was revealing the identity of CIA agents who were still active. Most journalists regarded it as a minor miracle that they hadn't all long since met with serious accidents in the Athens traffic.

"What you don't know, I'll fill in on the flight," Ryder said. "The important thing is that one of the ID people, a guy called Ray Truscott, wants to come back into the fold. He doesn't like the world outside the Company. His price is information about a document he says the ID leader, Philip Ackerman, has come by. Truscott has never seen the contents but he claims it names the Starburst mole and tells the whole story. Now, thanks to your beloved Seagull, I have clearance to launch a little raid."

He grinned. "Much as I love you, John, that was why I woke up Momma Ross at three o'clock this morning. Now, do you still want to go and sit in your nice cozy World News Building?"

"No," I said. "I think I'd rather go a-hunting."

Ryder led me out onto the airfield and I saw Cox hurrying down by the side of the building, carrying a U.S. Air Force bag. I waved and Cox saw my smile but he didn't return it. I took him quickly aside and said, "What's the matter? Something wrong?"

"Nope. I'm just worried, that's all."

"What about?"

"It's that cat-with-the-cream look on your face. I could tell at fifty yards that Ryder's told you about Paul Sellinger."

"He's already briefed you?"

"Yes."

"So what do you think?"

"Chief, when we were in St. Tropez," Cox said seriously, "you made me keeper of the royal objectivity. So I'm telling you: Don't prejudge. You hate him too much. He's the only enemy you want or need. Well, maybe it is him. But there's nothing unusual about vodka–cola contacts. He could have been on a secret mission for the Sellinger Corporation. Shit, corporations are so fucking cynical, he could be looking for a site to build a Starburst plant."

"And what about the rift between Paul and Robert?" I said.

"Two brothers hate each other. So what else is new? Chief, just get on the plane and wait until you see the document. Okay?"

"You're right, of course," I said.

"Natch. I've a genius for being right. That's why execs like me end up feeding penguins in Reykjavik."

16

"If the ID people operate out of Athens," I said, "what the hell are we doing in Rome? Are we refueling?"

The question brought laughter from all around the cabin of the Grumman Firestream, but I noticed that the six men making up Ryder's special assault squad waited a respectful split second for him to laugh first. It was obvious that I'd hit on some CIA in-house joke, but Bob wasn't ready to enlighten me. "No, we're not refueling," he said. "This is the end of the line. I'll explain it when we're at the base house."

It had taken me several minutes to work out where we were as the plane taxied down the tiny military airstrip. We could have been on the industrial outskirts of half a dozen European cities, but it certainly wasn't Athens; the hill configurations around the field were all wrong for that. Eventually, I recognized Parioli, the eighth and least-known hill of Rome. From the airstrip we were seeing it from its unfamiliar side, as a nondescript hump at the edge of a plain given over to light industrial factories and warehouses, but I knew the district well and I spotted some apartment buildings on the crest which I knew formed part of the Anglo-American residential ghetto that covered most of the hilltop.

It was almost six o'clock. The small Grumman had taken almost six hours to reach Rome, and on the flight Ryder had apologized, saying he wanted to use a very small strip and hadn't wanted to change planes at any of the major airfields en route. I'd gathered that the mission was not only secret, it was also barely official within the Company itself. Ryder had what he called personal authorization from the director's office, but I had the distinct feeling that if the raid went wrong the authorization papers might just mysteriously become missing. Ryder had brought six men from England but others would be joining the team from the CIA Rome station. Cox and I were to take no part; in fact, Cox was not going farther than what Ryder referred to as the base house. Cox was disappointed, but I wasn't entirely unhappy; if something did go wrong, the less direct World News involvement had, the better.

The base house turned out to be a part of an anonymous, modern housing complex at the edge of the industrial area. It was detached, and cut off from the surrounding houses by a high walled yard. The houses were even less Italian-looking than the industrial area; they were in a hollow at the foot of a scrubby cliff and looked as though they had been assembled in factory-built kits. The hollow would be a sun trap in the morning, but now it was in shadow and the solitary umbrella pine gave nothing of the Mediterranean look of the usual Roman suburb. The rest of the trees, like the houses, could have been "Euro models" and the little enclave might have been in Munich or Brussels or Amsterdam.

When we were inside, I asked again why we were in Rome. Ryder grinned and I noticed a slight touch of gentle malice in his voice as he said, "You're about to learn one of the best-kept secrets in the intelligence business. The IDs' Athens HQ is strictly for the benefit of the media. The ID people appear to operate out of Athens, but they actually live in Rome."

When he explained it to me, I couldn't help being a bit irritated. The CIA, it seemed, fostered the myth that the office in the Athens suburb where the ID people gave their monthly press briefings was also their base, because they wanted to carry on their own dealings with the dissidents, free of the prying eyes of the media. I didn't like the idea of the press being fooled that easily, but I admit I was fascinated by the curious symbiotic relationship that apparently existed between the CIA and the dissidents.

Bob described the ID organization as a way station for waverers who were disillusioned with intelligence work but couldn't cope with life out in the cold. Such people gravitated naturally to places where other ex-intelligence people gathered, looking for somewhere to reattach their umbilical cords. Many had regrets and tried to buy their way back in to the Company with information picked up in this fringe network of dissaffected agents.

There were, he said, several such organizations, but the ID people were the most valuable to the CIA, ironically, because ID's anti-CIA successes had given it real credibility and had drawn to it the disaffected of other, hostile intelligence agencies. Its leftist inclinations also plugged it into Europe's urban guerrilla and terrorist networks and it had become a clearinghouse for information from a whole web of subversion throughout Europe. By subtle manipulation of the waverers, the CIA was also plugged in, but the price it had paid was the inability to head off the exposure of its own agents.

When I asked Bob what would happen to the IDs after the raid, I gathered he had not personally favored the Company's tolerance of the organization. He said abruptly, "We lost one too many good buddies because of that bastard Ackerman. Some people in the Company got greedy; they were getting too much good material. There were people in the Director's office who wanted to gamble that Ackerman would run out of names."

The leader, Philip Ackerman, was not, in anyone's book, a waverer. According to Ryder, he had been pushed out of the CIA with a dishonorable discharge after a mission failure which had cost the lives of four of his men, and he had inverted his guilt into a passionate need to blame the CIA for all the sins of the U.S. government and the Western world at large.

"It sure as hell isn't the way the media sees the ID people," I said, when he'd finished. Ryder shrugged. "This is a private war. Company versus the IDs. Private wars need private battlegrounds."

"I don't like private wars much," I said.

"A lot more about my trade is private than you realize," Ryder said, unapologetically. "It's the nature of the beast. There's a public mythology about spying and there's spying. They're not the same. Sorry, old buddy."

I still didn't like it, but I had even more of a shock when

155

Ryder took a reconnaissance trip to check on the preparations for the operation and I discovered that the building where the ID people had their headquarters was not much more than a block from the apartment of the World News chief Rome correspondent.

As chief of correspondents, I'd been there often when Ray Swallow had been bureau chief, and from the balcony where I'd listened to Ray's good-humored griping about the Rome allowances, I could have thrown a stone onto the ID people's rooftop.

After a quick circuit of the hill we parked at the edge of a small ornamental garden, where we might have been admiring the view over the eastern slopes of Parioli, and watched the entrance to the ID headquarters.

"The tricky part of the raid is getting in," Bob said. "Being ex-agents, the ID people have some pretty bright security ideas." He gave me a quick summary of their defenses. There was no front or back door to the ID building; the windows had been sealed and barred and the windowsills removed to make it harder to climb the yellow brickwork of the outside walls. From the street, the main entrance and the side door appeared quite normal, but the glass lobbies led nowhere, except to blank, bricked-up walls. No one ever entered the building on foot, which explained why successive WN chief correspondents had managed to live practically on the same street without recognizing a face as well known as Philip Ackerman's.

The only entrance was through the garage which was below road level, down a steep ramp. According to Ryder's surveillance reports, cars entered the ramp, went through an electronic security screen when they were halfway down, then the garage doors opened very fast and closed again equally fast once the car was through. When I asked Bob how he planned to get in, he said enigmatically, "We're going to ride in on Mr. Ackerman's coattails."

I caught a smile on the face of the young Texan driver and once again I had the feeling that I was not going to be made part of the in group, despite my friendship with Bob. "Don't try to do anything," Bob had said. "Just accept that you're an observer, with the correspondent's ringside seat, only this time you're getting a bit closer up than usual."

Since we'd left the base house Bob had, in fact, been treating me quite distantly. He wasn't cold exactly, but he had withdrawn into a shell which included the rest of the assault team and excluded me, and I suspected that he might just be bothered by some residual memories of the West African business. It seemed important to him to emphasize the difference the years had made. When I had saved his life he had been a vulnerable kid without too many physical skills, on a first assignment that no one had wanted him to have. Now he was one of the CIA's folk heroes and I didn't blame him for being a bit reserved with me; it's always difficult to be a myth figure when you're with someone who's seen the other side of your face.

I noticed too that he had the extra responsibilities that came with hero worship. The members of the assault team were all very young. I suspected that for most, this was their first operation and they were drawing a lot of reassurance from Ryder's reputation. If Ryder had told them, on a whim, to swim through the sewers to Trastevere, they would only have paused long enough to ask where to draw their wet suits, but it was obvious there were going to be no whims. The raid had been meticulously planned, long before Seagull's innocence had allowed it to go ahead.

On the tour of the hilltop, Ryder had indicated two vans. One had the markings of the City of Rome urban maintenance department, the other appeared to be an ambulance belonging to the emergency services. There were two men in each cab and presumably more inside, and the ones who were visible looked far more Italian in appearance than the team from London. "They're the Rome station people," Bob said. "With a bit of luck we won't need them," he added, but without explaining.

I gathered that we were waiting for the arrival of Truscott, the ex-agent who had given Ryder the original tip. "He won't be coming on the raid," Bob said. "He's going to point out Ackerman's car. It's better if he doesn't go along after that."

Again he didn't explain, and again I caught a little smile on the driver's face.

Then a few minutes later, Truscott arrived and I understood: he looked as though he were barely holding himself back from a nervous breakdown. I may have been projecting onto him everything Ryder had been telling me about the schizophrenia of

157

the ex-agents in organizations like ID, but it seemed as though Truscott's personality had not just split but had fragmented into a dozen facets, and he seemed to jump about from one to the other. One minute he was being deferential to Ryder, talking about old times and hinting with almost palpable yearning about good times to come when he was "back in the Company." The next minute, he was attacking the policies of the administration with a venom that made his hands tremble.

His appearance didn't help either. I doubt if he was much over thirty, but he had a sallow face and drawn eyes. His hair was carrot-colored and he had a beard made up of reddish whiskers of two different shades, neither of them exactly matching the hair, which added to the wild and unstable look. No personnel manager would have hired him as an elevator operator, but Ryder chatted calmly with him as though he were only days away from being reinstated into the very highest echelons in Langley, and I sat quietly praying that he hadn't hallucinated the document naming the Starburst mole.

From the talk, I didn't learn much more about the operation, but I did build up a picture of the inside of ID headquarters. It had once been a three-story apartment building set into the hillside, with the top floor at the level of the steep road that wound down Parioli hill. The ID people had apparently gutted it and turned it into a minifortress, joining all the apartments together. It was run like an officers' mess, with a bar and lounge and a number of bedrooms that ID people could use for short or long stays. In the back of the first level were Ackerman's own quarters: an office where the safe was located, with an annex which he used for conferences, and a bedroom and bathroom which formed his private quarters. The building had been under surveillance for some time and I gathered Ackerman usually came into the building in midevening. He varied the time and the car he used and though the surveillance team thought they had most of the vehicles pinpointed, it had been decided to use Truscott to make the final verification.

When Ryder was satisfied that everything was in position, we made a move that I hadn't expected: we switched from the small, anonymous dark-blue Alfa Romeo into a large, cumbersome black Cadillac with smoked windows.

When I commented that it was a very conspicuous vehicle,

Ryder said, "Not particularly. Don't forget, this is still film-star and rock-group country. But there are other reasons."

In the final deployment, Truscott and a second driver stayed in the Alfa and I went with Ryder and five other agents in the Cadillac. I was told to sit in the back and I was surprised to find that all the rear seats had special safety harnesses, cross-webbed and padded. Ryder, who was in the front passenger seat, turned and leaned over the heavy leather partition. "John, when we go into action," he said, "I want you to keep your body relaxed and fold your arms across your face, to give yourself maximum protection. You're going to get a bit of a jolt back there, but the padding on the rig will take care of most of it."

We moved out onto the hilltop with the Alfa about thirty yards ahead. I noticed with a touch of wry amusement that we were following what Ray Swallow used to call the blue line. On the maps provided by real estate agents in Parioli, the bus routes to the American and English schools were marked in red and blue respectively, and it was well-known that apartment rents were forty percent higher within a block of either line. In the distance, I could hear the faint crackle of gunfire from the fashionable Parioli sporting club; there, wealthy Italians practiced for their annual massacre of everything that flew, ran, or crawled through the countryside. There were very few pedestrians in the street, and despite the warm evening sun, hardly anyone was sitting on the balconies and terraces of the secluded apartment buildings. Parioli had always been a secretive area; among the film families and the diplomats was a good sprinkling of Middle Eastern exiles and high-class mistresses, and with the constant risk of Red Brigades kidnapping, the life-style of the hilltop had become almost completely introverted.

We cruised once around, then the car intercom crackled. The driver of the Alfa was signaling that Truscott had spotted what was probably Ackerman's car and was moving in for a closer look.

Ryder turned around. "Harness okay?"

I checked the straps and nodded.

"Okay. Hold on to your hat."

We followed the Alfa along the crest of the hill, past the convent school and the little park where, in pre–Red Brigade times, nannies used to take their children to watch the sunset. Then the Alfa driver relayed a message from Truscott that it *was* Ackerman's car and our driver gently put his foot down. At the top of the road leading down to the ID headquarters, the Alfa turned off into a side street, leaving us to pull into position behind Ackerman. He was driving a metallic-gray Fiat with Rome plates and he appeared to be alone. The Texan brought the Cadillac to within about thirty yards, then slowed so that the Fiat appeared to be pulling away.

"What do you think, Jake?" Ryder said.

"If he doesn't spot us, I think we've got him," the driver said. "And even if he spots us now, I think we've still got him, because he'll probably make a run for the garage."

Ackerman's Fiat continued on down the hill steadily and he gave no sign of any special interest in the Cadillac. When he drew close to the ID building, he indicated a left turn and slowed to swing into the ramp leading down to the garage. The five men in the team adjusted their harnesses and from beneath their seats brought out short-muzzled Uzi machine guns.

"Here we go," the Texan said. "Fourteen seconds to impact." As soon as the Fiat was on the ramp and partially obscured by the wall dividing it from the street, the Texan began to count: "One thousand, two thousand, three thousand, four thousand . . ." Immediately I guessed what "going in on Ackerman's coattails" meant. Each thousand was one second, marked off against the time it took for the Fiat to complete the security procedure that would open the garage door. I could see the Texan's foot poised on the large rectangular accelerator of the Cadillac. Then, at the count of "nine thousand," he put it down hard.

The thick padding of the seat seemed to scoop me up like a gloved hand and propel me against the harness. I sucked in my breath and, ignoring Ryder's warning to cover my face, stared fascinated through the windshield as we swung first left, then right to make the swaying S turn into the ramp.

The Fiat was already at the bottom and the security gate was open. The Texan slammed his foot straight to the floor; the Cadillac screeched down the ramp and smashed into the back of the Fiat. For a second I closed my eyes, fearing flying glass.

There was a body-jarring thud and when I opened them again, we were inside the garage, locked hard onto the crumpled tail of the Fiat.

The Texan's timing had been impeccable: we had shoved the Fiat right through into the garage and followed it, without even grazing the electronically operated gate which had closed smoothly behind us. Ryder's squad had released their harnesses and were out of the Cadillac while I was still fumbling. They ignored the Fiat and ran toward the small staircase which led up into the apartment building.

Ryder himself ran toward the Fiat, where Ackerman was slouched against the wheel. He ran swiftly but with the curious lopsided gait dictated by his limp and flung open the door on the driver's side. He pushed a pistol to Ackerman's head, jamming it hard up against his ear, and with his other hand, he reached in and switched off the ignition. In almost the same movement, he started to drag Ackerman out of the car. Ackerman was a heavy, shambling man and he was still stunned from the crash. I moved forward to help, but Ryder waved me back. The Texan didn't move either; as soon as I was out of the Cadillac, he did a swift three-point turn and parked sideways, blocking the entrance, paralled to the garage door.

By hammering the gun barrel against the side of Ackerman's face, Ryder forced him into semiconsciousness and half-dragged, half-manhandled him out of the Fiat and up the narrow staircase. From above, I heard a muffled shot, then a second. After that there was silence, except for the sound of scuffling feet. Ryder seemed to have memorized the layout of the building exactly, as we found the office without Ackerman making any guiding gestures. The door to the office was open. Ryder pushed Ackerman through and one of the squad came running along the corridor to report that everyone was under control upstairs.

Ryder almost threw Ackerman into the big leather chair behind the cluttered desk and told me to lock the door behind us. The room was small and dark and showed the same signs of schizophrenia as Truscott had; on the walls were various Marxist and anti-American posters, yet if you had taken them away and tidied up a bit, the office would almost have fitted into an American Embassy. Ackerman sprawled dazed in his chair;

his forehead was badly cut and there was blood streaking down his nose and onto his chin.

He was in his mid-thirties, with a chubby, innocent-looking face and receding curly hair, and he seemed to have put on weight since the photographs I had seen of him were taken. Ryder stood beside him, a few feet away with the pistol centered in the middle of his chest. Ryder's eyes showed no emotion at all; he seemed to be completely absorbed in perfecting his aim. Slowly he moved the pistol downward, passing over Ackerman's stomach. Ackerman flinched and trembled as Ryder paused with it aimed directly into the groin. The pistol continued its downward track until it was aimed at Ackerman's thigh. Ackerman stared at Ryder with pleading eyes, as though appealing to some unwritten code that you couldn't injure someone who was already hurt. Unemotionally Ryder pulled the trigger. I flinched as the shot tore into Ackerman's leg, sending him back a foot in the chair. Ackerman screamed and put his hands over the wound, then looked up at Ryder in fear and disbelief.

"That was a present," Ryder said coldly. "A present from Sol Weizman. When they took him down to the security headquarters in Kampala after you published his name, the Ugandans broke seventeen bones and damaged five vital organs. I have other messages, from other old colleagues of yours. Whether I deliver them depends on you."

"What do you want?" Ackerman was almost sobbing. He rocked forward as he tried to staunch the blood welling from the wound in his thigh.

"I'll tell you first how this operation is going down," Ryder said, in a voice like a whipcrack. "It's briefing time. Now you listen good. In the back of that Cadillac you so clumsily ran into is an oxyacetylene cylinder. It's already been unloaded and put on your garage workbench. Five minutes from now, there's going to be a workshop accident and the cylinder is going to blow, causing a lot of noise and a lot of damage. The noise will cover the plastic charge that's going to be put on that wall safe. Out in the street up there, the Rome Emergency Services Department is going to thoughtfully cordon off the street for us, so we can leave with the contents of the safe. Now you'll be praying that it all goes off quickly because if I have to do the operation that way, I'm going to put a slug deep into your groin first—with the compliments of Al Menady of our El Salvador office—to keep you occupied while we work.

"The alternative is for you to open the safe."

Ryder lowered his pistol a few inches.

"I'm not going to bother counting. One decision. Yes or no?"

Ackerman just managed to drag himself to his feet. Ryder didn't move as he stumbled over to the wall safe. He kept the pistol trained on Ackerman's back, unwavering in a two-handed military grip. It was chilling to see all the Doc Holliday jokes turned into reality. This was a Ryder I'd never seen: a machine for killing and winning, a man a lifetime away from the young zealous patriot I'd known when he first joined the Company.

When Ackerman reached the safe, Ryder made a clicking sound with his teeth. It was enough to make Ackerman's fingers fly to the dial. The safe door swung open and Ryder said, "You know what I want."

Ackerman rifled through some papers and pulled out a yellow manila envelope-folder tied around with blue tape. Ryder took it, opened it quickly, then put the papers back.

"That's fine. Now you have a job to do."

"What?" Ackerman said hoarsely. "For Christ's sake, I think I'm going to pass out."

"No problem," Ryder said calmly. "You can start when you come around. Close down ID. Disband it. Your lease has been terminated. Open season has been declared. If you don't disband, either I or someone else will be back. There'll be nowhere to hide. You'll never take another safe step. Close it down. That's final."

Ryder didn't wait for an answer. He signaled me to open the door. One of the squad men was outside with a machine gun at the ready. Ryder pushed me ahead of him down the stairs to the garage and into the car. The Texan was standing near the garage door, beside an electronic control box positioned on the wall. The box was open, and the Texan had rigged it with wires across two of the terminals. When Ryder signaled, the Texan triggered the mechanism and, as the door started to rise, he leapt into the Cadillac, reversed and turned, then roared up the ramp.

Once we were back on the hilltop, I wanted to reach over and grab the file that was resting on Ryder's knee, but Ryder was going through a checklist of moves to round off the operation and I couldn't interrupt. The members of the raiding team were making a big point of acting cool. You could feel their exultation at having pulled it off, but it was strictly an undercurrent; on the surface, they were reviewing the operation while the Texan made radio checks with the other vehicles.

When there was a pause, I asked Ryder what he thought Ackerman would do.

"He's no hero," Ryder said quietly. "He'll do as he's told and wind the organization up. He knows he's been lucky. A cut forehead and a flesh wound in the thigh are a small price for what he's done." He paused. "Mind you, now his operator's license has been sort of canceled by Langley, there's no guarantee he won't run into problems down a dark alley one night anyway. The people he named have a lot of friends. But that's his problem. We have other things to worry about."

Ryder kept up the same stone-faced calm until we were back in the safe house, then, after a final debriefing session, he took me into a dark, sparsely furnished lounge and finally allowed himself a little grin of satisfaction.

"Well. Did you enjoy the ringside seat?"

I was going to say something about preferring the young, naive Ryder of long ago but I decided it wasn't the moment.

"It was fine," I said, glancing at the file, "but now I think I'd like to just curl up and have a good read."

Ryder tossed the file on the table.

"I should really read it first, you know."

I grinned. "You try and I'll break your goddam arm."

"Okay, we'll do it together. You'd better get started. I'll go and see if Cox is back."

"Where's he gone?"

"I asked him to call London, to check the situation in World News. See what Paul Sellinger's up to. He said he could do it without anyone knowing where he was."

"Yes," I said, "that's right." I tapped the dossier. "But with a bit of luck, we won't have to worry about Paul Sellinger for too much longer."

I waited until Ryder had gone before opening the file. I wanted to be alone to savor the moment when I first read Paul

Sellinger's name. I didn't know what form the document would take: whether it would constitute proof, or whether there would have to be a long investigation. But it didn't matter. I just wanted to see Paul Sellinger's name, to be certain that, finally, the right enemy had come into focus.

I opened the file and found about twenty pages, typed neatly, but on an old manual typewriter with uneven keys. There were no title and no headings and I couldn't immediately gather what the document was. I found myself skipping down the first page looking for Sellinger's name, but instead I found a name that made me catch my breath, because it was so unexpected. It was in the first paragraph: Claire Dahran, a wealthy Lebanese exile whose family had been in England since the war. She'd been a friend of Nancy's since before we were married and when I saw the name, I could picture her sitting by the fireplace at the dinner parties we used to give at Samman's, chatting about Middle Eastern cooking, which seemed to be her only passion. Her English had never been good and I realized immediately that the document had been written by her. The flowery, overdramatic style, full of grammatical mistakes and odd turns of phrase, was unmistakable. Reading it was just like hearing her speak.

The first page was a letter, but there was no heading to indicate to whom it was addressed. It wasn't easy to follow, but I gathered that Claire had been forced to leave England for some reason. She didn't want to go, she said, but she had no choice. She had been "betrayed by the cowardice of others" and "blamed for their weaknesses." As far as I could grasp from the rambling, bitter wording, she was determined not to take the blame for whatever was causing her to leave and the rest of the document was, as she put it, "proof that I am being unjustly persecuted."

Then I turned the page and the first paragraph gave the explanation: Claire Dahran had been a Soviet agent since 1954. Now she was being recalled to Moscow in disgrace, and she had fled "elsewhere," apparently to avoid punishment by the KGB for failing in her mission. "I have been destroyed by the vacillation and dereliction of another," she wrote, "and I have prepared this file so that she will not go unpunished."

As I turned to the third page, my hand was already trembling, knowing the name I was going to read, and it was there right at the top in a bold underlined heading:

File of State Security Agent B584R: *Nancy Westlake; by marriage Nancy Railton; later Nancy Sellinger.*

The file said that Claire Dahran had recruited Nancy in 1959 when they both had been studying at the University of Aix-en-Provence. The first page described in great detail the circumstances of the meeting. It said that Nancy had returned from a long holiday in Morocco in a state of shock. She had fallen in love there with a young left-wing student who had been arrested for subversive activities and had died under torture. She blamed the CIA for the arrest, claiming the student's political party had been disbanded because of a joint anti-Communist investigation done by American and French security. The details of the Moroccan's death were meticulously recorded and there were notes on Nancy for a seven-month period as Claire satisfied herself that Nancy's hatred of the United States was strong enough to justify risking an approach on behalf of the KGB.

When we were first married, Nancy had told me about an unhappy love affair during her year in Morocco. She had never gone into detail, but she'd talked about "getting into a bad scene because of some Frenchmen," and I knew that her dislike of France stemmed from that period.

The file showed that Nancy had hated Aix-en-Provence and because she was determined to leave, Claire had followed her and finally risked an approach—apparently with success.

Then my name was mentioned for the first time. For ten or eleven pages the file went on to summarize Nancy's activities as an agent, and it was like seeing our life together through a vicious distorting mirror.

The details were chilling. The file showed that Nancy had been systematically passing on to Claire the insider's version of every sensitive story I had ever covered. It was full of names and contacts, sources I had talked to; my dealings with the British and American embassies in the posts I'd held for WN; assessments from the Western side of numerous wars and revolutions—all material that would have been invaluable to Soviet intelligence in the Third World.

It scared me all the more because it wasn't like the file on Seagull. It was too personal, too real. Nancy seemed to come to life in the pages and as the events were set out year by year, I could picture her vividly in the different countries where I'd been assigned. But the later pages were worse. During my period as chief of correspondents, there was material prepared from dozens of debriefings I'd done with returning correspondents. Reading it, I felt tired and sick. If it was true, then my life was a disaster. I had been a pawn; I might as well have been an agent myself.

Attached to one of the pages was a photograph of Nancy dressed in a way I'd never seen her. She was wearing a long granny dress, of the kind fashionable among hippies in the 1960s, and she was in a group of young people. The file said the photograph had been taken at the Copenhagen People's Progressive Congress, a rally of Left-leaning and ecological "green" parties which, the file said, Nancy had attended to give a special briefing to senior Soviet officials. The Congress was in 1969, during our marriage, and I could have sworn that Nancy had never been near Copenhagen, but the page contained photostats of Danish passport stamps and of a pass giving her American observer credentials at the congress.

As I was staring at the photo, Ryder came into the room. He saw my face and, without speaking, looked over my shoulder and when he saw the picture, he said softly, "Oh, sweet Jesus."

I was too stunned to say anything. Ryder sat down and I passed across the pages I had finished reading and turned to the end of the file.

It covered the period of the divorce and I gathered that Claire had been jubilant, especially when Nancy reported to her the first sign of a romance with Paul Sellinger. Claire had urged her to break with me as quickly as possible. When the possibility of marrying Paul was mentioned, Claire described it as "a greater opportunity for service to the State than had ever been possible with me." My career was in decline, Claire said; Nancy must accept Paul's proposal.

Then, in the final two pages, the tone changed completely.

167

Claire began whining and carping at Nancy, accusing her of losing enthusiasm just when the possibilities were greatest. Starburst was mentioned several times and the drift was clear: Nancy was supposed to be getting information on Starburst but she hadn't produced. Nancy was claiming she couldn't get access to the information; Claire was accusing her of backsliding, of cowardice, of not trying hard enough. Claire kept urging that Nancy must act now: the decoy (obviously me) was ready. But Nancy didn't like the plan, and she didn't want to use me as the decoy. She claimed that it couldn't be done convincingly, but Claire had accused her of being sentimental and stupid and making excuses for her failure to obtain the Starburst information. It was clear from the tone that Claire was becoming frightened. She was being blamed by Moscow for upsetting Nancy and being responsible for the failure of the mission, and relations between the two women were becoming severely strained. At one point, Claire found herself justifying Nancy to Moscow, pointing out that she had been useful in giving information which had helped the Soviet side prepare for "secret trade negotiations" with Paul; but Moscow had replied that this was only marginally useful. Only Starburst mattered.

By the last page, Claire was accusing Nancy of deliberately lying in her reports and exaggerating the difficulties. She claimed Nancy was disillusioned with Communism and was planning to make Paul throw her out so she would be no further use to her Soviet masters. As I read it, I remembered Nancy's behavior at Samman's and wondered whether, in a final nerveless maneuver, she was going to try to use me to get her out of a situation she couldn't handle.

If the file was correct, then Nancy could herself be in considerable danger. Moscow had threatened Claire for upsetting Nancy and Claire had fled. Now Claire was doing her best to expose Nancy in revenge.

But how far had it gone? Was the file that Ackerman had acquired the only copy? Did Moscow know about it? If they did, they would certainly move quickly.

I sat back against the hard sofa and watched Ryder reading the last of the pages.

When he'd finished, I said, "So much for the right enemy coming into focus."

Ryder nodded. "We have to make some quick decisions, especially with the situation in London."

"What situation?"

Ryder did his best to give me a little grin of encouragement.

"I know this isn't the time to break this, old buddy, but there's trouble there too. The World News technical unions have filed a formal grievance against you and gone on strike. Your U.K. operation's at a standstill and Paul has made a formal request to the board for your resignation."

17

It was the low point of my life. The period before the divorce had seemed desperate enough, but now there was nothing left. I'd been used as a puppet by Nancy for most of my professional life and whether any legal moves were made against me or not, I was finished. She had humiliated and destroyed me and now Paul Sellinger was about to organize the burial of the wreckage. She had fooled him too, of course, and that was a weapon with which I could fight back, but I had no will to fight. I really no longer cared and I couldn't bring myself to deal with the trap he had sprung on me.

Paul had acted as soon as he had discovered that Jennifer was innocent. He had filed a formal motion with the board asking for my resignation on the grounds that I was not in a suitable emotional state to hold the office. Cox had been in touch with the company secretary, Nick Jopling, who was an old friend and a close ally, and been told that the motion was expressed in only vague terms. "According to Nick, it's a very short formal request which talks about your poor management judgment under stress," Cox said. "Sellinger has told Nick that he'll be preparing a memorandum before the next board meeting setting out the reasons in detail, but apparently he's working mostly by telephone and contacting each of the board members directly."

Most of the complaints against me were predictable. Sellinger had apparently been talking about my absence from

Brussels, having managed to eradicate all trace of his promise to stand in for me, and rumors were flying that I'd simply "gone off screwing in the south of France" and let the EEC negotiations collapse. Word was also out about the fight on the way from the airport and Paul had started fueling speculation that I was acting unstably because I was under great personal stress. There were no prizes for guessing the next step. Thus far the Allenby business hadn't been mentioned, but as the board meeting approached, the cause of the stress would start to be spelled out and details of the party and the sleeping-bag game would start to emerge.

But Paul was too shrewd to rely just on that to prove a case of instability and poor judgment against me. He knew very well that innuendo and rumor are fine, but it helps if you can dramatize events and bring them to a head. So he had provoked the strike—or rather he had made it appear that I had provoked it.

In typical Sellinger fashion, he'd gone straight for the jugular, plunging into our most sensitive area: our shaky relations with the technical unions. It had always been delicate ground. World News was an acknowledged leader in introducing new technology and we had survived a number of neo-Luddite onslaughts from the unions, only because of the negotiating skills of our former Personnel Director, Geoffrey Haycroft. But there was one issue that was more fraught with danger than all the others: the introduction of the Datavol X-13 news processor, and it was there that Sellinger had chosen to attack.

The Datavol technology was complex but the issue was simple. The X-13 processor could shrink the entire World News distribution operation by more than a third. It eliminated technical jobs, cut across union demarcation lines, and because it was a self-monitoring cybernated system, it also played havoc with maintenance-staff levels. More threatening still, it could make the central newsroom instantly transportable to another country with the flick of a switch. If the London unions threatened to go on strike, we could switch the news-processing operation to Amsterdam or Zurich or New York within twenty minutes.

With prayer, patience, and a half-decent successor to Geoffrey Haycroft, I had hoped that we might be able to start introducing Datavol peacefully within two years, but Sellinger had decided that I should not wait that long.

As far as Cox could reconstruct it, word had been allowed to leak out in New York that I had personally placed an order for twenty-four Datavol X-13 processors in Los Angeles two weeks ago. A photocopy of a purchasing request, apparently bearing my signature, had mysteriously come into the hands of the secretary of the American Technical Workers Union. Half an hour later, after some quick transatlantic phone calls, the London newsroom had come to a complete standstill.

It was a brilliant move by Sellinger. If I *had* placed such an order at a time when relations with the unions were so sensitive, it would be ample evidence that I was behaving rashly and showing poor business judgment. Coupled with all the other signs of my "instability," it was a masterstroke.

But I just couldn't be bothered. Ryder tried to talk to me about the document but I wouldn't listen. Cox came, but I turned him away, and finally they left me alone in the miserable little lounge of the base house and I stared at the walls, not even thinking about what to do. The only drink available was bourbon, which I'd never liked, but I took the bottle and sank three in quick succession to keep the bitter tang from lingering on my tongue. The lounge looked as though it had been furnished in one visit to a cheap Italian chain store by a man whose only home had been military quarters. The furnishings were completely spartan and unimaginative and they fitted my mood perfectly.

A fourth bourbon was just beginning to ease the pain when Cox came back a second time. He walked in and closed the door behind him, deliberately ignoring me as I waved him away.

When I looked up, he said: "I have a few things to say."

"There's nothing to be said."

"Yes there is."

"Like what?"

"Like I am getting pissed off," Cox said abruptly. "While you've been sitting in here for the past hour wasting good bourbon, which I know you don't even like, I've been trying to run World News, which I'm not being paid for and I'm not qualified to do. Look, Chief, I didn't ask to be your exec. You asked for me. I'd have been perfectly happy screwing around in Tehran or Rio or somewhere chasing fires."

I looked at Cox hard.

"It won't work, you know, the shake-the-chief-out-of-his-self-pity routine. I'm not in the mood."

"You always taught me that mood didn't matter," Cox said. "Let me quote you some of the Railton words of wisdom for rising executives. When the situation is a shambles, isolate the different elements and deal with them separately. That way the problems become more tractable. Sound familiar?"

I smiled. It certainly did, especially as Cox had managed a passable imitation of my own voice.

"And what would you suggest, Cox?"

"First things first, Chief," Cox said seriously. "We're leaving for London in half an hour. We can deal with WN on the flight. First Nancy . . ." He saw me flinch and said quietly, "Look, Chief, you've got to face it. May as well be now. I'll get Ryder."

While Cox was gone I gave myself a talking-to. He was right. My entire life I'd based my career on finding out what needed to be done and then doing it. And now here I was cradling a bottle instead.

When Bob arrived I said simply, "Sorry. I had what the Victorians used to call a transient attack of the vapors. I'm okay now. Go ahead. Separate the elements. Let's see how the situation looks."

"To be completely callous," Ryder said, "the situation looks more promising than it did this morning."

"What!"

"Well, I'm sorry, we're talking about Nan," Ryder said coldly, "but if it is Nan, she's apparently not going through with the Starburst number and that's good news, John, however you may feel about her."

"You say 'If it's Nan,'" I said. "Do you doubt the letter?"

"I don't know. It could be a fake. A few tapes of this Dahran woman to get her verbal style plus a raft of confidential information from your files. A topflight writer to craft it all together. Yes, it could be done. It's not likely, but it's possible. That has to be our next move. Finding out."

"How?"

"I've given it some thought while you've been brooding," Ryder said. "The most direct way is for you to confront her. Accuse her. We'll tape you. Put it through Voice Stress Analysis. It won't be one hundred percent foolproof, especially if she is a pro with a lifetime of experience, but it's our best bet."

"Why me?" I said. "Why don't you confront her?"

"Because, old buddy, if she is a Soviet agent, and Claire's right, she's trying to quit. You might be the one to help her."

"Why the hell should I help her?" I snapped.

"I could say because she may still be fond of you and because I suspect you still care for her a bit despite everything. But quite frankly, John, I don't give a shit. What I care about is saving the Starburst program from being scuttled by the Soviets. I don't really care whether she loves you, hates you, despises you, or is totally fucking indifferent to you. Or how you feel about her. But if there is a chance—even a small chance—that she does care for you, and that can be exploited, then I want it exploited. Okay?"

I grinned. "Well, thanks for sparing my feelings anyway. Incidentally," I said, "since you're allowing for the possibility that Nancy could have been framed too, I presume it has occurred to you that this file has made its appearance at a very convenient time for Paul. Just when we were suspecting him seriously, up it turns. It even confirms that his visits to Moscow and Prague were for nothing more serious than secret trading contacts which Soviet intelligence apparently wasn't very interested in. Nothing to do with Starburst. Very convenient."

Cox put his arm on my shoulder.

"Chief," he said seriously, "do me a favor."

"What?"

"Stop clutching at fucking straws. We don't know if the document's genuine. You're going to see Nancy to find out. Just wait, will you? For Christ's sake," he added, mimicking one of my own moments of exasperation with him, "how long is it going to take me to train you?"

It was agreed that Ryder should set up a meeting with Nancy later that day, if possible.

"We'll touch down at Whitestones by breakfast time," Ryder said. "I'll give you the morning to sort out your problems with World News. Then Nancy. Deal?"

"Terrific," I said. "A whole morning to deal with an all-out strike of the London headquarters and a formal demand for my resignation."

After that, I deliberately put Nancy out of my mind and didn't talk to Ryder about her or the document for the whole of the flight back to London. Of the six hours in the air, I spent four gratefully asleep and two discussing the World News situation with Cox. At the end of it, I still wasn't sure how to deal with the union situation, though a few ideas were beginning to form, but I knew that, in any event, it would have to take second place to the resignation demand. If I knew Paul, he would be filing a special request for an emergency board meeting. Since the World News directors were about half British and half American, the normal notice required for a special meeting was ten days. There was a procedure by which he could demand a meeting within five days, if he could prove there was a major crisis, but if I could get the support of five members to oppose it, then Paul would have to wait the full ten-day period. Buying those ten days was the first step; after that, I'd take a look at the strike situation.

In dealing with both the unions and the board, mood was probably even more important than substance. If I had tackled either problem in the mood I was in after reading the file on Nancy, I would have been beaten whatever the rights of the issue. I'd been away five days and there were rumors that I was behaving erratically and that I'd been screwing around when important World News matters needed to be settled. If I gave the slightest impression of slinking back, it would be quickly taken as confirmation, especially by my enemies. It was—if ever there had been one—a moment to return to Fleet Street with colors flying.

When we reached Whitestones, I had myself driven straight to Claridges and sent Cox to my flat to pick up my smartest clothes and order the company Rolls-Royce, which I used only on the most formal occasions.

At Claridges, I had a luxurious shower and barber shave, my hair trimmed and my nails manicured. When Cox arrived, I dressed myself with meticulous care in a dark-gray Dior suit and glistening white shirt with a Per Spook tie to add a touch of more noticeable elegance. It was nine-thirty and I knew that

175

Sellinger was already in the World News building, but I made a point of having a slow and self-indulgent breakfast, then ordered the Rolls to the hotel entrance and set off for Fleet Street, in a mood to cross any picket line.

I arrived at the WN building at ten-thirty and though the morning traffic was thinning out a bit, there was still some confusion caused by the squad of police who were keeping the pickets confined to the apron of the building.

The TV news crews were in fact causing more of an obstruction than the demonstrators, but as usual they had made their peace with the officer in charge and were even allowed to interview me in the middle of the street—and block traffic as far as the Aldwych and Ludgate Circus—because the point where I had stepped out of the car didn't give them a good enough angle.

As I answered the questions, I spotted the Technical Union General Secretary, Joe Billingsly, among the protestors; when the interviews were finished, I walked straight over to him and repeated my little set piece about misunderstandings having arisen, and managed to avoid showing any irritation when he dropped into the stilted "speak-your-weight-machine" language which has somehow become received trade-union English. At the top of the steps, I paused by the bronze World News plaque. Before the TV crews could notice the gesture and make a big production out of it, I gave the plaque a quick rub for luck. When I had first joined World News, I had been so proud of entering the building, I sometimes used to linger by the plaque in the hope of being noticed by passersby in Fleet Street. I'd lost a lot of innocence since then, but the plaque was still my private talisman.

In the entrance hall, the commissionaire saluted and gave me his usual cheery greeting, as though he hadn't even noticed the turmoil outside. I gave him a message for Nick Jopling and went with Cox straight to the newsroom.

The main World News newsroom occupied the whole of the fifth floor of the building. Like its New York counterpart, it was nowadays quiet and cool; computer-based equipment simply cannot survive in the stuffy, airless hothouses that were the traditional newsrooms in the industrial age. The journalists' union had not yet joined the strike and about seventy men

176

and women were sitting beside the silent VDUs or talking in small groups. Their relations with the print and technical unions had always been as uneasy as the management's and each new dispute intensified the lingering conflict over union solidarity.

I glanced around and saw that the father of the journalists' union chapel was on duty and I chose a route to the editor's office that went past his desk. I paused just long enough to let him know I was hoping for a breakthrough soon, but not long enough to embarrass him by making him appear too friendly before the dispute had been judged, then made my way quickly to the editor's glass walled cubicle in the corner of the newsroom.

The editor, Nye Harzman, looked harassed, but then he always did even when the newsroom was running as smoothly as he liked it to. There were no greetings; we always went straight into his laments about coverage and he gave me a hand-wringing rundown on the way our emergency cover out of New York wasn't holding up and we were being murdered by AP and Reuters on the Starburst row.

There was no reproach in his tone. I knew he wasn't really realizing that he was talking to the man who was supposed to be responsible for the stoppage. Unlike the correspondents, for whom events were real and directly related to people's lives, Nye lived in a detached world and though he was credited, rightly, with an astonishing "news sense," that too was an almost abstract gift for assigning weights and values to information that flashed across his monitoring screens.

"It won't be long, Nye," I said soothingly. "We'll sort it out. What's happening with Starburst?"

"Total bloody chaos. Half of Europe's up in arms over the NATO test, but the President won't back down and neither will Bonn or Westminster. The Dutch are going bananas and there's one report they'll pull out of NATO, then ban Starburst from flying over their territory."

I thanked him and went up to my top-floor office where Nick Jopling was already waiting for me.

He was looking worried and I grabbed him cheerfully by the arm before he could begin to lay out the seriousness of the problem. I knew his analysis would be accurate to the last subtlety, but in boardroom confrontations his mood was more important than detail too. Nick was one of my strongest allies in World News, but he needed buoying up when Sellinger was in one of his harassing moods. Nick was a quiet, diffident man whose hobby was collecting china horses and who, I'd always believed, liked to get his excitement vicariously through the turbulent and disorderly lives of the correspondents.

The staff all respected him and vied with one another to invent jokes about his parsimony. According to one currently going the rounds, Nick had invented reusable toilet paper but had lost out on a fortune because he'd been too fastidious to patent it. My own favorite was an oldie, alleging that Nick had been in World News five years before he had understood that when you bought someone lunch on expenses, you were supposed to eat yourself. I enjoyed the jokes like everyone else, but I also knew that it was Nick's sense of financial discipline that had saved the company during my predecessor's tenure.

"Sellinger is still doing his round robin of the board members," Nick said. "So far he's been preaching mainly to the converted but he's starting on your people now. He went to Howard Branston first. They're up in his office now. Paul said he wanted a meeting as soon as you came in."

It was a development I hadn't expected. Lord Howard Branston was no friend of Sellinger's, and on the Datavol issue I would almost have expected him to favor the kind of "boots in first" approach that Sellinger had made it appear I had chosen. Branston was a man of sixty with a dull mind and very little common sense, who had managed to construct the media empire that was his personal plaything by having unlimited funds to cushion his mistakes. If you are ambitious but intellectually handicapped, it helps to have a personal inheritance which includes almost a quarter of the land in the West End of London.

His favorite stance was, "Let's show these union people what we're really made of," and I wondered what piece of Sellinger deviousness was behind the latest move. But I didn't show any concern to Jopling. I had his secretary call Sellinger to arrange a meeting in the boardroom, then allowed myself the luxury of being two minutes late and strode down the corridor, doing my best to carry Nick along in what Dr. Richardson had called my air of masterly calm.

I was in a perfect mood for confrontation—the staff of Claridges had done their work well—but when I opened the door of the boardroom I found that Sellinger had set out the pieces for an entirely different kind of game.

Lord Branston was sitting at one end of the oval boardroom table in his usual pompous position, arms resting firmly on the table to give an air of solidity to his flabby figure. Sellinger was standing behind him, half-blocking the light, and they were both looking at a large black-and-white photograph on the table. I walked down the room and as I greeted them, I looked down at the photo and recognized my own naked back. I might not have been so quick to place it if I hadn't instantly recognized the context: I was kneeling between Seagull's thighs. She was sitting naked on an upright chair, her legs folded around my shoulders. With one hand she was stroking my hair and the other was holding a joint to her lips—even through what was obviously a long telephoto lens, the angle of her fingers left no doubt that it wasn't just a cigarette—and beside her on the table was a large glass of red wine.

I recognized immediately a situation that had become a friendly, loving ritual between us. It had begun once when she had come back to her Hampstead flat feeling fractious and ill at ease in her skin. As part of the process of gentling her out of her mood, I had placed her in that position; at first she had resisted, saying it was too self-indulgent to accept it all so lazily: the wine, the grass, and the tongue. But I had insisted, and over the months she had grown to love it and had designed what she called "mood-lifting rituals" for me in return.

In the background of the photograph there were shadowy figures, suggesting that other people had watched the scene. But that part I knew was faked. The photograph had been taken through the window of Seagull's Hampstead flat and I stared down at the table unable to believe that anyone could have recorded such a private moment.

Then Sellinger broke the silence. "John, I'm afraid some of these party photographs have started to circulate already. I think we've caught them all, but it's a very awkward situation."

179

And so the trap was sprung. The photograph hadn't been taken at the party, but a simple denial wouldn't be strong enough. I would have to tell the board who it was and about the affair and I could imagine the absurd conversations I would be dragged into:

"You say the photo is faked?"

"Yes."

"But it is you?"

"Yes."

"And there was sexual activity between you and this woman at the party but not of this particular kind? . . ."

Once in the public domain, sex always became unreal. And Paul had chosen his man well in Howard Branston. He was one of the strongest advocates of a return to public decency, but worse, I had glimpsed the private side of his face. Once, on a Concorde flight to Bahrain for a special meeting of the board, I had chatted with Branston when he was slightly drunk. The defender-of-family-life mask had slipped just for a few moments and he admitted sadly how much he regretted having been born too late to enjoy the permissive society. With that kind of conflict in his soul, there was no way of even guessing what fantasies were being triggered as he stared down at the photograph. He couldn't take his eyes off it and he paid only scant attention as Sellinger went through the ritual incantation of my sins.

Sellinger listed the symptoms of my instability almost sympathetically: Brussels, the St. Tropez trip, the fight, my clumsy handling of the technical unions. As he went through the litany, he was careful not to diminish me too much in Branston's eyes. Sellinger always operated on the old principle of Washington politics that a man is measured by the stature of the enemies he destroys. I was about to be defeated, so I must be allowed enough stature to be worth defeating. Sellinger's tone was one of sorrow: I was the great leader falling because of private weakness. My anguish that photos like this might start to circulate explained everything.

I looked at Branston and saw that it was working. The oldest cliché of Fleet Street was true: a picture *was* worth a thousand words. I could imagine it circulating and being discussed at urgent private consultations between board members and I could hear the jokes and the sanctimonious rubbish that it would automatically trigger.

Just for a moment, I had an urge to take Paul aside and tell him about the dossier on Nancy, to shake his oily complacency at the brilliance of his gambit. But I remembered Cox's words: Don't prejudge. A step at a time. Though I would never have admitted it to anyone, there was still a corner of me that believed in Nancy, in the face of all the evidence; and even if I didn't, I would never sell her into the hands of Sellinger, even now.

It was time for a strategic retreat. There was no point in arguing now. The picture was dominating the meeting.

"Howard," I said, "I think we'd better have a private chat. There's a lot more to this than is apparent."

"Yes, of course."

Branston barely lifted his eyes from the photograph and I saw Paul smile.

"I'll be in touch," I said. "And I'll also prepare a written statement before the ten days are up."

"Sorry, John. It can't wait that long. I've asked for the five-day rule to apply."

"That's impossible," I said shortly.

Sellinger didn't argue. He knew that the issue wouldn't be decided here and talk was pointless.

He made a point of showing me to the boardroom door. When we were in the corridor, I let Jopling go ahead then I said quietly, "Paul, you're in the process of making a fool of yourself. Jennifer's innocence didn't end it, you know. Don't you care anymore about finding the mole? Doesn't Starburst count?"

"We've lived with the threat of a Starburst leak for a long time now," he said blandly. "We'll just have to go on living with it a bit longer, won't we."

I walked back along the corridor and as I approached my office, I saw Cox signaling that he wanted to talk to me before I rejoined Jopling. "Ryder called," Cox said. "The meeting with Nancy's set. In France. This afternoon."

"In France!"

"Ryder says it's safer. And he's right. Nancy's flying over after lunch. She does most days. Ryder has it fixed pretty neatly. She flies to a little airstrip in Normandy called Chantelux. Ryder's going to arrange to have it blocked. She'll be diverted. You'll be waiting."

"All right," I said, "I'll deal with it."

I went into my office with Cox and found Jopling waiting. At first, Nick wasn't sure whether to refer to the photograph in front of Cox, but when I showed that I didn't care, Nick still hesitated and I could see he was embarrassed.

"John, it looks bad. Really bad," was all he could say.

"Nick, trust me," I said. "That photo is a phony. I'll deal with Branston—and Sellinger. Just buy me the ten days."

Nick looked surprised. "You need five directors with you. You'd better make those calls yourself. Much safer."

"I'm sorry, Nick, I can't," I said. "I just haven't time. I'll have to rely on you to round up my allies."

"Yes, of course. The union business. That's a nasty one too. When will you be seeing Billingsly?"

Nick looked so solemn that just for an instant I had an urge to say, "Haven't time, old boy. Matter of fact, I'm popping over to France for a chat with my ex-wife," but I resisted the temptation. Nick's sense of humor wasn't his strong point and I hadn't forgotten how close I'd been to losing my own in Rome.

"I'm going to delegate the union business," I said. "I have no choice."

"Huntsman's not really up to it," Jopling said cautiously.

"Yes, Nick," I said, "I know."

I picked up my direct line and asked Marge on the switchboard to get Geoffrey Haycroft at home.

Jopling looked startled.

"John, you can't do that," he said. "Not even for a situation as bad as this."

I ignored him and waited for the call to come through.

"John, you're not usually that cruel," Jopling insisted. "You really mustn't call him. You can't."

I knew that Jopling was saying the call might just kill Haycroft, but it was a chance I had to take and I told myself it was for the sake of World News as much as for myself.

I couldn't handle the Datavol issue. I had to go to France. If I walked now into the pressure cooker of union negotiations,

I would do nothing else for hours and perhaps days. But we had no one else who could go in my place.

Haycroft's heart attack had left the Personnel Division in disarray, even though we had all known it had been coming for years. Haycroft was the company's master negotiator and Milner had used him mercilessly as a buffer against union hostility brought on by his own incompetence.

One especially cruel irony was that I had acquired the reputation of being an even better negotiator; it wasn't true but my successes had been achieved in colorful settings from Bulgaria to Hong Kong and had ended in spectacular new contracts which could be announced at press conferences and state banquets.

Haycroft meanwhile had lived with the thankless, punishing round of daily arguments with the technical unions. He had spent most of his adult life forcing people to do things they did not want to do, and reasoning with unreasonable men had finally sapped his energy. He had held on to his post because he wanted to, and at his request, Dr. Richardson had concocted medical reports of Chinese inscrutability so that no one would have to face the fact that Haycroft was slowly burning out.

I had watched him aging at twice the calendar rate and tried several times to persuade Milner to give him generous early retirement before it was too late.

The heart attack had finally settled the matter and Haycroft was on extended sick leave which would go on until he qualified for his full pension.

When the call came through, it was his wife Mary who answered and I could hear the fear in her voice.

"Mary, it's John Railton. I'd like to talk to Geoff."

"No, I'm afraid you can't." Her voice sounded bitter, determined.

"Mary, I just want a quick word. Some advice. It won't take a minute."

"I know about the strike. It was on the radio. When he heard it, Geoff went into the garden. He doesn't want to talk . . ."

"John?" It was Haycroft interrupting, I guessed, from the extension phone.

"Yes. Geoff. We're having a few problems." I told him about

the forged purchase order, speaking quickly before Mary cut off the call.

When I'd finished he said, "Tricky little bastard, isn't he? Do you want me to come in?"

I heard Mary gasp and tried not to look at Jopling as I said, "We could use the old warhorse, yes, but only if you feel up to it."

"I'll come right in."

"Geoff, I'm grateful," I said. "I'll send a car." And I put down the phone quickly, aware that, though no guns or blows were involved, it was the most ruthless thing I had done since the affair had begun.

18

On the flight to France we were diverted over Sussex
because of troop movements toward the Channel ports and
even Ryder's security priority wasn't high enough to avoid the
delay. As we circled the alert zone, we saw the nucleus of an
anti-Starburst protest march, one of dozens which were forming
and following routes to various military installations in southern England. Announcements were being carried on the pop
radio stations and the marchers were stopping, village by
village, to hold rallies to try to build up their numbers. The
biggest protests had been in Suffolk because of the large number of American military installations, but the marches were
aimless because on one knew for certain where the missiles
were.

Demonstrators were beginning to flood in from the Continent too. The European disarmament movement had sensed
that if the test was to be stopped, the place to try was Britain,
where the launching was to take place, but no one seemed
certain where the protests would be most effective. Two gigantic tent cities had sprung up as the protesters deliberated
what to do: one near Heathrow to house the more affluent
members of the Movement for Nuclear Disarmament who
were coming in daily by charter plane, the other near Dover for
the boatloads of protesters who were crowding the decks of the
cross-Channel ferries. The government had pressured the local
councils into allowing the tent cities because they wanted to

keep the protesters together, in areas where they could be supervised. The MND executive had called another mass rally for central London, but already there was talk of getting bigger groups out across the country because the police had security and crowd control too well organized in the capital. The lack of focus for the protests was helping the militants win a bigger voice, and leaflets were beginning to circulate calling for more spectacular protests which would bring home the dangers of nuclear weapons more effectively than dignified marches and rallies.

Nearer the Channel coast, we flew over military columns heading for Folkestone and Dover on their way to embark for the European maneuvers. They were mostly territorial units, swollen to record numbers by the unemployment crisis and a hard-sell recruiting campaign promising camaraderie and excitement instead of the boredom of the dole queues. The protest marchers too were attracting large numbers of young people who wanted a focus for their alienation from a government they blamed for failing to provide jobs. From the air, the lines of traffic almost crisscrossed in patterns—military and antimilitary—getting in each other's way in dangerous polarization.

Then, halfway to France, the weather began to change. Most of Europe had had sunshine for weeks and though the forecasters had warned of approaching rain, they had as usual underestimated the speed of the moving front; before we had crossed the French coast, our tiny four-seater was being buffeted by squalls so heavy that they bordered on sleet. We landed safely at the tiny Vaudur airstrip where we were going to wait for her, but Nancy was only just due to leave Ashford and we learned from the tower that small planes on the British coast were turning back or delaying takeoff to await the passing of freak winds.

It was already half-past three. Since Nancy made the crossing almost every day, it was conceivable that she would simply cancel, if the delay took her landing into the evening. I sat with Ryder in a small outbuilding watching the rain blow across the meadows, almost obscuring the little grass strip. Two other CIA men kept in touch with Chantelux where Nancy was due to land; the diversion there was ready but there was no news from Ashford of her departure.

"Damn the blasted weather," I said. "We have to get this settled tonight."

I still wanted desperately to believe it was another hoax but Ryder had run a wide-ranging check on Claire Dahran and both MI6 and the West Germans had her on their suspect lists.

"She'll come," Ryder said. "If she loves flying as much as everyone says, she won't be put off by a few squalls."

Eventually, the news came. The weather had eased on the British side of the Channel and even though the rain was still sweeping across Vaudur, the reports began coming in that the skies were also brightening nearer the French coast.

Then things started to move swiftly. First there was confirmation that Nancy had left Ashford, then an hour later, word was flashed urgently from Chantelux. Nancy had been diverted to Vaudur but there had almost been a tragedy. The driver of the fire truck that was supposed to overturn and block the runway had misunderstood his instructions and Nancy had had to perform a dangerous last-minute maneuver to avoid hitting it.

Twenty minutes passed, and finally Nancy's little Piper came into view on the gray, rain-swept horizon. It seemed odd watching her land; a reminder that I was dealing with a woman I no longer knew very well—or indeed might never have known at all.

Her approach was neat and she skimmed down onto the sodden grass with only the slightest wing waver when she hit the crosswind from the mouth of the tiny valley. As she stepped out of the plane she looked ever more remote, dressed in a light one-piece cotton overall similar to the one I had seen on the magazine cover in St. Tropez. But Ryder didn't give me time to think about it.

"Get her before she gets to a phone. We don't want her calling to get picked up."

The rush made it easier. I sprinted out onto the field and as I reached her I said, "Nancy, I need to talk to you. I'll explain later. Come on."

But she didn't move. Her surprise registered briefly, then she said angrily, "John, did you arrange that shambles at Chantelux? You almost made me wreck my bloody plane."

187

"I had no choice. I had to see you without Paul knowing."

"You could have tried a phone call."

"I had to be certain. It's important."

I decided to try to soften her anger. "After the other day at Samman's, I thought you might not mind too much."

She looked at me curiously and I noticed her glancing around the airfield, and I smiled.

"I've arranged rooms at the Auberge de la Vallée," I said.

"Oh."

"For you to change. I thought we could have dinner and talk." She hesitated and I saw she was glancing around the field again. There was nothing to see—Ryder's men were well out of sight and I knew that the bugging equipment they were planning to use was ultrasensitive at very long ranges—but she was a very quick, intuitive woman and, I thought bitterly, possibly well trained also.

"All right," she said. "But if you'd wrecked the Piper, it would have taken more than dinner to put it right."

Vaudur was famous for its Auberge de la Grande Vallée, a seventeenth-century stone hospice at the head of a long wooded rift on the Solan escarpment. The hotel was only a short ride from the airport and Nancy said very little on the journey, and I could feel her distrust. In the lobby, she handled the staff with the kind of elegant arrogance that the French instantly respect, but she left me to deal with the formalities at the desk and she chatted with the manager coldly when he insisted on showing us upstairs personally.

I had booked a suite consisting of two bedrooms, with a common lounge between them. When the manager had gone, leaving behind a bottle of champagne with the compliments of the Auberge, Nancy said casually, "Why don't you pour us a drink while I get ready?"

As she changed, she treated me like a Victorian maid, a person without sex or eyes who made drinks, helped unpack, and handed her garments as she showered and put on a pale pink summer dress. She was neither discreet nor flaunting. Once I glimpsed her naked except for a pair of rainbow-colored Gucci briefs, but she gave no sign of even noticing that the bathroom door was ajar.

Finally, she came out of the bathroom and sat down on the broad, oak-backed settle. "So it is official," she said quietly.

"What do you mean?"

"John. Give me credit for knowing a little bit about you after all the years we were married. If you were following up on what happened at Samman's you'd have made a move by now."

"Nan, I did like what happened at Samman's," I said, "but there's something we have to clear away first." I hesitated. I'd already considered several ways of trying to bring up the material in the Dahran file obliquely, but there wasn't an easy one.

"I want to talk to you about a trip to Copenhagen. Five years ago."

She gave me an odd look. "That would have been a very fair question if you'd asked it two years ago," she said. "Now, you have no right to ask it."

For a second, I was caught off balance by the ease with which she brushed the question aside.

"Nan, I wouldn't be asking if it wasn't important," I said. "Just tell me about it, please."

"No. Not until I know exactly what this is about."

"What do you mean?"

"John, World News is a powerful organization, but it doesn't have the authority to overturn fire trucks on Chantelux airport. This has to do with your problems. Now why do you want to know about Copenhagen?"

"You don't deny going."

"I'm not saying anything until you explain."

I knew the look. Nothing would budge her until I answered.

"Nan, since this business began, there have been security checks done into everyone who's ever been near me. Colleagues at World News, friends . . . and, of course, you. The CIA and Military Intelligence have dug up suspicious-looking material on several people. Most of it turns out to be rubbish. But it has to be checked. They're bothered by the Copenhagen conference. It was a left-wing, a Communist meeting. It wasn't the kind of place anyone would expect you to go. It came as a shock to me that you went. I couldn't explain it. Now that Jennifer's been cleared, everyone's pretty anxious to find a new suspect."

189

"And I've been elected?"

"No, of course not. But I didn't want the Copenhagen business to become an embarrassment. I said I'd ask you, so you wouldn't have to be asked formally."

"Good God," she said quietly. "How much you must have thought I hated you."

"Nan, I . . ."

"John, I'm not a fool. I know this isn't a casual security check. This is the big time. Diversions in foreign airfields. Special confrontations in remote hotels. I knew we weren't alone at Vaudur, I could feel it. How many agents are around us now, John? Are we on candid camera? Or is it just microphones?"

"Nan. Just tell me about Copenhagen."

"You really thought that I'd been betraying you to the Russians all these years?"

"I'm trying not to think," I said, "until I hear your explanation."

"You won't like it."

"But I have to have it."

"Yes, I suppose you do. Do you remember who covered the Congress for World News?"

"No."

"Think," she said. "It couldn't be a very big list. Grade C assignment, or B possibly if done solo."

"I can't remember," I said. "Somerville? Stevens?"

"Would it help if I told you it was a man with a staircase?"

I stood quite still. "Graham Loftus?"

"Yes."

Loftus was an amiable, easygoing rogue who had the reputation of being what the American side of the agency called the champion pussy hound of World News. In his flat in London, the bedroom was a converted attic with access up a steep wooden ladder. He had kept many a World News dinner party in stitches with accounts of how the ladder was a recurring obstacle to his seduction routines.

"Always have to get them up the steps before I'm too drunk. Trouble is, I soften them up, then have a few too many glasses myself. So I have a trick. I stare up their skirts while they're climbing; focuses the mind marvelously. Stopped me slithering down base over apex many a time."

"You know the ladder," I said throatily.

"Yes, damn you. I know the ladder. I climbed it one night when I was so goddamn fed up with you and your obsession with World News," she burst out. "You don't remember the time of the Congress, do you?"

"I was in Madrid."

"No. Before that. You were in Monaco, and so was I, except that I might as well have been in Timbuktu."

The memory came back instantly. I had been sent to cover the Grand Prix, and to apologize for too many weeks of neglect I had taken Nancy with me. Two Formula One drivers had been killed on the first night and the routine coverage had turned into a week of round-the-clock reporting.

"Yes, I can see you remember it," she said bitterly. "The first time we spoke, practically, was the fight on the plane back. Then do you remember the Saturday? The cocktail party for the head of the Economic Services which we were going to call in at for ten minutes on the way to a nice intimate dinner at La Terrazza—until you were called away to interview the Soviet President at Heathrow? I spent two bloody hours listening to Econ small talk, until finally Graham took pity on me and filled me full of white wine and pizza. I climbed that ladder gratefully, John Railton, and I was glad he looked up my skirt because at least somebody thought it was worth looking up. And I was so goddamn mad at you, I went to Copenhagen instead of going home for a cutesy week with Mommy."

"You had observer credentials," I said feebly.

"They'd cordoned off the Congress Palace. I had to have them. But even then, I slunk around in a stupid granny dress and kept away from the press box so as not to embarrass you."

"Did you enjoy it at least?"

"If you mean is he good in bed, the answer's yes. If you want a technical appraisal, he's excellent but he's too lazy and he drinks too much to be outstanding. Next question?"

I decided to try for a shock reaction.

"The next question is about Morocco," I said. "Your Moroccan lover. How did he die?"

Nancy looked at me in amazement. "Sidi? He drowned on Casablanca beach. But what in God's name has that got to do with anything?"

I didn't know what the Voice Stress Analysis machines had registered, but I knew I believed the surprise was genuine.

"He drowned?"

"Yes."

"How long after he was arrested?"

"Sidi was never arrested."

"Detained then. For left-wing activities."

Nancy laughed. "John, you really are coming out of your tree, my love. Sidi's only ambition, apart from laying every foreign woman who set foot on the beach, was to become a banker like his father."

"Nan, can you prove that?" I said urgently.

"No, of course I can't," she said. "It was almost twenty years ago. I was on holiday and I had a fling with a Moroccan kid who drowned in a swimming accident. I've no idea where his family are, or even if there's anyone left. John, you've got to explain this. It's getting too crazy."

"All right," I said. "The truth is that they're investigating Claire Dahran. There's reason to believe she was a Soviet agent. And that's not craziness. The suspicions about you have come out through her."

"John, that's totally ridiculous. I have no special connection with Claire. I knew her in Aix. We kept in touch. She came to a few parties. You must remember her."

Nancy smiled. "She did try to seduce me once. After the divorce. She must have thought I was on an anti-men kick. It happened at the Kingsmills'. After a swimming party she got too close in the showers. There was a bit of a fuss when I showed her I wasn't interested. After that she more or less dropped away."

"Tell me," I said, "did Paul know about Claire?"

"Yes. He was with me at the Kingsmills'."

"And Sidi?"

"Yes. I've mentioned him, I guess. But anyway, I'm pretty sure he had me investigated before the marriage." Nancy smiled ruefully. "I think it's an old Sellinger family custom."

I hesitated. I wanted to say so much more, but I knew I had to have clearance from Ryder.

"Nan, I have to leave you. I'm expecting someone downstairs."

"You mean you have to see how the security boys think I'm doing."

"You always were too goddam sharp," I said.

"Perhaps. But I understand. Go ahead. I won't try to go anywhere."

I ran down the great circular stone staircase and spotted Ryder as soon as I reached the lobby.

He was smiling and before I could say anything he pulled me into a small side room.

"Well," I said urgently, "did you get all that?"

"Sure did."

"And?"

Ryder grinned. "We've been had for suckers. The VSA analyst says he has no doubts at all. None. She isn't lying."

"And she's not hiding anything either? She couldn't have had the affair with Loftus to give her a genuine excuse to make the trip?"

"Nope. I brought the best expert the Company has. He's given her a clean bill."

"Can I talk to her freely?"

Ryder shrugged. "You sure as hell may as well. Or we could be playing ring-around-the-rosy forever."

"No, not forever," I said. "It has to be Sellinger, doesn't it? It just has to be. No one else could put this whole thing together. Seagull. Nancy. All the stuff from my files. It just has to be."

"Yes," Ryder said, "I guess it does. But we have to prove it. Go and see if your good lady can help us."

19

"Brother against brother?" Nancy said. "Yes. It's possible. The rift in the Family is deep enough."

She stirred in my arms and pulled a corner of the sheet from under my stomach so that nothing interfered with the contact between our bodies.

Two hours had passed since I'd talked to Ryder. The first had been spent hesitantly, trying to heal the breach of suspicion between us as I told her everything about the contents of the Dahran file. The second had been spent making love, with a beauty and frenzy we hadn't shared since the early days of our marriage.

Now, finally, we felt close enough to talk about Paul without constraint, but we were getting nowhere.

Once she had heard the whole story, she too believed it had to be Sellinger.

"He's the only one who could have designed that file so perfectly. And using the ID people to leak it is just his style. And yes, he would destroy Starburst. For revenge. Or for profit. But not for ideology. If he's working with the Russians, it's for his own purposes, not theirs."

She confirmed that the tension between Paul and the rest of the Family seemed to be growing.

"There have been terrible fights over who will run the Sellinger Corporation if Robert goes into politics," Nancy said. "You know he's being touted for Secretary of Defense. Paul wants the presidency of the corporation but Jacob's blocking it. Says he wants to keep Paul free as the family troubleshooter and there's talk of putting in a nonfamily chief operating officer. The truth is that Jacob's afraid of Paul. He recognizes another predator like himself. He knows he wouldn't be able to run the corporation through Paul the way he has through Robert.

"The family's been getting Paul pretty angry lately," she went on.

"Real anger, or the rough-tough angry performances he gives at the office?" I asked.

Nancy smiled. "I'd forgotten. You don't know the private Paul Sellinger, do you. It's very different. You'd be surprised."

As she talked about Paul, I realized that I had never really glimpsed behind the public mask. In his business dealings his lapses in control were rare and momentary, but not, apparently, in private. In public, he accepted the Sellinger mystique which required a perfect and disciplined performance for every appearance, but he apparently found it much more of a strain than I had realized. In private, Nancy said, his idea of luxury was to be moody and he was given to alternating bouts of manic activity and black depression. In recent weeks the moods had grown worse, and he had been particularly bad since the announcement of the Starburst tests in Europe. But it was all circumstantial and not even particularly damning: she knew nothing of his travels or his business contacts. It was maddening to be so certain and yet have so little to go on.

Nancy stroked my hair and let her breasts slide playfully across my chest.

"Nan, I'm sorry I suspected you," I said, "even if only with part of my head."

Nancy grinned. "You never did understand women very well, did you. Paul—if it is Paul—has really had you harassing your females, hasn't he? First your Seagull. Now me."

She paused and eased herself up onto her arms.

"Tell me. Am I a match for your Seagull?"

"Oh Nan, what a question. You can't possibly compare women."

Nancy laughed. "John Railton, you are a slithery, hypocritical diplomat. You know damned well you compare women. Everyone does. But I forgive you. I know I can compete now.

195

Wives are right to fear mistresses. A mistress can focus on sex so much better, excluding all the day-to-day worries that get in the way. But I'm not a wife anymore and I can focus on it too."

She smiled. "If it's any consolation—and it probably is— Paul is an absolute disaster in bed. He's the original two-minute wonder. And before you start fishing, yes, I did miss your loving, you old stud. And I'm not ashamed to admit it."

"Nan, why did you marry him?" I said. "I swore I'd never ask, but I'd like to know."

"You mean what's a tough, independent lady like me doing hanging around a shit like Paul? Well the truth is, I wasn't the tough lady then. I've been through the fire in the past year; the clay's hardened a bit. When you were away so much, I felt neglected. Unfulfilled. I had no career and no kids. I didn't really blame you, I just fell out of love with myself. Paul flattered me. He offered me a role: a Sellinger lady. It wasn't a career, but it seemed so much bigger than being a neglected World News wife. The big stage; independence, some power.

"All an illusion, of course. I was leaving him anyway, before this. But I was doing it my own way. I'm using his money quite ruthlessly, I'm afraid. I've fallen in love with flying and I'm spending more on logging hours than is decent. I was going to get him to give me the plane . . ."

"Nan," I interrupted gently. "I'm sorry I neglected you. I should have given you a life in World News."

She looked at me curiously.

"As what—a good World News wife? Eventually to become the president's lady and hostess-in-chief?"

Taking me completely by surprise, she reached down and seized my shoulders, shaking them angrily.

"You stupid, stupid man, John Railton. You really believe that's what it was about, don't you? That if you'd let me give a few more dinner parties and you'd come home a bit more often, everything would have been okay. Dammit, don't you understand I wanted to be a correspondent? I could have been a fine one, as good as you. And as good an executive. You really don't see, do you, that in a differently ordered world, *I* might have been chief executive of World News. It never crossed your mind, did it? I can think as well as you, perceive as well as you. With training, I could write as well as you. Don't you see, we're interchangeable, you and I."

Suddenly, I felt her hands relax and I saw she was beginning to laugh. I knew the switch so well. Her sense of humor had always been one of her finest graces; she despised people who took themselves too seriously, and rarely did herself for long.

"Jesus," she said, "this is a funny way to run a reconciliation."

I smiled. "Maybe. But it's true—I never did think of you that way. And I'm ashamed."

"Well, don't be," she said. "At least not now. I shouldn't have started ranting. Let's see if you're still ticklish instead."

She made a grab for my midriff. I yelped, knowing how quickly she could plunge her fingers in, and seized her in a playful bear hug. I didn't apply much pressure; it was a hold I'd put her in a hundred times when we used to wrestle around in bed, but she winced and I saw her face constrict with pain.

"Nan, I'm sorry," I said. "I didn't mean to hurt . . ."

"It's okay," she said. "It wasn't you. My back's a bit sore, that's all."

"Here, turn over. Let me have a look." Reluctantly, she turned on her stomach and I gently examined her back. Just over the kidney, I saw some pale subcutaneous bruises.

I stopped smiling. "Was this Paul?"

"It's nothing . . ."

"Nan," I said, "I didn't spend two years in the military police without knowing about hitting people without leaving marks," I said. "How long ago was this?"

"A couple of days."

"You mean after I came to Samman's?"

"Yes. He pretends it's a love spank, then he says he's sorry afterwards."

"Nan, you don't play-spank someone on the kidneys. Does he do it often?"

"No, only when he's very angry. That business with Sally Menzies really got under his skin."

"Nan, it can't have been that. Sally can't have been that important to him. It must have been because of me."

197

"Perhaps. But it was Sally he was ranting about when he slammed me in the back."

"It doesn't make much sense," I said. "Have you any idea what it was about?"

"Not really. I think it had something to do with Chad."

I grinned. "Nan, you must have gotten that wrong," I said. "Paul would never go to Chad. He's as likely to make a trip to the Falkland Islands."

"Maybe." Nancy paused. "John Railton, I'm going to end this conversation right now. I did not agree to climb back into your arms in order to discuss my husband's trips. Now you're not a two-minute wonder and I intend to make the most of that. So lie back while I do some revival work and after that . . ."

She eased herself down the bed and settled herself comfortably, with her head nestled against my thigh. I lay back savoring the delicate movements of her tongue. I knew the route the exploration would take. It had been a long time, but I could remember every exquisite stage.

Then I heard the scraping sound outside the bedroom door. Another moment and I certainly wouldn't have noticed it, but in that first moment of luxurious pleasure, I was sensitive to every sound in the silent room.

What flashed through my mind was pure instinct. The thoughts came so fast that it was like one single idea: The only sensible course for Sellinger now is to kill us both. He tried with Seagull. He must try with Nancy. If she were dead, the Dahran file would still be damning. If they were going to attack, it should logically be from the garden. The windows were open. A grenade tossed in would be the simplest way. No, that wasn't right. Ryder and his men were in the garden with the bugging equipment. The best way was from the landing.

The whole sequence of thought seemed to last only a split second. I grabbed Nancy's head between my hands and held it still, pushing her away from me.

She thought I was teasing, and tried to force herself back down on me, but I pushed harder and held her still in an iron grip.

The rustling sound was a little louder. What would they

be doing? The doors in the hospice were of massive oak with big locks and this one was bolted from the inside. They couldn't force them open to lob a grenade. They would use plastic on the lock to blow it open, then a grenade. Two moves and it would all be over.

There was no time for countermoves. I hurled myself upright, forcing Nancy violently backward. She let out a yell and I grabbed her and shouted, "Come on, quick. The window."

I ran across the room dragging Nancy behind me, onto the balcony. "Jump," I shouted, "jump!"

She hesitated, not understanding, poised naked on the edge of the balustrade. If I was right, there was no time to argue. I scooped her up in my arms, aimed her as well as I could, and virtually threw her down into the garden one floor below. In a second I was after her and I landed sprawling beside her in the flower beds in front of the hotel.

I pulled myself up to a kneeling position, feeling my legs sinking into the soft flower bed. I looked across at Nancy. She didn't seem to be badly hurt, but she was bleeding from a big scratch on her hip where she had scraped against a large thistley plant. Already, people were beginning to run out of the hotel entrance. I looked up and saw that the bedroom was completely quiet and peaceful.

I stayed very still, feeling totally and abjectly stupid. There was nothing I could say, but Nancy managed to grin and said quietly, "John, if you didn't like the sex, you only had to say. You didn't have to throw me out of the fucking window." She leaned forward and touched my arm. "It's okay," she said. "I know you're jumpy. Let's get some clothes on before the management starts selling tickets."

I was just about to make a joke about the leap looking terrific on a report to the World News board when the explosion rocked the front of the hotel. The noise was deafening and the bedroom we had jumped from vanished in a red flash and a swirl of smoke and flying debris. I threw myself on top of Nancy and tried to spread my body as far as I could over hers. As the hail of masonry and broken glass cascaded down, I could feel the sharp fragments biting into my back.

All around, there were screams and shouting and when I

looked up, I saw that half the wall of the hotel had collapsed and crumbled completely away.

Then I heard Ryder's voice, "John. Quick. The car on the driveway," and I pulled Nancy upright and started to run.

20

When I got back to the World News building in London, I announced that before anything else was done, I wanted a detailed inquiry into the firing of Sally Menzies.

No one questioned the decision openly. When I saw that even Cox was trying to humor me, I decided that it was time to announce some other decisions I'd taken on the flight back from France.

I waited until Ryder was back from installing Nancy in a CIA safe house outside London, then I called Cox, Jopling, and Pike into my office and asked them all, slightly formally, to sit around the conference table.

"Gentlemen," I said, "I don't want this little speech to sound ungrateful. But it has to be made. Since this Starburst thing began, every one of you has helped me in ways which can't be repaid adequately with thanks." I turned to Ryder. "Bob, you saved my neck in the first place. Without you, I'd have been arrested and the game would have been over before it began. And I haven't forgotten that, but I've decided that as of this moment, I'm taking sole charge of my side of the Starburst affair.

"In the past few days, I've yo-yoed around the world responding to pressures and theories from the intelligence community. I've almost been killed twice, and I've been led into believing that two women I love had both betrayed me. I've been threatened with exposure as a drug addict and a lecher and portrayed to my own board as a violent and unstable idiot who isn't fit to manage a hamburger stand.

"I'm completely and totally satisfied in my own mind that Paul Sellinger is responsible for all this, and as of this moment I'm going to proceed as I think best to prove it and to find out how and why. Bob, whatever the intelligence community feels it must do, it must do. But it can do it without me. I'm taking charge of my own campaign. The shadowplay is over; it's time to bring things out into the open."

I turned back to the rest of the group.

"Now, the first thing I want done is to find out why Sally Menzies was fired. I'm following a hunch. The same kind of hunch that kept me alive in the Auberge de la Vallée. I decided on the flight back that I haven't been following my hunches nearly enough of late.

"We'll set up our base here. Nick has been briefed fully and he's on the team from now on. My information is that Sellinger is at Samman's Farm and he's canceled his appointments for the day. I want instructions given to all my personal staff that no one is to communicate with him. I want him kept guessing about what happened in France. Total blackout. Not even to say who is in my office. Understood?

"Now the cover for all this is simple. If anyone queries anything I ask any of you to do, you simply let it be known that I've declared war finally and definitively on Paul Sellinger. My back's against the wall. He's asked the board for my resignation. I'm fighting back. Doing anything I can to get the dirt on him."

I tapped a sheet of memos and printouts from the E Net that were lying on my desk.

"Now I'm aware that there are pressing matters needing my attention. Geoffrey Haycroft has managed to get the unions back to work provisionally, but he wants to consult me on several points in the negotiations. Nick has been in touch with seven board members and some are wavering. They'll be calling, wanting meetings. There are twenty other matters that have been neglected while I've been chasing around Europe. For the moment, I do not care. I want to know about Sally Menzies. I want to know why Paul Sellinger has gotten so worked up about her firing and what the hell Chad has to do with it. It may have nothing to do with the Starburst business. That's my responsibility. Now, are there any questions?"

Ryder eased himself out of his chair.

"Nope. No questions," he said. "I know you in this mood. All I can say is, God help Paul Sellinger. I'll be at the Embassy. We've had a first report on the attack in France. No arrests and no clues. It's being treated as a terrorist attack against the hotel. I'll stay in touch."

When he had gone, Pike said, "You know, if I were you, I'd bring your Seagull in on this. She's a very bright lass and she's getting damned bored at the flat."

"Fine," I said. "Fetch her personally, would you, Jim, and brief her on the way."

When Seagull arrived, she looked as cheerful as if she'd just been let out of prison. When I introduced her to Jopling, I couldn't resist a little tease. "Jennifer," I said, "this is Nick Jopling. Nick, I believe you know Jennifer from her photograph." Nick blushed and Seagull grinned and said, "I know it wasn't very good. I always did look better in profile."

When Nick had moved away, Seagull took me aside.

"I gather your sex life got a little hectic in France. That'll teach you never to go back to old wives." I was trying to think of something to say when she grinned and said. "It's okay. I'm just glad you're all right."

When everyone was assembled, I set up the operations center in the annex that I used as an extension of my office for bigger conference meetings. Cox arranged a VDU and a bank of telephones, and before we began, I added one last detail which I knew could well be the most important.

I called the World News butler and asked him to select a dozen of the company's choicest wines and prepare them as a gift case. When they arrived, I told Cox to take them down to Marge. "Tell her we're choosing sides for a war and the wine is better on our team," I said.

Marge was the supervisor of the World News telephone exchange, which was known throughout the media as the magic switchboard. Marge's personal nickname was the Eye of God, because, it was said, she always knew where everyone was at any moment and she could find you whether you were in the wrong bed or the wrong country. Her passion was wine and I told Cox simply to give her the case and say it was my personal wish that Paul shouldn't find out what was going on.

Nick Jopling, who always loved a chance to play journalist, took over the VDU and got on line to the World News reference library to call up all the information we had on Chad.

Cox brought Sally Menzies' personal file from Personnel and immediately we hit our first snag. Officially she hadn't been fired, but she'd obviously left in anger and she had asked for no reference and left no forwarding or contact address.

But the file did show a mother in Scotland.

"Wouldn't you know it'd be in the Orkneys," Seagull said. But Cox grinned. "It's a helluva lot better than Glasgow," he said. "Marge won't even take off her warm-up suit for that one."

The mother wasn't at home, but Marge found her in three calls and put me through to her on the village store telephone in Stornaway against the background of a howling wind. She didn't know where Sally was exactly. She was hitchhiking but she wasn't moving all the time, and she was picking up mail in Basel but not for another week. When I asked her about boyfriends or companions for the trip, she got a bit huffy but eventually she agreed that there might be a boy with her and she gave us an address in Grimsby. Cox called the home but the boy was there; he'd broken up with Sally and didn't sound very happy about it. Seagull came on the line and coaxed the boy into telling us a bit more. There'd been a fight. Yes, there was another boy. Someone in London—and we had another name. We found the boy's address and his father gave us the employer; the boy was on holiday, but his workmates said he hadn't gone anywhere. Seagull again got the next link—a pub where he might be drinking. Two calls and we had the boy and he gave us our first breakthrough. He had meant to go with Sally but hadn't had the money. She'd said, "If you get any later, meet me in Strasbourg"—and the rendezvous day was tomorrow.

That narrowed it down, but not far enough. She could be already in Strasbourg or a day away. We tried Strasbourg first and finally had some luck. Cox got a guidebook from the WN library and we called every hotel we thought she might be able to afford. It wasn't done slowly and painstakingly, it was done quickly and painstakingly: thirty calls on six lines in twenty minutes, made by two French-speaking correspondents rounded up from the newsroom day shift, from among those I could trust.

We found the hotel, but not her. She had gone out to lunch, they thought. The guidebook again. Twenty restaurants and we found her in the eleventh. I talked to her personally and we put the call on tape and on the speaker phone. As I listened, I felt the familiar shiver. We had our break and, finally, somewhere to start.

She had been fired because she had failed to destroy some documents and she was furious because she still didn't know why it was important. She said there was a standing instruction among Sellinger's personal staff that no travel voucher or credit-card slip should ever be kept in the files; he hated anyone having any record of his movements, and if any came in, they were handed to him personally. There had been a letter, from a bank in Ndjamena, saying that there had been a mistake in an over-the-counter transaction exchanging dollars for CFA francs. The bank owed Mr. Sellinger fourteen dollars. Where should they remit? Sally had ignored the letter, leaving it at the bottom of a nonurgent in tray. Sellinger had found it and forced her to quit in a fit of fury.

"Was the problem that he didn't want anyone to know he had been in Chad, Sally?"

"It had to be," she said. "But it was so silly. No one would think anything about a stupid mistake of fourteen dollars."

"Do you remember the date?"

"July 1977. But I don't remember the day."

"Sally, I'm grateful," I said, "and I'm sorry about the fuss. If you want a reference or a job, you can have either. I'll see to it personally. Thanks and have a good trip."

Cox helped Jopling operate the VDU and at first there were no clues. The stories all related to the guerrilla fighting in the north, then Seagull said suddenly: "Testing ground. That was the year I left the Institute. The Black Eagle consortium was going to lose its testing ground in Libya. They were trying to get into Zaire; maybe they were also trying to get into Chad."

"It would be Chad," I said. "It's one of our few weak spots. Our routine coverage is lousy; we only staff for revolutions and big stuff."

I called Robert Messenet, the director of the Agence France Presse in Paris, and passed the problem to him. I didn't tell him why—only that it was personal and not news—and asked him for the name of the correspondent they had had in Chad during that period. He called back ten minutes later. The man, Christian Brovelli, had resigned and now worked for ORTF. Four more calls and we traced him to the Rome bureau. He was at lunch but he had left a contact number. After that, we really started to roll because Seagull had guessed right: a mission from the Black Eagle consortium had taken a look at Chad. They wanted a site for the early tests and Chad had the right combination of forest and desert. But it had fallen through and they'd signed a deal with Zaire instead.

We still had a long way to go, but Brovelli gave us ten names: businessmen, journalists, and tradesmen who knew the Chad scene well at that period. It took two hours for Marge to find them all, and one—a retired hotelier called Andre Buisson—had the piece we wanted. He had run the Hotel des Chasses in Ndjamena in 1977 and he remembered Paul Sellinger and his meeting with the Black Eagle people. At first, he was reluctant to name any consortium members, but eventually he gave us two, and at that point Nick Jopling took over. He stopped playing journalist and used the magic switchboard to plug into his private accountancy network. As a journalist, Nick was an intelligent dilettante who had observed professionals a long time; but as an accountant he was a wizard, and his network of contacts spread far out of London to all five continents. But that didn't worry Marge, who had the magician's gift of turning night into day. She simply ignored time zones. If a respondent growled that it was five o'clock in the morning in Sydney, she didn't argue. She knew it was five o'clock; she had banks of clocks showing the world's time zones right over her switchboard. She simply gave them eight seconds to wake up and said, cheerily, "Thank you," and connected the call.

I made Nick work alone, which took longer, but there were still early breakthroughs. Nick was told by a friend in Bonn that he ought to look at the share prices of the companies connected with the consortium over the past two weeks. Nick looked and wasn't certain, so he called in Joss Myers in the Economic Division. Myers decided that there was something wrong. Not a striking thing: the companies had been depressed after the successful firing of Starburst, but not quite as much as should have been expected. What was bolstering confidence in them? Nick looked at the possible sources of funds and slowly, fragment by fragment, the picture came together.

At one point Pike took a break from his position at Jopling's elbow and as he drank a cup of coffee, he said admiringly, "You never can tell, can you? For a man who collects china horses, that's one helluva rough operator."

Nick almost purred at the compliment and I thought, Yes, it's true. There's a psychopath lurking in all of us. The little man of violence waiting for an excuse to have his day.

This was accountant's violence and Nick knew the weaknesses and pressure points of his colleagues as surely as any martial-arts expert. In his gentle, educated voice, he blackmailed, threatened, and cajoled. Cox fetched and carried data from the Economic Division and finally, Nick looked up and said, "Well, I think we have it. We can't prove it all yet. But I think we have the picture."

I called Ryder. When he arrived, I left the briefing to Nick; it was his moment, and I gave him my chair and stood behind him as he arranged his pages of neat handwritten notes on the table in front of him.

He coughed, and said, "I admit I'm a bit in awe. I detest everything Paul Sellinger stands for, but I have to admire his artistry in my field. It's a masterpiece. It really is. A delicate, intricate masterpiece."

As he began to outline it, I remembered Ryder's phrase: "People like the Sellingers walk the world believing they are giants." The scheme was monstrous in its arrogance; it took no account of East or West, or nations, or politics, or the aspirations or the safety of peoples. It was, quite simply, a project for profit and revenge. Revenge on the brother whose ascendancy he resented came with the destruction of Starburst, the decline of Sellinger Defense Industries, and the eclipse of Robert's political career. That was half of the mosaic; the other was the delicate, subtle insinuation of funds into the companies connected with the Black Eagle consortium without disturbing the market.

"It really is an astonishingly difficult technical exercise," Jopling said. "With Starburst in the ascendancy, the Black Eagle group shares fall. It's a perfect situation for buying in with insider knowledge—in this case the knowledge that Starburst is heading for cancelation. But if there's even the tiniest whisper that someone is moving in money, the word will amplify instantly: Why? What's happening? Who knows something we don't know? Sellinger's got about twelve groups acting for him as intermediaries and straw men; but he goes about it so obliquely, it really has style."

Nick picked up one of his pages of notes. "This one is typical. When the Starburst test firing at Fort Benedict was declared a success, one of the companies badly hit was the firm manufacturing the lightweight plastic for Black Eagle. Their shares slipped badly. Paul could have made a killing. Instead, he waited to see how the plastic company was planning its own survival. They chose diversification and announced plans to merge part of their operations with another firm outside the defense field. Paul used that piece of news as a cover and bought in quickly, so it looked as though the shares were responding to a well-thought-out self-rescue operation. One of his groups is now close to a majority holding."

When he had finished his summary, it was obvious that Sellinger had succeeded almost perfectly: the share movements had been only fractionally uncharacteristic, but thanks to Jopling's perceptiveness and his network of contacts, we had enough to be confident.

I'd been listening very carefully to Nick's briefing and as he talked I'd been making a few notes on my own. When he'd finished, I said, "Nick, we're still one stage short. Do you think you can take it a bit further?"

Pike let out a chuckle. "Christ, mister, you really want jam on it, don't you."

"Maybe," I said, "but knowing what Paul's doing is beautiful. The question is, how do we stop him?"

"Expose him," Pike said.

"Not so easy," I said. "What would happen, Nick, if we shouted this from the housetops?"

"The evidence would disappear like summer snow. The syndicates would break up and there'd be so much shuffling of paper you'd never know who bought what from whom, and you'd probably be accused of slandering Sellinger out of personal hatred."

"That's right," Ryder said. "The rest of the scheme couldn't be proved either. We know what Paul plans to do, but he hasn't actually done anything. He hasn't leaked any information about Starburst to the Soviets. Dammit, he hasn't personally even bought any Black Eagle shares. In his own name, that is."

"I agree," I said. "I think Paul planned to move very slowly. I think he has a strictly long-term game plan. If I had to stick my neck out, I'd say it went something like this: I think he intended to set me up as a traitor, with Jennifer as my contact, then have us both killed so we couldn't disprove it. When he failed to get us in St. Tropez, he put Nancy up as next in line. The next step was to leak the information and have the Soviets make it so widely known that the Starburst program would have to be canceled as useless.

"But I don't think Paul would have moved in with Black Eagle. I think he'd have stayed within the bosom of the Sellinger family and consoled poor Robert for his lost political base and, probably, his political career. I think he'd have helped pick up the pieces within the Sellinger Corporation and gradually worked his way toward Black Eagle. You can imagine the rhetoric a year from now: The West needs a defense system; Black Eagle is the obvious choice and it's got support in Europe already. With an operator like Paul, I wouldn't put it past him to arrange a merger—Sellinger Defense Industries with the Black Eagle Consortium—he'd have enough clout in the consortium to rig it any way he wanted it. Three years from now what would you have? Another missile program. Black Eagle is ready—bigger, better, more beautiful than Starburst. The West is safe for another decade. Only this time it's Paul at the top, not Robert."

Ryder grunted. "John, I have to give you top marks. Now do you want to try for the grand prize and tell me how we stop him?"

"Not by a simple exposé," I said. "Nick's right. He'd just

fold his tents and steal away. But there has to be leverage against him, if only from inside his own family."

"How do you mean?" Ryder said.

"If Paul has bought himself far enough into the Black Eagle consortium to be close to indirect control, he can't have been using just his own personal fortune. He must have been using Family money, at least as collateral."

"That takes a bit of nerve," Jopling said. "But I agree. It has to be."

"So how would it be if we went to the key bankers and brokers in the scheme and put the word out that he's not using authorized funds? Threaten them with legal complications? Demand a freeze?"

"It would be fine," Nick said, "except that I couldn't pinpoint the key people for you. I could make a few guesses. But no more."

"Could anyone?"

"Neville Farmer could probably make the best guess, but he wouldn't do it."

Farmer was the head of the World News Economic Services, but he had come from Global and he was a committed Sellinger man who had strongly opposed my appointment.

"You're right," I said. "Neville knows Paul's mind inside out but he wouldn't help, and if we approached him, he'd run straight to Paul."

"So what do you propose?" Ryder said. He grinned. "Since you haven't done half bad since you took control of your own destiny, as you called it, do you have any suggestions?"

I grinned. "Yes," I said. "I have one very specific one. The great principle of American business is always try to go to the top man. Nick, I think it's time you booked yourself a seat on the Concorde and went and had a talk with Mr. Jacob Sellinger to let him know what his son is up to."

21

Meanwhile, Paul proceeded as though his only purpose in life were to oust me as head of World News. Even I had to admire his cool. He must have known he was in the middle of a major crisis. He knew I was alive and that Nancy probably was, too. The potential usefulness of the Dahran file was fading rapidly and though he couldn't have known how much we'd found out already about his financial dealings, he must have realized from the activity inside World News that I was pulling out every stop.

But he behaved as though I were the one on the run and he had only to press home for his advantage.

He stayed at Samman's and avoided any direct contact with the World News building, but I found out how active he had been as soon as I went back to my office.

My secretary had been told not to disturb me in the annex, but when I came out she was looking worried.

"Lord Branston's been trying to reach you," she said. "Then he tried Mr. Jopling. Then you again. When I said you were both tied up, he said one of you should contact him immediately. He'll be in his office for the rest of the afternoon, then he'll be dining at the Braganza in Soho. He sounded very severe," she added. "Not friendly as he usually is."

"Nick, find out what that's all about," I said. "I want a word with Haycroft about the union negotiations."

But I didn't get as far as seeing Haycroft.

I was in my office, preparing a list of negotiating options, when Cox came in with Pike.

"Chief. More trouble," he said. "Wint's been at it again. He's called the *Mirror* and the *Sun* and told them he has more stuff about the Allenby scandal. Says he has a guest list for the party which he'll sell to the highest bidder."

"Right," I said. "We'll just see what Branston's up to, then I'll deal with Mr. Wint personally."

Nick came back and he looked downcast.

"Paul's been very busy," he said. "I think he's bought Branston."

"Nick, how the fuck can you buy someone who already owns half of London."

"With a seat on the board of the New York Metropolitan Opera. Branston's life ambition. I couldn't get Howard right away so I talked to someone I know in his organization. When I did get Howard, he gave me the complete cold treatment. Said he'd consider the matter carefully and decided there was no point in arranging a meeting with you. He said evidence like that photograph couldn't be faked, it simply wasn't possible. He felt he had no choice but to argue strongly for your resignation. He has a lot of friends on the board, most of them your friends, too. He can be very dangerous to you."

"Yes, I know. But I'll sort out Lord bloody Branston. If he can switch his support from me for the sake of a seat on the Met board, then he has a very sharp comeuppance due to him. Cox, call Simon and Medlar, the advertising agency. The number's on my pad. Ask for Ronald Simon, personal from me. Branston's dining at the Braganza, so tell Simon to meet us at the Fox and Grapes in Wardour Street. Seven o'clock."

"What if he isn't free?"

"He'll make himself free. If he argues, tell him I said it was grateful time." I turned to Jopling.

"Nick, get your backside onto a plane and get to New York. Call me every three hours to report developments. Come through the switchboard. Marge will arrange to keep the calls private.

"Jim, now that Seagull's with us, can you spare two men?"

"Yes."

"Good. Put one on Branston's tail and set the other one digging. I want everything you can get on Branston in the next few hours. Cox will help. He'll give you everything we have from the World News side."

"What about Wint?" Cox said. "The *Mirror* and the *Sun* won't waste time starting to bid. The *Mirror's* considering now. I had the tip from a friend in their features department."

"Don't worry," I said. "I'm going to see Mr. Wint right now. I've had enough of that bastard, along with all the rest of Mr. Paul Sellinger's acolytes and business associates."

"Are you planning on going by yourself?" Pike said. "Ryder was telling me about Wint. He sounds like a real tough boy. The SIS people sweated him hard. He wouldn't give them anything."

"Oh yes, I know all about Mr. Wint," I said. "He has some lovely tricks. Like pretending to be drunk, then beating the hell out of some soft-bellied innocent in the Press Club, then saying later it was all a drunken mistake and he didn't mean it. Knocked eleven teeth out of a kid from the *Standard* just a few weeks ago."

"You could try to buy the list," Jopling said tentatively. "If he'd accept a reasonable figure."

Cox laughed. "That's the Nick we know and love. Even with the West in the grip of Ming the Merciless, he still wants to keep the expenses down."

"Don't worry. I'm not going to pay anything, Nick," I said. "And I know what a gesture of friendship it was for you to suggest it. I'm going to deal with Mr. Wint personally. Alone. On my own responsibility."

Pike looked doubtful. "You think you can handle him alone? You're not as young as you were and you're a gentleman now."

"I *was* a gentleman," I said, "until I got finally and definitely pissed off lying bareass naked in a flower bed outside a French hotel being sprayed with broken glass."

I winked at Pike. "For Christ's sake, stop being a mother hen. I had this friend in the military police who taught me never to get into fights." I gave a passable imitation of Pike's growling tone. "When you're dealing with a real hard man, mister, never get into a fight. Get in control."

Wint had an office in a warrenlike building on Ludgate Hill called Allbury House which was used mainly by foreign correspondents whose organizations couldn't afford the rents at the International Press Center, and by freelancers who just wanted a place for a phone and a typewriter.

I had Cox check that he was there, and Pike drove me across in his Rover. He had parked at the top of Ludgate Hill and as I was getting out he tapped a large briefcase resting between his legs.

"I've been keeping this around in case we needed it," he said. "Do you think you can make use of it?"

Inside was a military police nightstick; it was white and highly polished to indicate it was a "special," hollowed out probably, and modified with lovingly balanced bits of lead. Seeing it brought back instantly all the horror of life as a redcap: the boredom and the brutality of depot life, the savage jokes, brass polish on the testicles, and the smell of sawdust and vomit on barroom floors during the nightly round of brawling.

"No, Jim, I'll pass," I said. "I might just kill him with it. I'll just give him a Pike special."

Jim nodded. "How are you going to get in? There's a security desk."

I grinned. "This is my world, Jim. Don't worry about it."

I took my jacket off and left it in the car, rolled my sleeves up to mid-forearm, and loosened my tie. At a coffee shop opposite the building, I bought a coffee, specifying triple cream. The girl sniffed and made me pay extra for the cream and I put a lid on the plastic cup and carried it across the street. At the entrance, I nodded to the security guard and walked straight to the elevator. He barely gave me a glance and I rode straight up to the fourth floor. On the landing, I checked the directory for Wint's room, took the lid off the coffee, and knocked on his door.

When Wint opened it, I gave him the coffee straight in the face. The triple cream had been my concession to gentlemanly conduct. The coffee wasn't hot enough to scald, but it disoriented Wint as effectively as any stun grenade. While he was still coughing and spluttering, I kicked him in the groin, and as he doubled up, I waited until his head was low enough, then I put him into a neck lock and spun him around and onto his knees. I'd known so many men like Wint—dangerous, deadly fighters because they were instinctively brutal and had a high tolerance for pain. But Jim Pike had had a motto for that too: "If you're dealing with someone who has a high tolerance for pain, mister, the best way is to give him a lot of pain to tolerate."

For that, there is nothing like the "bow." I'd had it used on me during a session of barrack-room brutality and the memory of the pain was still imprinted almost twenty years later. I held Wint's face against the edge of the desk to muffle the screaming, then applied the hold. Left foot at the back of the calf to keep him locked in the kneeling position; leg in the small of his back, choke hold on the Adam's apple, and arm across the shoulder to provide the leverage, when the twist on the spine was applied.

I did it only once and very briefly. Then I let Wint go and let him slide to the floor cursing and sweating from the pain.

"Where's the list?"

Wint was almost crying with the pain. I moved as if I were going to reapply the hold and he shouted, "No. Jesus. Don't." He unlocked the top drawer and handed me an envelope.

"Who gave it to you?"

Wint's eyes looked frightened. "It came in the mail. Everything did, with a phone call first. I never knew who it was."

It was what I expected. I didn't argue.

"Wint," I said, "you're a lucky man. You're going on an assignment. In an hour's time, you can go to the Renway Freelance Syndication office in High Holborn. You'll be given a one-way ticket to Australia and one hundred pounds' expenses for a story on the family life of wallabies. You'll get the return ticket, one day, maybe, when Shaun Renway, who's a very good friend of mine, is satisfied that your story is acceptable. If you go to the police or contact any papers, I'll find you again and break your back. That's a promise. It'll be an accidental injury incurred when the middle-aged, gentlemanly president of World News was desperately trying to defend himself against a known sadist and street fighter. Get the picture? Goodbye, Mr. Wint. Enjoy the wallabies."

When I got back to the car, I winked at Pike. "I think he'd have liked a battle of the giants," I said. "Unfortunately, there wasn't time to oblige him."

I opened the envelope and examined the list. I didn't know

215

most of the people and there were only a couple I'd remembered seeing at the party.

"I'll deal with this later," I said. "Right now, I'm going to have a word with Geoffrey Haycroft and then we'll see about the good Lord Branston, my fair-weather friend."

I spent two hours with Haycroft and mapped out a strategy to deal with the union crisis. Haycroft had wanted to tell Billingsly confidentially that I'd been tricked by Sellinger, but I wouldn't hear of it.

Instead I told him to call Los Angeles and talk to the president of Datavol, Jake Hyman. "The order for the X-13s would be worth over two million dollars if it was genuine. Tell Hyman I'll make it genuine on two conditions. I want a letter specifying that I asked for a delivery date specified not less than a year from now, and an escape clause after three months if union negotiations were not completed satisfactorily. Tell Billingsly that I had to place the order or lose my turn in the line. Say I was gambling on his good sense and on his understanding of the future needs of the company. *Then* start negotiations."

Haycroft grinned. "You're taking a risk."

"I'm in that kind of mood," I said. "But you're sure you're fit? You won't have a heart attack on me in the middle of the negotiations?"

Haycroft laughed. "No. I really hated being at home, you know. I suppose it's become a kind of drug. Negotiating is my life." He grinned. "And this one's going to be fun."

After that, I refused all calls and rested for an hour, then had Pike drive me with Cox to the Fox and Grapes.

Ronald Simon was already there, looking prosperous and stylish but very uneasy. He was dressed in a rich-looking blue suit with a soft sheen to it and a monogrammed pink silk shirt under a bold St. Laurent tie.

As soon as I walked in, I commented on the suit, ordered a round of drinks, and introduced Cox and Pike.

"When I first knew Simon," I said, "he was wearing transparent shirts open to the navel and gold medallions on his hairy chest." I smiled. "And sunglasses. You should have seen those shades. Beautiful. You should try the gear out on your clients. It'd make quite a hit."

Simon winced. He had never seen me in this brash, false-hearty mood and he knew it could only mean serious trouble. He was head of one of the most prosperous advertising agencies in London and one of the most respected members of his profession. Very few people knew, as I did, that he had once called himself Rinaldo Simoni and had been one of the most unscrupulous and unprincipled of the paparazzi—the street photographers who work the Rome nightclub circuit for gossip and scandal about the jet set.

Far worse, from Simon's point of view, he believed, wrongly, that I had evidence of embezzlement that could have put him in jail. In fact, I had no such evidence. Simon had been involved in shady dealings with a television news syndicate associated with World News, and I had helped the WN Rome Bureau chief to extricate himself from guilt by association. Simon had gotten out too, and he'd believed that my silence had helped. I was too contemptuous of him to bother telling him otherwise and I'd never had any intention of using the hold I had over him. But as the French say, great ills need desperate remedies, and I probably had less than a day to deal with Lord Branston.

I could see Simon was terrified. The Italians also have a saying: "If a man does you a favor, make sure you know his price." Simon knew I was there to rake up the past, and I had one of the best-known ex-policemen in London with me. He had no idea what I wanted and I let him sweat a little, as we chatted in a quiet alcove of the pub.

Finally I put him out of his misery.

"Jim," I said, "a long time ago I was able to do a small favor for Ronald and now he's very kindly agreed to pay me back." I turned to Simon. "Ronald, you know Lord Branston, I'm sure."

Simon nodded nervously.

"Well, Howard is being very awkward about some photographs he has. They're photographs of me. Rather tasty ones actually, except they're faked. Now the problem is that Branston is claiming that you can't fake photographs." I grinned at Pike. "I'd love to hear Howard Branston tell that to Ronald here. Do you know what Ronald once did? He was hanging around outside the Piper Club in Rome one night when Richard Burton and Liz Taylor were the hottest tabloid story in the world. They just came out onto the street. Side by side. Not drunk. Just standing there. Very disappointing, no story there at all. So you know what Ronald did? He paid a little kid to race down the pavement and stamp on Liz Taylor's foot. Liz screamed with pain, and grabbed hold of Burton's lapels to stop herself losing her balance. Simon snapped the shot and sold it around the world with the caption 'I'm leaving you, screamed Liz.' It was a terrific photo. Liz's face all contorted, Burton looking upset. Ronald's a real genius."

Simon swallowed hard.

"What do you want me to do?"

"Nothing very serious," I said. "A joke, really. Howard Branston is trying to maintain that you can't fake photos. I want you to show him that you can. Only I want more than photos. I want a little dossier put together on Branston's private life."

"When?"

"Tonight."

"Christ."

"Yes," I said, "I know it's a bit rushed. But Branston's around the corner having dinner at the Braganza. You could start right away."

"I don't have a camera."

Cox tapped the bag at his feet. "Nikon. Motor wind. All the trimmings. No problem."

Pike nodded. "We'll give you a hand," he said gruffly, "seeing as how it's just for a joke. One of my boys has been keeping an eye on his lordship. Let's go and take a look."

We finished our drinks and I led Simon out to Pike's Rover. We cruised slowly around the block and picked up Terry Mitchell, who had been assigned to Branston.

"What's the score, Terry?" Pike asked. "This is Mr. Simon. Put him in the picture."

"Not much to report, Jim," Mitchell said. "Branston often comes to the Braganza because it's near where he lives. Usually walks home. On his way he calls in to see his mother who has a flat in Soho Square, then he continues over to Headcorn Street."

Soho Square, despite its name, was completely respectable. It was on the fringe of the area of strip clubs and porn houses which made up most of Soho, but the square itself contained a private hospital, several smart apartment buildings, and a few business premises, mostly connected with the film industry.

"Not very promising," I said, "but that never worried Ronald." I laughed. "You know what he used to do in Rome? On his way to work, he'd stop outside a cinema where they were showing blue films. In his car, he used to keep a movie camera and he'd slap an RAI State Television News sticker on the side and start filming the line. There was no film in it, of course, but the men in the line didn't know that. They thought they were going to end up on the eleven o'clock news lining up to see *Lust on Two Wheels* or whatever. So they'd all get the hell out of there and the theater manager would try to chase Ronald off. But he's a very persistent fellow, our Ronald, and he'd end up getting a few thousand lire lunch money to go play in the next street. Genius. Absolute genius."

Simon was looking really sick by now and he knew that I had enough stories about him to pass away a whole evening.

"Where's this apartment building," he said.

"Right in Soho Square."

"That's nearly next to the Braganza. He won't walk through Soho at all."

"No, that's right."

He turned to me. "You want the fakes to be embarrassing?"

"As embarrassing as possible," I said.

I pointed through the car window. "Something along those lines would do fine."

We were passing The Fetish House, which advertised "Films, videocassettes, and magazines for all kinds of specialist interests."

"Pictures and what else?"

"Anything you like," I said. "I'll leave it to your imagination."

Simon turned to Pike.

"We're in West End Central's police district, aren't we?"

"That's right."

"What would happen if someone, an ordinary citizen, filed a complaint about a flat or an apartment building, claiming it was being used for immoral purposes?"

"It would be investigated."

"How long would the investigation take?"

"Depends how busy the station was. Could be right away. Could be a week or more."

"If there was such a complaint made tonight, could you arrange for West End Central not to bother with it for a while?"

Pike nodded. "Yes, I know the guvnor down there very well. Yeah. We could fix that."

"There you go, Ronald," I said, half pushing him out of the car. "Once you set your mind to it, I know you'll come up with something beautiful."

Simon hesitated as he stepped out of the car.

"After this, are we quits? And no stories about me around the street?"

"Not a whisper, Rinaldo," I said. "You have the word of an English gentleman."

22

The package from Simon arrived just in time. It came at nine-thirty the following morning, ten minutes after I'd received a message from Paul Sellinger peremptorily "inviting" me down to Samman's for a meeting with Howard Branston. When I'd examined Simon's handiwork, I called Sellinger to accept.

"I wanted to spare you the embarrassment of a full board meeting," Sellinger said. "I think Howard will convince you there's no point in trying to hang on."

"Yes," I said coldly, "a meeting is a good idea. We have a lot to say to each other, you and I."

As I put down the phone, I wondered how soon Paul would hear what was happening in New York. Jopling had arrived and had already had two meetings with Robert Sellinger. The story had "shaken the poor bastard to the core," Jopling said, and now a meeting with Jacob was scheduled for nine o'clock, New York time.

That was two o'clock London time, so I agreed to come to Samman's at four. With a bit of luck and some careful management, it would all come together nicely.

Next, I called Branston and suggested that we have lunch together on the way down to Samman's. At first, he refused, as I'd expected. But I knew how to tempt him. "Howard, it's not just for my sake," I said. "The woman in the photo wants to meet you. She has something to say about all this. I'm sure you feel that's fair." I was sure that would do it. Branston would never refuse such a meeting. When he accepted, I wondered what he was imagining. A desperate, tearful appeal? An offer of her body even? Whatever he fantasized, it was sure to be a situation which put him in a position of power, and that was a temptation Branston could never resist.

We arranged to meet at a country pub called the Red Lion in a village in Kent about ten miles from Samman's. I'd known it well in the old days and there was a very cozy, private back room that was ideal for the meeting.

I called and booked it, then spoke to Seagull. I'd slept the night in the office, partly because I wanted to catch up on a week of missed work and partly, I admit, from caution. Seagull had said she didn't mind about my resumed relations with Nancy, but I didn't know how Nancy would feel about Seagull and I decided it was safer to place a moratorium on my sex life until the Starburst affair was over.

I hadn't fooled Seagull, though, and she teased me mercilessly for several minutes before listening to what I wanted her to do.

Then she really laughed. "Now that is worth coming out of hiding for," she said. "Send the package over, to give me a bit of time to rehearse."

For the hell of it, I decided to take the Rolls to drive down to Samman's. If the schedule held, I'd be able to dispose of Branston over lunch, just in time for a telephone call from Nick in New York to tell me that the Family was ready to put the screws on. And I would be there first, to add a little retribution of my own.

Ryder was also poised. The director of the CIA had been briefed and he had agreed to hold back his report to the President just long enough to be sure of Jacob's reaction.

Everything was set, but at the last moment I almost didn't make it down to the Red Lion. We began the journey in almost skittish high spirits, with Walker driving the Rolls and Mitchell riding shotgun, and Pike and Paddy following in the Rover.

The heat wave had returned and the Kent countryside was looking almost tropical in the baking sun.

With the air conditioning of the Rolls on full, the landscape seemed completely unreal, as though it were being back-projected onto our personal television. Then, without warning, the peaceful image was transformed and an antinuclear march erupted in front of us.

It was the Rolls which provoked them. They had been trudging along the dusty lane, keeping close into the hedgerow to use what shade there was, when suddenly we had turned the corner and the sight of Seagull and me kissing in the luxurious air-conditioned comfort of the Rolls was too much. We learned later that they were already in an angry mood. They had been heading for Colemarsh Camp, which was being used as an assembly point for the troop movements to the Continent. The marchers had wanted to disrupt a territorial column which was making for Dover, but they had been turned back by police and dispersed into the countryside.

With Pike's help, we managed to maneuver our way out without getting the car damaged, and found a long detour free of any further pockets of straggling protesters. The incident was a useful reminder, though: Starburst was still what this whole business was about. As usual, in my obsession with Paul Sellinger, I'd been close to forgetting that.

Despite the detour, we arrived at the Red Lion on time and I immediately spotted Howard Branston standing beside the small ornamental lake. Walker parked the Rolls and I introduced Jennifer. As we walked into the pub, I noticed Branston's eyes covering every inch of her figure, with an extra lingering glance at the line of thigh that was showing through the slit in her carefully chosen, skimpy mauve dress.

The Red Lion, like Samman's and most of the buildings in the area, was a sixteenth-century structure with low, timbered beams. George, the landlord, came through to greet us and led us toward the special back room. In the main bar there was a group of very loud, noisy men in too-new country clothes, with several women who looked as though they would be more at home in the Hunter's Den. Through the window I could see two Range Rovers—one of them with leopard-skin seat covers—which obviously belonged to them.

"Croydon car dealers gone horsey," George whispered as we walked through. "Don't worry, Mr. Railton, they won't disturb you."

We settled in the back room, which was cozily furnished with high-backed oak settles with good thick cushions around an unpolished table.

Branston settled himself into a corner and looked Seagull over once more. "Well, young lady, nice to meet you. Sorry about this business. Damned sorry. John said you wanted to see me. Can't do much to help, I'm afraid. Hands are tied. Anyway, lunch first. May as well make ourselves comfortable."

"I think we'd better talk," Seagull said. "I'd like to get this over with." She hesitated. "It's a bit embarrassing."

"Yes, of course, my dear. But let's have some drinks at least." Branston summoned George and when we all had glasses, Branston turned back to Seagull.

"Now, my dear, what do you want to tell me?"

It was an invitation for a confession and I could see Branston waiting with wet-lipped anticipation.

"It's the photograph," she said. "John told you it was a fake. It wasn't taken at the party. Nothing happened at the party remotely resembling that."

Branston coughed and I could see he was preparing to enjoy himself.

"You say nothing like that happened."

"No. Nothing at all."

"But there was some"—he coughed again—"sexual activity?"

"What happened there is no concern to anyone who wasn't present."

"Well, that's not quite true, my dear. The photo does rather make it a bit public."

"The photo is a fake," Seagull said.

"So you say, my dear . . ."

She looked at him steadily. "Lord Branston, I said the photo was faked. If you'd stop staring at my tits for just a minute, you'd be able to concentrate better."

Branston hesitated. The change in Seagull's tone was unmistakable, but I could see he wasn't sure whether she was losing her temper out of fear. He looked at her carefully and her eyes told him to be careful.

"Lord Branston, how would you like it if your private life was exposed to the board of World News?"

"My dear, that isn't the point. And anyway, I'm afraid no one

224

would find the private life of an old fogey like me very interesting," he added with a smirk.

"Not at all," Seagull said. "I found it fascinating." Branston looked startled, but Seagull went on calmly. "I thought it was only fair. You seemed determined to take an interest in what I do in my leisure time. I returned the compliment, especially after what you left behind at World News."

Jennifer opened the large brown envelope Simon had provided and pulled out a magazine. It was a copy of *Spanker's Choice*. On the cover was a picture of an elderly man, sprawled improbably over the knee of a woman wearing high boots, black briefs, and a narrow mask. She was holding a heart-shaped paddle poised over his buttocks, apparently waiting for a fifty-year-old schoolgirl in a straw hat and gym slip to finish taking down his trousers.

"Good God, what's that?" Branston said.

"A friend of mine in World News said you left it behind by mistake last time you were over there. She asked me to return it."

Branston turned angrily on me.

"Railton, this is preposterous," he said. "You put her up to this. I've never even looked at a magazine like that. It's disgusting. Abominable."

"Yes, of course, there could have been a mistake," I said. "The affidavit makes that quite clear."

"Affidavit? What affidavit?"

Seagull slipped her hand into the envelope and pulled out a sheet of paper. It was the photocopy of an affidavit, dictated by Pike and signed by a girl friend of Cox's who worked in World News. It said, in the ponderous, labored language of affidavits, that she had found the magazine and believed it could belong to Lord Branston, as it had been found in an office he had been using.

Branston read it and his face turned purple. "Railton, this is libelous, criminally libelous. It wouldn't stand up for one second."

"No," I said, "not on its own, but it does seem to fit in with a few other things in that envelope."

Seagull dipped her hand in again. This time, it was a photocopy of a document, under the heading of West Central Police

Station. It was a formal complaint, filed by a woman identified as Mrs. Mary Whitstable, alleging that 419 Soho Square contained apartments which were used for practices of a sado-masochistic nature. The complaint was set out neatly, on a Metropolitan Police form, and countersigned by the detective constable who had typed it and the desk sergeant who had accepted it.

Seagull passed over a pile of photographs, showing Branston entering a building on which the plaque reading 419 Soho Square was clearly visible.

"Dammit, that's where my mother lives," Branston roared. "How dare you suggest . . ."

"I'm not suggesting anything," she said calmly. "This just happened to come to my attention, that's all. Along with these."

She took more photographs from the envelope and pushed them across to Branston. This was the *pièce de résistance*, the culmination of Rinaldo Simoni's years of experience in the sleaziest end of the world's photographic trade.

They were all photographs of Branston, taken, as I well knew, on his innocent walk home from the Braganza on the previous evening. But the backgrounds had all been doctored. Instead of strolling down Frith Street, on his way to call on his mother, Branston had been resituated in virtually every fetish shop in Soho. In one he seemed to be staring directly at a blown-up picture of a woman being whipped by a masked black slave master. In another he was passing through a narrow doorway in a fetish movie house under pictures of a man tied naked to a tree trunk with women dressed in assorted rubber garments dancing around it.

Branston looked at the pictures, then at Seagull, flushing a deep shade of scarlet.

Seagull continued to stare at him, apparently unconcerned by the photographs. Then she smiled. "My private life begins to look almost innocent, don't you think, my lord?"

Branston started to splutter, but I broke in quickly.

"Howard," I said, "let's get this over with quickly. This isn't blackmail. You can have all the photographs. It's just a joke. But it has a very serious edge. Half an hour ago, you were preparing to crucify me. For the sake of a seat on some bloody operatic board, you were prepared to help end my career, while sitting on your fat arse and passing around photos of me you knew damned well were phony.

"Well, Howard, I'm afraid I'm a very difficult man to fuck over, and I'd be obliged if you'd remember that.

"Vote against me by all means, when the matter comes to discussion. But vote on the issues. And if you have the nerve to maintain that evidence of this kind can't be faked, I'll make you the laughingstock of London. The man who did this will be happy to tell the tale. And I doubt if you'll walk into a club in London to your dying day without hearing it. Now, Howard, I'm off to see Paul. Do you still want to come?"

Branston sat back in the settle and I thought for a moment that we might have pushed him too far—a heart attack wasn't on the schedule—but Branston managed to pull himself together. Still looking at Seagull, he started putting the photographs and documents back into the envelope. "No, Railton," he said, "I won't be coming down."

"Can I take it you're prepared to wait ten days before this matter comes to issue?"

"Yes, damn you."

"Good," I said. "I'm grateful. I think you'll find that by then it will all be settled anyway."

As we left the Red Lion, George came hurrying over.

"What's up, guv? Don't you want any lunch?"

"No," I said. "Not this time. But you might be able to sell a couple of reviving glasses to the gentleman in the back room."

It was a splendid moment. Another hurdle cleared. Now all that was missing was the phone call from Jopling.

It was still only half-past two, and we drove quickly to the Shabby Poacher, a pub about a mile up the road, and ordered drinks and a sandwich just before closing time.

From the garden at the back, there was a view all the way down the valley and I saw that some kind of campsite seemed to be set up in one of the fields near Roland's Hollow. I asked the landlord and he said, "It's the MND people. They were getting a bit touchy, so the police fixed them up with a campsite. They've got singers down there and grub from Boxhill Farm. I wouldn't be surprised if the coppers didn't turn a blind eye if the Jug and Hoops stayed open a bit late."

"Only in England," I said. "Thank God we still have a few police around with a bit of imagination who can think beyond water cannon and riot shields."

I sat with Seagull in the garden for half an hour after the bar had closed, drowsing in the shade and talking about the old days in Hampstead. But as half-past three approached—the time of my call to Jopling—I could feel my anticipation growing.

Finally, I was going to come to grips with Paul Sellinger.

I made the call from a box in the grounds of the pub and had Marge call me back as soon as she had made the link to Jopling.

When Jopling came on the line, I said, "Well, are we set? Is Jacob ready to lower the boom?"

There was a moment of silence, then I heard Jopling's voice, worried and angry, even through the transatlantic static.

"It didn't work," he said. "Jacob won't act. The Family's closing ranks. They're flying to London for talks with Paul. I think they may even have left already."

I listened for fifteen minutes as Jopling gave me the details, and when he'd finished, I knew the fight was a long way from being over.

When I put down the receiver, I found another coin and dialed the number of Samman's. The meeting had to go on. I was determined not to run away from it, but when the receiver was picked up, the butler's voice came on the line.

"Mr. Sellinger left a message for you, sir. He's afraid he's had to postpone the meeting. I'm not sure when he'll be back, sir. I believe he's gone to Heathrow."

23

That night, I again slept in the World News Building. This time, I wasn't concerned with avoiding Nancy or Seagull; I simply wanted to be alone to rest and to think. Cox stayed with me, but I hardly saw him. At first, he dozed on a couch in my secretary's office, but when he realized that I'd gone into what he always called my trance, he found a pillow and some blankets, settled in his own office, and slept soundly.

I slept too, but only for the four hours I needed in order to stay alert. For the rest of the night, I quietly reviewed everything that had happened since the affair began. Then I thought about the showdown and tried to put myself into Paul Sellinger's head, to look at myself through his eyes and try to decide how he would close in for the kill. Jopling had called again before leaving New York, and this time the message had been even clearer: the Sellingers weren't coming to London to defend Paul. They were coming to get me.

At about four o'clock, I started to write. I prepared two memoranda, one for Cox and one for Jopling, writing in clear longhand so there could be no dispute about their authenticity, then I made photocopies and locked them in the safe.

At five o'clock, I called Ryder on his emergency number and told him I wanted to see Nancy. I knew she would be awake; this was her best time of day and I remembered how she used to love to wander through the gardens at Samman's, listening to the dawn chorus and taking note of which beds needed weeding or which plants needed attention.

We met at the American Embassy. She could not come to the World News building and Ryder would not let even me know the location of the safe house, so we talked, finally, just after six o'clock, in an office that smelled of old leather and pipe smoke, looking out over the treetops of Grosvenor Square.

When I told her how I wanted her to help me, she said, "John, I do still love you. I'm sure you realize that. But you're still asking a lot."

"Yes, I know that. But it's a weapon I need. The fight's going to be very bloody."

"When will it begin?"

"Tomorrow. They'll want to see me today, but I won't agree. It'll be tomorrow."

"That gives me a little time to think."

"No. I need to know now whether I can count on you."

Nancy smiled. "I'm not used to dealing with you in your executive incarnation. You're very direct."

"It's better."

"Then I'll try to be direct too," Nancy said. "Yes. I'll help you. I'll try to do what you ask. I just hope I'll have the courage to go through with it when the time comes."

I made a move to touch her arm, but she drew it gently away.

"Better not. Stay in your executive incarnation." She smiled. "By the way, I was going to offer to help with something else. It seems pretty small stuff now, compared with what you had in mind."

"Every little bit helps," I said. "What is it?"

"Bob told me about the guest list for the party, the one you got from Wint. Are you doing anything with it?"

"It's pretty hopeless. We're trying to find someone who knows how the hell Louise Allenby really did die. There's not much chance. Kent Allenby's had private investigators on it. They found the man who took her to the party. He was clean. What we really need is the man who left the party with her."

"Are you sure it was a man?" Nancy said.

"What do you mean?"

"I think if you look very closely at Louise's private life, you'll find she was AC-DC. You'll have to look really closely, though.

It's not well-known. In fact, it's not even gossiped about. But I think it's true."

Nancy paused. "I asked Bob to show me the guest list. I know a few of them. There's one woman on there who might just be Louise's type. The list calls her Campbell, Beth Campbell. I knew her at school in New England. Campbell's her maiden name, but as far as I know she's still married to Johnny Corcoram, the sugar millionaire."

"Would she talk to you?"

"She won't want to." Nancy grinned. "We loathed each other at school. Spent most of our time pulling each other's hair in the locker room. But I'll try."

"And the others too," I said. "Anyone. I can use any tiny bit of ammunition." I hesitated. "Jennifer is going to go through the list this morning, with Jim. You wouldn't consider working with her?"

"Why the hell not? I've often thought I'd like to meet her."

"In other circumstances, you could easily have been friends."

"We may be yet." Nancy laughed. "The question is where do we meet. Her safe house or mine, as we say in spook country."

"Fix it with Bob. But Nan, no risks. I need your help, but if Paul finds out where you are, he'll come after you."

"Bob will take care of me." Nancy smiled. "And don't worry, I won't exchange any girlish confidences with your Seagull."

Before I left the Embassy, Ryder asked to see me alone and we talked in another, more spacious office along the hall. The Stars and Stripes on the mahogany stand in the corner had been dismantled for cleaning; it had been draped over the table and it looked as though someone were preparing for a burial.

"We've got surveillance on Samman's," Bob said. "They're all there. Jacob, Robert, and Paul. Only about six support staff. By Sellinger standards, they practically sneaked into London. They usually need a floor of the Connaught just for their PR men. They've put the word out that it's strictly a private visit. Usually, they expect the ambassador to start jumping the minute their plane lands. This time, they haven't even contacted him."

Ryder paused.

"I don't mind telling you, he's not sorry. And the director is cowering on the sidelines too. John, old buddy, I'll level with you. My people are putting you up at bat. The Company's made what it calls contingency plans, but no one wants to be the first kid on the block to take the axe to the Sellingers. Around Washington, their people and the President's are intertwined like old lovers. On the Hill. Everywhere."

"Terrific." I gestured down at the flag. "Even if you're going to throw me to the fucking wolves, there was no need to start preparing for the body."

Ryder laughed. "It's not that bad. We'll move if we have to."

"But you mean you'd rather I did the dirty work."

"Something like that."

"I don't suppose your surveillance people have fixed up any audio by any chance?"

Ryder shook his head.

"We've tried. Total jamming. The Sellinger Corporation's developed its own antibugging systems. Just for Defense Industries."

"You've finished sweeping my shop at least?"

"Yeah. You're clean."

"Then we're off," I said. "But I just have a few little tricks to organize first. I've decided it's time we started playing by Sellinger rules."

When I got back to the office, it was already eight o'clock. Cox had shaved and changed and looked more rested than I'd seen him in days. I called him into my office and handed him one of the envelopes I'd prepared during the night.

"What's this?"

"Instructions," I said. "Very detailed instructions."

Cox looked up. "You don't usually spell things out in writing. What's the matter? Am I losing my grip?"

"No," I said. "This is different. This is to cover you. Anything you do from here on in is strictly on my responsibility."

"You mean when they come to take me away, I clutch the envelope, click my heels, and scream, 'But I voss only obeying orders!' "

"Something like that. In the envelope there's a list of six names. I want you to find out which of them's available. I only need one. Maybe two of them at most. I want you to make sure they're in London by tomorrow morning if they're not already here. If you've any preferences on the list, feel free. You're the one who'll be working with them. With the list is a memorandum setting out what I'm authorizing you to tell them. But not till I give you the word."

Cox opened the envelope and glanced at the names.

"Jesus H. Christ," he said quietly. "You really want this?"

"Yes."

He gave me a hard look.

"Chief, are you sure this is best for World News? Not just for getting Paul Sellinger?"

"Yes, I'm quite sure. It'll have to happen in the end. I may as well use it as a tactic."

Cox glanced down the list again.

"Yeah," he said. "I guess you're right. It is going to come to that in the end."

Next, I walked down the corridor to see Jopling. He was in his office having breakfast, and his personal bone china tea service was set out fastidiously on a little side table beside the electronic calculator which was his favorite office toy. He too had shaved and changed and I could see he was making an effort to hide his disappointment.

"John, I'm sorry," he said, when I walked in. "That call yesterday must have pretty well shattered you."

"For a while. It passed. I suppose I always knew it couldn't be that easy." I handed him the second envelope.

"Nick, I'm sorry to scramble your brains with jet lag, but I need you back over the Atlantic. I want you in Toronto by tonight. Earlier if you can. Take the morning Concorde to New York, then the Air Canada shuttle. You know whom you'll be seeing."

Nick stood up. "Yes, I thought it might come to that. I wondered if you'd have the courage. I should have known you would. You know what this might mean for you."

"Yes. It's all covered in the envelope. It's all set out. If it all goes wrong, it's my head."

"I won't have an answer before tomorrow."

"I know that. That's why I'm going to stall the Family. I won't see them before tomorrow morning. Oh, and Nick," I said, "those notes you made on Paul's share dealings—the Chad business and buying into the Black Eagle consortium. I've

233

copied them out in my own handwriting. I want to show them to Neville Farmer."

Nick looked surprised.

"He won't help. It's pointless."

"Yes, I think he will," I said. "I'm going to have to make him. I'm afraid I'm going to play it the way Paul would."

Jopling sighed. "God, it's become a dirty business."

"Yes," I said. "But do your best in Toronto and it may just come out clean in the end."

I sent a message asking Neville Farmer to come to see me urgently, and as I sat in my office waiting, I thought how much I hated operating like a Sellinger. I'd been very glib with Bob and with Nick about playing by Sellinger rules, but I'd spent a working lifetime fighting against that way of running an organization. I was about to deal with Neville Farmer exactly as Paul would have, by pressure and threat, mixed in with tempting promises or at least hints of career rewards.

Farmer didn't deserve it. He was a Sellinger man, but it wasn't his fault. He fully deserved his position as head of Economic Services, the third most senior post in World News; no one could have filled it better, yet without Paul he might never have come anywhere near to that level. Ten years before, he had been a thirty-year-old American commercial reporter, kicking his heels around Brussels, covering the European Community's wrangling over farm prices which none of the papers in the United States cared about anyway, and playing a lot of tennis to cover his boredom.

Paul Sellinger had met him accidentally and seen his potential immediately. After only one meeting, Paul had spotted Farmer's commercial shrewdness and realized that he was languishing because he was in the wrong field: he should have been a salesman, not a reporter.

Paul had hired him for Global and taken him back to the States and set him up as marketing manager of a then almost nonexistent department of computer-based information services for banks, corporations, and stockbrokers. Five years later, Farmer was a vice-president of Global and head of the biggest revenue-earning segment of the agency, and after the merger I'd been grateful to have him as head of the two agencies' combined commercial operations. But our relations had never been easy. Partly, I think, he associated me with his days as a nonentity, which he wanted to forget, and perhaps too he blamed me for not recognizing his talent as Paul had. Also, I knew he had decided that, eventually, I was going to lose the "war" and his future—perhaps as the head of World News—rested in the gift of the Sellingers. He was—and he could hardly be blamed for it—totally a creature of the Sellingers, and because Paul believed he had him bought and paid for, he confided in him more than anyone else in World News. Neville knew more about Sellinger's financial situation and the interlocking ties which bound WN to the Sellinger Corporation than anyone else, outside the Family, and that was the knowledge I needed now.

When he arrived, he looked slightly ruffled. I didn't usually summon people as senior as him at short notice; that was more a trick of Paul's and he did not like it from me.

"Neville," I said, when he was seated, "I'd better get straight to the point. The 'war' is coming to a climax." I gave him a faint smile. "I don't need to tell you which war I'm talking about. Paul and I are about to lock horns—probably for the last time."

"John, I really think it's best if I don't get involved," Farmer said, eyeing me cautiously, aware that I wasn't usually this blunt about my relations with the Sellingers.

"It probably is better," I said, firmly, "but I'm afraid it's not possible. We're choosing sides. There's no middle ground." I gave him another faint smile. "I'm afraid the middle ground has suffered a scorched-earth policy."

I could see Farmer thought I was bluffing. If Paul had said it, he would have taken it seriously immediately, but he regarded me as the softer—and therefore the safer—of the two to cross. As I looked at him, I decided that was really why I could never warm to Farmer, even though I respected his talent. It's very hard to empathize with someone who has you tagged as a loser, and Farmer was convinced that was what I was.

It was time to change his mind.

I opened a folder on my desk and passed across the desk the notes that Jopling had prepared on Sellinger's financial juggling with the Black Eagle consortium, which I'd recopied in my own handwriting.

"Neville, I'd like to read you this," I said. "It's something I want your help with."

Farmer took the pages and started to read. Halfway down the first one, he looked up, startled. "Is this serious?"

"Read it all first," I said. "Then we'll talk." When he'd finished, he said, "Are you saying this has happened? Frankly, I don't believe it's possible." Even as he said it, I could feel his doubts and decided to press home quickly.

"Neville, you and I have never gotten along all that well," I said. "I know you don't think of it as a personality thing. You think I'm a general newsman who doesn't really understand your problems as well as I should. I would deny that, of course, but that isn't the issue here. Answer me one question. From your experience of me, would you say I'd be likely to invent something like this, to score over Paul Sellinger?"

Farmer hesitated. "No, I wouldn't have said that."

"Then let me ask you a second question. If what was on that paper were true, do you think it's likely Paul Sellinger would be allowed to survive—in World News, or elsewhere, for that matter?"

"No, I wouldn't say so. But can you prove this?"

"Not entirely, no."

Farmer started to get up. "Then it *is* better if I don't get involved," he said. "I don't know whether it's true and frankly, I don't want to know."

"Sit down, please, Neville," I said firmly. "I don't think you have the position clear. Paul Sellinger is about to go down the tubes. His men will go with him."

"I'm not just his man," Farmer snapped. "I built Econ. I sweated for five bloody years. I've earned my position."

"I hope the board sees it that way after the Sellinger shambles is over. I'll do my best to reassure them. It could be difficult. You're known to be very close to the Family."

"Are you so sure you're going to survive? You could both be out, you know."

"Perhaps. I admit that backing me isn't a racing certainty, but frankly, backing Paul is an absurdity if you even half-believe what's on that paper."

"And if you win?"

"There'll be many changes in the company. New opportunities. In the restructuring, Economic Services may gain in prestige. I'd like to think you'd be around to enjoy the fruits, after all your years of work."

"What do you want?"

"Very little," I said. "I just want you to speculate for me. If Paul Sellinger had done exactly what is on that paper, whom would he have used?"

Farmer looked at the notes. "You've practically got them already. Whoever did this knew what he was talking about. I presume it was Jopling."

"Practically isn't good enough," I said. "I want names. I want three or four people Paul would rely on to do the wheeling and dealing for him. That's all I want, Neville. A bit of speculation. Three or four names." I looked at him squarely. "Names you're willing to bet your career on."

Farmer took the paper and was about to start to write. Then he changed his mind. "You'd better write them," he said. "The main one has to be Billy Slade. Has to be. This has Billy's name written all over it. Karl Rathburg. Joe Kaminski. Ray Weldon."

I made him give me the names of the firms and the addresses, then I read them back to him to make sure there were no mistakes.

"Neville, there's just one more thing," I said, as he got up to leave. "I won't reveal this conversation to anyone. You have my word. If it comes out from your side, I'll have to assume that you were in collusion with Paul in the dealing. If that were believed on Wall Street, we couldn't just be worried about your future in World News. For both our sakes, don't let it come to that."

Next, I decided to see if Nancy and Jennifer were making any progress with the list. I dialed the flat, but it was Pike who came on the line.

"Best not interrupt for the moment," he said. "We've had a bit of luck. Nancy's here. Ryder's people brought her. And there's another woman. Beth Campbell."

"She was on the guest list," I said. "What's happening?" I heard Pike chuckle softly. "Right now, your two ladies are in the process of putting the screws on Miss Campbell. Christ, they'd be a credit to the squad. Talk about a tough interrogation. That Nancy, she's a real so-and-so. They've got a Mutt and Jeff routine going. Jennifer's all sugar and spice and 'Please won't you help us, oh please, Beth.' Then Nancy gives it to her in the ribs and threatens to tell her husband all kinds of shit about the party. Beautiful stuff."

"Shall I come over?"

"Not yet. Leave it to the lasses. I'll call you when we're ready."

I waited almost an hour and when I did finally go to the flat, I immediately recognized Beth Campbell. I'd never actually met her, but I had glimpsed her, at about three o'clock in the morning on the night of the party. I had left Jennifer in the sleeping bag in the attic and gone quietly down to the kitchen to look for some food. Beth Campbell had been on the same mission but while I had dressed to come down, she had wandered in wearing only a towel. She'd been clutching it around her body but she'd been too high to realize that it had slipped around to the side, and I'd had in my mind ever since the party the haunting image of a luxuriant pubic bush in a V-shaped frame formed by the two edges of the towel.

When Pike let me in, I saw the woman sitting with Seagull but before I could go in, Nancy came into the hall.

"Be very careful," she whispered. "Be nice to her. Take Jennifer's side. I'm being the heavy. Use all your charm. I think she's about ready."

When I went in, she showed no sign of recognizing me. Seagull explained who I was and that I was in the same position they were, and I really needed her help.

"Beth, tell us again about the sleeping-bag game," she said. "What happened with Louise."

"Louise was high. She agreed to play and she wound up with Rex Stainton. They stayed together for a while, but Louise didn't want to carry on . . . she . . ." Beth broke off. "I really don't think I can go on with this."

"Beth, for Christ's sake, stop being so coy," Nancy broke in sharply. "Tell John what you told us. That Rex is a lousy fuck and Louise got bored and threw him out of the bag. Then what?"

Beth hesitated for a long moment, then she said nervously, "I was bored too. I went off with Louise."

238

"Off where?" Nancy snapped.

"To my place. We went home together."

"Then what happened finally?" Seagull said soothingly. "Just tell us the last bit. About the supermarket."

"We didn't have anything for breakfast. Louise was hungry, so we went down to the Asian supermarket to get some food. Louise was still a bit hung over. She wasn't really awake properly and she just stepped under a bus. She was killed instantly."

"Just as the police report said."

"Yes."

"Then why in God's name didn't you say so?" Nancy said. "You've never told the police that."

"I ran away. I didn't want to admit I was at the party. My husband didn't know . . ."

"But he does now."

"Yes."

"So why didn't you tell them when they came back to you?"

Beth sat very still, looking down at her knees.

"I didn't want my husband to know Louise had been with me. He knows . . . he knows I get fed up with men sometimes."

Nancy flashed me a quick glance and I knew it was time to pick up the cue.

"Beth," I said gently, "I really don't think that's the issue here. You and Louise were two friends who met at the party and went home to rest afterwards. There's nothing very wrong about that. Whatever happened in your flat is strictly your business. All that matters is that you saw Louise knocked down by the bus. Would you be willing to testify to that much?"

"Testify where?"

"Just an affidavit," Pike said quickly. "It would never need to come to court."

Beth looked nervously at Nancy.

"I suppose I must."

"Yes," Nancy said firmly. "You're damn right you must."

I left them to prepare it and Pike took me back into the hall.

"I'll get it to Kent Allenby," he said. "And a copy for you."

"Thanks. It could be a winner."

Pike grinned. "Don't thank me. Thank your womenfolk.

Christ, I hope they never get together and gang up on me. Or you, for that matter."

Pike opened the door.

"Well, mister, are you ready for them?"

"I wouldn't say that," I said, "but I'm as ready as I'm going to be."

24

As I watched Jacob Sellinger's limousine coming down Samman's Lane, I thought: "Christ, in the old days, the potholes would have broken both his legs." Anyone who had ever done business with the Family knew that the back of the huge Cadillac was padded with thick foam rubber to prevent Jacob from injuring himself. No one knew exactly what disease the old man suffered from, but it had caused wasting of the bones until his frame was as fragile as an anorexic's. He also suffered bouts of faintness and sometimes, while out driving, he would simply keel over and disappear onto the floor of the car. Out of pride, he refused to travel with a nurse in attendance, but after one particularly serious fall, the Family had forced him to accept a compromise. Now—in a bizarre twist on the usual recruitment of security personnel—the Sellingers had hired a driver who looked rugged enough to be a body-guard but was in fact a male nurse.

I watched the car come down the lane from the east wing of Samman's, where I had been installed with Cox for the past hour waiting for negotiations to begin. A fire had destroyed the center of the old farm sometime in the eighteenth century and it had been rebuilt almost in two separate parts, the east and west wings. They were joined by a long corridor, which swelled in the middle into a large drawing room with views over both sides of the estate.

Now we were arranged like knights before a tournament,

241

each with one wing as his tent, preparing to lunge down the corridor to clash in the central drawing room. But thus far there had been no combat. I had refused an invitation to Samman's on the previous evening, then after much stalling and arguing, had agreed to come at nine o'clock that morning. I had brought no staff, other than Cox and one of Ryder's men who had swept our section of the house for bugs. The electronic expert had left and I was ready for the first meeting when Cox had spotted the patriarch's limousine leaving the main drive of the house.

We might have thought he was going away from the talks, had Ryder's surveillance team not briefed us about the comings and goings of the previous day. The limousine, I knew already, was the patriarch's sanctuary. In New York, it was his preferred place for doing business and he also used it to drive around Manhattan, thinking or working on his files. Ever since his illness, he had come to hate offices. He could no longer walk and he felt his wheelchair humiliated him, and the limousine had become his symbol of freedom. At ninety, he always gave the appearance of spending his last day on earth, but it was said—as a grim joke within the Family—that he was planning to park the limousine at the graveside for the funerals of Paul and Robert.

At Samman's he had taken to going out with each of the brothers in turn. According to the surveillance team, the three had never been out together. It was always Jacob and Paul, then Jacob and Robert, separate and in strict succession.

"I know Jacob's problem," I said to Cox. "I used to have two dogs like Robert and Paul. They were too much trouble to be walked together because they fought all the time, but if you exercised one for a yard longer than the other, the jealousy was incredible and they'd sulk and bite each other, and me as well, if I didn't watch out."

But now they were coming back. This time it had been Paul's turn. The limousine pulled into the driveway and the wheelchair was brought to the west entrance. The driver and the butler had already mastered the routine and Jacob was taken into the house smoothly, with no jarring, even as the chair was maneuvered through the narrow, timbered entrance hall. Ironically, we had been allocated the better wing of the house. The lounge of the east wing, where we made our base, was larger and airier than the one in the west wing, and it had taken me a while to figure out why we had been given preference. Then I remembered the little twist in the corridor at our end of the "lists" and realized that the wheelchair would not go around it.

I did not need to be told that we would not be seeing Jacob immediately. He made use of his illness ruthlessly as a negotiating tool, using it to impose his own rhythm on whatever talks he was undertaking. I knew, too, that there would be some preliminary skirmishing and I guessed rightly that it would be handled by Robert.

Negotiating with any of the Sellingers always reminded me of repertory drama. The actors always knew their lines, and sometimes the performances were extremely polished, but they always seemed to lack the feeling of genuine emotion.

With the Family, emotions were as theatrical as the lines. Listening to them bargaining was like studying plays for an examination: "What was Robert Sellinger trying to convey when he lost his temper, or expressed sympathy with so-and-so, at such-and-such a point?"

In the first meeting I had with him in the central drawing room, he tried to convey two things: that they had a strong hand and were capable of doing me real harm, but that at the same time they recognized a worthy adversary and might well agree to an honorable compromise.

"John, I think what we're dealing with here is a major misunderstanding," was one of his opening phrases. It was a stock Sellinger line, as familiar as Robert's blue cashmere blazer and near-military tie—his summer campaign suit, a political commentator had recently called it.

Under the smooth politician's turn of phrase and the wary courtesy toward me, the content of what he was saying was totally preposterous, little more than a blatant trial balloon, in fact, to test my mood. The "misunderstanding" was that I was reading too much into Paul's determination to oust me as chief executive of World News. "Paul plays hard ball, sometimes," Robert said. "His tactics were rough, but he was acting in what he saw as the best interests of the agency. He believed you were not the man for the job—quite wrongly in my view," he added unctuously. "Clearly, he went over the top. The situation's gone sour. A lot of bad feelings all around. It might be best in everyone's interests if you both beat a retreat and called it a draw."

When I tried to probe what he thought a draw might consist of, Robert immediately became vague, but I gathered it could involve both Paul and me leaving World News. It wasn't specified what Paul might do, but some hints were subtly placed that there were at least two international media jobs about to become available, both more senior than my present one, and that might be a route that could be negotiated.

It was all so ridiculous that I didn't let it go on for more than about twenty minutes. I didn't lose my temper. I simply said that the problem, as Robert had presented it, didn't seem to cover all the issues, which seemed a mild enough way, even for me, of referring to two attempts at murder and a campaign to sabotage the West's most promising missile system.

Robert took the hint and suggested a short break. As I walked back down the corridor, treading the thick, rust-colored carpet Paul had laid in place of my old threadbare cream one, I noticed that the floorboard opposite the old rhododendrons still creaked. There are some things you just can't cover up, you old swine, I thought cheerfully, and I stepped down extra hard so that the squeaking sounded right down the corridor.

I knew it would be Paul's turn next and I was also ready for one of his usual touches of drama. I'd been around the Family so long now that I really was becoming used to their ways. I didn't always feel I understood them, but I always knew them in the way I had come to "know" the warring tribes in my early days as a correspondent in West Africa; I might not be close enough to them in background and upbringing to feel as they did, but I'd observed them so closely that I was rarely wrong when I predicted their patterns of action.

Paul's little piece of dramatics was to throw on the table in front of me a package of photographs along the lines of the one he had used with Branston. In each, Seagull and I were the centerpiece in various positions of lovemaking, and I could tell from the shade of the coverlet and the pillows that they had been taken through the window of her flat in Hampstead. In each, observing faces had been added to give the impression that we had been the focus of an orgy and had put ourselves on show with heedless abandon.

"Paul, you're a fool," I said. "You simply don't know when to quit."

Sellinger's eyes narrowed. "There are some things you can't run away from," he said, bringing out his old line. "You may have scared Wint off and intimidated Lord Branston, but the Allenby scandal won't go away. Wint only whetted the papers' appetite; their own people are turning up stuff all the time. When they have enough, pictures like this will be on sale on every street corner."

"Paul," I said shortly, "get Robert in here."

"What for?"

"Bring him, Paul," I said. "I'm saying nothing until you do."

Paul pressed an intercom switch and Robert appeared down the corridor. He saw the pictures and looked at me.

"Robert, I sent for you, because I don't trust your brother to report back to you what I have to say," I said. "But first, we have to dispose of this nonsense."

I gestured down at the photographs. "This kind of intimidation is pointless. Those photos are about as relevant as last week's weather forecast. The Allenby scandal is dead. No one's interested in the party any longer."

I opened my attaché case and pulled out Beth Campbell's affidavit.

"Kent Allenby has the original of this," I said. "And every editor who received the original Wint material has a copy also. You can keep the dirty pictures for your album, Paul. It's over. Now we can get down to the issues."

I looked straight at Robert.

"We're dealing here with the story of a prodigal son," I said, "and we all know that little parable. The prodigal son in the Bible was a pain in the ass too, and I've always felt sorry for the older brother. But the biblical prodigal only spent his time screwing around and generally enjoying himself before he was welcomed back in the fold, whereas this prodigal here has been plotting to destroy you. The issues here, Robert, are treason, greed, and treachery, and the question is, why the hell you're lying down for an agreement to cover them up."

Robert went gray under his suntan and I knew I'd hit home. Jacob was for the closing of family ranks; Robert would have handed his brother to me with an apple in his mouth if the patriarch would allow.

"I see," I said. "So it's Jacob rules, as we Brits say, okay? The ties of blood must bind. Well, all right. So let's take a look at what you're binding around.

"The issues were set out for you in New York by Nick Jopling: attempted murder, intent to commit treason, illegal stock manipulation, countless violations of international corporate law, and total, cynical treachery rooted in hatred of one brother for another."

To his credit, Robert recovered well. The audience would only have seen a momentary fluff—a few lines lost and a brief gleam of purest hatred as he looked at Paul—in place of the brotherly love of the script.

He had the reputation of being the better performer of the two, and Jacob's upbringing, combined with years of public relations and politics, saved him now.

"We've looked at the documents Jopling brought," he said. "There's not one damn thing in them to tie Paul in with what you're alleging. The material related to the Seagull woman and the material concerning Paul's wife are obviously fraudulent. We'll support a full investigation, as we have from the beginning. Our first impression is that the Soviets have moved in smartly to exploit a tense situation. The so-called 'war' between you and Paul was well-known. Not hard for any agent to make use of it. But that's your concern. The intelligence agencies will be questioning you closely. None of this concerns Paul."

Robert shuffled his papers again and produced photocopies of two large official documents. They were the reports of police investigations into the fire at St. Tropez and the explosion at Vaudur.

"Take a look," Paul said. "Then quit accusing me of trying to murder you. There is nothing, repeat nothing, in those investigations that leads anywhere near me. Look hard and you'll see they're as good as closed."

I'd already seen most of the Vaudur file, which Ryder had shown to me the previous evening, and I knew Sellinger was right. The police had cornered one of the men who had placed the plastic charge on the bedroom door and had put eleven bullets into him in a shootout in which one hotel guest and a valet had been injured. He'd been identified as a professional killer who had done political work for several terrorist organizations. The second man was believed to have already left France and there were no further leads. The St. Tropez file was even thinner. The fire marshal had returned a verdict of accidental fire setting and the police had closed the case. It was the price we had paid for getting out without being arrested ourselves.

"These are all dead ends," Paul said. "None of your allegations are leading anywhere."

"To use a phrase of yours, Paul," I said, "there are some things you can't just walk away from. Issues can be kept alive."

"Not these," he snapped. "You've seen the dossiers."

"There are other ways."

"Like what?"

"It's a point I'd like to bring someone else in on," I said. "They're close at hand. I'll send for them now."

We broke off again and Cox made a phone call to a coaching inn at Melford where one of our three groups was waiting. I went back to the central drawing room and watched with the Sellingers as the metallic-gray BMW slid swiftly down Samman's Lane.

Both scanned the passengers anxiously and when Paul recognized Nancy, he whirled on me.

"What the hell is she doing here?"

"As I recall it," I said calmly, "she owns the place. She's probably coming to see you haven't burned any cigarette holes in the carpets."

But it was the man with her who gave Paul the first indication of her real purpose. The stylishly waved gray hair and hooked nose, together with the slight stoop, were well-known as belonging to Sir Michael Tudor-Hyde, the leading divorce lawyer in London.

"What the fuck is this charade about?" Paul said angrily. Nancy stared back at him unmoved, looking cool and elegant in a plain navy-blue dress.

"It's not a charade, I'm afraid," Sir Michael said genially. "I

247

try to deal with these matters with as little acrimony as possible, but your wife has asked me to announce her intention to seek a divorce."

I could see that Robert was surveying the situation warily, but Paul plunged on.

"This is a business meeting." He glared at Nancy. "I'll talk to you later. Go and wait in the study."

Sir Michael glanced inquiringly at Paul, as though checking that he had finished, then continued, unruffled, as though nothing had been said.

"I believe the grounds for the divorce are the relevant point here," he said. "There'll be a number of items raised, but I'm afraid the principal one is that of attempted murder."

Nancy looked at Paul with a steady gaze. She was turning out to be the best performer of all of them, I thought. I had talked to her less than two hours before and I knew that she had been terrified.

"I'm very ashamed to be so scared," she'd said, with a little squeeze of my hand. "It's one thing to plan to take on Paul. When you have to face him, it's not quite the same thing."

But neither brother could have told.

Very deliberately, she took a step closer to Paul. "I'm going to use everything, Paul," she said, "starting with Vaudur. I'm going to explain in open court why I believed you tried to kill me and John. And I shall bring in the Dahran document and call Ackerman to testify. I may not prove it all, but by God I'll give it a good airing."

Paul started to take a step toward her. His fist was clenched and his eyes bitter and black. Both Tudor-Hyde and I moved to intervene, but it was Robert who got in first.

It was clearly time for a trip to the locker room, and while the brothers went to talk to Jacob, I led Nancy and Tudor-Hyde back to the east wing.

We stood around in an oddly formal group, as though we were already in the corridor of the law courts, and said very little.

Tudor-Hyde passed the time with a few pleasantries, and when the call came, we all walked back to the central drawing room.

"As far as we're concerned, this thing is over," Paul said,

248

before we were all settled in. "My father is leaving. He's not well. He's returning to New York for medical treatment."

"You can't run, Paul," I said quietly. "This time, it really won't go away."

"There's nothing *to* go away," Paul said. "Let it all come out." He looked at Nancy. "Go ahead, make a fool of yourself in the courts. We'll all enjoy hearing you describe your night back in the arms of your former husband. Great for establishing your credibility. All you have is allegations. No evidence and no witnesses. And don't count on Mr. Ackerman," he added with a sneer. "He was shot dead this morning."

"What!" I said. "How?"

"Who cares how?" Paul said contemptuously. "Ask your friend Ryder. There was an order out to blow him away."

"Which made him the perfect conduit for your file?" I said.

"Bullshit. This talk is air, strictly air."

It was the moment I'd been preparing for. Our bluff was now finally being called. I made a sign to Tudor-Hyde, who took up his cue smoothly.

"Mr. Sellinger," he said, "it is true that your wife's case is not yet complete. However, we expect with some confidence that supporting evidence will begin to emerge, once the general substance of our case is disclosed to the reporters assigned to analyze this situation. I think it wise to warn you that I've been authorized to make disclosure of our grounds to them."

"Who the hell are you talking about?" Paul snapped. "What reporters?"

"I can't tell you about that," I said. "It's really a question of pulling this whole thing together. What we have here is a very simple story. Paul, you tried to cause the cancelation of the Starburst missile program by leaking secrets to the Russians. To cover yourself, you tried to set me up as a traitor and you twice tried to kill me, as well as two other people in the process. You did all of this out of greed and out of jealousy of your brother, and the determination that you, not he, would be master of the Sellinger Corporation with all that the position entailed in American political and corporate life.

"A simple story, but unfortunately, with too many shadowy facets for a news agency to handle. Usually, I like World News to tell its own stories. I hate to pass over a good scoop to somebody else. But this is a special case. This story is better told by an outsider—someone who can look objectively at all the material we can make available."

I turned to Robert, ignoring Paul. "I think we're lucky that we've found the right man. He's here in Axton, having lunch at the moment at the Goose and Firkin. You all know Gerry Deighton. You'll agree he's right for this. I'd say he's the best investigative reporter working today and he's syndicated in the States and Britain. Plenty of good scalps under his belt. Multinationals. Drug companies." I smiled. "Made a bit of a dent in the Democratic party over the Hadcombe business, so no problem with his objectivity there."

"Jesus God Almighty," Paul roared. "You goddam stupid motherfucker! You mean you've talked to Gerry Deighton about this?"

"Not yet," I said. "I plan to brief him right after your departure."

Paul's mask had finally slipped, and it was almost a comic moment. His look of outrage had nothing to do with any stage-managed Sellinger performance. One of the most powerful figures in the world media had been totally uprooted by the idea that anyone might actually publish something. Watching his face, I really believe it hadn't occurred to him that this might happen. These were negotiations; the stuff of smoke-filled rooms and deals and trading for power and gain. Calling in Gerry Deighton was the ultimate act of sacrilege, and I knew I had finally gotten to him.

He was so angry he really couldn't speak, but Robert moved in swiftly. "Let's hold this right there while I go talk to Jacob," he said, and I knew I'd finally won my ride in the limousine.

When I was taken to the Cadillac, Jacob was already inside. I stepped in and sat beside him, and the driver pulled carefully away up Samman's Lane. To say we were sharing the back seat would be an exaggeration. I could have had almost nine-tenths of its width while Jacob's tiny frame, hunched in the corner, seemed almost to be perching on the huge, padded elbow rest. In silhouette against the sunlight, his parchmentlike skin was almost translucent and I noticed for the first time that his eyelids had a curious violet tinge to them.

He looked me up and down for a minute, then said in a

250

reedy, almost scratchy voice which still had traces of his original Swiss-German accent in it, "Mr. Railton, why are you so anxious to destroy me?"

As Paul and Robert must often have done, I wondered how many years Jacob would go on using his frail, dying-man routine.

"Because you've sired a worthless and treacherous son and if you're determined to protect him, you may have to go down with him," I said.

Jacob inclined his head slightly and seemed not to have heard the answer.

"And why do you wish to destroy yourself? Have you an answer for that too?"

"I very much don't want to destroy myself," I said. "I like to think of myself as a survivor."

"If you call in Gerry Deighton, you will not survive. If the story is told, it will include many things about you. You may have killed the Allenby story, but the party was real. People will enjoy reading about the sleeping-bag game. I enjoyed it myself."

"I would have to resign," I said. "I don't deny it. But you have a great deal more to lose."

I handed him a copy of the note I had prepared for Cox, setting out for him exactly what Deighton should be told. Jacob took it and unhooked a large magnifying glass from the pillar of the rear window.

I gave him time to read it, then took it from his hands and put it back in my briefcase.

"With that kind of material, you don't really need a Gerry Deighton," I said, "but Deighton's thorough. He won't let Slade and Rathburg and Kaminski wriggle away easily. And we'll give him help where he needs it—in Central Europe while he's looking into Paul's trips behind the Curtain, for example. When he publishes, the Family will break apart. You won't be able to keep Paul. Not even buried somewhere in Sellinger Defense Industries. You'll have to unload him."

"I do not wish to lose my son."

"But why," I said, "why do you want to keep a mole in the family?"

"I am to blame. I pushed him too far. I raised my sons to play rough. I pushed Paul too hard and he turned on me, and

251

on Robert. He fought the way I had taught him. I cannot blame him for that."

"I won't let him win," I said.

"No, I can see that. I accept that you must win. But you can do that without Mr. Deighton."

"I'm a survivor," I said. "I'd like to both win and survive. What are you proposing?"

"You want to keep control of World News. It can be arranged and in improved circumstances. Your contract will be bought out, which will be the equivalent of a substantial cash settlement, then renewed unbreakably for five years. The rest of the package will be generous. Paul will move out, into Sellinger Defense Industries. He will not have the top slot; there will be a period of penance first."

"And then you find some other way of meddling in World News," I said. "You'll still try to use us."

"The directors who are with us will support a reorganized structure. You can bring in a special advisory board of prestige names to guarantee the agency's objectivity. That's your own scheme, isn't it? You've always wanted it."

I sat back in the cushions. It was a beautiful offer. My own plans for the agency played back at me, with guaranteed American support. The Sellingers neutralized and the round-the-clock warfare ended. Time to concentrate on building World News the way I had wanted it. And though we hadn't spelled out the money, I knew we were talking about doubling my own remuneration.

I glanced at Jacob and I could see he was examining me closely as I thought over the offer.

He gave me a faint, mirthless smile. "I do not like to lose so much. But there are things a man must do for his son."

It really was a family matter for him, I thought. He really didn't care about Starburst or NATO or Western defense. The thousands of people who were roaming around Britain looking for somewhere to protest against his missile cared more about the issue than he did. Starburst was a private matter. Even the concessions to me were really concessions to Paul.

"No," I said. "I can't accept your proposal."

"What counteroffer do you wish to make?"

"I'll take you to the man who will make my offer for me. He's close by, less than a mile away. I think we'd better go and talk."

Jacob signaled to the driver and we turned down the tiny lane leading to Millards Cross. "He's at Chequer's Inn," I said. "Just by the bridge."

As we approached, Jacob made no attempt to scan the crowd of people who were enjoying the sun in the white-painted chairs around the ornamental fishpond, and I realized that he could not see that far.

I grinned at the thought that the old man was having to wait until the very last moment before seeing the huge, raw-boned frame of Andy Doyle, who was sprawled across two chairs under the oak tree, reading the local newspaper with a pocket tapemeasure in his hand, to measure off the column inches of advertising.

When Jacob finally saw him, he said, "So that's your position."

"Yes," I said. "I want the Sellingers out of World News, lock, stock, and every last barrel. Doyle's wanted World News for years. As of this morning, he has almost two-thirds of the British shareholding. Enough to give you a fight even without special circumstances. Don't fight him, Jacob. Do a deal. That's what I want."

I got out of the limousine and Andy grinned and stepped in to take my place.

The Cadillac moved smoothly away and I was left standing by the side of the ornamental pond.

In a few moments Pike's car appeared with Cox in the back seat and I got in beside him.

"How long will it take?" he said.

"Not long. They both have all the figures in their heads."

"What's Doyle like? Will they get on all right?"

I smiled. "As long as Andy doesn't accidentally nudge him," I said. "If he does, he'll break every bone in his body. Andy's fine, but a bit too hearty for my taste. The last time I was in Toronto, he wanted to take me ice-fishing."

"What the hell's that?"

"You go out and cut a hole in a frozen lake, erect a hut over it, then sit around it drinking bourbon with fishing lines dangling in. Someone said it's as much fun as getting drunk in an ice-bound privy, but Andy loves all that stuff. Snowmobiles, canoes, ocean racing. The great outdoors."

"What's he like as a publisher?"

"Very shrewd. Do you know how he started his empire? Bought a small paper in Ontario and said he was going to do it over. While everyone else was planning a dynamic new editorial policy, he designed a cover to keep the snow off the batches of papers when they were dumped in the rural areas. Tripled sales overnight." I grinned at Cox. "That's how empires are made."

"Is he right for World News?"

"Yes. He's completely straight, right down the line. No interference. Just don't waste money. He'll do just fine."

Cox heard the catch in my voice, but he pretended he hadn't noticed. I knew that the questioning had been to stop me from thinking of other things.

We waited for almost thirty minutes, then the Cadillac glided back down the hill and Andy Doyle got out.

Pike waited until the Cadillac moved off, then eased the Rover into the small, crowed parking lot.

Doyle strolled over and the grin of satisfaction on his face was obvious. "Hi," he said cheerfully. "You guys like a drink?"

Cox stayed in the car and Pike also made no move to get out from behind the wheel. Doyle took the hint and led me into a small orchard where we could be completely alone.

"Is it settled?" I said.

"Signed, sealed, and delivered. Good price. No hassling around."

"And does he know the bottom line?"

Doyle smiled. "No, I don't believe it ever occurred to him."

"There's no way he can wriggle out?"

Doyle's grin was broadening. "Johnny, when I get a pickerel on my line, he stays on my line."

"So there's just our part left."

"Yep. That's right."

"You have my letter of resignation already. You wanted suggestions for my successor." I handed him an envelope. "I've given you two names: one inside World News, one from outside. Equally good."

We shook hands and I went back to the car. "Cox," I said, "get over and see Deighton. It's time for me to break the news to the Sellingers that we're going to publish the whole story anyway."

25

Then I made a mistake: I got too cocky. I wanted to tell the Sellingers myself as a final bit of personal revenge, but I didn't go straight back to Samman's. I wanted to give Jacob time to brief his sons, so I asked the WN driver who had been standing by at the pub to drive me to Black Oak Ridge, and I went for a stroll in the woods to compose myself for the final confrontation with Paul. I intended to descend on the house just as the Sellingers were settling down to what Cox always called a Family Planning session, and break the news that the whole story was going to come out anyway and there was nothing for them to salvage and no deals to be made.

I thought I'd judged the timing nicely, but as we approached the end of Samman's Lane I saw Pike's Rover speeding up the ridge road.

In his hurry to cut us off, Pike almost skidded into the ditch. "Come on," he yelled. "Get in. I'll explain on the way."

As I got in the Rover, I saw that Pike was almost trembling with fury and frustration. "I still don't believe it," he said. "I just don't bloody believe it. John, I must be getting old. I don't know how I let them pull a stunt like that. Jesus Christ, I really must be getting past it."

Jim caught my look and broke off. He was too old a pro to waste time confronting his own mortality. As we sped down the road, he quickly recovered himself and gave me crisp summary of what had happened.

After playing her part at Samman's, Nancy had gone back to the country inn at Selleyfold where she had made her base; her lawyers had gone straight back to London. She'd just been about to sit down to lunch with Pike and Paddy when a Sellinger driver had arrived with a message from Robert, asking for a private meeting. "I wanted her to refuse," Jim said. "It didn't feel right. They'd found out too easily where we were, for one thing—but Nancy insisted. She said she'd always trusted Robert in the past and it could be important."

The driver had phoned Samman's from the car and Robert Sellinger had driven to Selleyfold to join them. "Then they worked a simple double block on me," Pike said. "The oldest gag in the book and I wasn't ready for it. Well, to be honest, I was ready, but they were damned good and it was the mood of the meet that threw me."

By Jim's account, Nancy and Robert had seemed to be talking like old friends. They were standing in the lane, close enough to Jim and Paddy to be reassuring without actually being within earshot. They had appeared completely relaxed. "Nancy even laughed at one point," Pike said, "and like a bloody idiot I let it lower my guard. One minute there were just the two of them having a nice matey chat; the next minute there was a Jag streaking out from behind the pub. It sent us skittering, then did a broadside skin and blocked the road right from one ditch to the other. They just abandoned it there. You know what these Kentish lanes are like. Paul grabbed Nancy and they were all away in his car. They really had us over. And now they're on their way to Heathrow."

"Heathrow?" I said, with a chill. "How do you know?"

"We've got Cox to thank for that," Pike said.

As Pike described Cox's moves, I couldn't help smiling for all my anxiety. He hadn't thought like an exec trained in administration; he'd done it the correspondent's way: cut corners, to hell with the rules. Just do it.

When Cox had realized that Pike didn't have any good contacts with the Kentish police, he had tried first to hire a helicopter from Biggin Hill airport. There wasn't one available, even with WN pull, so he'd used the phone in my car to call a friend at Capital-194 radio and gotten himself patched through to their weather and traffic helicopter. The pilot wouldn't come to fetch them, but he'd agreed to a quick detour and spotted the Sellinger car heading in a direction that could only have meant they were making for the airport.

"Cox took your Rolls, because of the phone," Pike said. "He's trying to organize something at Heathrow to delay them at the airport. I don't know what he's got in mind, but he's a resourceful young devil, Mr. Cox."

I trusted Cox's resourcefulness too, but it was infuriating not to be able to contact him. There was no telephone in the Rover and if we stopped at a phone booth, we would lose precious minutes. Jim drove almost as fast and as skillfully as Paddy, but there was only a token strip of airport motorway; the rest of the route to Heathrow was a series of suburban high streets strung together and described optimistically as an airport bypass. Without siren or flasher, there was no way of threading through easily.

Once he had given me the situation, Jim concentrated on his driving and I fretted and tried to anticipate the Sellingers' next move. Why the hell had they snatched Nancy? What good would it do them? I tried to get inside of Paul's head. They had to be heading for the United States. America was home ground. Whatever it was he wanted to do with Nancy, it was in the States that his influence was greatest. He obviously wanted to prevent her from exposing him in the divorce proceedings; maybe he had some courts in his pocket there. If he was pushed to extremes, he might even try to make Nancy disappear; they were still husband and wife and there were several places where no one might act on a missing persons complaint if none of the Family supported the complaint. But no, it still made no sense. I had to face it. With Paul, there was no longer any point in looking only at rational motives. He wanted revenge. He needed it. And harming Nancy was the surest way of getting back at me. The thing that puzzled me was, what was Robert doing involved in this harebrained scheme?

As we came nearer to the airport, the traffic began to thicken. "Jim, for God's sake," I said, "hurry it up."

He shrugged. "Nothing I can do, John. If I go up on the shoulder or off the roadway, I'll get stopped for sure and it'll take me longer to explain." He gestured helplessly. "Anyway,

258

look at that. That's not normal afternoon traffic, even for Heathrow. There must be an accident or something."

After one more forward burst, the line gradually slowed and finally we stopped altogether, just as we were entering the spaghetti jumble of roads on the fringe of the airport complex. We both got out and I ran up the shoulder to assess the situation. From the brow of the hill, I could see the reason: a group of antinuclear protesters were blocking the six-lane underground road tunnel which funneled the traffic into the Heathrow terminal area.

There weren't very many of them—twenty or thirty at most. They were mostly women and some of them were quite old. Two were obviously pregnant and several others had young children with them. They were sitting across the motorway in a pattern which couldn't easily be broken up without violence. Some police and airport security people had arrived but they were arguing indecisively and didn't seem sure what to do. Most of the police were young; they would have been children in the sixties and no one had trained them to deal with peaceful sit-ins. They were used to hooliganism and street violence and they would have been happier to have been able to go in with batons swinging.

Many of the people in the blocked cars had obviously decided that the police weren't going to act quickly. Those with drivers were beginning to leave their vehicles to try the last half mile or so on foot.

I left Jim to look after the car and sprinted toward the airport. The direct way was down one hill, then up again, across the huge grassy hummock over the motorway tunnel; it was steeper than it looked and the passengers struggling with luggage looked at me enviously as I raced over the sparse, shiny grass which had turned brown in the heat.

From the top of the hummock, I could see the main gates of the terminal area and I knew immediately that trouble had broken out inside too. There were policemen everywhere, and a path was being cleared through the snarled traffic to bring more reinforcements from the airport security headquarters on the other side of the cargo terminal.

At the gates, I looked around for Cox, but saw instead Tim

Osman. He was an old WN man who had been a friend for years; he had taken early retirement to found his own little airport news service which acted as our collective stringer at Heathrow. I noticed that he was carrying a small walkie-talkie of the type we had started issuing to World News teams on major assignments.

"Cox left me to wait for you," he said. "He's somewhere in the transatlantic terminal." Osman tapped the walkie-talkie. "I haven't been able to raise him for a little while but he's keeping in touch."

In the official parking area by the gate there was a small runabout van with Osman's agency logo on the side, but Osman ignored it. "Too much chaos to drive," he said. "Cox has quite a demonstration going."

"Cox has it going?"

Osman hesitated. We were old friends, but I was president of WN now and I could see he wasn't certain how far he should cover Cox.

"Well, he didn't actually organize the demonstration," Osman said with a half grin. "He just made sure they were here."

As we hurried toward the transatlantic terminal, Osman filled me in. Using the telephone in the Rolls, Cox had contacted Marge on the WN switchboard and had her radiopage Rex Turnstall, who was at the tent city near the airport, interviewing the antinuclear demonstators. After a briefing by Cox, Turnstall had asked the MND leaders there what their reaction was to the Sellinger mission. When asked what mission, Turnstall had explained that the Sellingers had flown to London to try to have the Starburst test brought forward right to the beginning of the NATO maneuvers. Now they were flying back to Washington to tie up the American end. What was MND's reaction?

Osman grinned. "You can imagine the reaction. They went absolutely ape. All hands to the airport. They've got a very sophisticated communications setup; they use CB radio mostly. They had a couple of hundred people at the airport within twenty minutes and more are coming all the time. There were some Animals too—you know, the antinuclear militants. They flew in from West Germany yesterday and they're just raring to go."

Osman pointed toward the entrance to the multistory garage. "There are some of them now."

A team of eight figures were walking in procession down the exit ramp of the garage. They were completely anonymous under huge death's head masks and they were carrying a coffin on their shoulders. The coffin, I noticed, was inflatable: a typical Animal touch. They specialized in what they called hit-and-run guerrilla theater, with instant props which could be easily hidden from the security forces.

The procession filed slowly across the crossing and I saw police moving into position to stop them from entering the terminal. The procession stopped, then with no warning at all they let the air out of the coffin and broke ranks, dispersing into the crowd. Then one of them stopped in front of a group of passengers who were loading suitcases onto a luggage cart. He pulled out an aerosol can, pointed it at them and shouted, "Radiation, radiation. You are contaminated."

At first nothing came out of the aerosol and the passengers laughed uneasily, trying to avoid a confrontation by sharing the joke. Then the man pressed again and a yellow streak of foam sprayed over one of the passenger's suits. The passenger started to yell abuse and moved forward with fists clenched, but he seemed reluctant to hit the death's-head mask, either from superstition or because it looked so hideous and rubbery —and before he could bring himself to strike a blow, the Animal skipped away into the crowd, pulling off the mask as he went. The other Animals did the same.

Several policemen dived into the crowd to chase the fleeing figures, but once the masks had vanished, there was no way of telling for certain where any of them were.

The main entrance to the terminal was still cordoned off, but Osman took us in through a side entrance. I followed him through a warren of corridors and up some stairs which brought us out in the upper level of the passenger terminal.

At first, everything seemed quiet. Loudspeaker announcements were being made, apologizing for delays in flights and promising that the situation would be restored to normal shortly. Then suddenly the loudspeakers were drowned out by the sound of a siren; it was a noise to send a chill through any one who had suffered an air raid. There was no panic. The crowd in the concourse froze, some of them looking upward expectantly. The siren stopped and a voice boomed out, amplified by megaphone, "Nuclear attack, nuclear attack. Take cover, take cover."

At first no one moved, then there was a soft, muffled explosion and a red mushroom cloud billowed upward from the refreshment area in the middle of the terminal. Fortunately anyone who had been near a television set in the previous week recognized it as what the Animals called their nuclear firework displays.

They had done simulations of nuclear explosions twice in the past four days, once in France and one in West Germany. The cloud was formed of a harmless red dye, but the ominous mushroom shape gave it an awesome look and people started to crouch down on the ground and hide under tables to try to protect their clothes from being stained.

The cloud smelled acrid and as it reached the roof of the terminal, it broke up and pockets of red smoke began to drift out over the heads of the crowd.

The confusion was total. Fearing panic, police opened all of the doors at the end of the terminal and passengers streamed out into the open air.

We waited on the upper level, close to an open window, scanning the crowd for some glimpse of any of Sellinger's people. Then the signal light on Osman's walkie-talkie flashed and Cox came through. For a second I thought we had our breakthrough, but his voice sounded depressed and anxious. He asked whether I had arrived and Osman reported our position. "I'm close," Cox said. "I'll be there in a minute."

When I saw Cox running up the stairs to the gallery, I knew he had found nothing. He was breathless and slightly harassed and the disappointment was clear in his face.

"Chief, we're stalled," he said. "There's no sign of them anywhere. The Sellinger jet's on the ground; no one's come near it. We thought maybe they were trying to decoy us and use a commercial flight instead, you know, drug Nancy a little, have her sleep the flight. Marge has rounded up four WN people. With Osman's men and Paddy, we've had eight people combing the terminal. And the demonstrators are looking too. Nothing. Zero. Nothing. We've covered every VIP lounge, all the airline offices. My own bet is that they're in a car somewhere in one of the garages. We're searching now, level by level."

I gave him a tight grin of encouragement. "You've done damned well," I said.

"I hope to hell no one gets hurt in all this," Cox said. "It was all I could think of, but these Animals are real crazies. I'm consoling myself with the thought that they'd have held their demonstration somewhere and it might as well be here."

"Whatever happens, I'll take full responsibility," I said. "But I don't think it'll turn nasty. The Animals are wild but they haven't hurt anyone in any of their demonstrations so far. Just ruffled a lot of people's dignity and spoiled a few suits."

"Yeah, I guess so." Cox shrugged. "Anyway, the question is, what now?"

"The main thing is to keep them from flying out," I said. "If they are in one of the garages, we haven't much chance of finding them until they come out. Our best bet is to keep an eye on their plane and watch all the terminals. We'll just have to cover all the departure areas as best we can."

I made it sound as encouraging as I could. Cox had done more than I had the right to expect of any exec and I wasn't optimistic. With the Sellingers' resources there were ways of cutting any corner.

"What about charter flights?" I said.

"I've had Chris Lewin checking all the private operators," Cox said. "By the way, he was on his way to Geneva with Paul Mills for the trade talks. We'll have to arrange replacements for them."

I smiled. "I'll make an exec of you yet," I said. "But later. The talks will hold. Right now, let's worry about Nancy."

"Okay, then, two to a terminal," Cox said. "A walkie-talkie for each pair. If anyone spots them—" He broke off. "I guess, report and improvise."

We were just deciding who should watch which area, when I hear my name called over the loudspeaker system.

"Paging Mr. John Railton. An urgent call for Mr. John Railton."

I thought at first it was Jim Pike trying to locate me, but when I found a booth and picked up the receiver, I heard Robert Sellinger's voice.

"John, we must talk. Urgently. There isn't much time."

"Where are you?" I said. "Where's Nancy?"

"Nancy's quite safe," Robert said. "There isn't time to argue. I'm at Terminal Four. On the upper level. Be as quick as you can."

I didn't bother to argue. I knew the Sellinger style too well by now. There was no point in worrying about traps. They had been preparing to offer a deal; now they were ready. And with them, a deal was always urgent to build up the pressure. The problem was, I had nothing to trade.

When I reported the conversation to Cox, he read the situation the same way. "One thing's odd, though," he said. "It's not like Paul to act through Robert. I'd have expected him to deal with you face to face."

"Yes," I said. "So would I. I think we'd better watch our backs."

Terminal Four was no longer in use as a terminal. It was scheduled for demolition to make room for an extension to the Atlantic building, but that project had been held up for lack of financing, and Terminal Four was being used only for administrative offices and as an overflow storage area. Everything about the building proclaimed its second-class status; it looked untidy and abandoned, but it was well clear of both police checks and demonstrators and Osman got me there quickly by a shortcut through the cargo handling area.

As soon as I entered the building, I saw Robert standing at the head of the main escalator, with two men who were obviously bodyguards.

I went up the escalator with Cox, leaving Osman in the empty concourse below. "I think we'd better talk alone," Robert said when we got to the top. "Cox can wait here. There's an office we can use."

I let him lead me through a door marked Trans-America— Bulk Cargo into a drab little room cluttered with papers and files.

"All right," I said when he had closed the door, "where the hell is Nancy?"

"Nancy's quite safe," Robert said quietly. "She's been safe all along. Your demonstration idea was very clever, but it was quite unnecessary. Nancy was never going to fly anywhere."

"What?"

"You're right to be suspicious," Robert said. "But there's no need. I've taken the problem of Paul in hand. It's a Family matter, but it's a mistake to imagine that all Family matters are settled amicably. Paul went too far. Much too far. But he's caused all the trouble he's going to cause. He wanted Nancy for revenge, but revenge is no longer appropriate. At least not on his part."

"You mean it's your turn."

"Yes," Robert said quietly. "I think we can say it's my turn. I agreed to seize Nancy because if I hadn't, Paul was going to do it. He'd gone beyond the bounds of rationality—it simply would have done no good just to tell him no. If he'd succeeded, it would have been disastrous, so I decided to head him off by pretending to go along. I told Nancy all about it at the inn, so she'd be prepared. She's at the Airport Sheraton. Paul is looking for her. He knows something is wrong. He doesn't know yet just how wrong." Robert paused. "You'll be publishing the story, of course."

"You realized?"

"Of course. It will start to leak eventually anyway. If it ever came out that World News covered up, the agency would be finished. I presumed that's how you would reason."

"Yes."

"Paul will say you destroyed yourself to destroy him."

"He'll be wrong."

"But you will resign."

"I've already done so," I said.

"Yes. Integrity carries a high price," Robert said indifferently. "That's your concern. Mine is Starburst. The European test will be canceled, of course. But the missile will survive. There'll be a high price for that too."

"Which Paul will pay?" I said.

Robert nodded. "Unfortunately, you have to be your own martyr. I have Paul. It's time for him to start making some sacrifices for the family."

All in all, I thought, it was a solid Sellinger performance. One of Robert's best. Calm, matter-of-fact; a realist accepting the inevitable. But I wasn't fooled. I was talking to a man totally consumed by hate. Brother had turned irrevocably against brother. Robert's vengeance on Paul would be greater than anything I could ever have achieved. I had no further role to play.

"I'll go and get Nancy," I said.

"Ask at the reception desk for Mrs. Cadbury. My people are expecting you."

I was about to leave when there was a knock on the door. One of the guards came in and there was a whispered conversation. When Robert turned back to me, there was a slight smile on his face. "I'm afraid Paul's martyrdom is beginning already," he said. "Do you want to come and see?"

I had never seen Robert run before. He was not as overweight as Paul, but his dignity vanished completely once he was forced to hurry. He obviously knew it, but he didn't care. If there was something happening to Paul that Robert wanted that much to see, I decided, then I wanted to see it too. I ran after him down the corridor which led to the far side of the terminal, with Cox close behind me. At the end, there was a glass wall, with views out over the runways. Below, only a few yards from the building, a gray Rolls-Royce which I recognized as Paul's had been forced off the road and was jammed up against the perimeter fence. Around it, a group of Animals in death's-head masks were circling and tapping on the windows. I could see Paul alone in the back, and a driver and one other man in the front.

I glanced at Robert. His face was impassive as he waited for his breathing to settle down.

"Paul's going to need some help," he said. The two guards with us moved as if to go down the staircase, but Robert held up his hand. "Not yet. The police will be here in a minute. Better leave it to them."

The Animals continued circling, then one of them pulled out an aerosol can and sent a yellow spurt of foam across the top of the car, then a second and a third, crisscrossing over the shiny gray surface.

When that produced no response from inside the car, one of the Animals produced a large pocket knife, opened it deliberately so it could be seen through the windshield, then started to cut a huge circle in the paintwork of the car.

He made a rough cut first, then widened it and deepened it, standing back from time to time to admire the artistry. Then he made more gashes and I realized he was shaping a nuclear disarmament sign. As he was completing the final cut, the men in the front of the car could stand the provocation no longer.

They talked animatedly with Paul, obviously arguing about what to do, then simultaneously they flung open the two front doors of the car. It was all the Animals needed. Their moves had obviously been rehearsed and before the guards were even halfway out of the car, a figure who had been crouching out of sight behind the vehicle darted forward and tossed a small metal canister into the car. There was a muffled crack and the car filled with red smoke. The guards tried to fling the doors fully open, but the Animals piled all their weight against them and the three men in the car were enveloped in the thick, choking cloud.

I could no longer see Paul clearly, but I could imagine the panic in the car, as the Animals leaned against the doors and pressed their skull masks against the windows. Eventually, they managed to get one of the car doors open. As the driver struggled out, he was met by a crossfire of yellow foam from aerosols aimed at point-blank range. Paul came out next. He saw the aerosols but was too desperate for air to put up any defense. Within seconds he was covered with foam and the Animals shouted and jeered as he stumbled about in the roadway, choking and gagging and trying to wipe the yellow froth from his mouth and eyes.

I glanced at Robert and saw his face had broken into a tight, humorless grin.

Deliberately and without any sign of urgency, he turned toward me.

"You'd better go and get Nancy," he said. "The police are not very quick off the mark. I think I'd better see if my brother needs some help."

26

The victory was complete, but the next morning it seemed hollow and savorless as I prepared to take my last look at the WN newsroom. Nancy was safe and I had spent the night in my office putting my affairs in order. Now it was time to take a firm hold of myself and give a Sellinger-style performance as I took a final walk as chief executive through the building I thought of as home.

Later that day, the announcement would be posted: that I had stepped down "in the interests of the agency" but would remain available in an advisory capacity to assist an interim committee, consisting of Don Westerman and Neville Farmer, pending the appointment of a new president. It was a good formula. There were a lot of issues to tie up, but it wouldn't be prudent to have me "in the shop window" when the full story broke. Deighton's story was superb and not sensationalized, but the tabloids would go berserk; a chief executive who smoked dope and enjoyed erotic games and beat up kids after car accidents would be a liability just when World News least needed it.

I glanced at the notice board where the board memorandum would be posted and saw a notice of a joint union chapel meeting to discuss the introduction of the Datavol X-13 processors. Haycroft was winning and I wondered for a moment if I should call his wife to reassure her, or send her flowers. No, I thought wryly, if I do that, I'll probably jinx the poor devil and he'll keel over at the feet of the father of the Technical Union chapel.

The dawn shift was just about to go home. I walked with Cox down the center of the newsroom and chatted with some of the younger subeditors who were being given extended periods of overnight work during the quieter hours of the dawn shift, so that they could be tried out on more senior duties. I knew they all hated it. Only a few journalists really liked the dawn shift, and often it was because they had problems at home or else had queer body-temperature cycles which made them natural creatures of the night. The younger men were impatient to become correspondents and see their own bylines, and as I stopped to give them a few words of encouragement, I remembered my own impatience to get on up the ladder.

At the end of the central news-processing layout—known in the newsroom as "computer alley"—I noticed the neck of a wine bottle sticking out of a wastebasket, half hidden among the piles of wastepaper. I made a mental note to draft an "It has come to my attention . . ." note for the log. It might just have been someone's birthday, but there was always risk on the dawn shift that a friendly drink behind the computers could become an accepted way of whiling the night away. I grinned as I remembered how alcohol had first come to be totally banned in the World News newsroom—even at Christmas and New Year's. Three crazy young subs had celebrated too hard one New Year and, while plastered out of their minds, had opened up the circuits to Australasia and sent their choicest drunken thoughts about life, sex, and newspaper publishers spilling into all the newspapers and radio and TV stations across the continent.

The ringleader had been asked in a written memorandum why he had—as a final act of lunacy—laid his two unconscious colleagues out on the floor of the editor's office. His answer had been, "It was the only office with a carpet." The reply had been framed and put on the personnel manager's wall.

Good times, I thought . . . but memory lane wasn't a very comfortable trip just at the moment.

Cox sensed my mood, but when he tried to cheer me up, I quickly covered it over.

"What were you thinking about, Chief?" he asked.

"I was thinking that you look too fucking respectable," I said. "Dark, sober suit, solemn executive look. The Econ job is going to be the death of you."

One of the things I had done during the night was to ensure Cox's own next assignment, so that he would not catch any of the downdraft from my resignation. I had offered him the choice of four major foreign assignments which were about to come open, but he had chosen instead to go to the Economic Services as deputy editor. It was an excellent move for him to make and he knew I approved of his choice, but I didn't want him losing the sacred fire and being caught in the promotion rat race.

But that would be my successor's worry. I had my own future to think about.

I looked at Cox and, just for a moment, I wished I could change places, then I put the thought aside and went down into the main lobby of World News.

It was almost seven o'clock. The day staff were starting to arrive, together with a handful of eager executives who wanted a quiet hour or two in their offices to clear their paperwork before the phones started ringing.

The commissionaire sent for my car and we chatted briefly about the weather and the next WN cricket match until the BMW arrived. Not for much longer, I thought. That was one thing I really was going to miss. A car and chauffeur in London was a priceless luxury, and I wondered what kind of car I should buy once I had to fend for myself. And what kind would I be able to afford? It was something I didn't want to think about too closely. There would certainly be severance arrangements, and Doyle had indicated he would be generous, but without the company flat in Little Venice and the car and the chief executive's expense account, it was going to be a very different world.

I left Cox in the lobby and made a point of avoiding any special leavetaking, and I waited until he had gone back to the elevator before I went outside. I didn't want him to see me rub the WN plaque for luck, and I couldn't have left the building at that moment without making that gesture.

I was about to have two breakfasts—one with Seagull and one with Nancy—but I wanted to drive a little first to clear my mind of World News. I was seeing Seagull first, then Nancy, and I'd thought about it on and off for much of the night. I didn't really know what I wanted to say to either of them.

God, it would be so much simpler, I thought, if I could be straightforward about it and admit that I wanted them both. It ought to be possible. They both had separate and independent lives and I was no longer committed to either but was in love, in different ways, with both. That was the great cake-and-eat-it fallacy, and it had been the downfall of more men in Western society than any other fantasy. It *was* possible to love more than one woman, but in practice it just didn't seem to work, once the three points on the triangle were linked.

But the daydream was still fun. I wondered suddenly if either Nancy or Seagull had ever put the three of us together in fantasy, once the two of them had met.

In reality, though, a triangle was as delicate to negotiate as any confrontation with the Sellingers. Even when all you wanted was to go on sharing your life with two human beings you cared for deeply, without having to make a choice, it had to be done one cautious step at a time.

The first step was to persuade Seagull to stay in England. At least now, I thought, I would have the time to let the relationship develop gently. Seagull hated hasty meetings and quick rushes into bed. Her idea of good sex was a luxurious and leisurely marathon, and I wouldn't have to go through contortions anymore to create an illusion of unhurried leisure in the middle of a lunatic World News schedule.

We were meeting in a little café on the Embankment. Pike was bringing her and he'd agreed to look after her for at least another week.

I had Walker drive me around Blackfriars until it was closer to the time we had set, then, as we started down the Embankment, I saw Seagull standing on the pavement. Immediately I noticed something different about her. She seemed preoccupied and distant.

As she got into the car, I said, "Seagull, what's the matter? Are you all right?"

"Yes, I'm fine really. I'm just a bit shattered, that's all. John, look, I'm sorry, I shouldn't be laying my private problems on you. It's Hughie. My son. I have a chance to take him back.

This whole affair set me thinking about him again and what I'd left behind. Last night, I phoned my aunt. She's having problems with him. I think I could persuade her to let me take him back. I'm not sure if I should. I don't know if it would unsettle him."

"I don't know what to say." I smiled. "As you know, that's a part of your life I never knew much about."

"It's been on my mind for months, but our talk the other day really got me going. Look, John, I'm sorry. Would you forgive me if I just left? I know we have things to say to each other, but I have to get this settled. He's in Northamptonshire. Jim said he'll drive me."

I kissed her and gave her a little hug.

"I'll think about you when I'm worrying about homework and stuff like that," she said.

"That lovely tan will fade."

"Yes. But now the old life's been reopened, I have to find the guts to plunge in. You held me in your arms once when I faltered, and I was grateful, but I have to do this myself now."

So much for fantasy, I thought, as I watched Pike's Rover drive away, and I felt nervous suddenly, knowing that I had no reason now to hold back with Nancy. I was sure she had wanted us to get back together; I'd felt for months that it wasn't just I who regretted the break. But would it be different now that I was no longer chief executive of World News? Jesus Christ, I thought suddenly, not only was I worrying about how to ask Nancy to remarry me, I had to worry too how to explain away my prospects.

I'd arranged to meet her in Covent Garden. Usually we would have met in one of the cafés near Fleet Street, but I didn't want those kinds of old memories getting in the way. I felt suddenly as though I were offering a very naked John Railton—a middle-aged man, stripped of the trappings of power and achievement—and it wasn't a comfortable thought.

It helped, though, that she looked gorgeous. She was wearing a lavender-colored silk suit and her hair was set in the loose, easy style that had always suited her best.

"Nan, you look fantastic," I said as she came into the café and joined me in the polished wooden booth.

"I made an extra effort," she said. "I didn't get much sleep last night, and I look a bit ragged under the makeup."

"Has something happened?"

"No. I was up most of the night thinking."

I touched her hand gently. "I did quite a lot of that too," I said.

"Yes, I thought you might. That's why I feel so bad. John. I'm not as good as you are with words. I've been rehearsing like mad on the way here. But it all keeps coming out wrong, so I'd better just say it as best I can. I feel as though I've used you. Led you on, almost. And I didn't want to do that. When things got bad with Paul, I let myself slip back to the good times we'd had, before it went wrong. I do love you, you know. I always have. I love being with you, and I love making love with you, but I don't want you to ask me to come back to you. You remember Mike Harding? Several times, he's offered me a job, and this time I think I'm going to take him up on it. He has an air charter business. I'm going to run it for him. I'll do some flying too and try to build up enough experience to get my commercial license. It's just bush flying. They probably won't let me carry anything more valuable than old oil drums first, but it's a chance to do what I want to do most . . ."

She touched my arm. "John. I'm sorry. But I don't ever want to marry again. I'll be your lover, any time you want me. But I've made the break. Inside my head. I can't go backwards, even for you."

One, two. It was almost funny. And it served me right for my grand fantasy. "I don't think this is going to go down as one of my better days," I said, with a smile. "But I'm glad for you. I mean that, I really am."

"Do you have any plans yet?" Nancy said.

"No, not really. I suppose I could write my memoirs, but the best parts are going to be in the papers on Sunday anyway."

"John, stop feeling sorry for yourself," Nancy said. "You're one of the most talented men I've ever known, and what you did was incredible. When the dust has settled, all kinds of people will come looking for you."

"Yes," I said. "I know that. There'll be some offers . . . but being head of World News is a bit of a tough act to follow."

273

"What you need is a mistress," Nancy said playfully. "I'm available, and I bet Seagull is too."

The joking helped and I could see Nancy realized it. She went on teasing me gently, and I was just about to find out how serious she was about being available as a mistress, when Walker came into the café. I didn't want to break the mood and I made a sign to him not to interrupt. But he walked over to the table anyway. "Mr. Railton, could you come outside for a moment?"

"Not right this minute," I said, "but I won't be long."

Then I looked beyond Walker and saw Andy Doyle in the doorway. He gave me a wave and seated himself on a stool at the counter.

"It's okay," he said. "Take your time. I just wanted a quick word."

I turned back to Nancy, but she grinned and said, "Go on. Get it over with. I'm not going to get much of your attention until you find out what he wants."

I slid out of the booth and went over to the counter.

"I've got the proofs of Deighton's first article," he said. "You know I've bought the rights for some of my own papers."

"Yes," I said. "I heard."

"Have you seen it?"

"Cox showed me a draft early this morning."

"What did you think?" Doyle said.

"Brilliant. Exactly what's wanted."

"Yeah. I think so, too," Doyle said. "But there've been a couple of changes. I wanted to clear them with you."

"What are they?"

Doyle grinned. "The bit about your resignation, mainly. I've changed it to an explanation of why you offered your resignation and I've inserted three grafs about why I refused it."

I could feel my hand trembling on the counter. I was ashamed of it, but there was nothing I could do to stop it, and Doyle appeared not to notice.

"I've been over the story, line by line. You come out of it pretty well, Johnny, and frankly I don't think that screwing around at a party and smoking a bit of dope should rule you out of court." He grinned. "Matter of fact, I've tried a couple of joints myself. My kids gave 'em to me. I still prefer booze,

274

but grass is no big deal in my book. So what do you say? Will you stay with me? I'll get you a good package. More than you've been used to."

"Yes," I said. "And thanks."

"Great. The first thing is Datavol. I liked your approach to the union hassle. Haycroft told me about it. It was a smart move, but we can go faster. We've got 'em on the run. I figure we can get the X-13s in in six months. I'll be in L.A. myself on Wednesday. I'll see if I can light some fires. You'd better come over and join me. I'll take you back to Toronto with me. Best if you meet a few of the boys."

"I'll take a look at my schedule," I said. "But I want to be in London when the story comes out. The press are going to be around World News like a pack of mad dogs and I want to be there to handle it."

"Good thinking," Doyle said. "Okay. See you in L.A. Wednesday."

When he'd gone, I walked back to the booth. "I don't have to ask what that was about," Nancy said with a grin. "Your face says it all."

"Somebody up there apparently still likes me," I said. "They heard that one of my mistresses has gone broody and the other loves me but would rather be a bush pilot, so they offered me a consolation prize."

"John Railton, you're a fraud. You know you love World News better than either of us. But if you do want a consolation prize, I've got just the thing. You can have this."

She pulled a small package out of her bag.

"What is it?"

Nancy laughed. "I got it from Ryder. It's a tape of us making love in Vaudur. It's very amusing. I never realized that you talked so much . . . and I make a funny kind of whistling sound."

"I'd rather have a live run."

"So would I," Nancy said, "but if I know you and World News, playing the tape on that little office machine of yours is about all you're going to have time for."

275

NORMAN HARTLEY

In a tradition which Ian Fleming began and Frederick Forsyth continued, Norman Hartley turned to writing thrillers after a career with Reuters. For ten years, he covered mainly violent events in Africa and Europe, including eleven coups d'etat while Reuters chief correspondent for West Africa, and the beginnings of the current political and student violence in Italy while chief correspondent in Rome in the late 1960s. Later, he traveled extensively in the United States and Canada as a reporter for the Toronto *Globe and Mail* and broadcasted for the Canadian Broadcasting Corporation. During this period, he wrote his first thriller, *The Viking Process*, which has since been published in fourteen countries, followed by *Quicksilver*. He has now returned to England and lives in Kent with his wife, Christina, and their two daughters.